PRAISE FOR *THE SHELL HOUSE DETECTIVES SERIES*

Praise for *The High Tide Murder*

'*The High Tide Murder* confirms Emylia Hall's place as the queen of the Cornish crime series. I loved this book for its intelligent plotting, its bursting heart, its clever surprises, and its company of characters who have fast come to feel like family. Few writers can pull off a devilishly twisting mystery while infusing the story with such soul; I savoured every page of this wonderful, life-affirming read and cannot wait for the next one.'

—Emma Stonex, author of *The Lamplighters*

'Atmospheric, propulsive, and menacing – plus all the deliciously cosy Shell House vibes – *The High Tide Murder* is the perfect mystery to curl up with this autumn.'

—Lucy Clarke, author of *One of the Girls*

'Windswept and utterly unputdownable, this is the perfect winter read. The Shell House Detectives are fast becoming my favourite literary duo and Emylia Hall is a genius. Brilliant!'

—Veronica Henry, author of *The Impulse Purchase*

'A new Emylia Hall novel is always such a treat, and *The High Tide Murder* did not disappoint. I was gripped from the very first page, unable to put the book down until the end. A brilliant cast of characters, brimming with emotion and intrigue, all set against an escapist Cornish backdrop. What more could you want?'

—Libby Page, author of *The Lido*

'A fantastic Cornish crime series that just keeps on getting better. I couldn't put this latest instalment down and read long into the night to finish the last 100 pages, equally gripped and moved.'

—Kate Riordan, author of *The Heatwave*

'An absolutely stellar read. Emylia Hall's writing is standout and this story is packed with genuine suspense, beautifully drawn characters and yet another stunning setting for a terrible crime. I can't recommend the Shell House Detectives series highly enough.'

—Rosie Walsh, author of *The Man Who Didn't Call*

'Another generous slice of cosy brilliance. To be a Shell House fan is to be continually (and delightfully) wrongfooted. Each time I think I know the killer, I have to think again. Each time I think I've found my favourite in the series, I have to think again. Long may it continue.'

—Jo Harkin, author of *The Pretender*

'Another great mystery from Emylia Hall in an evocative setting, I devoured *The High Tide Murder* and already look forward to the next.'

—Heidi Perks, author of *Now You See Her*

Praise for the series

'A cleverly plotted and thoroughly enjoyable book about dark deeds in beautiful places.'

—Elly Griffiths, author of the Ruth Galloway series

'A total delight.'

—Sarah Winman, author of *Still Life*

'Exquisitely written, set in Cornwall, great characters, and a gripping plot. Who could ask for more?'

—Jill Mansell, author of *Promise Me*

'This beautifully written cosy coastal mystery packs a real punch! With wonderfully atmospheric prose and twists and turns aplenty, the plot will have you riding a wave of suspense long after you've turned the final page. If you love Cornwall, you will adore this book.'

—Sarah Pearse, author of *The Sanatorium*

'Suspenseful, twisty and unputdownable . . . Loved it!'

—Claire Douglas, author of *The Couple at No. 9*

'Clever, plotty and compelling.'

—Jane Shemilt, author of *Daughter*

'If you're looking for a new favourite cosy crime series, here it is!'

—Libby Page, author of *The Lido*

'Emylia was born to write detective fiction.'

—Veronica Henry, author of *The Impulse Purchase*

'An expertly plotted and hugely compelling murder mystery . . . Crime fans are in for a treat.'

—Lucy Clarke, author of *One of the Girls*

'An absolute treat from start to finish! A wickedly plotted whodunnit with a cast of suspects fit for any Christie, all written with Emylia's trademark heart and humour.'

—Hannah Richell, author of *The Search Party*

'A big-hearted page-turner with twists you won't see coming and the best pair of amateur sleuths I've read in a long time. I loved it!'

—Lucy Diamond, author of *Anything Could Happen*

'My favourite new crime series.'

—Ginny Bell, author of the Dover Café series

'Sensationally good: utterly gripping, beautifully written and brilliantly clever. I was up reading way past my bedtime and could not unravel Emylia Hall's fantastically plotted mystery for love nor money! Set in gorgeous Cornwall at the peak of a heatwave, with her best cast of characters yet, this book oozes confidence, style and sparkle, with Emylia's trademark warmth and humanity. I absolutely loved it.'

—Rosie Walsh, author of *The Man Who Didn't Call*

'Gorgeous writing and a plot crammed with suspense, this is your perfect new crime series.'

—Kate Riordan, author of *The Heatwave*

'Beautifully written, gripping, and so atmospheric . . . One for fans of Richard Osman!'

—Emily Koch, author of *What July Knew*

'A clever and complex whodunnit, a deeply compelling human drama and a gorgeously imagined love letter to Cornwall. Every brushstroke is the work of a master . . . and I adored it.'

—Emma Stonex, author of *The Lamplighters*

'A treat of a book: immersive, suspenseful, full of twists and turns . . . It's as captivating as a Cornish summer. I loved it.'

—Susan Fletcher, author of *The Night in Question*

'*The Shell House Detectives* is a hug of a book that is transporting and full of love, with a humdinger of a mystery at its big heart.'

—Amanda Reynolds, author of *Close to Me*

'Captures the magic and beauty of Cornwall wrapped within a warm and engaging detective story. I loved it.'

—Rosanna Ley, author of *The Forever Garden*

'These mysteries are never less than gripping, but are told with so much heart, and with such a vivid sense of place, that each one is a breath of fresh air. I recommend them to all my friends, and can't wait for the next instalment!'

—Kate Webb, author of the DI Lockyer Mysteries

'An intriguing mystery that perfectly captures how a seaside community is rocked by murder.'

—*Sun*

'Mystery with heart! Fans of intriguing crime mysteries will adore this brand-new series, which is just crying out to become Sunday evening television.'

—*The People's Friend*

'Engaging and enjoyable.'

—*Daily Express*

THE LONE ISLAND MYSTERY

ALSO BY EMYLIA HALL

The Shell House Detectives Mystery series

The Shell House Detectives

The Harbour Lights Mystery

The Rockpool Murder

The Death at the Vineyard

The Arts Trail Killer

The High Tide Murder

Women's Fiction

The Book of Summers

A Heart Bent Out of Shape

The Sea Between Us

The Thousand Lights Hotel

THE LONE ISLAND MYSTERY

Emylia Hall

THOMAS & MERCER

This is a work of fiction. Names, characters, organizations, places, events, and incidents are either products of the author's imagination or used fictitiously. Any resemblance to actual persons, living or dead, or actual events is purely coincidental.

Published by Thomas & Mercer, Seattle

www.apub.com

EU Product Safety Contact:
Amazon Media EU S.à r.l.
38, avenue John F. Kennedy, L-1855 Luxembourg
amazonpublishing-gpsr@amazon.com

ISBN-13: 9781662533891
eISBN: 9781662533907

Cover design by Will Speed
Cover illustration by Marianna Tomaselli

Printed in the United States of America

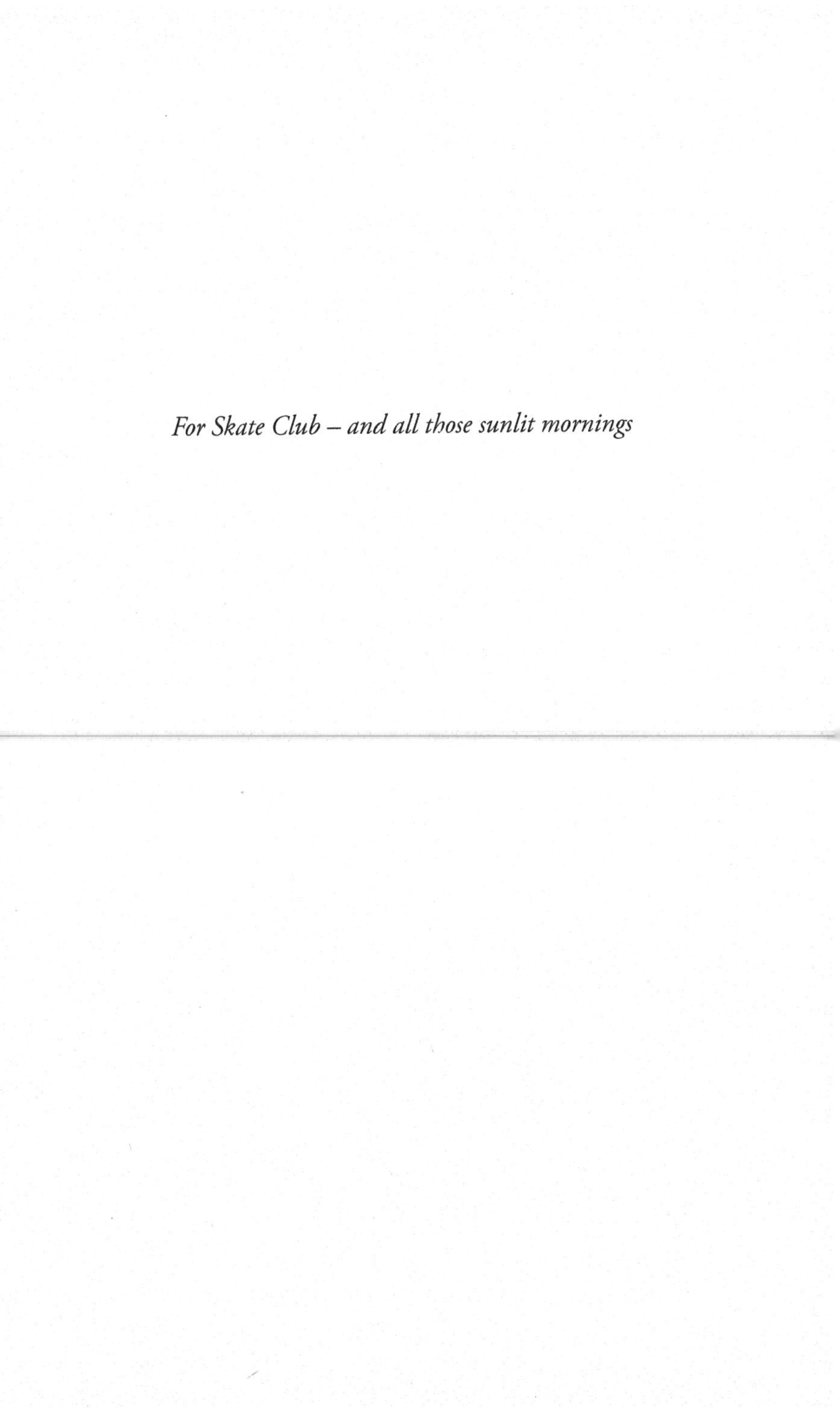

For Skate Club – and all those sunlit mornings

Prologue

Axel knows death. He knows what it is to face it, and he knows what it is to cheat it. He knows, too, what it is to want death; to hold his hands steady and close his eyes tightly and not think of anything, anything at all, except oblivion.

But this is different.

As Axel surfaces – his mouth gaping, gasping; the pain white-hot in his skull, his ribcage, his hip, his shoulder – he's struck, above all, by the sensation of surprise. For this was a danger that he did not anticipate; not for one single second. But surprise morphs quickly into fury. Fury, and fear. And as salt water burns in his throat, and his whole body blazes with injury, the two feed off one another. They're old foes – this fury, this fear – and he knows which one he'd rather. He knows which is more useful.

Axel kicks hard with his one good leg and he cuts through the water with his one half-good arm. He makes for the hulking shadows that must be the cliffs, understanding – instinctively – that they're both his best option and his worst; his only, either way.

There's a sudden drop in the waves then. A God-given lull. And maybe this is it, his moment of grace. Axel Marks, defying the odds. Well, why not? Once upon a time, he thought he was invincible.

The moon turns the sea silver. It's almost beautiful, this metallic, drenching light.

But the pain in his skull is taking over now, and somehow he's sucking in water. His limbs are flailing, failing. The cliffs – those dark, shifting forms – are further away than ever.

And that's when desperation hits.

Because Axel wants this life of his. Misshapen as it is, he wants it.

I have things to live for. I have someone great to live for. I have—

Then he's slamming into rock. Slamming with his whole body.

And time stops.

Axel sees dust; billowing clouds of it. It's in his eyes, his ears, he tastes it at the back of his throat. He feels the throbbing heat of the desert. Smells burning flesh. Everywhere, an Afghan sky so hopelessly blue. An explosion so loud it shakes the distant mountains. So loud that it still rings in his head; not every day, not now, but most.

How strange. And yet . . . how not strange.

To be back in the place he has never really left. *Some corner of a foreign field*, as Edward Grey read to him once, years back when he was a boy; the two of them in Porthmerrin's library with a book of war poetry. Slanting sunlight, the tick of the clock, and Edward talking of fighting with courage and dying with valour and most of it sailing clean over young Axel's head.

He's floating now. And it's as if he's driftwood; scorched and sea-bitten. Body useless. The ocean will do what it wants. The current takes him this way and that, this way and that. Axel is no more than a fallen leaf: flattened, shredded. From far away, maybe as high as the stars, he hears Edward's voice – Rupert Brooke's voice – blending with so many others: *If I should die, think only this of me . . .*

But think what?

Before Axel can summon an answer, he slips beneath the surface. It is over so quickly, in the end.

1

Ally is already on her second coffee of the morning when she reads about the body found on the beach. Lone Island lies to the east of Porthpella, about a mile offshore. From a distance it appears as neat and round as a cupcake; a clump of rock, topped with foliage. And save for a tiny cottage used by the appointed wildlife warden, Lone Island is uninhabited. Most would consider it an isolated outpost – in high seas, a mile offshore might as well be a hundred – but Ally can imagine how wonderful it would feel: a world unto itself, at one with nature. The utter peace.

Until the tide brings in a dead body, that is.

The article in the paper is short, with no more than the facts. The man has been identified as thirty-four-year-old Axel Marks. He was reported missing yesterday morning, after friends grew concerned for his whereabouts. His death is not being treated as suspicious.

Ally folds the paper and sits back in her chair.

Gone are the days when she could read such an article and simply think, *Oh, how sad.*

Her eyes move to the window, her mind working. She dwells on who might have found the body; the moment of disbelief – and horror. There of all places, where intrusions are scarce, and one could almost believe that the real world – with all its mess of people and problems – has ceased to exist entirely. Ally pictures the police boat taking the narrow channel between the rocks, officers splashing to shore. CSIs leaving their footprints in the sand. Then the bereaved – the reeling, desperate, left behind – wanting answers to so many questions, but above all this: *Why?*

Outside Ally's window, Porthpella is enjoying a bright spring day. The blue sky is rippled with soft cloud, and beyond the dunes, the lighthouse gleams in the sunshine. White-tipped waves race into the bay. On the surface, it appears all serenity, but Ally knows that this great blue blanket of sea will trip you, and smother you, at the drop of a hat. Was Axel Marks's death a mishap, an error of judgement, an underestimation of the ocean's power? Or a different story, one of desperation and sorrow, the water an all-too-willing accomplice? Lone Island can't be seen from here – Ally would need to round the headland, and then the next – but she and Bill took a trip there once, before the boats stopped running. It was a choppy crossing and Bill – never much of a sea dog – feared he'd see his breakfast again. But it was worth it for the dolphins that played beside them, breaching in silver spray; the seals that lolled on the rocks, doe-eyed and whiskered. Then the glimpse of the cottage through the trees, with its black slate roof and salt-crusted windows. A place to capture the imagination. *Don't get any ideas,* said Bill. *Our Shell House is wild enough, Al.*

Now it's four years since Bill died, and more than four decades since they moved to The Shell House together, and these numbers don't make sense to Ally because it all feels like yesterday. And there is both comfort and disbelief in that. Another source of disbelief? The detective work. Since joining forces with Jayden, there's an unpredictability to her days. And Ally wouldn't have it any other way.

The sound of her phone interrupts the reverie. The name *Ray Finch* flashes insistently.

Ray is her art school boyfriend – before there was a Bill – from nearly half a century ago. Ally never thought she'd see him again, but then Ray came to Porthpella for the Arts Trail last spring – quite out of the blue – and Ally wasn't prepared for her reaction. Ray, on the other hand, seemed to take this rekindling of their old flame quite in his stride. They embarked, in a loose sense, upon a relationship – though, a year on, Ally still struggles to define it as such. Occasional weekends in each other's company, mostly at his Suffolk cottage but also, memorably, at The Shell House, not long after her last big case with Jayden in the autumn.

'Ray,' says Ally. 'Good morning. It's a beautiful day here.'

'It's a strange day here. Wonderfully strange, I think. I hope.'

Ray's voice sounds different. There's a crackle in it, somewhere between excitement and . . . something else.

'Someone's made me an offer I couldn't refuse, Ally.'

He proceeds to tell her that the other evening he came back to find a card slipped through his letterbox. It was from a couple looking for their forever home and they'd decided it should be his cottage. Would he be tempted to sell? How about if they offered above market value, and completed the sale privately? They had, they said, fallen in love with the dusty-pink rendering, the dumpy thatch that's as neat as a hat, even the profusion of roses at the front door.

'The note was so effusive, Ally. Anyway, I called them back, out of interest more than anything, and turns out the woman is a successful romance novelist. An extraordinary person, actually, given to spontaneous gestures, following the heart, that sort of thing. I'd have felt like a party-pooper not going along with it.'

'What, so . . . you've agreed to sell?'

There's a note of incredulity in her voice – and, Ally's surprised to realise, a tinge of disappointment too. How many times has she stayed? Perhaps just five or six? But she's grown quite attached to Ray's place. The uneven flagstone floors, the fireplace as big as a room, the rambling garden with its wigwam beanpoles and strawberry bushes. The coast a short drive away, down green-tunnel lanes.

'Indeed I have,' he says, delivering it like a punchline. 'Ally, listen, I've decided it's fate.' His tone changes now, becoming altogether more serious. 'The same kind of fate that first brought me to Porthpella. And to you.'

Ally can feel herself smiling.

'It seems like an opportunity to make a big change.'

Last winter, they had fish and chips at sunset in Southwold, bundled up in coats and scarves, with a thermos of hot cider. Ray pointed out an old tar-black wooden house located just steps back from the harbour. How the light would stream in through the enormous windows; the clinking of rigging a bedtime lullaby. Perhaps he'll leave a note of his own.

'And I'm weighing up a couple of options,' he says. 'You know Lucy's baby's due in May, and she keeps hinting that she wishes I was closer.'

Ray's daughter, a university lecturer, lives in St Andrews.

'But I can see through that one a mile off, of course,' he goes on. 'Grandaddy day care. I mean, it would help if I was into golf, but there are worse places to lay a hat, I suppose.'

He waits a beat.

'But the trouble there is . . . it's a long way from anywhere. And it's a bloody long way from Porthpella, Ally.'

'It is, but . . . not as far as Sydney.'

Ally's daughter is on the other side of the world, and over the years – especially since Bill died – she has refused various entreaties to emigrate. As much as Ally loves her daughter and her grandsons, a granny flat in the Sydney suburbs holds no appeal. Nor can she imagine, in truth, being anywhere but Porthpella.

‘So I’ve been thinking,’ says Ray, ‘and the other option . . .’

And Ally has the impression of a car changing gears, a shift in the engine’s tune.

‘. . . is that I head west.’

‘West?’

Ally feels strangely suspended, caught between currents.

‘Cross the Tamar, once and for all,’ he says. ‘How would you feel about that?’

2

'Do one-year-olds really need birthday parties?' says Jayden.

Benji is currently rolling around on the carpet, bellowing incomprehensibly, waving his legs in the air. He looks a lot like the kind of person that, in Jayden's old life – patrolling Leeds city centre on a Saturday night – he'd have had a few words with. Only, really cute.

'Of course they do,' says Cat. 'Jazz loved hers. And check him, Jay. Life and soul.'

Benji is indeed the life and soul. He skipped walking and, a month ago, jumped straight to running – and now there's no stopping him. He thunders through the rooms of their small cottage, and at every opportunity he's out and across the farmyard, heading for the barns. Jayden's father-in-law is so impressed with his spirit he's decided that Benji's going to run the farm one day.

Funny, he's never said that about me.

Not that Jayden wants to run a farm. Like, ever. When Cat first pitched the idea of them moving into the little cottage at Upper Hendra, Jayden presumed it was a temporary thing. Get out of the city, find their feet, have some help with their baby daughter. But three years later, they're still here. And their business is here too: the campsite will be expanding into another field this summer. Cat shows no signs of wanting to shift, and after the tough time she had following Benji's birth, Jayden will do anything to make life easier and happier for her. Though even if they wanted to move, they couldn't afford it. The prices round here are silly, and while the campsite turns a good profit in the high season, the detective work doesn't exactly bring in the big bucks. Although their last major client – Louisa King at the High Tide Hotel – did write them a sizeable cheque back in November. Jayden's share is earmarked for the campsite's toilet block expansion.

Glamour, glamour.

'Let's get everyone down, Jay,' says Cat. 'Your mum and dad, your sister, the kids.'

'Where will they all stay?'

Jayden's mum and dad got on fine with Cliff and Sue at their wedding, but he can't imagine them all bunking up in the farmhouse together.

Cat looks to the window. 'A day like this, it feels like we could open the campsite early.'

And it's true that the sky is fully blue. But Jayden knows that if he steps outside, a lively breeze will take this illusion of summer and kick it all the way back to winter. He's come to realise that spring in Cornwall is an unpredictable month.

'Yeah, Mum and Dad aren't really the camping type,' he says. 'They'd do a B&B though.'

But already he's thinking of his curmudgeonly father-in-law and his eternally optimistic dad sharing a couple of uneasy beers, trying to find common ground by way of crop rotation and jazz patterns, but mostly failing. His mum probably remarking how weirdly *white* this corner of the world is, and Cat's mum no doubt saying how she felt the exact reverse when she went to London for a stage show that one time. And his sister Ella, just finding it hilarious that Jayden, once a city boy through and through, now has sand in his shoes, or cow dung on a bad day, and is his Leeds accent morphing into something a little bit bumpkin?

Bring it on.

Plus, Jasmine, their daughter – a mighty three – would love a party for her little bro.

'Obviously we'd invite people round here too,' says Cat.

'How big is this thing getting?'

Cat takes his hand. 'I feel like I want to celebrate. For us too, you know?'

A few weeks after Benji's birth, Cat struggled. Jayden didn't realise how her mental health was dipping, and then felt guilty when he did, because he knew what it was like to be laid low and how could he not have seen it? When they first moved to Porthpella, he'd felt bleak. His friend and partner in the police, Kieran, had died while the two of them were on duty. Jayden knows Cat thinks it was being in Cornwall – away from the city, away from the crime scene, away from the job, away from basically everything – that helped Jayden find his way through the grief. But it was just time.

Time and – maybe a little bit – the detective work.

'I get that,' he says. He pantomimes checking his watch. 'Alright, we've got two weeks to organise a party to remember. For *us* to remember. Because, yeah, Benji's one. It's all lost on him.'

Their little boy barrels into their legs then, throwing his arms around both of them and gazing up with a look of such pure love that Jayden is instantly liquid.

'Don't count on it, Jay,' she says. 'Anyway, you've got time on your hands, right? Things are quiet with Ally?'

'Yeah, things are quiet.' Though, like always, he's hoping they won't stay that way. 'I'll take a look at some B&Bs.'

'Or there's that new self-catering place just off the coast road that's supposed to be good,' says Cat. 'Something Barns. Spindrift Barns?'

'I'll check it out.'

Jayden reaches for his phone, because he wants to look willing – and the thought of his family piling down from up north is kind of a nice one. They've never all been in Cornwall together, and as improbable as it once felt, Cornwall's his home.

He's about to tap in *Spindrift Barns* when he sees a Google alert. He clicks.

> Body found on Cornish island in search for missing man.

'Found it, Jay?'

'Lone Island,' says Jayden, his eyes scanning the piece. 'That's near here, right?'

'Lone Island?' Cat scoops up Benji, plants him on her hip. 'What made you think of that? You can't stay there, Jay. There's like one tiny cottage and they don't rent it to randoms.'

'They've found a man's body there,' says Jayden, eyes scanning the piece. 'Axel Marks. He's thirty-four.'

Just then Jasmine hurtles into the room, her dark curls flying, the closing soundtrack of her favourite TV show drifting through the living room door. Then Benji's hollering to be put down. And Cat's face is concerned.

'Washed ashore? How sad.'

Jayden nods, reads aloud, '"The circumstances surrounding his death are currently being treated as unexplained but are not thought to be suspicious." Axel Marks. You've never heard that name, no?'

Because round here, it's a small, small pond. But Cat shakes her head.

'Suss-pish, suss-pish,' Jazz starts chanting.

It can't be the first time his daughter's heard the word *suspicious* living in this house, but it feels all wrong.

'Anyway, Jay, not in front of the kids,' says Cat. She clicks back to her bright voice. 'So, Benji's party. Are you telling your parents, or am I?'

3

Saffron opens the windows wide. Delicate sunlight streams into the café, illuminating the walls that are patched in surf stickers and skate decks, the tie-dye cushions, the jungle-like foliage of the cheese plant. Saffron has filled jam jars with daffodils and set them on every table; the yellow heads are electric. She turns up the music and breaks out a few moves.

Spring is here. Finally.

Saffron's always glad to see the sunshine. If she's thinking commercially, the beach is much busier than on a grey-sky day, which means Hang Ten is busier too. She kept the café open through the winter for the first time this year, and let's just say the decision had its peaks and troughs. Peaks? She and her ex-boyfriend Broady, owner of the surf school next door, successfully ran not one, not two, but three Winter Waves and Wicked Warm-ups sessions together. It was a concept she came up with on the fly, mostly as a way to improve relations between them, and it turned out to be a hit with the die-hard cold-water surfers as much as the shivering beginners. Hang Ten was as rammed as in midsummer – misted windows, tunes pumping and the delicious aroma of coconut dahl. And there were more peaks. Like the time she skated to the café on a true-blue winter morning, clouds of white breath as she laughed on the turns, then propped her board on the decking to watch a pair of seals playing in the bay. The time a walking club of mums and babies came in – bobble hats and carriers; tired eyes and coffee fever – so happy to find the place open that they then came in every week, rain or shine, and Saffron knew to double her baking.

But there were troughs too. Horizontal rain. Mists so thick she couldn't see the shore. Winds that threatened to take the roof off. What that meant was all she got through the door was a bedraggled dog walker, if she was lucky, or a grizzled surfer who looked like they'd gone ten rounds. Thank goodness for her friends dropping by out of kindness. Like Gus, without fail. Because he loves her flat whites, but also, he really likes stepping away from the novel he's been writing forever.

And Constable Mullins.

Mullins, whose new thing this winter was running. That first time he came in, flash in a new tracksuit, cheeks red from the cold, let alone the exertion. A warm-up run before a shift, a shake-it-off run after a shift; Mullins told Saffron he runs on the beach seven days a week, but she can't vouch for that as she's only been open for four this winter. It's not that she doesn't believe in his commitment, but Saffron can't help feeling he's got something to prove. And guys like Mullins tend to add a little embellishment when that's the case. Still, he paid for his post-run coffee and brownie every single time. Which is more than he used to do.

Poor Tim, she heard Gus mutter once, but Saffron didn't probe it. The guy was getting fit. Okay, so progress in that department was compromised by all the baked goods, but maybe he's in it for the mental more than the physical.

Saffron moves into a patch of beautifully warm sunshine and closes her eyes. On the stereo, Desmond Dekker starts singing 'You Can Get It If You Really Want'. And in the quiet of the café, she thinks about what *she* really wants. Some people feel new energy on January the first as they make their resolutions, or in September, with that back-to-school, new-pencil-case vibe – but for Saffron, it's always the first sign of spring.

That's when she starts fizzing.

The door clangs, and she turns with a smile, ready to bring full-beam brightness to her first customer of the day.

'Morning!' she sings.

But the woman hovering in the doorway of Hang Ten looks as if that one word, that single greeting, is gale-force. She ducks her head, saying something inaudible in reply.

Okay, I'll tone it down.

Saffron smooths her denim apron and steps out from behind the counter.

'What can I get you?' she asks with an easy smile.

The woman wears a too-big navy-blue raincoat, and her fair hair is wild and windblown as if she's been at sea. She rubs her hands together like she's cold; her fingers look red, work-sore.

'I'm hoping you can help me?' she says.

And her face is all worry: her eyes wide as moons, lines criss-crossing her forehead. Even without the question, she seems to radiate need.

'Always,' says Saffron.

The thought lands that she might be a rough sleeper, and Saffron tries to make her smile as welcoming as possible.

'I'm . . . I'm actually looking for Ally Bright and Jayden Weston. You don't know where I can find them, do you?'

4

Ally sets off from The Shell House, taking the same sandy path through the marram grass that she's followed for what feels like forever. More or less the same path, anyway. The dunes rearrange themselves through the autumn and winter gales. The beach is never still, and that's part of why she loves it so much. The fact that life is always moving at the coast fills Ally with vitality.

Fox walks beside her. Gone are the days when he shot through the dunes like a bright-red fireball. Her best little friend is an old boy now, and sometimes Ally finds herself slowing and waiting, as he lays his small pawprints in hers. Together they crest the dunes, and Ally is hit with the full, wide vista of sea and sky and lightly sketched cloud formations. She tips her head back and takes it all in.

I said the wrong thing.

That's the thought that's darted into her mind and lodged. That's why she's come out here to walk, to think. She said the wrong thing to Ray, when he told her he was considering moving to Cornwall. Or, more accurately, she just didn't say much at all.

We've been seeing each other for coming up on a year, Ally, said Ray. *That's nothing short of miraculous, as far as I'm concerned.*

It's been a great surprise to her too. Only Ally's not sure she'd use the phrase 'seeing each other'. Is that part of her problem, her lack of willingness to define what they are? *We enjoy each other's company*, is how she explains it to Evie. *That's all.* And Evie always takes issue at 'that's all', responding with *It's a big deal, Mum. In a good way.*

And Ally can't refute that. Lord knows she's thought on it often enough. The first time Ray stayed at The Shell House, she felt like a stranger moving through her own home. It didn't feel wrong that he was there, just different. But then he drove back to Suffolk, to his fruit trees and his cat called Alf and all the usual patterns of his east coast life – and her own rhythms resumed too.

Ray selling up and moving to Cornwall? That would change everything.

'This way,' she says to Fox. 'Let's get a coffee, shall we?'

But she will absolutely not be mentioning Ray's announcement to Saffron. The girl's natural exuberance will have her already planning a welcome party. And St Andrews is still very much on the table, isn't it? The pull of his daughter and brand-new grandson must surely be stronger than Ally and Porthpella. But Ally knows Ray. And the way he said it? She thinks she can tell where his heart lies. She can also tell that he was disappointed by the hesitation in her response.

I know, he said quickly, *it is a bit of a bombshell. But if you think about it, so was everything that happened this time last year, Ally. The two of us getting back together after nearly half a century was about as improbable a thought as any I've ever had. And . . . look at us.*

Ally can see All Swell up ahead. *Gus.* Her neighbour in the dunes. He first came into her life at the same time as Jayden, three years ago now. Gus was the first man to make Ally feel something since Bill's death. The smallest flickering at first, a far-off storm lantern on a dark night. But it was a shock to realise that even that was possible; that through her continued grief she could come to feel such tenderness and fondness. Desire too. But events

– emotions – conspired, and they are settled as friends. Good friends. Dear friends.

As if there's been a conjuring, thoughts of Gus make actual Gus appear. He's hauling a bright-striped wooden deckchair on to the sand, and she smiles at the sight. Gus is one to make the most of a patch of sunshine: fill a glass, take a book, and go and sit in it. He's like Bill, in that way.

'Good morning,' she calls out.

'Ally,' he says. 'Can I get you a chair? I've a matching pair. End-of-summer sale and all winter I haven't had a chance to use them.'

'It's a beautiful chair, Gus.'

'Think I'll need a blanket, though – it's a bit chillier out here than I thought. Dickens, wasn't it, who said springtime is summer in the sun and winter in the shade? I think in Porthpella it's still resolutely *spring* in the sun.' He grins. 'Anyway. Coffee?'

'I was just on my way to Hang Ten, but . . .'

Fox has already settled in the sand, nose on his paws, as if his mind is made up. There was a time when Fox used to growl at Gus. Perhaps he's decided he's no longer a threat. Fox is, Ally has noticed, largely indifferent to Ray, as though he hasn't considered him at all.

'I made a carrot cake yesterday. Took me ages too. All that infernal grating isn't for the faint-hearted. I was actually going to ring and see if you wanted to take a slice or two off my hands.'

Ally smiles, narrows her eyes. 'Baking? Presumably that means your deadline is approaching?'

He huffs a sigh but his eyes dance. 'How did you guess?'

Gus came to Porthpella to write a novel. A year ago, he was actually signed by an agent, but the commercial interest seemed to slow him down rather than speed him up. Gus finally let Ally read his efforts back in the autumn, and she told him she thought it was fantastic. What she didn't tell him was that the parts she liked best were when she could see and feel actual Gus on the page. It didn't happen all that often, almost by accident, as if the author dropped the veil of fiction and showed his true face, through occasional expressions, or the tastes of certain characters. It was inexpressibly charming, to get these glimpses of her friend in the dunes, through the prism of an Oxford-set police procedural.

'I'm just pushing on with final edits from my agent,' he says, 'which should be exciting, I suppose, but it rather feels like I'm heading towards execution. So . . .' He grins. 'Coffee and carrot cake?'

But Ally's distracted by a woman who appears to have stopped on the beach perhaps twenty yards away. She holds up one hand, shielding the sun from her eyes, and is staring directly at the pair of them.

'Morning,' calls out Ally. Because it feels strange not to.

'Morning!' Gus follows. Then, quietly, 'Friend of yours, Ally?'

'No,' says Ally. The woman's walking towards them now. Perhaps she's looking for directions. But as she comes closer, Ally has a sudden feeling. It's hard to articulate. Not a bad feeling as such, but one of graveness. And certainty.

This woman has sought me out.

'I'm sorry but . . . you're Ally Bright, aren't you?'

The question feels almost inevitable. Ally nods.

'The girl at the café said . . . Well, I was on my way to see you. But then I thought I recognised you. From your picture.'

She's perhaps in her forties. Her face is faintly tanned and lined, as if she lives her life outdoors. As she looks down, her fair hair blows about in the wind. Her heavy boots are sunk deep in the sand.

And Ally can feel the sadness pouring from her like water.

5

Jayden scrolls through the playlist. It's coming together. The kind of tunes the toddler crowd can get behind, as well as the older generations. He adds Sister Nancy, Saffron's favourite, and grins thinking of their first Christmas party together – *sorry, Tom Bawcock's Eve party* – at The Shell House. Mullins in his reindeer jumper. Ally and Gus nodding along to 'Bam Bam'. Turned out Porthpella was full of surprises.

Party planning doesn't give Jayden much of a buzz, but putting together a decent playlist? That he's on board with. And it's why he's got right on it instead of his actual work – which, today, is making some updates to their website ahead of the new camping season. *No contest.* Jayden eyes his list again. How much Trojan Records is too much Trojan Records? Yeah, no such thing. But he adds Pharrell's 'Happy' just to mix things up a bit. Then he finds himself clicking back to the news. Back to *Body found on Cornish island in search for missing man.*

He eyes his phone.

Cat's taken Jazz and Benji across to the farmhouse for an hour.

He makes the call.

'Mullins, what's up?'

'Alright, Jay.'

'Busy?'

'Always.' A beat. 'Actually, yeah. But you know, right? That's why you're calling me.'

Jayden hesitates. 'I could have just been calling you for a chat. Suggesting a beer.'

'When have you ever suggested a beer?'

And Mullins says it so quickly, it makes Jayden think that it's a *thing*. Does Mullins want to go for beers? Is Mullins vexed because it's never happened?

Hold on, it must have happened. At some point. Surely?

'Anyway, there's not much to write home about,' says Mullins. 'Bloke reported missing, vulnerable sort, more or less homeless. Substance-abuse issues. All that.'

'Who reported him missing?'

'The Grey family over at Porthmerrin House, if you must know.'

'Am I supposed to know who they are?'

'Landed gentry, Jay.'

Jayden wrinkles his brow. 'How come these "landed gentry" reported him missing? Are they his family?'

'No, his van was just parked up on their land for the night. All above board: they invited him. His mum used to work there back in the day, but she passed away years ago. As far as we know he's got no next of kin. Anyway, the Greys were concerned that he'd walked off in the night, worse for wear, and gone over the cliff. Turns out they nailed it, because a few hours later we're getting a phone call from Lone Island, of all places. Lady over there found a body on the beach.'

Jayden's tapping *Porthmerrin House* into Google, zooming out and seeing the map of the coastline, Lone Island about a mile offshore.

'She's the island warden,' says Mullins, 'the lady who found him. Her and her husband look after the place for a private wild-life trust. Only the husband's none too plussed with island living and has done a runner. And I tell you what, Jay, I don't blame him either. There's remote, and then there's being the only people on a sad little rock in the ocean. No thanks.'

The only living *people at least.*

'So the warden was on her own when she found the body?'

'Yup,' says Mullins. 'And *freaked out* is not the word. It's two words.' He chuckles to himself. 'Anyway, I haven't got all day, Jay. I know you and Ally like to chase an ambulance, but there's nothing here for you this time.'

'Chase? The ambulances come to us, Mullins. So listen, in the paper it basically says the death is unexplained but not suspicious.'

'So you can read. Gold star.'

'Does that mean you're closing the investigation?'

'Not yet, but we're close. The bloke went through it, didn't he? First he falls off a cliff, then he's tossed around in the ocean, smashed on the rocks. Obviously, the corpse is showing all kinds of serious trauma, but nothing that doesn't square with all of the above . . .'

Jayden can hear Mullins hesitate.

'And yet?' he offers.

'The lady who found him is a little bit out there.'

'Out there?'

'Too much time on the island on her own, I reckon. She's calling foul play, with nothing to base it on except for a "feeling".'

'And what do you think?'

'I think . . .'

Again, that hesitation.

'Jayden, what I think is that I've got a shedload of paperwork to do, and playing Twenty Questions might be your idea of fun, but . . .'

'Why was Axel Marks invited to Porthmerrin House? I mean, *specifically* why. Beyond the connection with his mum.'

'Wouldn't you like to know?'

'That's why I asked.'

It's true that with their last case at the High Tide Hotel, Mullins surprised them both with his incisiveness, but sometimes Jayden thinks talking to the constable is like talking to his children.

No, that's not fair on the children.

'Listen, pal. Skinner's happy that everything's in order. So go back to whatever it is you were doing before you started fantasising about a little island adventure. It's not those Famous Five books you read when you were a kiddie, you know . . .'

'I was never into the Famous Five, Mullins.'

'Yeah, well. We've got a drifter who parks his van way too close to the cliff edge, then drinks himself silly. Doesn't take a genius to figure out what happens next. And, with respect, a mad lady out on a rock isn't going to be able to add anything, even if she thinks the corpse spoke to her.'

Jayden's eyes widen.

'What, he was alive when she found him?'

'You missed seeing my air quotes, Jay. Big massive air quotes. But, to clarify, no, the corpse did not have the power of speech. Hence the use of the word *corpse*.'

'Alright, Mullins,' says Jayden. 'Thanks, as ever, for your open-minded and—'

'Yeah, yeah. Over and out.'

Mullins has hung up.

Jayden clicks back to his work-in-progress playlist, and hits play on Pharrell. Music fills the room.

'Now maybe I'm about to say something crazy too,' he says, a beat behind the song. 'But there's at least three weird things in that story.'

And so he calls Ally.

6

Pippa Grant folds her hands around her mug. They're shaking slightly, and she doesn't want to look chaotic; she really doesn't. She tries to focus in on the coffee. It's good: rich and deep. It is, she thinks, a good house too. Warm, welcoming, a place of real love. Did she have that feeling when she stepped through the door of Lone Cottage? Not as such, but, nevertheless, a sensation that she was home.

It felt right. And that's the heartbreak.

The Shell House isn't fussy, but care has been taken with the interior. An artist's touch, with the white-painted wooden boards, the bright seascapes on the walls, the shelves of beach finds: bowls of shells; a perfect starfish; the delicate architecture of a mermaid's purse. Pippa's eyes go to the photograph above the fireplace, a smiling man in a striped apron presiding over a summer barbecue. Ally Bright's late husband, and his smile is all kindness.

Pippa did her homework, before she came here.

She lowers her shoulders and evens her breathing, trying to let the calm of this house in the dunes quell her hectic thoughts. But all she can think about is the dead man on the beach. And how it means the end of everything. *Unless . . .*

'Oh, Lone Island is beautiful,' says Ally.

'I fell in love with its name as much as anything. It spoke to me.'

It's been such a long time since Pippa has sat and talked with another woman like this – across a kitchen table, mugs, a coffee pot – that she's sure she's forgotten how.

'It's the most beautiful place in the world,' she says.

It comes out with too much fervour, like she's at a rally with words on a placard. Like she's *fighting*. But that's how it is, when something is being taken away from you. Something that you couldn't have looked after better or loved more. That's how it is. And her eyes burn, as if they're wide open in salt water.

Pippa shifts beneath Ally's quiet, assessing gaze. It's gentle enough, but there is scrutiny too. Of course there is. The woman's a detective. She might have become one by accident, but there's been no chance element since. Pippa has read about the cases that Ally has solved. If anyone can help, Pippa is certain it's her.

'How did you first come to be on the island?' asks Ally.

Pippa resists the urge to say, *What's that got to do with anything?* Because she needs to keep her on side, this Ally Bright. Pippa has no money to pay her, and she wants so desperately for her to take the case. So she tells her, taking it all the way back to the beginning. Well, not the *beginning* beginning – she has no intention of opening up old wounds. Instead, Pippa tells of an advertisement, an interview, and then another; an offer letter arriving in the mail. The packing of bags. The little boat out, lifting up and over the waves, the way her stomach pitched and tossed too, but her heart – her heart was singing. How the island looked so featureless from afar, no more than a rock, but then the sand underfoot, a mosaic of exotic shells and spilled sugar and pebbles as smooth as coins. Rhododendron flowers so rich and ripe she felt like they'd stumbled into the Amazon. Cascades of the sweetest-smelling honeysuckle. A single palm tree, as round and fat as a pineapple. Cormorants as bent and angular as old men, huddled with their heads together. Seals that lifted a languid flipper, then flopped from the rocks. A jellyfish, big as a bedside lamp, flowing into the cove. The symphony of birdsong.

Then, the cottage. Cold, even in summer. The most basic of bathrooms. A Dark Ages kitchen. A flagstone floor that sloped like the deck of a ship, and a tiny winding staircase that creaked as if each step was breaking underfoot. But the view from those upper salt-crusted windows.

All that blue.

Ally listens as if she's spellbound, and Pippa begins to think she might understand after all.

'They warned us that it'd take some adjusting to,' she tells Ally. 'The isolation. How when things go wrong, you're on your own. How sometimes even the boatman won't go out, and then it's weeks on end. But honestly, we loved it. I love it.'

Pippa sees Ally note the change of pronouns.

'Fergus, my husband, he's more sociable than me. He missed people. So he went back and forth from the mainland more.'

'Was Fergus with you when you found the body, Pippa?'

'No, he wasn't.'

And Pippa explains that, actually, Fergus has left the island. That he's been gone for a while. That he is, in fact, probably never coming back. She feels her eyes sting again, her throat burns too, and it's not because of the loss of him – *well, it's a little to do with the loss of him* – but rather the loss of everything else.

Her island life is over. *Unless . . .*

Pippa watches Ally process this detail of Fergus leaving. It's not the first sad story of Pippa's life. And it's not the worst, not by a long chalk.

'Will you stay on?' asks Ally.

'I want to.'

But wanting something and getting it are two quite different things.

'The trust will only employ a couple. But if I can persuade them that I'm up to the job on my own . . .' Her voice falters. 'I have to at least try.'

Again, Ally looks as if she understands. Living here in the dunes is a cushioned sort of existence compared to Lone Island, but the woman must appreciate wildness, nevertheless. She must enjoy solitude. For a second, a fractional second, Pippa imagines laying it all bare. How it might feel, to fill this woman's arms with all that she's carrying.

But instead she says, 'I know about being on my own. My first husband died.'

It's the line Pippa prepared, but the taste of it in her mouth is all wrong. Her eyes flick to Bill Bright's picture on the wall.

'I'm sorry,' says Ally.

Pippa waits. What did she expect? For Ally to clasp her hand and say, *Oh, mine too, dear.* If there's kinship there, it's muted.

'Tell me how you found the body,' says Ally.

And it is why she's here. Perhaps Pippa doesn't need to offer Ally anything more.

'I couldn't see him at first,' she says, looking down into her coffee. 'He was on the strandline. The way the currents run, the south beach is always strewn with wreckage. Driftwood as big as a wardrobe. A forest's worth of bladderwrack. But then I saw his blue jacket.'

Pippa's clutching her mug as if she wants to break it. She puts it down before Ally notices the white press of her fingertips, her red knuckles.

'When I was a child, I used to imagine what it'd be like to find a body,' she goes on. 'I suppose I'd watched too many dramas on television. You know, if it opens with a dog walker going through a forest, you just know that dog's going to find something, that the owner's going to call and the dog's not going to come, because it's too busy dragging out a thigh bone, or . . .'

Macabre.

'. . . but nothing can prepare you for what it's actually l-like.'

Pippa stutters to a stop. She hasn't stammered in years, but every so often it surfaces, like a single raindrop out of a grey sky. The trick is to pay it no heed. Don't, whatever you do, stop and hold your hands up and say, *Is that rain?*

'It must have been shocking,' says Ally.

Pippa wonders if Ally has ever found a body. Being a detective, the likelihood is higher, probably, than average. *And then there's her husband.*

'Of course, on the television they always scream, the people who find the bodies,' says Pippa. 'And what's the use of that, on an island where no one can hear you? So I didn't scream. I cried. I sat down and cried.'

There beside him; this stranger, washed up on the shore. His shredded tracksuit jacket. His torn jeans. His broken, busted face. Pippa sat down beside him and wept.

'It was the tattoo that did it. His jacket was ripped, and I could see his bare arm. He had this tattoo. "Swift and Bold", it said. And I thought, is that what you were once? I hope you were. I hope you knew swiftness and boldness. It struck me as the saddest thing.'

Pippa sits straighter in her seat. She takes a deep breath and feels it judder in her chest.

'And that's why I'm here,' she says. 'That's why I came looking for you.'

For this is where no one has listened to Pippa before. Where those police officers looked at her as if she'd started talking of angels or devils or any such thing that they wanted no part of.

'I'm a practical person. I'm not religious, or even especially spiritual.'

Pippa feels like she needs to say this. Perhaps it's how she should have started with the police, but she was too jittery to set up a rational argument. And now? Pippa knows nothing of Ally Bright's beliefs, but she knows she can't afford to be written off by her too.

'But I do believe in feelings. I do trust in mine. And I got such a strong feeling from this man, Ally.'

Pippa can hear the crack in her voice. It hasn't left her, the feeling from the beach. If anything, it's intensified.

'I felt that someone had done him a great wrong.'

She lets the words settle. Ally is a good listener. Pippa can see that she absorbs the significance of what she's saying, but she doesn't press for more.

In your own time.

The words of the kindly female police officer, all those years ago, rise in Pippa's mind. And how, against all the odds, that phrasing felt like a crumb of power handed back to her. As if time was something Pippa owned, perhaps even had control over; when she felt she had control over nothing, and clocks were just another thing to smash at the wall.

Pippa has come such a long way to be at Lone Island. Her job – as long as it lasts – is to take care of the place, and all of its creatures. And that is what she's doing now.

'He didn't want to be in that water, Ally. He didn't want to be dead on my beach. That's what I felt, so very strongly. That someone had sent him there.' She can feel her voice rising; her heart flutters like a trapped bird. 'That it wasn't suicide, or a tragic accident. It was murder. Axel Marks was murdered.'

7

After Pippa leaves, her story stays within The Shell House. Ally can feel it settling around her, as light but drenching as mizzle. The details of the torn tracksuit jacket. The words *Swift and Bold.* The bladderwrack wrapped tight around his legs. His face, damaged by water and rocks, but his deep brown eyes – *soft eyes, Ally, soulful* – appearing to gaze deep into Pippa's.

He spoke to me, she said.

The first thing Ally did was call Jayden and she waits for him now, out on the veranda. In classic spring-day style, the weather has turned jumpy. Clouds crowd the horizon, but there's enough blue for the sun to still hold. Ally has donned a jumper, though – one of Bill's, as it happens, a navy fisherman's jersey – because it's chilly, sitting waiting. But she wants the clean, crisp air. The fortifying sunlight.

Because the trouble is, she's not quite sure what she thinks.

Ally identifies with Pippa's appreciation of her island home. And then the trauma of such a brutal interruption; how that must have felt to be a woman alone, so far from anyone, discovering the body. What Ally finds harder to identify with is Pippa's certainty that Axel was murdered.

Ally is a little suspicious of certainty. She admires conviction, in the right places, but when people don't acknowledge the possibility of doubt, a small alarm goes off inside her. Is it the same alarm that also sounded as Ally saw Pippa's eyes go to the photograph of Bill, as she mentioned her first husband having died? Pippa must have read a newspaper article online, referencing Ally's connection to the force; there are a couple out there, from when her and Jayden's cases started hitting headlines locally. Perhaps it was natural for Pippa to offer this point of connection. But it felt rather out of the blue.

Ally opens the newspaper again and rereads the article. *The circumstances surrounding his death are currently being treated as unexplained but are not thought to be suspicious.* Then she takes out her phone and searches for the deceased's name online. *Axel Marks.* She finds slightly different iterations of the same article, but even in the comments sections – where opinions are ventured freely and seemingly without much basis – there is little to support Pippa's theory.

Pippa's feeling.

Ally's philosophy is one of 'never say never'. There have been moments, particularly since Bill's death, when the lines between this world and the next – *and don't ask me what 'next' means because I don't know* – have seemed to blur. She has stood on the beach at sunset, the sea and sky all flame and colour, her spirit soaring; felt the dance of magic in the luminous light. Or in the depths of night, her head tilted to watch a sky loaded with a number of stars, a full-bright moon, a scene so dizzying that the earth falls away entirely.

Wonder, everywhere. Sometimes the fact that this world, and any human being in it, exists at all feels like a miracle. Not in a religious sense, but rationally, surely? The extraordinary gift of it. And so much still not known.

Who is Ally to say that Pippa didn't feel something? There are infinite things that Ally does not understand. And is a 'feeling' so very different from the 'instinct' that Jayden talks of, so important in detective work? How Jayden's old partner Kieran used to say that it was what made the difference between a good officer and a great officer.

Perhaps Pippa – this windblown woman, her eyes so sad, her need so apparent – simply has great instincts.

Ally sees Jayden appearing over the dunes and stands up, her hand raised. His tall, slender frame, his loping stride. He has a coat slung over his arm; he'll have charged down here from the farm, driven by the thought of a new case.

A possible new case.

'Al!' says Jayden, bursting through the gate. The sun-faded buoys swing on their ropes – a decorative touch that Bill always rolled his eyes at – as the gate shuts behind him. The abundant rosemary brushes his legs as he makes his way up the path.

'Do you believe in serendipity, Al?'

And here was Ally thinking Pippa's basis for their case might be a hard sell for Jayden.

'Actually, nothing serendipitous about it,' he says, going for a knuckle-bump.

A Shell House knuckle-bump, as Constable Mullins calls them. Three years on, Ally has stopped feeling completely ridiculous as she holds up her fist in response. She now feels only mildly ridiculous. But it always makes her smile.

'So, I see a report in the paper and get on the phone to Mullins. That's just due diligence, right? Meanwhile you get a new client through the door because we're not the new kids on the block anymore. All totally logical.' He grins. 'Is there a coffee going?'

'There's always a coffee going.'

'What about one of those ginger biscuits?'

'You know the tin.'

They go inside together.

'You've saved me from website wrangling,' he says. 'It's the countdown to opening the campsite and we've decided the site needs a refresh. Website, I mean, not campsite. Though that could do with one too, to be fair. Cat's got planting plans. She wants a tropical garden for people to hang out in. Drinks beneath the palms, that kind of thing.'

'She's welcome to some cuttings,' says Ally.

'That would be awesome. Sue's got a bunch of succulents but they're not looking that . . . succulent. Oh, before I forget. Benji's having a party. Two weeks on Saturday. First birthday. We'd love you to be there. Obviously bring Ray, if he's down.'

If he's down. Jayden's head is tipped to one side, his eyes enquiring. Her young friend has never probed the parameters of her and Ray's relationship.

On another day, Ally might have talked to Jayden about Ray's house plans – and how the first emotion she felt, one Ally hasn't fully got to the bottom of, surprised her. Through the intricacies of their investigations, and the meshing of their personal lives alongside, there's little territory that they're not comfortable covering and she can always count on Jayden for a measured and open-minded response. But now? There's a case.

A potential case.

'The first thing to say,' says Ally, getting the stovetop coffee pot going, 'is that Pippa, the island warden, has no funds to pay us.'

'Okay.'

'So, she said she'll understand if we can't take the case,' says Ally, hearing the caution in his voice. 'She said she simply had to tell us about it, because she felt like we'd understand, and want to help.'

'Going for the heartstrings, then?' says Jayden, one eyebrow raised. 'Sorry. Bit cynical.'

'I don't disagree, but . . .'

She thinks again of Pippa's mention of her late first husband, the pointed look towards Bill's photograph. Is Ally overthinking things? It has become, perhaps, an occupational hazard. As much as

Ally thinks she has good judgement, the detective work has taught her to be cautious of trusting too easily. She now believes that, given the right circumstances, almost anyone is capable of almost anything. But what possible reason could Pippa have for wanting to hire them, beyond one of good intentions?

'She seemed very sincere. And almost . . . somewhat haunted.'

'"Out there" was Mullins's verdict.'

'That doesn't surprise me. But I think that says more about our friend Mullins than Pippa Grant.'

'Yeah, but what was surprising was that part of Mullins was genuinely interested in Pippa's reaction. He didn't say that as such – I mean, this is Mullins we're talking about – but I could tell that it was kind of bugging him. Did Pippa talk about the Grey family, and Porthmerrin House?'

'She said the police confirmed that they were the ones who'd reported Axel Marks missing.'

Ally thinks of Pippa's face as she talked about Porthmerrin. The tightness to her mouth.

'I was wondering if she had an axe to grind, that's all,' says Jayden – and it's as if he's reading Ally's mind.

'I didn't get that impression. At least, not as a reason for why she's so sure it's foul play. But she did tell me that Lone Island used to be part of the Porthmerrin estate, and it was gifted to a wildlife trust several generations ago. Edward Grey used to make it his business to meet all the wardens, apparently, but he's elderly now, and so when they first arrived, he sent his gardener to meet Pippa instead. I sensed she didn't particularly enjoy the experience.'

'Oh yeah? How long ago was that?'

'Pippa and her husband Fergus moved to the island six months ago.'

'That's a lonely life. Mullins said the husband's no longer in the picture too.'

The coffee pot starts whistling, and Ally gets two mugs. 'It sounds like our constable friend was rather forthcoming.'

'Yeah, hardly,' laughs Jayden. 'Just my expert interrogation skills.'

'Pippa's husband left two weeks ago, and apart from anything else, she's worried that that means the end of her time on the island. Apparently, the wildlife trust will only employ a couple, or two people anyway. It's a one-bedroom cottage.'

'What, for Health and Safety? I guess I wouldn't want to be on that island all by myself.'

Ally smiles. For a tough ex-cop, Jayden can occasionally be unsettled by aspects of rural living.

'I think I'd rather like it. But it probably is a two-person job, monitoring the wildlife, maintaining the island itself.'

Jayden takes his coffee and raises it in a 'cheers' motion. Then as he has a sip he says, 'Ahh.' Just like Bill always did – coffee, pints, a glass of cold water on a hot day.

'So this Pippa's marriage has broken down,' he says, 'and it looks like she could lose her job too.'

'And her home,' says Ally.

'And her home. That's a triple hit. It makes sense that her emotions are running high right now.'

The same thought has crossed Ally's mind.

'Then she has the trauma of finding the body on the beach, and she's all on her own,' says Jayden. 'So maybe she's catastrophising . . .'

Ill winds blowing in every direction, so why not for Axel Marks too? Laid bare like this, Ally can see why Jayden would doubt Pippa's word. *Her feeling.*

'But . . .' says Jayden, 'all that aside, this case does have my interest, Al. It's that mix of Axel Marks and the people up at Porthmerrin House. Mullins described Axel as "more or less homeless". His mum used to work for the Grey family, apparently, but she died some years ago. And as far as the police know, he has no next of kin. Maybe the Greys are socially conscious, maybe they wanted to offer him a place to park his van overnight. No skin off their noses, is it? They've enough land – I mean, they're giving away islands, right? But, and maybe I'm being cynical, I don't see it.'

'Did Mullins know why Axel Marks was at Porthmerrin House?'

'He does, but he wasn't sharing that with me.'

Ally takes a sip of coffee and looks to the window. A windsurfer tracks across the bay, the sail as bright as a butterfly.

'So Mullins and Skinner have presumably interviewed everybody,' she says.

Jayden nods. 'Yeah. And obviously no alarm bells were ringing. Whatever Pippa's saying about it being murder, presumably it can't be backed up by physical evidence, so the police aren't thinking it's credible. The body was well battered by the elements, and the rocks. Mullins basically said that the post-mortem supports the thesis that he fell from the cliff, sustaining violent injuries, and then suffered further trauma being washed from the mainland on to the island. But there's no evidence of injury being inflicted from another source. Not enduring evidence, anyway.'

'Lone Island is very rocky,' says Ally. 'And the waves were high two nights ago. It would have been terrible. Did the cliff fall kill him, Jayden, or did he drown?'

'Mullins didn't say.'

They swap a look, both no doubt thinking of their first case, the one that brought them together: Lewis Pascoe, and the cliff fall.

'Whatever happened, it was the middle of the night, Al. According to the news, Axel Marks was reported missing more or less straight away, yesterday morning.'

'And Pippa found his body yesterday afternoon.'

'Did you like her, Ally?'

'Pippa?' She hesitates. 'I think so.'

'That's not a yes.'

'I liked her well enough. I feel sorry for her, certainly. And I believe that she believes what she's saying.'

Jayden narrows his eyes.

'Is that enough for us, Al?'

'To take the case, you mean?'

'To take the case. And not be paid for it.'

Ally thinks of Lone Island, feeling a prickle of anticipation. She imagines the pair of them taking the boat, pacing the beach, looking across the water to the mainland and the imposing sight of Porthmerrin House. Asking questions, looking for answers, trying to understand the life of a man who is gone, and to piece together his last movements on this earth – and in the water. Late-night sessions in the thinking room, coffee and theories flowing; the pursuit of crystalline truth – and wading through great swathes of the unknown to get there.

And – Ally has to admit – being so thoroughly occupied that she'll have little time to think of anything else. Not least Ray's disquieting proposition.

'It would be for me,' she says, feeling guilty at this last thought. 'But Jayden, you've got a family to take care of, you've got other responsibilities, and—'

'Al' – Jayden holds up his hand – 'it's good.'

'So, you do want to take the case?'

'I always want to take the case, Al,' he says with a grin.

8

'Okay,' says Jayden, 'let's start with the facts that we have.'

They're in the thinking room. Bill's old office, a space that Jayden knows is special to Ally. So special that, for the first year and a half of their work together, Jayden didn't know it existed – even though The Shell House is not the biggest place in the world. It was almost as if it was only when Ally truly believed herself to be a detective that she felt it was okay to wipe clean that whiteboard, pick up those markers, sit in that leather chair of her late husband's. They've had some decent breakthroughs in this room. Case-changing moments. Jayden feeling that electric charge of different investigative strands fusing; the pieces of a puzzle clicking together, the picture clear to see.

'Well, we don't know very much at this point,' says Ally. 'Only that Axel is thirty-four years old and it was the Grey family at Porthmerrin House who reported him missing.'

'His mum used to work for the owner, Edward Grey, but we're not sure in what capacity. As far as the police know, Axel's got no living family.'

'He parked his van on the Greys' land for the night,' says Ally.

'And on that, Mullins called him "more or less homeless". We don't know if he lived in his van full-time, if he based himself in

Cornwall or was passing through. Actually . . . what am I saying? You don't pass through Cornwall. It's the end of the line.'

'So the big question is why he was at Porthmerrin House.'

'I want to know more about his relationship with the people there too,' says Jayden. 'If he was a frequent visitor, or if this was a one-off.' Jayden pauses with his marker pen. 'I think there's going to be a lot of legwork with this one, Al. Because the trouble is, Pippa doesn't know anything about the victim either. We've never started a case with less information.'

'You never know, Mullins and Skinner might be willing to share what they know.'

'Al, hardly. And remember, they think we've lost our touch, right? Or Skinner does anyway, after what happened at the High Tide Hotel.'

Their last major case, in the autumn. Ally and Jayden got their answers, but at the end there was something of a gap between them and the police.

'But Mullins knew better,' she says, 'didn't he?'

'Yeah, we've never gone there with him, though, have we? And I don't want to either.'

The funny thing is, Jayden felt sure that Mullins would enjoy holding what happened with the High Tide Hotel case over them. But he never has. Which either speaks to a greater human understanding than Jayden might have credited Mullins with, or . . . he's saving it for a rainy day.

'What if you and Mullins went for a beer?' says Ally. 'Talked informally about this case.'

Beers with Mullins. Why does that keep coming up?

'Because, Jayden, the police already have so much of what we want to know. I'm trying to picture us catching up on our own, walking up to a place like Porthmerrin House, and . . . Well, what's our angle?'

'Same angle as always. We're private investigators. If people don't have anything to hide, then they won't take issue with answering a few questions.'

But Jayden's travelling hopefully. When you carry the badge, people have to give you the time of day. Private detectives, though? You're dependent on goodwill, or curiosity. People connecting with some kind of civic duty.

'You're right,' says Ally. 'Okay. And we'll do some groundwork first. I bet Wenna will be able to tell me more about Edward Grey and any other Porthmerrin residents.'

'For sure.'

Wenna, aka The Oracle, has run White Wave Stores for the last thirty years. Even if the Greys, this family of landed gentry from fifteen miles up the coast, have never darkened the door of her shop, she's sure to have the basic facts – and probably some juicy gossip too. The difficult bit will be getting away once she's started talking.

'So, if I'm going for a beer with Mullins, do you want to talk to Wenna?'

Ally smiles. 'That seems a fair division of labour.'

'Alright. Can we talk about Pippa for a minute? We don't know very much about her.'

'No. She told me all about Lone Island, and it's obvious she's very at home in nature. But her life before she came to the island . . . we didn't go into it.'

Jayden rubs the back of his head. 'I mean, we've got to consider the possibility that she might have an ulterior motive here.'

'But what could that possibly be?'

Good question.

'She might want the attention,' says Jayden. 'She might be feeling . . . voiceless.'

'Voiceless?'

'Her husband's left and now her job and her home are compromised. That's a lot, right? And maybe she's not in control of any of it. Suddenly she finds herself bang in the middle of this drama, police turning up on the island, taking her statement, making her feel important. Only they're not listening to her.'

Jayden starts pacing, warming to his theme.

'We know how that feels, right? Our first case, when I saw Helena Hunter running in the dunes? Skinner couldn't have been more dismissive if he tried. And it made me feel rubbish. And Pippa, maybe she's already feeling rubbish. And she's scared too. I mean, she's just found a dead body, and she's on that island on her own. She wants someone to listen to her, to pay her attention, to feel like there's someone *in this* with her, you know? And so she comes to us. And you're kind. You give her coffee. You gave her coffee, right?'

'I gave her coffee.'

'And suddenly she's not alone anymore. And she's being taken seriously.'

'But even if all that's true, it doesn't alter the fact that there *could* be more to this.'

'True,' says Jayden. 'And that's why we're taking the case. But for me there's a question mark around our client too.'

'But that question mark should fade once we get to know her better, shouldn't it?'

'A hundred per cent.' He stands back and looks at the board. 'Okay, so, basically . . . right now we don't know anything about our victim.'

'He had a tattoo on his arm, Pippa said. "Swift and Bold". She was moved by it, given the context.'

'Okay, so we know he had a tattoo.'

Jayden writes *Swift and Bold* on the board. The two words look so sad up there – so far from their meaning. He gets why they struck a note with Pippa too.

'And we don't know anything about our suspects,' he says. 'Yet.'

'But we do have suspects?'

Jayden draws a circle around Porthmerrin House. 'We begin at the source, Al.'

9

Porthpella's main square isn't quite ready for the tourist season yet. The winds are too brisk for Wenna's postcard racks, and even though it's a bright day there are no sun umbrellas outside The Wreckers Arms; no one wants shade, unless they're prepared to add some layers. Nevertheless, the blue sky brings a festive air to all beneath it. In the depths of winter, the grey stone buildings, with their bright painted doors and window ledges, appear to huddle together, but today it's as if they're standing tall, holding their faces to the sun. The palm trees look right at home, their spiked shadows dancing on the pavements. And everywhere Ally looks there are profusions of daffodils.

Across the square, Sunita's Bluebird gallery is a beacon of colour. One of Ally's vivid collages fills the window: sea thrift, wide skies, the coast path going up and over the headland, all made out of tiny pieces of plastic she cleaned from the beaches up and down the area. Working in her lean-to studio, back at The Shell House, is one of Ally's great pleasures; as is wandering the shoreline, looking for natural treasures too.

Before the detective work, Ally's days felt filled with this occupation – but perhaps a murder investigation isn't so very different. During a case she moves slowly, eyes down, searching for details of interest. Spotting what others don't. Then she holds her finds up to the light: might they form a part of a picture? What happened to Axel Marks is a mystery. How his body ended up on Lone Island is a mystery. But if she and Jayden do all the things they've done before – walking the strandline of the case, with care and attention – Ally knows they'll get there. In the end.

They're just crossing the square together – Ally on her way to Wenna's, Jayden headed for The Wreckers for some desk research – when a sign catches Ally's eye.

For Sale.

Lighthouse Cottage. A little white-stone place with a grey slate roof. Olive painted windowsills and a whale knocker on the front door. She knows how it looks inside too: charming, if a touch too polished for Ally's tastes, as if someone has gone through a catalogue and picked everything out in one fell swoop. It's a holiday cottage owned by out-of-towners – and this time last year, give or take a few weeks, it was rented by Ray.

Ally realises she's stopped in the middle of the road.

'You alright, Al?' says Jayden.

Is it a sign?

Surely, with all Ray's talk of a move to Cornwall – *and there is St Andrews too, St Andrews is still very much under consideration* – he wouldn't be thinking of Porthpella itself? But Ally is certain that if Ray mentioned to his buyer – the romantic novelist who apparently lives by her heart – that the moment he decides to sell up, the very cottage he stayed in a year ago, the one where he became reacquainted with an old love, suddenly comes on the market . . . well, Ally knows what the woman would say. What anyone would say, really.

It's a sign.

Jayden is still looking at her quizzically.

'Yes, sorry, just . . . I noticed the "For Sale" sign.'

'You're not interested, are you?' he says, surprised.

'Of course not. I'd never leave The Shell House. No . . . Just . . . it always surprises me when holiday houses go up for sale. I imagine they're good earners.'

Ally has given very little thought to the income from holiday lets before – but the answer seems to satisfy Jayden.

'It'll be silly money,' he says. 'Meanwhile someone like Mullins is still living with his mum. Though actually, I think he *likes* living with his mum, but that's not the point. Speaking of, he's up for a pint later, so I'll be back here again. Alright, good luck with Wenna, Al. Come over to The Wreckers when you're done. Hopefully I'll have dug up a bit more background for us.'

With a last look towards the 'For Sale' sign, Ally dips her head and makes for the store.

The bell jangles as she enters, as loud as church bells. It's cave-like inside, with everything from everyday groceries to holiday souvenirs to a sprinkling of artisan, locally sourced items.

'Oh, hello Ally love.'

Wenna's jaws are always moving with some sweetie or other, plundered from the rows of glass jars behind the counter, and if Ally had to guess today, she'd say mint toffee.

'How are you keeping, Ally? Makes ever such a difference seeing the sun, doesn't it? We're simple really, aren't we, us humans? All we ask for is a bit of brightness now and again. Mind you, I wouldn't go out without my cardie on yet. Not on your nelly.'

Ally moves along the shelves, because she can't not buy something. Information in exchange for a box of Cornish fairings. A bottle of wine. A bunch of bananas.

'Wenna, I wanted to pick your brains. Do you know the people at Porthmerrin House?'

'Porthmerrin?' Wenna shakes her head. 'You've heard too then, have you? News travels fast, and perhaps sad news fastest of all. I didn't know Edward Grey personally – he wouldn't have exactly rubbed shoulders with the likes of me and Gerren, would he? But I knew *of* him, of course.'

'Was Edward Grey close to Axel Marks, then?'

'Axel Marks? Oh, you mean the poor bloke they found out on Lone Island yesterday.' Wenna looks confused for a moment, her brows knitting. Her glasses pitch down her nose. 'I was talking about Edward. Seventy-five years of age, which is nothing these days, is it? But he was down to bone by the end. Probably a kindness, him passing.'

Ally puts her groceries down on the counter.

'It was Ginny who told me,' Wenna runs on. 'Gerren's sister's niece. She saw the ambulance going up to the big house, and she doesn't hold back in getting the goss, that one. He passed with his family around him, and that's all anyone can ask for really, isn't it? In the end.'

Which only makes Ally think of Axel being all alone.

'Sorry, Wenna,' she says, 'I'm a bit behind here. When did Edward Grey die?'

'This morning, dear.'

However interested Ally was in Porthmerrin House, she's even more interested now. Could two deaths, in such quick succession, simply be coincidence? Was the elderly man's demise sped by the upsetting events of yesterday?

'I'd have thought you'd have heard the news, Ally, a big noise like Edward dying. Though I suppose you're not into all that, are you? Neither am I, if I'm honest. I don't need A-listers in my little black book, do I? And Edward did live very quietly, for all his money. It wasn't as if they opened up the house for village parties or anything like that. And of course, if he'd been doing his shopping, he'd have gone to Merrin, wouldn't he? Not Porthpella. And I love The Wreckers to pieces but it's not worth a twenty-odd-mile drive for a ham, egg and chips, is it? Even their crab sandwich would be pushing it.'

Ally attempts to get Wenna's darting mind back on track.

'So Edward Grey was ill?'

'On his last legs, apparently, and had been for a while.' Wenna turns, her hand going to the sweet jar. 'Why would you be asking about that poor chap with the funny name, though?'

'Axel Marks? He was reported missing by the Grey family, Wenna. Would that have been Edward, do you think?'

Wenna pops the toffee in her mouth and sucks for a moment, a rare instance of silence. *Well, not quite silence.*

'Now, that's a turn-up. I shouldn't have said it was Edward. I shouldn't have said he'd have had the wherewithal to notice anyone was missing. No, it would have been his son if it was anyone. Blow me if I can remember his name, though. He lives upcountry.' Wenna frowns. 'But Ally, why would someone like that bloke they found on the island matter to a family like the Greys?'

Exactly.

Although Ally doesn't care for Wenna's tone. She seems to have more compassion for the elderly patriarch who died with his family around him than for the man who was washed out to sea. It's also when Ally realises the limits of the shopkeeper's knowledge: Porthpella is a small pond, and while Edward Grey sounds like a big fish, his habitat was some miles away. A different pond altogether.

'I tell you what, Ginny would know, though. Gerren's sister's niece. She's got a cleaning business, which means she can tell you most things about most people.'

'Does she clean for the Greys?'

'No, no. Holiday lets. Doesn't want people watching her every move, and I wouldn't either.'

'I don't suppose you'd put me in touch with Ginny, would you, Wenna?'

Wenna pushes her glasses up her nose and regards Ally steadily. 'Is this you and Jayden at it again?'

Ally gives a small smile. 'It might be.'

'But Edward Grey was terminal. So . . . it's the island bloke then, is it?' Wenna's brow furrows. 'Reading between the lines, he was a drifter, Ally. His home was a van – at best. You live on the edge like that, well, it's not going to be a surprise if you fall off it, is it?'

10

'Talk to me, Mullins.'

Mullins takes the proffered chair in Detective Sergeant Skinner's office, shooting his boss a wary look at the same time. The sergeant's mood has been thundery the last couple of days. Thundery, without any of the pizzazz of lightning or release of rain; just a low-grade, ominous, bad mood.

'Well, Sarge,' he says carefully, 'I could have told you it was coming. You saw his statement. Poor old bloke was on his way out, wasn't he?'

Edward Grey was a shadow when Mullins spoke to him yesterday. He felt sorry for the old fella, because it was clear he really did care about Axel Marks. *Plus, he was dying and all that.* Edward's nurse was tough as a bodyguard; if Mullins hadn't had a badge to flash, she wouldn't have let him through. And she stood there listening the whole time too.

It hasn't quite left Mullins yet, the feeling of being in that room in the big house. It's found its way into him, like fumes. The curtains were closed, just a thin stream of light filtering through. A wooden bed as huge as a ship, and Edward Grey lying in it, small and shrivelled as a newborn in a paisley dressing gown. The machine next to him – wheezing and beeping – that Mullins found he couldn't quite look at.

He's seen more than his fair share of dead people. *Comes with the territory.* But dying people? That's a whole other thing.

Afterwards, as Mullins left the room, he wanted to gulp in big breaths of fresh air or run straight into the sea and wash it all off. Not that he's the kind of person to run straight into the sea. He was supposed to have surf lessons with Hippy-Dippy last winter but, somehow, they never happened. Probably because Mullins realised how cold the water actually was. Or maybe because Hippy-Dippy laughed it off, like the surf lessons were never a real thing anyway, when she was the one who'd suggested them in the first place.

But Mullins doesn't like to think about that, because it's muddling. And he's muddled enough by Saffron Weeks at the best of times.

Mullins felt bad after leaving Edward Grey. Someone else's imminent death being something that you want to shake off or run away from is just insult to injury, isn't it? If Mullins was on his way out, he'd want someone – anyone – by his side. Holding his hand. Saying the right things. *What are the right things?* At least Edward Grey will have had that. His bossy nurse for one. His son for another. That glamorous daughter-in-law of his. There was a lot of love for the old boy up at the house.

And Axel Marks should have been there too.

'The smart money says it's connected,' says Skinner.

He's sitting forward in his chair, hands steepled. His forehead is as deeply grooved as a just-ploughed field.

'You mean what happened to Axel Marks, and the old man's death?'

'The shock of it tipping Edward Grey over,' says Skinner. 'Never underestimate the physical impact of emotional disturbances, Mullins.'

And the lines on Skinner's forehead seem to intensify.

'If you want my opinion,' says Mullins, 'by the time we knew what'd happened to Axel, I don't know how much Edward Grey had left in him. I don't know how much of it he took in.'

But Mullins can remember the silver tear that ran down the old man's cheek. It was one of the saddest things he'd seen: a crying, dying man.

'Anyway, at least they both died happy,' says Mullins, with a cough.

'In what possible interpretation of the word was Edward Grey "happy"?' says Skinner, his disdain popping 'happy' like a pin in a balloon.

Mullins is temporarily thrown. What did the word *happy* ever do to hurt Skinner?

'Well, Axel came to see him, didn't he?'

Jayden wanted to know the reason why, but Mullins wasn't spilling. Because if he and Ally knew there was a will involved, they'd put two and two together and make any number but four.

'Axel showed Edward how much he cared, didn't he? And Edward got the chance to say his piece, before it was too late. Whatever happened afterwards, at least Edward knew that when Axel went to bed that night, he was on top of the world.'

And then he fell off it.

But Skinner hasn't noticed the clumsy phrasing. He's switched from scowling at Mullins to staring out of the window, taking his bad mood out on the fire escape, the motley red-brick wall, the station car park, instead.

11

Jayden zooms in on a picture of Edward Grey at Porthmerrin House. He looks like a cartoon drawing of a country gentleman, with corduroy trousers, green wellies, a wax jacket and a flat cap. He stands with confidence, looking square at the camera. Sharp cheekbones, a smart smile, his imposing house behind him. The master of all he surveys. *Not short of a bob or two* would be his father-in-law Cliff's assessment. Cliff's a fan of the green-wellies-and-wax-jacket look too, but there's bona fide cow dung in his tread, and loose threads in his coat.

Jayden's search for Porthmerrin House didn't bring up much beyond basic listings in various historical-interest sites, but this article about a Cornwall-wide Open Gardens weekend – from eight years ago – is useful, because it means he gets a good look at the owner too. For the first time, Porthmerrin House was taking part in the Open Gardens weekend, which earned it a mention, and a photograph, in a piece on notable venues. But beyond Jayden learning that it's a big house, it's got a big garden, and the owner was, for this one weekend in July 2018, happy to share them with the public, there's not much to know.

He takes a sip of Coke and looks across the bar, wondering if there's anyone in here whose brain he can pick. When the place is jumping, it can be a hive of information. Gossip swirls around the countryside, and there's no better place for it to settle than in a pub like The Wreckers. Between them, the old boys at the bar probably know everything about everybody – or reckon they do, anyway. But not quite lunchtime in March, the place is as good as dead. Two hikers sit at the table in the window studying menus. The barman himself is just covering – while Lou's in hospital getting a hip replacement – and he's already told Jayden he's from Taunton and doesn't know anyone round here.

Wenna will deliver, he's sure; she'll make it her business to know about someone like Edward Grey. And while part of Jayden wants to shoot up to Porthmerrin House and start forming his own opinions, he knows it makes sense to wait for the debrief from Mullins later. Okay, 'debrief' is probably pushing his luck. Try: irritating but weirdly enjoyable chat that might contain some useful kernels if he's lucky.

His phone starts buzzing beside him and he thinks it'll be Ally, but no: Cat.

'You won't believe this, Jay.'

It's her outraged voice. He doesn't hear it very often.

'What's happened?'

'Mum and Dad are going to be in Gran Canaria for Benji's birthday.'

Jayden feels a little flood of relief. He thought she was going to say something really bad, like they'd lost all their campsite bookings, or Jazzy's preschool was closing, or . . . something else.

'I can't believe they're missing his party,' she says.

Cat is, Jayden thinks, one of the best-adjusted people he knows. But when it comes to her parents, sometimes she can't help slipping into entitled-teenager mode.

'We can always tweak the date, babe.'

'But they know when his *birthday* is, and they booked to go away anyway. I just thought . . . after, you know . . . they'd want to mark it with us.'

He hears a true bit of sadness in her voice then, and Jayden thinks maybe it's about more than Benji. That maybe it's about the tough start Cat had as a second-time mum too, and them all getting through it together.

'Look,' he says, 'we'll just make sure we—'

'Dad hates holidays too,' Cat cuts in. 'He never wants to leave the farm. But then Mum said these friends of theirs invited them, and it was a last-minute thing, and they thought they'd be impulsive for once in their lives. Which, you know, I *get*. But . . . still. It's rubbish. Your mum and dad are in, though, right? And your sister?'

Jayden picks up a beer mat, turns it in his hand.

'They will be.'

'You haven't called them yet? Jay, please. Before they book a holiday too.'

'I will. I'm on it. Cat, the party's going to be great. I promise. Even if it was just us four, it'd be great.'

After they hang up, Jayden takes a minute or two to reset. He won't call his parents – they'll want to get into a long chat – but he taps out a quick message to his mum. Then sends more or less the same one to his sister.

Done.

'Axel Marks,' he says with renewed purpose. 'Okay.'

He's already looked for him online but he's proving hard to trace. Axel wasn't on social media. He's not featured in the 'Meet Our Team' pages of any companies. No mentions in local papers – not beyond his death. Often, with the report of an incident like on Lone Island, there'll be a photograph of the victim, but not in this case.

Is it this online invisibility that makes Jayden feel a pull towards Axel Marks? A man not easily found, until his body was washed on to a beach and Pippa Grant, for whatever reason – and that still nags at Jayden – cared enough not to let it go. To not let his death be left as 'unexplained but not suspicious'.

Swift and Bold.

Jayden wonders what meaning those words had for Axel. And, straight away, Google offers up an explanation: 'Swift and Bold' is the motto of The Rifles, an infantry regiment of the British Army. Jayden reads on; with no other avenues to explore – the words don't seem to have other connotations – he's all in on this one. He reads of The Rifles' deployments in Afghanistan and Iraq. Flicks through images of soldiers in camo, in dress uniform on parade grounds, Prince Philip or Queen Camilla looking on. When he searches *Axel Marks Rifles* and *Axel Marks soldier* nothing comes up. Ironically, if Axel had served a hundred years ago, Jayden could have accessed service records through any number of historical archive sites, but in the last couple of decades? Nothing.

Was Axel a soldier? Perhaps not recently, because that kind of detail would likely have been included in the news report, but at some point in his life? Mullins's assessment was 'more or less homeless', and Jayden knows first-hand from his time in Leeds that there are a disproportionate number of ex-servicemen on the streets. He thinks of the rough sleeper who got into a fight with some partygoers on Call Lane during Jayden's last summer on the job. An Iraq veteran and a drug addict. Kicked to pieces, by a bunch of lads with too many drinks inside them, something to prove and nothing to lose. *I wasn't ready for them*, the man kept saying afterwards, *I wasn't ready*. As if that was the senseless bit, his lack of preparation.

But Jayden saw it go the other way often enough too. Squaddies blazing into the pubs and clubs like they wanted to set them alight, knowing there would always be some commanding officer who'd show up in court, decked out in uniform, and get them off the lighter charges. *What's a bit of drunk and disorderly when it's someone who next week is going to put their life on the line for Queen and country?* the chief super used to say with a headshake.

'Jayden.'

He didn't hear Ally come in; he was that lost in this other world.

'You won't believe this,' she says.

'Weirdly enough, Cat just said the same thing. And I *did* believe it.'

'Edward Grey is dead.'

Jayden can actually feel his jaw drop, comic-strip style.

Ally takes the seat across from him. Sunlight streams through the window, striping the wooden table. He realises his ice has melted, and he's barely touched his drink.

'Apparently, he'd been ill for some time,' she says. 'It was anticipated.'

'But the timing, right?'

'I know.'

They stare at one another.

'Apart from anything, it makes it harder for us to turn up and start asking questions, doesn't it?' says Ally.

'It'd look like an intrusion.' Jayden picks up his Coke. 'I think we need to wait to hear what Mullins has to say anyway, otherwise we'd be turning up blind. But even so, I want us to get up there tomorrow. However sketchy Mullins's info might be.'

'I just had a quick chat with Wenna's husband's sister's niece.'

'Say that again, Al? Actually . . . don't.'

'A young woman called Ginny. She lives a couple of miles from Porthmerrin House and Wenna thought she might know something about the family. But she didn't have a lot to tell me, except there's a son called Lucas who lives somewhere near London. And he rarely visits, apparently. Though presumably he's here now.'

Jayden holds up his phone with the picture of Edward in his garden.

'That's Edward Grey. Eight years ago.'

'Funny, he looks just how I imagined,' says Ally, peering close. 'By the way, I rang Pippa just now, to tell her we'll take the case.'

'Was she surprised?'

'She was grateful. Also . . .' Ally hesitates. 'She sounded almost trepidatious. As if she was setting something in motion that . . . she's not sure about.'

'She's going back on this "feeling"?'

'No, not that. More . . . she was aware of the gravitas of being the one who's pushing for answers.'

Jayden waits for more, half thinking that Ally's projecting how she'd feel in this situation, reading too much into Pippa's tones. He needs to meet this woman for himself, because otherwise he's going to keep feeling sceptical. Even though, every minute that they're on this case, he's wanting to know more about Axel Marks and the Grey family. And experiencing a stirring of his own: the instinct that there's a bigger story here.

'Is Pippa still on the mainland?' he asks, looking at his watch.

'Ah, now that's what I was coming to. Jayden, how are your sea legs?'

12

Donna Goode lets herself into her room, breathing a deep sigh of relief to be on her own at last. Emotions are running high in the house, and the only good thing is that there's no bad feeling coming her way. *You were wonderful with my father*, Lucas said earlier. *I can't thank you enough for that.*

If it weren't for Axel Marks, Donna would be thanking Fate for bringing her to Porthmerrin House.

She moves to the window and plants both hands on the sill. It's not the best view – that's from the master bedroom; Edward's room, of course – but it's still a beauty. Crane a little and Donna can see the stretch of green lawn, as neat and even as a football pitch, and the strip of sea beyond. She can see Robbie working in the gardens, his sleeves rolled to the elbow; that way he has of stretching his stiff back out midway through a job, making her want to run down and lay her healing hands on him, work out all of his knots.

They haven't put a label on this relationship of theirs yet, but for Donna it's more than a fleeting romance. And if she's reading him right, it is for him too. At least she hopes so, because there's nevertheless something impenetrable about Robbie Cassidy. Thirty-three years old, and Donna wonders if she's ever really been in love.

Though I thought I was once.

She shakes her head, pushing the thought away. The scene through the window blurs a little as Donna refocuses. *Think of good things. Look at what's in front of you.* That's what her brother used to say: *Look at what's in front of you, Don.*

So she does.

The leaded windows make Donna feel like she's in a fairy story, and the four-poster bed is the cherry on the cake. She's been happy here. So what if the mattress is hard as concrete and there's woodworm in the frame? It still looks the part. For the last few months, she's had a taste of living like the other half. She's even found her Prince Charming – though how Robbie would laugh at that one. And, as patients go, Edward was a dream. They're not all – and why should they be? When a person has been dealt body blows, Donna can understand why they might fight back in any way they can. In her time, she's nursed the surly, the unpleasant, the downright spiteful. And she's tried her best to smile through it: brisk, bright, ever-efficient – that's her setting. It's one that she's cultivated over time, as much a part of her CV as any medical qualifications.

Donna clearly remembers her first-ever job as a live-in carer. It was in Torquay, a white sugar cube of a house, with a garden full of conker trees and a pond that shimmered with koi carp. But her elderly patient's tongue was so relentlessly sharp that Donna felt each cut. Donna got that she was sad, got that she was angry, got that she was in pain – but why be so mean with it? Though even then, Donna knew why. *Oh, I knew.* She'd been there herself, after all. Mental pain is every bit as harrowing as physical. Donna has had days, weeks, whole months where she's woken up seething, and God forbid anyone got in her way.

Edward Grey, though? A puppy dog. A gentleman. Her friend, by the end. Perhaps he wasn't always that way, but in his decline, he was a dear old man. His eyes twinkled even as his body failed around him. Seeing his distress over Axel's death was a knife in her heart. He'd been so happy the day before. Perhaps he was, Donna thinks, ready to go after that. As if there was simply nothing left to live for.

She turns from the window and drops into a chair. A Queen Anne, with split leather, but soft as a doughnut to sit in. She rests her head on the wings.

I'll miss him.

And I'll miss all this.

Because without a patient to care for, Donna has no place at Porthmerrin. Lucas has said there's no rush for her to leave, that she's welcome to stay until she's found her next posting, that it's what his dad would have wanted for her. And it's a really generous offer. Robbie's smile went off like a firework when she told him.

But after everything with Axel?

Donna doesn't feel like she deserves any of it.

13

As they draw closer to Lone Island, Ally feels a quickening in her chest. What is the particular magic of such places? Perhaps it's because of her own island view in Porthpella: the bright white lighthouse is part of the iconography of home. Or maybe it's all the adventure novels she read in childhood, full of sea swims and hidden coves. Or does it go back much further than that, something evolutionary almost? An ancient voyager seeing a landmass rising from the ocean, an untouched place at which to drop anchor.

'No way I could live somewhere like this,' says Jayden, beside her.

He lists with the boat as it meets another wave, while behind them their skipper stands impassive in his shades and baseball cap. Once upon a time, occasional boat trips ran out to the island, but they've all stopped now. Pippa gave them the number of Trent Simms, the man she uses whenever she needs to get off the island.

A boat did come with the cottage, she told Ally, *but unless it's dead calm I find it too scary to go around the island, let alone back to shore.*

Jayden turns towards Trent.

'Do you know Pippa well?' he asks, his voice barely audible over the roar of the outboard.

'She's not a talker,' he says. A little pointedly, Ally thinks, as though that's the way Trent prefers all his passengers. 'Not like her husband,' he adds.

'Fergus? He's left the island, we heard.'

'Has he?' Trent tweaks his cap. 'Not in my boat.'

Jayden looks to Ally. Behind his sunglasses, she knows his eyebrows will be raised.

'Spooked by all the silence, maybe,' says Trent. 'Fair enough.'

When Ally called Trent about the boat, he asked if they were journalists. Not in the mode of a gatekeeper, more out of interest.

'I expect you've had the police coming and going,' says Jayden.

'Not as much as you'd think.'

'He'd been reported missing, hadn't he?' says Ally. 'The man they found.'

'That's what I hear.'

Ally looks back towards the mainland. The cliffs are sheer, the rocks dramatic. Slabs of black stone, wave-lashed and formidable. Here, it's the sort of coastline that makes you want to stand further back, grateful for the solid ground beneath your feet. The beach at Porthpella is, at first glance, a caress; a gentle, sweeping golden landscape. Of course the waves climb high and are thunderous with power when they want to be, but nevertheless the place has the illusion of gentility. The coastline near Porthmerrin House can make no such claim.

Ally shivers, thinking of Axel Marks falling from such a height. The sharp-toothed rocks below. The thrash of untameable water. *Swift and Bold.* Jayden told her the possible significance of the tattoo. No one, not even a highly trained soldier, could survive a situation like that.

From here, Porthmerrin House is just visible. A grey stone oblong. Ally raises her binoculars to her eyes, but the boat is lifting and dropping too much for her to focus. Delicate sea-spray coats the lens, as if her eyesight's failing.

'Do you know the Grey family?' asks Jayden.

'I know they used to own this place once upon a time,' Trent says, nodding to the island. 'Edward liked to visit every so often. I'd happily run him out.'

'What about Edward Grey's gardener?' asks Ally.

'Robbie? Yeah, I know him a bit. Look, there she is waiting for you.'

Pippa stands on the shingle beach. A glint of light shows she's watching their progress through binoculars, but as they move closer, she tucks them inside her coat and zips it up. She wears black wellingtons that seem too big for her; her hair blows across her face.

'What time do you want fetching?' asks Trent, as the boat noses on to the beach. 'I've got my godson's birthday later.'

Jayden checks his watch. 'What do you reckon, Al?'

'They won't need more than an hour,' calls out Pippa, instead of a greeting. Then, looking to Ally, 'I wouldn't have thought.'

'An hour?' says Trent. 'I might as well stay here, then.'

And he slides his phone from his pocket, as if it offers all the entertainment he needs.

Pippa frowns, and Ally has the sense that the woman is caught between two evils and is unsure of the lesser. Is two people on the island for two hours worse than three people for one hour?

'Pippa, we'd like to see all of the island, if you're willing to show us,' says Ally. 'It'd be good not to rush.'

Pippa nods. 'We'll call you then.' She turns to Trent. 'If that's alright?'

'Alright by me. But if it's after four, I'll be eating jelly and ice cream.'

'It won't be,' says Pippa firmly.

And the woman waits until Trent and his boat are firmly on their way before she says another word at all.

Ally is all too aware that this new pro bono client of theirs isn't oozing welcome.

'Pippa,' she says brightly, 'this is my partner, Jayden.'

'Hello Jayden,' says Pippa. 'And sorry, you must think me rude, just . . . the last couple of days, I feel as if I'm only just getting the island back.' She exhales slowly, her eyes closing for a second. 'But I'm glad you're here. Glad and grateful. It's important you see the place. To understand, I suppose.'

'Understand?' says Jayden.

'That it's different here. The elements are all you have, so you trust them. Instinct rules.'

'You're talking about your feeling when you found Axel,' says Jayden, watching her carefully.

'Not when I first found him, but when I sat with him. When I let his voice be heard.'

Ally glances to Jayden, and she's grateful to him for maintaining a steady expression. While Constable Tim Mullins is capable of occasionally surprising them, she can imagine what his face would be doing now.

'Thank you,' says Pippa, 'for listening. For taking the case. If I could pay you, I would. Or offer payment in kind. But I don't think I have anything that someone else could ever want, or need, I—'

'It's okay,' says Jayden. 'We're intrigued.'

'*Intrigued?*' Pippa says it as though she doesn't like the word.

'We want to understand what happened,' says Jayden levelly.

And Pippa nods, satisfied at that.

'Is this the beach where you found Axel?' asks Ally.

She turns, taking in the horseshoe cove, the heaps of seaweed and the pebbles as rounded as hens' eggs. A narrow path leads up through the rocks and disappears.

'No,' says Pippa. 'That's this way.'

And she strides ahead, wellingtons slapping as she goes. They follow, Ally not wanting to hurry. The path climbs, skirting the edge of the rockface. It's steep, and she wonders how it would be hefting groceries and supplies up here; especially on days when the wind is whipping off the water, pushing and shoving everything that gets in its way. Not an easy place to make a home.

'It's the next cove along,' says Pippa, over her shoulder. 'It runs with the currents, but the rocks are treacherous, so the coastguard had a job getting in.'

They step from the path and clamber down a steep slope of loose stones and coarse tufted grass. Ally holds her arms wide for balance as, beside her, Jayden skids in his trainers.

'Here,' says Pippa, stopping suddenly.

The beach is tiny, no more than a slice of shingle at the end of an inlet. The sea pushes in and pulls out with an almost desperate sort of relentlessness. Spray fizzes high from the rocks.

Axel Marks's resting place.

There is nothing to show that he was here. No crime scene tape, no traced outline of a body in the sand. But then a flash of colour catches Ally's eye. As they make their way on to the beach, Ally sees that there's a jam jar wedged between the rocks and filled with daffodils, the most delicate little narcissi. Fairy flowers, Evie used to call them as a little girl. Pippa notices Ally looking.

'I had to do something,' she says. 'As long as I'm here, I'll make sure he always has fresh flowers. It feels as if we're all that he has.'

Ally can see that Jayden is looking across the water, where – distant, but distinct – there's a clear view of Porthmerrin House. She raises her binoculars. It takes her a moment to focus, as her vision bounces from cliffside to treetops to grey stonework. A tall chimney and dark windows. She can see three cars parked up, the light beaming off their bonnets.

'The Grey family cared enough to raise the alarm,' says Jayden.

'They did, didn't they?' says Pippa, and there's something deliberate in the way she says it.

'Have you ever met Edward Grey?' asks Jayden.

Pippa shakes her head. 'He's elderly, not in good health. I told you, didn't I, Ally? That he sent his gardener to check up on us, when we first arrived.'

'To welcome you to the island?' says Jayden.

'*Welcome?*' Pippa raises an eyebrow. 'I suppose so. Though it belongs to the wildlife trust now, which makes it no more Edward Grey's business than anyone else's. But aristocrats can't help clinging to the past, can they? Anyway, it was a brief visit. He didn't seem to want to be here. He was just under orders.'

'The gardener's called Robbie, isn't he?' asks Ally.

'Something like that.' Pippa pushes her hair from her face. 'I'm sorry if I sound unfriendly, but that big mansion house sticks out in the landscape rather forbiddingly and . . . I don't know. Some days out here, I feel rather watched. When the police officer, the young one, said that Axel Marks knew the family, that he was spending the night on Porthmerrin land in his van, something just seemed to . . . click into place. I thought, "Of course he was."'

Ally lowers her binoculars.

'What do you mean?' says Jayden.

'It's hard to explain. But he was dead, here on my island, and he'd come from that house of all places. It just made a grim sort of sense to me.'

'Well, there's logic to it,' says Jayden. 'It's probably the nearest house. The Greys probably own the land right up to the water. If that's what you mean.'

'Yes,' says Pippa. 'There is logic to it.'

Ally goes back to her binoculars. She travels back towards the cliffs, the movement jerky and disorientating. She glimpses a white van and holds steady.

It has to be Axel's.

She can't tell at this distance, but it looks like he drove it up and over grassland to get to where it's parked. She can't see a track. She wonders how long this ownerless vehicle will be there for, whether it'll be towed away.

'I can see the van,' she says, passing the binoculars to Jayden. 'Here.' Then she turns to Pippa. 'Pippa, did you not think to go to the Greys first? Before us, I mean.'

'Why would I do that?'

'Because they were the ones who first raised the alarm,' says Jayden. 'They're invested.'

Pippa pushes a hand to her forehead, as if she's trying to think.

'If I'm honest, I thought it was strange that they didn't come here straight away. I phoned the police, and they came immediately. They took away the body. Then he was identified, presumably by the Greys. I was expecting a boat to land with the Greys, or at least their gardener again, but I never heard a thing. They think they're important, people like that always do, and they had absolutely no interest in meeting me.'

Ally can't help but think of Jayden's comment about Pippa possibly feeling overlooked. She wants to be listened to, to be taken seriously. And here they are, out on her island. Listening. Taking her seriously.

'We heard that Edward Grey died this morning,' says Ally. 'He'd been ill for some time. Perhaps they intended to but were preoccupied. They still might.'

'They could have phoned me, couldn't they? A basic courtesy?' Pippa stops. 'Did you say Edward Grey's just died?'

'This morning,' says Ally. 'He'd apparently been ill for a long time.'

Pippa gives a just-perceptible nod. She offers none of the usual platitudes.

'You found Axel yesterday afternoon, right?' says Jayden. 'So when did you decide to contact us?'

Pippa hesitates. She looks down at her wellingtons.

'Honestly? Almost as soon as the police left. Because I knew they wouldn't take me seriously. But then I saw the write-up online. "Unexplained but not suspicious". Those are the words the police are using. Would you want that on your gravestone? Would anyone?'

14

Jayden ducks his head as they go through the door of Pippa's cottage. He expects it to feel ancient inside, but *dated* is more the word. The dark-green carpet is worn bare in places, with stains in the shape of continents. The furniture is cheap pine. A stiff-backed sofa faces the fireplace, without looking even slightly cosy.

'It's not much to look at,' she says, 'but the house was never the point. Tea?'

The kitchen is a galley, only big enough for one person at a time. Pippa fills the kettle then turns to stare out of the window as it boils. It's a perfect square of two shades of blue: the horizon line splicing the sea and sky. A living picture.

Ah, that's the point.

A few months into their relationship, Jayden spent a weekend at Cat's family's farm. *You need to see where I come from*, she said. They'd met at a friend's barbecue in Chapeltown and Jayden would have guessed her for a city girl, then. But surrounded by green and blue, by rolling fields and wide-open sea, he soon saw that this was her natural habitat. It was like she went from standard definition to high.

'Pippa, where did you live before this?' he asks.

'Reading,' she says. 'Berkshire.'

Somehow, it's not the answer he was expecting.

'There was never enough sky for me there,' she says, taking a carton of long-life milk from the fridge.

'Do you know where you'd go next?' asks Ally.

Pippa shakes her head, a teaspoon paused in her hand.

'I can't imagine,' she says. Then, 'I mean, literally, I can't imagine. That's the trouble with a place like this. Once you've had such an extraordinary existence, it's very hard to picture yourself anywhere . . . ordinary. But I haven't given up all hope of not having to leave. Not yet.'

'Have you asked to stay on, then?' asks Jayden.

She holds a mug out to each of them. 'Well, I've made my case. I'd already asked Fergus to do me one favour, to avoid formally resigning until I'd had a chance to . . . adjust. We're not paid until the twenty-eighth, see. It's not as though it was fraudulent, and I'm covering all the work he would have done. But then, when I found Axel, I knew I had to tell the police the truth, that I'm the only one here. And as soon as I'd told them, I had no choice but to tell Mike too. Mike's my contact at the trust. They've given me a month. One month, and then I have to leave too. But I'm making an appeal.' She darts a look at them both. 'This might help, you see. The fact that I'm showing initiative, bringing you both in. My job is to take care of Lone Island and all of its creatures. And Axel Marks came to the island. So, I'm trying to take care of him too.'

As Pippa dips her head and pushes her fingertips to her eyes, Jayden nods to himself, and feels a flare of cynicism again. *Now I get it.*

'You've been through a lot,' says Ally.

Pippa looks like she's about to say something but then changes her mind. 'Yes,' she says quietly, then gestures to the living room. Jayden takes a seat on the hard sofa, Ally beside him. Pippa draws up a chair.

'Where will you start the investigation?' she says. 'I know I've given you nothing, really.'

Jayden looks to Ally. 'Al?'

And Ally looks moderately surprised that he's deferring to her.

'Well,' she says, 'we'll probably cover similar ground as the police initially. They'll have taken a statement from whoever raised the alarm at Porthmerrin House, and anyone else who might have come into contact with Axel in the hours leading up to his disappearance. That's right, isn't it, Jayden?'

'That's right.'

'And then?' says Pippa.

'To understand Axel's movements, and what might have happened to him, we need to know more about him. At the moment—'

Ally stops, as somewhere in the house a phone starts ringing.

'That's mine,' says Pippa, but she makes no move.

'It could be the police,' says Ally.

And at that, Pippa gets to her feet and hurries from the room.

Jayden looks to Ally. 'So now it makes sense,' he says quietly.

'What do you mean?'

'She wants to save her job. And she thinks by hiring us, her employers will see that she's got this place under control all on her own.'

'Is that what you think?'

'She said it herself, Al.'

'But she also said she knew the police wouldn't take her seriously, so what choice did she have?'

Jayden cocks an ear to upstairs. Above their heads, the floorboards creak.

'I don't know,' he says, his voice low. 'But I don't love the spin she's putting on it. This guy dies, but then because of the way she handles herself afterwards, she might just keep her job? She's already eyeing the silver lining.'

'I don't think that's what she meant. The flowers on the beach, Jayden. That's genuine.'

'I'm not doubting that she's cut up about it. Look, don't worry, I'm still all in. Just . . . We're paying attention, right?'

'Right,' says Ally, without a great deal of conviction. 'I think we should go to Porthmerrin House straight after this.'

'You mean before my full briefing with Mullins at The Wreckers later? Yeah, I hear you. Mullins might decide to be tight-lipped, in which case we'll have lost time for no reason. You're no longer worried about intruding on them so soon after Edward Grey dying?'

'It's being here, Jayden. It's only a mile offshore but it feels so far from anywhere. There are tangible connections with Porthmerrin House, though, aren't there? Lone Island used to belong to the Greys. And Axel was staying there when he went missing. I do agree with Pippa that it's a little strange that no one from Porthmerrin has been in touch.'

'Even with Edward Grey's death?'

'Well, perhaps that's strange too.'

Jayden rests back in his chair.

'The truth is, Al, once we're fully in the middle of this, we may be no more enlightened. What actually happened to Axel could be a black hole.'

'Isn't that the same with every case?'

But it's not the same. Often, it's the corpse that holds the answers – or at least confirms the questions that need to be asked. But Axel was battered by a cliff fall and the ocean. Somebody could have grabbed him by the shoulders and pushed him over, but DNA traces can't survive the waves. Someone could have taken a rock and struck Axel over the head, but how could such a strike be isolated from every other rock that he hit on the way down?

Thinking like this, how can they hope to prove anything? But maybe that's the appeal. That perhaps there's someone out there thinking they got away with it – and he and Ally aren't going to let them.

'I think with this case . . .' he starts to say, but then looks up at the sound of fast feet on the stairs. Pippa comes back in the room. She looks uncertain, almost like she's surprised they're still here.

'That was the police. The Greys want my phone number. Well, Lucas Grey does. Edward's son. You're right, Edward died this morning. I said they could have it. Was that the right answer?'

'Course,' says Jayden. 'You wanted to speak to them, right?'

And he's wondering if it even occurred to Pippa that the reason the Greys might not have been in touch with her was that they didn't have her number.

She looks to the clock on the wall; it's the sort of functional thing you'd get in a doctor's waiting room or a classroom or a police station.

'Time's getting on,' she says. 'You'd better call the boatman, hadn't you? And I'd better wait for this phone call.'

With so little to go on, Jayden wishes he could listen in.

15

After the short return boat trip, they sit a while in the car. White clouds skim the horizon, and from here, the island is an ink blot, its features impossible to distinguish. You'd never even know there was a cottage there. Meanwhile, Porthmerrin House is just a ten-minute drive away, an imposing landmark of a place, high on the clifftop. From the sea, it's visible from miles around, but from their current standpoint, it's as if it doesn't exist at all.

'I don't think Pippa's reaction is wrong,' says Ally.

Jayden shifts in his seat. 'Keep talking.'

'I mean, if I'd found a job – and a home – that I loved, then I'd do everything in my power to keep it. And she's right, she's the warden. It's her duty to protect the island.'

'I don't disagree, Al.'

Ally isn't quite sure of the point she's making.

'Look,' says Jayden, 'we're investigating through choice, right? And we reserve the right to stop investigating at any point too. That's true of any case.'

'Yes. Good.'

'I know you haven't got Pippa fully figured out, Al, but that's okay. You don't need to. Not unless she becomes a suspect.' He grins. 'I'm joking. But look, our duty is to the victim. It always is. We're doing this for Axel Marks.'

They sit quietly for a moment, Ally still trying to make sense of her unease. Pippa's drive in hiring them, but then her reluctance for them to linger on the island any longer than was essential. The flowers in the jam jar, the way Pippa's eyes filled with tears. Ally had hoped spending more time with Pippa, and having Jayden meet her, would make things clearer. Instead, she feels a lack of clarity – and it's as light, but as definite, as sea mist.

'Okay, let's decide how we play this with the Greys,' says Jayden. 'Treading carefully, given Edward's death, obviously.'

The energy in his voice is, as always, infectious.

'Well,' says Ally, 'if I reported someone missing, I'd want to know all I could about what might have then led to that person's death. I'd be reassured that people were continuing to investigate it.'

'Unless you had something to hide.'

'Or were focused on other things, perhaps. Like Edward's death. It's understandable if they see our visit as an inconvenience.'

'Agreed,' says Jayden.

'Why don't we simply say that Pippa wants us to put the pieces together. That after finding Axel's body she wants to understand more about him and how he died. I think that's a very reasonable response, actually. It's probably how I'd feel in her shoes, Jayden.'

It was three years ago now, but Ally can remember exactly how she felt when Lewis Pascoe was found lying at the foot of the cliffs, just hours after he'd knocked on her door asking for help. Their first case. There was guilt, possibly an element of self-preservation, but also something akin to a moral obligation.

'Even without the "feeling" factor. Yeah, agree again, Al. And put like that, it's not suggesting any suspicious circumstances. Just that there are blanks to be filled in.'

'You know they could be talking to one another now,' says Ally. 'Pippa and the Greys, I mean.'

'And who knows, maybe we'll get a call from Pippa telling us to call the whole thing off. She has answers enough, and she's shown her employer that she's capable in a crisis. But even if that happened, I want to make my own mind up. Don't you?'

'I do.'

Ally sees him hesitate.

'Do you think it's weird that Pippa's husband left the island, apparently for good, but their usual boatman wasn't the one to take him?'

Ally's brow crinkles. 'It's not that far offshore. Any number of people could have collected him.'

'Fergus Grant. You looked him up, didn't you?'

'He's a freelance graphic designer in Reading, but his website says he's currently on sabbatical.'

'Pippa hasn't said where he's moved to, now he's left Lone Island, has she?' says Jayden, looking thoughtful. 'She hasn't said much about Fergus at all.'

'I can understand that, though. Their relationship's broken down, and she's been left high and dry. It's perhaps not a comfortable subject for her.'

And as much as Ally believes this, her mind dwells on the possibility of connection: Fergus and Axel. Lone Island. One man missing – well, not missing, a man who *left* – and one man dead.

'Fergus Grant's departure strikes me as an anomaly,' says Jayden. 'Don't you think?'

'It could be,' she says carefully.

'I don't know about you, Al, but I want to start getting some facts in this case. Let's go and meet the Greys.'

They pitch into lanes so narrow that there's a generous strip of green in the middle, neat as a table runner. They climb and climb, then the entranceway to Porthmerrin House comes upon them and Ally almost misses it. They pass between two grey-stone pillars and continue down a pitted driveway, tall pines marking the edges of the track. There are sheep grazing behind an electric fence, and two crows bounce around a piece of roadkill – a rabbit, maybe, or a squirrel. From here, the views are vast, the sea spanning out before them. Lone Island looks like no more than a rock.

The house appears almost out of nowhere, a granite hulk. Not delicate or beautiful, but built to withstand the assault of the weather in this unprotected spot.

They pass through a second gateway, their tyres crunching on the gravel. The driveway is well tended, with no weeds between the ash-white stones. Two cars and a Land Rover are parked at uniform angles. The trail of a hosepipe leads around the corner, and it's from this direction that a man appears. He's in heavy boots and khaki-green shorts, a t-shirt despite the chill; a baseball cap on back to front and a straggly beard. He eyes them dispassionately. Perhaps people have been coming and going all day.

'Hi,' says Jayden, leading the way as they climb out of the car. 'We're looking for Lucas Grey.'

'In the house,' the man says. 'Who's asking?'

His voice has a faint accent that Ally can't place. Perhaps Midlands? His eyes, up close, are dark as conkers. He must be the gardener that Pippa mentioned.

'Jayden Weston and Ally Bright. Lucas doesn't know us,' says Jayden. 'It's in connection to Axel Marks.'

Jayden says it casually enough, but Ally sees the way the man stiffens.

'Do you work here?' she asks.

'What's the connection?' he says, ignoring the question. Then, correcting himself, 'Yeah, I'm the gardener.' He holds out his hand and they shake. 'Robbie Cassidy.'

'We know the police have taken statements from everyone,' says Jayden. 'You too, Robbie?'

'I told them what I knew. Which wasn't much.'

'Would you be open to telling us too?'

Robbie rubs his jaw with a hand. Ally notices a faded blue tattoo running across his knuckles. She can't make out the design.

'Going to need a bit more information before I do, mate.'

So Jayden uses the line they agreed on in the car: Pippa's desire to know more. And Ally's surprised by how quickly Robbie's demeanour changes in response.

'Okay.' He nods towards the house. 'The family will give you what you need.'

'You met Pippa, didn't you?' says Ally. 'When she and her husband first took on the warden jobs.'

'Yeah, I met her.'

And he looks steadily back at Ally, offering nothing more. She has the impression that Robbie's willingness has a limit – and it's Axel they're here to talk about, not Pippa.

'What about Axel?' says Jayden, evidently thinking the same. 'Did you know him?'

'Know him? No. But we did meet.'

Ally glances up at the house, hearing a noise; the click of a window or a door opening.

'He said he liked what I'd done with the gardens.'

'So he'd been here before?'

'Been here?' says Robbie, eyeing them levelly. 'You could say that. The guy used to live here.'

16

As the gardener takes in their surprised faces, there's something slightly hostile in his expression.

'Everyone's got a story,' he says. 'Bloke like that, you can't go making presumptions.'

'Hey, no presumptions,' says Jayden. 'We're at ground zero. And right now, we don't know much at all about Axel Marks.'

'Like I said,' says Robbie, starting to turn away, 'the family will fill you in.'

Jayden can't work out if he's reluctant to talk about Axel because he doesn't think it's his business, or he genuinely doesn't know much.

'Did Axel work here too, Robbie?' asks Ally.

Robbie tugs at his beard. He looks like he's turning something over.

'No, just his mum. Years back.' He jerks his thumb. 'They lived where I live now.'

Jayden and Ally look where he's indicating and see the roof of a much smaller building, partially hidden by trees. Jayden has fifty questions, but opts for one with a simple answer: 'Were you here when the Greys raised the alarm about Axel going missing?'

'Yeah, I helped look for him.' Robbie nods towards the house. 'Here's Edward's son now.'

Lucas Grey hovers at the top of the steps. He's tall, slightly built, and looks as if he's stepped from a boardroom, with a sharp shirt and trousers, black shoes that glint in the sunlight. But as he moves towards them, Jayden sees that the polish is exterior only. His eyes are rimmed red, dark scoops beneath them. The man looks haunted.

'Can I help?' asks Lucas stiffly.

Jayden explains why they're here, using the same terms as with Robbie. He makes sure to offer his condolences too, and Lucas nods at that, rubbing one cheek with his hand as if there's a pain there.

'I've got work to do,' says the gardener, and, without waiting for a response, goes back the way he came.

Jayden watches Robbie's retreating back, thinking of all the things he still wants to ask him. But then he refocuses on Lucas Grey.

'I just spoke to Pippa Grant. It's rather off that she didn't mention hiring you.' Lucas shakes his head, as if the thought doesn't matter in the scheme of things. 'Anyway, I'd been meaning to call her since the news came in. What a nice woman. She got quite upset, talking to me. Perhaps it shouldn't surprise me that she's finding it hard to move on. Or that she'd want you involved.' He hesitates. 'Though it feels rather surreal, hiring private detectives. Like something out of a film. Or is it that you're already friends of hers?'

'We only met her this morning,' says Ally.

'Well, proactiveness is to be applauded. The police have been frustratingly oblique, but I suppose in a situation like this, they can't do much more.'

He sighs, and his whole body seems to sag. He looks, Jayden thinks, incredibly tired.

'We'd love to ask you some questions,' says Ally, 'but we're mindful of the timing. The last thing we want to do is intrude so soon after your father's passing.'

'Thank you, but we were expecting it. My father had been ill for a long time. Axel, on the other hand, was a terrible shock. I just wish we could have shielded my father from it. It meant a huge amount to him that Axel had finally come home. Seeing him again, my father was brighter than he'd been in days.'

Axel had finally come home.

Jayden wants to jump on that, but it feels right to talk more about Edward first.

'Did your father know that Axel was missing?' he asks.

'Yes,' says Lucas quietly, 'and I wonder if I made a huge mistake in telling him. But he was asking for Axel, that was the thing. I couldn't lie.' He worries at his thumbnail; bites it like a child. 'And then I had to tell him that he'd been found. And . . . how. Again, I regret that. I honestly didn't know what to do, but I spoke to Donna, and—'

'Donna?' says Jayden.

'My father's nurse. Wonderful woman. I asked her what she would do, and she felt it was wrong to hide it from him. He's a tough old boot, my father, and . . .' His voice cracks. 'But if I'd known that telling him Axel had died was the last conversation I'd ever have with him, I wouldn't have done it. I'd have told him something good instead. Cricket scores, or . . . I don't know.'

Jayden notes the contradiction. That Edward's death was anticipated, but that Lucas still hadn't thought it was about to happen. But no matter how prepared we are, death is always a shock; the only inevitable thing in life, really, and yet the fact of it startles and defeats us every time.

'I'm sorry you're having such a difficult time,' says Ally.

Lucas nods and pushes his hand through his hair distractedly.

'Sorry, I should have asked you both in. Did you want to . . . ?' He looks from one to the other. 'Like I said, I'm grateful to Pippa Grant for finding Axel. If his body hadn't come ashore on her island, it would have been a kind of purgatory. The perpetual not knowing. I'm happy to tell you anything I can. Though I must admit there's still quite a lot I don't know about Axel. His life had its challenges since he lost touch with us. Come in and have a pot of tea.'

They follow Lucas towards the house, their reception already much smoother than Jayden anticipated. He glances to Ally, and she gives a quick nod in response. *She's on the same page.* As they head up the steps, Jayden turns back and sees the quick movement of a shadow on the grass, as if someone just stepped back around the corner of the house.

Robbie?

'My wife's here somewhere,' says Lucas, over his shoulder. 'She's taken my father's death hard. He had a soft spot for her. Comparatively speaking, anyway. Elspeth!' he calls out, and from somewhere deep in the house there's a faint response. 'She's rather got her hands full with Donna. My father's nurse? Yes, I told you that. She's been live-in, you see, so naturally she's worried about what her next step is. I get the impression that she doesn't have too many options, so of course we've said she can stay here as long as she wants.'

Lucas shows them into a vast kitchen. Weirdly, it reminds Jayden of a super-sized version of his in-laws' kitchen. Not the newest fittings, despite its grandeur. Windows look out over the immaculate gardens, the sea a band of blue.

'Where do you live, Lucas?' asks Ally. 'Here with your father?'

Lucas laughs. 'God, no. Sorry. He'd have laughed to think that. No, I adored him, and I had a glorious childhood running around the estate, but . . . I'm a town mouse at heart, not a country mouse. We're in Windsor. So, you see, it really would suit us to have Donna stay on anyway. Someone to keep an eye on the place. And Robbie's here, of course. Tea for you both? Or coffee?'

They both opt for coffee.

'I feel rather a duty of care to them both,' Lucas goes on, 'but we'll have to sell up eventually. It's a great shame, but it just wouldn't suit us to live here. Not like Axel. Axel would have been perfectly at home. He always loved Porthmerrin. That's half the tragedy of it, really.'

'What do you mean?' asks Jayden.

'Oh, of course. Sorry, I presumed you knew. But then perhaps you private detective types work independently from the police. Porthmerrin House was going to be Axel's.'

Jayden feels his eyebrows shoot up.

'My father split his estate in two. The house to Axel, and all other assets – including the contents, his antiques, his art – to me. And with all due respect, I know who got the better end of the bargain.' He smiles sadly. 'My father was a very wealthy man, but he didn't spend a lot of money on maintaining this place. I'd have seen it as a monkey on my back, but Axel was astonished by the gesture. Overwhelmed, actually. It was very moving.'

Lucas looks from one to the other.

'I need to start at the beginning with this story, don't I? Otherwise, none of it will make sense.'

'Please,' says Ally.

Jayden silently applauds her composure. Personally, he can barely keep his face straight. Axel, who apparently lived in a van, was set to inherit this massive pile? In what universe could the police have known that and not thought his death suspicious?

17

Lucas struggles with the plunger on the cafetière as coffee grains dance up into the jug. Just like everything in this place it's in dire need of updating and there's obviously a tear in the mesh. His visitors will be picking bits out of their teeth for the rest of the day.

He knows he dropped a bombshell just now, but honestly? Lucas rather enjoyed the moment – and he didn't expect to be enjoying anything today. But what on earth are two private detectives doing here? The woman on Lone Island sounded so guileless, but she obviously operates on multiple levels. Perhaps she's a conspiracy theorist, looking for intrigue and corruption everywhere. It's not beyond the bounds to imagine a person like that, secreted on that lonely isle, as paranoid as they come.

Because if Porthmerrin House is the ends of the earth, what about Lone Island?

Whatever made his grandfather donate it to the wildlife trust all those years back, Lucas is happy that he did. How he'd have hated being dragged there for perpetual picnics and camp-outs and terrifying cliff-path jaunts – or whatever Boy's Own adventures Edward would no doubt have masterminded. Not that it stopped Axel. Any chance he got, he was on that island. Perhaps there's a grim kind of synchronicity in him ending up there.

No, Lucas can't wait to get back home and retreat firmly into his own life. The immaculate Windsor house, where things just *work* – and Lucas knows exactly who he is. That said, he's doing rather well with these two nosy parkers. He managed to sound upset about Axel just now, when, quite honestly, he can't help feeling as if it's the universe correcting itself.

If anyone's to blame, it's Donna. Because it was Donna who drew out all those nonsense nostalgia stories from Lucas's father. Getting him thinking how much he wanted to see Axel again. She had no idea what Edward had up his sleeve with his will, of course. None of them did. Even so. It was embarrassing that he should confide in a paid employee – *boo hoo, poor Axel Marks* – and not his own son. A case of Lucas's father chronically underestimating him. *Plus ça change.* The fact is, Lucas was prepared to go along with this great reunion. He was the one who did the legwork in tracking the fellow down. He was even prepared to accept the terms of his father's ridiculous will. Not that there was any choice in it.

It's all change now, though, isn't it?

'I can't vouch for the quality, I'm afraid,' he says, pouring the coffee into three mugs. 'Donna's been doing the shopping around here, and I don't think she's a connoisseur, as such.'

But these two look like they couldn't care less about the coffee. *Just give us the story!* Some private detectives: they didn't know the first thing about Axel Marks. Mind you, Axel was a slippery customer. Untraceable on social media. Lucas only found him by using his father's email address. And three weeks later, Axel replied.

'Axel was a couple of years younger than me, but we grew up together, in a manner of speaking,' he says. 'His mother was the housekeeper. Lovely lady. Jeanie Marks. I liked her a great deal, as a boy. She made a Victoria sponge to die for.'

Lucas would sit in the kitchen of The Nook – the tiny estate cottage that Jeanie and Axel stayed in – a wooden spoon in his hand, scraping the buttercream bowl as Jeanie laid strawberries on top of the cake as carefully as embroidery stitches. The two of them singing along to some tinny song on the radio. Where was Axel in such moments? Oh, with Edward, of course. Bent over a table together, lining up those horrible toy soldiers that left your hands smelling of metal. *Why, but it's the Battle of the Bulge! Can't you see it's Trafalgar?* Or striding the estate together in all weathers, Axel like a straggly little dog at his side. A stray – with pretensions.

'And your father took an interest in Axel?' says Ally.

'Very much so. Axel was obsessed with my father's antique weapons collection, which of course my father loved him for. I don't mind telling you I'm not going to waste any time in selling the lot. Never my cup of tea.'

'So you were quite different, as children?'

'It was nice having another child about the place,' he says, 'but we were hardly two peas in a pod. I left home for university. Then, when Axel was seventeen, he joined the army. And that was it. He never came back.'

Lucas notices a look pass between Ally and Jayden. So brief, like a note passed in class between experts. *But I saw.*

'He never came back here?' says Jayden. 'Not even on leave?'

Lucas rubs the back of his head. 'Well, to be fair to him, I suppose it was rather complicated. He'd barely qualified, or whatever the terminology is, and before long he found himself in Afghanistan doing God knows what. Then Jeanie, his mother . . . Well, she passed away. Very suddenly. It was heartbreaking. It was not long after Axel left the army, actually. He did one tour and that was enough for him. He came back here, quite honestly for the first time, I think, and within a month or so Jeanie was dead.'

It was heartbreaking.

Lucas was in Oxford. It was autumn. He remembers fallen leaves the size of dinner plates, as yellow as rubber ducks. Then his phone ringing and his father's voice, as hard as a brick wall. *The funeral is family only*, he said. But as far as Lucas knew, Axel was Jeanie's only family, so how could that be? *You're joking, aren't you?* he said to his father. Because Lucas knew he wasn't Axel's favourite person in the world, but Lucas couldn't conceive of Axel organising a funeral for his mother without Edward Grey being present. For moral support – on top of the obvious financial contribution.

'In retrospect,' says Lucas, 'I think the army rather made a mess of poor Axel. "Medically discharged" was the phrase he used. I didn't pry. But with his mother dying at more or less the same time, it was all too much, I think. He turned his back on us all. He turned his back on the entire duchy. He went to London and that was it. Cast himself adrift. He quite possibly would have stayed that way – well, best-case scenario, if you know what I mean. But it seems he'd started to get himself back on track and returning to Cornwall was a part of that. He told me that he'd been living out of his van along the coast for the last two months. First time back in fourteen, fifteen years. It made luring him to Porthmerrin a hell of a lot easier, I can tell you.'

Luring him. That came out wrong.

'What I mean,' says Lucas, being careful to meet the pair's eyes – their very sharp and questioning eyes – 'is that if he was still submerged in London, then no matter how good of a rope I threw him, I don't think he would have taken it. But he was here. And he was sorting himself out. He was in good spirits, and he assured me that he hadn't felt that positive for a long time. The news my father gave him was the absolute cherry on the cake. My God, it blew his mind, quite honestly. A man in a van, and he's handed a house like this? It's a dream come true, isn't it?'

Lucas stops waxing quite so lyrical. For a moment he's forgotten himself. Whatever Axel's dream might have been, it certainly didn't come true.

'Anyway,' he says, taking a sip of his drink. 'God, this coffee's dreadful. Apologies. What I mean to say is, this was Axel's home. And even though he forgot that for quite a few years, I managed to get him back here in the end. And my only consolation is that I managed to do so before my father's death.'

No, that doesn't sound right either.

'What I mean is . . .'

Then it hits him afresh, and his eyes sting with acid tears.

'For a brief moment in time, my father was happy, and Axel was happy, and if it weren't for the absence of Jeanie, it'd have been just like the old days.'

18

Ally knows that it's only once she and Jayden are alone together that she'll be able to process everything that Lucas has said, but her instincts, honed now, after all their work together, are clear.

Axel Marks served in Afghanistan, faced untold perils – was medically discharged – but he ended his days drowning here, just hours after learning that he was set to inherit Porthmerrin House.

Beside her, she can feel Jayden practically vibrating.

Ally watches Lucas keenly. His upset is obvious. But is that emotion entirely for his father, rather than some part of it for Axel Marks?

'Can you tell us about the day before Axel went missing?' asks Jayden. 'What was his mood like?'

'Like he'd been handed a winning lottery ticket,' says Lucas. 'That's the thing. If the situation were different, any one of us might have thought he'd decided to end it. He had his demons, Axel, that much was clear. But reconnecting with my father, with me, meeting my wife, it was like he had a family again. And then the really wonderful part . . . My father gathering us around him and telling us his intentions.'

'How did Axel take it?'

'Honestly?' Lucas passes a hand through his hair again. 'He said he couldn't accept it. That it was too much. He didn't need it.

He was very modest, actually. Self-effacing. But once my father was set on something . . . well, that was it. There was no changing his mind. My father got rather agitated, actually, said that he wanted to make amends, and this was his way of doing that.'

'Did you ask either of them what was meant by that?' asks Ally. 'Or did you already know?'

Lucas puffs out his cheeks. 'We don't come out of this especially well.'

Ally takes a sip of her coffee, affecting to be casual.

'My father knew how hard Axel took his mother's death, you see. And I think we both suspected he came back from Afghanistan traumatised, to a degree. He was an angry young man, an unwell young man too, though whether physically or mentally I don't know. He never let us in. And I suppose we let him rage. And . . . didn't try to help. My father was hurt, I think, that Axel turned his back on us, and at the time he couldn't quite get past that to understand the true reasons. With hindsight, he, and I, should have tried harder. We should have been there for him. So, this gesture . . . it was recompense, I suppose. And to show him that he was valued. Loved, even. Yes, loved.'

Lucas looks down at his hands.

'What about the evening before he disappeared?' says Jayden. 'How did Axel spend it?'

'I had visions of it being like old times, a big dinner here at the house, talking into the night. But my father was too frail for anything like that, of course. Axel and I, though? And Elspeth? I rather thought we might. But in the end, everyone was tired. It'd been an emotional day. We had a simple supper. Rather too much wine. I brought out a bottle of whisky, thinking we might have a nightcap, but Axel said he wanted to head back to his van. He asked if he could take the whisky with him and . . . I said yes, of course. Not exactly good manners, in my opinion, but I had to cut him some slack. His life had gone in quite a different direction after leaving Porthmerrin. I mean, my God, we can't imagine, can we? And that was the last I saw of him. Walking across the lawn in the moonlight, a two-hundred-quid bottle of whisky under his arm.'

'Was he drunk?' asks Ally.

'Yes, but not blind drunk. Not then. But when I dropped in on him the next morning his van door was open. I had a look inside – curiosity, I suppose – and saw the empty whisky bottle. And honestly? That's when I started to worry. More or less instantly.'

Lucas shakes his head at the memory.

'The police thought I was barmy, reporting him missing so soon, but when they sent someone up here, they understood why. He'd parked his van what I can only describe as *perilously* close to the cliff edge. I mean, I can't stand heights, but I'd call it death-wish territory, personally. I suppose he wanted the views. He was always mad about Lone Island as a boy. And he was a daredevil, of course. I can just picture him, sitting with the back of the van open, working on that whisky, feeling like the whole world was at his feet . . .'

Jayden nods. 'So the position of the van, and his drunken state, made the police consider him high-risk.'

'That's it,' says Lucas. 'That's exactly the phrase they used. I had to tell them about his background too. Axel spoke of it a little over supper. There were spells of homelessness in the last decade or so. I suppose he was technically homeless now. He certainly didn't have any bricks and mortar to call his own, and that van looks like it's on borrowed time to me. As I said, I didn't probe as to the exact medical reason why he was discharged from the army. I got the impression he didn't want to talk about it. But, thinking about it, I do suspect it was mental rather than physical. I dare say the police have run their checks and it'll be on his record somewhere. It's a perfect storm, isn't it? When it's put so plainly.'

Ally looks up as a woman enters the kitchen. She has bobbed blond hair and a neat figure. Ally would guess her as mid-thirties, a similar age to Evie. She smiles as she sees them, and although she looks tired, she's considerably less drawn than Lucas. But it's not her father who's just died; it's not her childhood home that's fundamentally altered. And the chances are she met Axel for only a few hours.

'Hello,' she asks, one hand still on the door. 'Am I interrupting?'

'Not at all,' says Lucas, waving her in. He smiles to Ally and Jayden. 'My better half, Elspeth. Ellie, these two are private detectives. They're looking into Axel's death on behalf of the woman who found him. Pippa Grant. The poor thing's quite undone by it all and hates that the police have rather drawn a line under it.'

Elspeth stands beside Lucas, one hand on his arm.

'She's hired you?'

Ally nods.

'Well, that's one reaction,' she says, her eyes wide as a cat's. 'Sorry, I mean, it's such a difficult thing to accept, that someone can be here one moment and gone the next. With Edward . . . well, it's different, isn't it, Lucas? He faded away. Gently, actually, in the end. But . . . to fall from the cliff. To drown. It's so sudden. So violent. And perhaps that makes it easier for the police, but for most people, it's—'

'Very hard,' says Lucas. 'Hard to accept.'

'Years back, Lone Island used to belong to this estate, you know,' says Elspeth, nodding towards the wide windows and their view of lawn, of thicket, of distant sea. 'I imagine that living on the island, even as a tenant, you'd feel a great sense of ownership. It was as if Axel came to Pippa Grant's door, wasn't it? In a manner of speaking.'

'Is Pippa paying you?' asks Lucas suddenly, as if the thought has only just occurred to him.

'Lucas, that's a crude question.' His wife frowns, her smooth brow wrinkling. 'The fact is, whatever the police say, a man like Axel will be low-priority. Because of who he was, I mean. As if someone like that' – and she puts air quotes around the words – 'would inevitably meet a sticky end. Imagine the furore if it'd been your father, or one of us had gone off the cliff, Lucas. No. I'm glad that resources are being bolstered.'

Lucas frowns. 'But no one's saying there's been foul play. That's not what this Pippa is getting at, is it?'

'She has questions . . .' Ally starts to say.

'It's more the principle of the thing, isn't it?' says Elspeth. 'That's how I imagine Pippa is seeing it. Axel Marks has no family. He was a lost soul. And he came here to stay with us in good faith, and . . . lost his life. Lucas and I can't help feeling responsible. And so I can understand why it matters to Pippa too, being the one to find him. Lucas, we should invite her here, before we go home. Let her know that we're grateful. Without Pippa, he could have been lost at sea forever, with none of us ever knowing, couldn't he?'

'I'm the one who brought Axel here,' says Lucas quietly. 'If it's on anyone, it's on me.'

'At your father's request, darling.' She squeezes her husband's shoulder, then looks to Ally and Jayden. 'You know, of course, about Edward's intentions?'

'I've told them about the will,' says Lucas stiffly.

'It's been a rollercoaster.' Elspeth bites her lip, then laughs softly. 'Sorry, you're going to think me callous but . . . I suppose we'd always assumed, as Edward's only child, that Lucas would inherit. Then suddenly it's Axel. Axel or any of his descendants, in fact. And then . . . well, quite against Edward's true wishes, it's back to us again. Which leaves rather a sour taste, but . . .'

Beside her, Lucas is shaking his head. 'I never assumed anything.'

'Sour because you know Edward didn't want you to have the estate?' says Jayden. 'Or sour because you feel it was rightfully Axel's?'

'Aren't they the same thing?' says Elspeth, with a little one-shouldered shrug. 'Entwined, certainly. I didn't know Axel at all, but . . . that's not the point, is it?'

'Did you say that the house would have gone to any children of Axel's too?' says Ally.

'Yes. Which goes to show how much Edward wanted to make amends with him, doesn't it? Even if Axel had turned out to be dead after all these years – which of course there was every chance, living the way he did – then his offspring would have got the keys.' She shakes her head; laughs lightly. 'Sorry. I know I sound like a terrible person. Lucas can pretend that it wasn't a hurtful move from Edward, but—'

'That evening we spent with him,' says Lucas, cutting in, 'Axel told us that he'd like to be a father but that he didn't trust himself to do it right, so he wasn't ever going to take that risk. Not with another person's life. Parents, they don't realise the impact they have . . .'

'Which I actually thought was remarkably self-aware of Axel,' says Elspeth. 'Sad, but . . . knowing.'

'If he'd had a kid, they'd have been welcome to the place,' says Lucas quietly.

Elspeth looks to Ally, rolling her eyes, as if Lucas is a child acting up. Then she catches his arm. 'Oh, Lucas, by the way, Donna wanted five minutes with you. I think she'd like something in writing about staying on here. Which of course we can authorise now. Though I'm sure Axel would have had the same response, wouldn't he? Especially given their special connection.'

Ally hears Jayden set his mug down hard on the counter.

'What was their connection?' asks Ally.

'Oh, didn't you say, Lucas? Turns out Donna's brother was in the same regiment in the army. Such a coincidence. Axel looked like he was about to faint when he realised.'

Ally glances at Jayden, and he sends her a pointed look.

'I think the army's a small world once you're in it,' says Lucas, with a wave of his hand.

'We'd like to speak to Donna too,' says Jayden.

'Be my guest. It's not as if she's very busy, now that my father—' Then he stops; looks to them both apologetically. 'Sorry. I think I'm running out of steam here. These last few days have been exhausting, and—'

'Before we talk to Donna, can we take a quick look at Axel's van?' asks Jayden.

'Head across the lawn and into the field at the end. You can't miss it. The police have inspected it – the tape's gone. I suppose I'll have to organise to get something done for that too . . . Get it towed, or . . .'

'A job for another day,' says Elspeth, squeezing his arm. Then she looks up at Ally and Jayden, her face suddenly full of alarm. 'But whatever you do, please don't go anywhere near that awful cliff edge.'

19

Jayden just about manages to wait until they're well clear of the house, then he turns to Ally.

'We need the thinking room, big-time.'

'We do.'

'And we need a whiteboard the size of a football pitch, Al. What we just got there . . . It's a lot.'

They walk quickly, all the energy from this new information going into their stride.

'It is a lot,' says Ally. 'But . . . presumably it's nothing that Mullins and Skinner haven't heard.'

And yet the line is this: *unexplained but not suspicious.*

'Yeah, okay, but when's that ever stopped us?' says Jayden, nudging her arm.

They're following the path that trims the lawn, past the kind of tropical-style planting that Cat wants for the campsite. The lawn itself is emerald green and buzz-cut: a football-playing kid's dream. Jayden imagines Lucas and Axel growing up here, the housekeeper's son and the little prince. But all this – the house, the land, the endless view – would have been Axel's.

'Tell you what,' he says, 'Elspeth wasn't shy about addressing the elephant in the room, was she?'

'You mean the inheritance?'

'Specifically, who stands to inherit now that Axel is dead. In their words . . . them. Did you see how uncomfortable Lucas looked? It's a huge detail. Axel, this man who has, on the face of it, not much at all, who hasn't seen the family in years, was about to be handed a mansion. I mean, that's massive. But if his death is a crime, and that's the reason, it's seriously stupid. Because the motive's so obvious.'

'And so sad,' says Ally.

'Really sad. You know what, though, it's not even actually that stupid. Because from what Mullins said, the state of the body makes it very difficult to prove anything.'

And that's the problem, thinks Jayden. Elspeth seemed genuinely concerned and Lucas seemed genuinely upset. But then the death of Edward Grey confuses things. What if Lucas's emotion for one event is masking indifference – or worse – towards the other?

'Elspeth obviously thought it strange that Axel was included in the will at all,' says Ally.

'She's a step removed, though. Perhaps she's never realised how close Axel and Lucas's father were once.'

Jayden glances back towards the house. From this distance, there are no signs of life. The windows throw back the sunlight: anyone could be watching them.

'Whatever Elspeth thinks, she's not looking at her husband like she's worried he's hiding something. The story that Axel drank too much back at his van and stumbled off the cliff edge in the dark makes sense. And that's where the police are, right? But then there's Donna.'

'Edward's nurse. Goodness, yes. The army connection.'

'My first question there is, when did Donna find out about the army connection?' says Jayden. 'Did she put it together talking to Edward, or did she figure it out sooner? Elspeth called it a coincidence but that's an assumption. Or maybe it's the impression

Donna wants to give. When we're done at the van, Donna Goode's got to be our priority.'

As they cross the end of the lawn, the turf springs under their feet. Jayden turns again, catching a movement in his peripheral. By the pale stone wall, back near the house, he sees the gardener with a pair of cutters, reaching up to some bright-leafed climbing plant.

'What did you make of Robbie?' he asks, dropping his voice.

'He wasn't particularly pleased to see us, was he?'

'Nope. And he didn't try to hide it. But maybe that's just his style.'

'Which corresponds with what Pippa said about the time he went out to the island.'

They pass through a gate and into a field of longer grass. Jayden can just make out a strip of white metal up ahead. The field must pitch downhill; the van parked on the lower level. He runs his eyes along the perimeter hedge and sees another five-bar gate further down: the entry point. So instead of electing to stay in the house – *or was that not offered?* – Axel chose this distant spot. But as they draw closer, Jayden can see perhaps why.

'What a view,' murmurs Ally beside him.

From this vantage point, the sea spans 180 degrees; on a day like this it's endless, and insanely blue. The only interruption to the smooth surface of the water is the bobble of Lone Island. Further to the west, and out of sight, is Porthpella. It's a timeless view, and if Axel was feeling nostalgic about his boyhood, then Jayden can imagine the years slipping away as he stood here. An effortless act of time travel.

And his van is parked just a few steps from the edge.

'What was he thinking, Al?' says Jayden. 'Even without the whisky, it's madness. If the handbrake failed, or—' He stops. 'Hear that?'

For all the deceptive serenity of the open water, there's the loud crash of water on rocks. From the boat earlier, they both saw how jagged and harsh the coastline is here; no one's putting it on a postcard any time soon. Jayden walks forward and peers over the edge of the cliff. He's cautious, aware of every millimetre shift, but still his heart bangs in his chest.

'If the ground was damp,' says Ally, behind him, 'it'd be incredibly slippery. It wouldn't take much to go over. Jayden, please step back. It's making me nervous.'

And it's making him nervous too; his body sending danger signals.

'It'd take nothing,' he says, moving away. 'And if it was dark, and if you'd drunk the best part of a bottle of whisky . . .' He pushes a hand to his forehead. 'You know what, if Pippa came and stood up here, that feeling of hers would make all the sense it needs to.'

They both stand quietly for a moment. The fizz and growl of water on the rocks far below makes the hairs on the back of Jayden's neck stand up. Somewhere behind them, gulls fill the air with their plaintive cries.

'Maybe Axel wasn't as happy about returning here as the Greys implied,' he says.

'And then he learns that he'll inherit the house.'

'Which could feel like a complicated proposition.' Jayden turns his back on the water. He suddenly doesn't want to look at it anymore. On a good day out walking – let alone a bad day; a day when life seems too hard – it would be so easy to die in this spot.

'Occam's razor, Al.'

She looks quizzical.

'The theory that the simplest explanation is often the likeliest. Axel slipped and fell. Or Axel jumped. Not that Axel was murdered. But . . . I want to see this through. All the way. Because apart from this newly formed connection with the Greys, who else did Axel have? I don't think the police have turned up anyone. The guy was all on his own. Who's fighting his corner?'

'The Greys?' says Ally. 'Edward would have, certainly.'

'And Edward's dead. And Lucas and Elspeth . . .' Jayden wrinkles his nose. *Check your inverted prejudice.* 'Well, maybe they're just talking a good talk. Elspeth said Axel was a lost soul, but she sounded so chirpy about it, you know? As if a guy like that coming into their orbit is a novelty, and his death is sad and everything but . . . it's not really going to touch their comfortable lives. Not for long.'

He shrugs. It's hard to explain, but it's this clifftop. This van. The thought of a man not much older than himself, here on his own, standing at the edge.

'I want to see it through, Al,' he says again.

'I'm with you, Jayden. I want to see it through too. Whatever Occam or his razor have to do with it.'

She gives his arm a brief squeeze and Jayden smiles gratefully, then moves towards the van.

'Come on. Let's look inside.'

'Lucas says it's open.'

It's not one of the sleek Transporters you see parked up in all the surf spots. Axel's van is a battered old Ford. Rust bubbling at the panel edges; dents in the fender.

As Jayden pulls the side door wide it's like peering inside an ordinary wardrobe and finding a whole other world beyond. There's a faded chequered duvet across a tiny bed, and a stack of four or five folded blankets. A guitar and a skateboard. A twist of fairy lights. A smiley-faced Nirvana hoodie, improbably on a coat hanger.

And it's all so neat. Neat as a pin.

'Axel's home,' says Jayden.

The emotion is sudden as a punch, right in his solar plexus.

They climb inside, treading carefully in the small space. Jayden can just about stand up without hitting his head, and with Ally beside him it's tight. The whisky bottle Lucas mentioned is on a flip-down sideboard. There are a few millimetres left in the bottom, if that. No sign of a glass. The lid is off, and no sign of that either.

Ally nods towards his bed. 'He was a reader,' she says.

There's a stack of old-looking paperbacks. Albert Camus. Jack Kerouac. Ernest Hemingway. Jayden picks up *A Farewell to Arms* and flips through it. *50p* is written in pencil on the inside cover.

'Literary tastes,' says Jayden.

The guitar is a cheap-looking acoustic. The skateboard, propped beside it, looks both well loved and well used. He runs his finger over the grind marks. This was a board that saw action.

'It's not what I expected,' says Ally.

'How do you mean? How tidy it is? That's an army thing, I bet.'

'Well, that too. But the way Lucas talked, I imagined Axel would have very little. But this van, it's full of the things he loved. Isn't it?'

Good things too. Books, music, skating. Jayden's never stepped on a board himself, but Saffron would approve.

He nods. 'No photographs up, though. No pictures.'

'Perhaps they were all on his phone. I wonder if he had it with him when he fell.'

'It's on my list of questions for Mullins later.'

Phone records would be good to see. Email too. How he'd love to see the communication between Axel and Lucas.

Jayden opens a small wooden cupboard. It looks as if it's made from reclaimed wood and is a little uneven; the catch sticks. Inside there's a pencil case stuffed with yellow-and-black-striped pencils and a metal sharpener. A pad of lined paper. And a biscuit tin, which he takes out and opens. *Photographs.* Straight away Jayden recognises the backdrop of Porthmerrin House in one. A woman standing on the lawn, a wicker basket over one arm. The sun is in her face and she's squinting. She has curly brown hair and a skirt that falls like a triangle from her narrow waist. He holds it up to Ally.

'Axel's mother?' he says.

Together they look at the rest of the pictures. There aren't many, and they're mostly of Axel's mum: holding up a glass of wine with a paper hat balanced on her curls, the twinkle of a Christmas tree behind; sitting on a sofa, her knees together, a sleeping cat draped across her lap. And then there's Axel.

It's the first time Jayden has seen a photograph of him, and again he feels that punch of emotion.

Mum and son have their arms around one another. His mum plants a kiss on his cheek, while Axel looks directly into the camera. His head is shaved and somehow it makes him look vulnerable, not tough. His cheeks are sprayed with freckles, and his eyes are a deep dark brown. He has a chipped front tooth and a wide grin. He looks about sixteen or seventeen.

He looks happy.

Madly, easily happy.

'Oh,' says Ally quietly. 'The two of them.'

'I wonder who took this picture,' says Jayden. 'Lucas didn't mention Axel's father being around. Long shot but . . . what if it was Edward Grey, and that's the real reason that Axel got the house?'

He can see Ally turning the thought over. 'And perhaps Lucas knew that?'

'Or suspected it. Maybe he even pushed his dad on the point, right at the end. I doubt the police have swabbed any of the Greys for a DNA match.'

'Because of this,' says Ally, waving her arm towards the open door of the van. The grass slopes straight to the cliff edge – the sheer drop. You could run and jump and fly.

Not fly.

Jayden takes out his phone and photographs the picture of Axel and his mum. Then he looks back to the tin. There are no more photos, but there's a folded piece of paper. He takes it out and opens it up.

It *is* a photograph.

A woman – maybe in her late twenties – hugs a skateboard to her chest and laughs into the camera. She has pale-blond hair that falls past her shoulders and, even with this poor-quality print, arresting green eyes. Maybe the location of the photograph adds to the effect – an urban skate park covered in graffiti, a tower rising behind like a lone bowling pin – but she doesn't look like someone you'd mess with. Her cheekbones are sharp as blades; her arms are skinny but muscled.

'Girlfriend?' he says, holding it up to Ally.

There's no way of knowing what period of Axel's life it dates from, or the location.

'She's significant,' he says. 'She's the only other person he has a photo of. A printed one, anyway.'

And he takes a photograph of it. Then another, zooming in on her face.

'What if it's recent, Jayden? What if she doesn't even know that he's dead? If you're not tuned into Cornwall news, there's every chance you wouldn't know anything about what happened on Lone Island.'

Jayden opens up Google and taps in *Skate park tower in background UK* then scrolls through the images. Loads of tower blocks, but nothing like this. He tries again, this time swapping *tower* for *chimney*.

It's a direct hit.

The distinctive red-brick tower. *Okay, chimney.* The windowless buildings either side, top to bottom in graffiti. The configuration of sloped ramps. Walls of colour. It'd be like walking into a painting.

'Dean Lane Skate Park in South Bristol,' says Jayden. 'That's where this picture was taken.'

'It could be years old, couldn't it?'

'Or months.' An idea strikes. 'We can date it from the street art. It's always changing, right?'

He thinks of Saffron's on–off boyfriend, the street artist Milo Nash, and the piece he sprayed on the side of Broady's surf school last spring, only for it to be gone a few days later. If you came across a photograph of that piece of Milo's, you could date it to not just the year but the month. The week.

'Fancy a deep dive into the Bristol street art scene, Al? We work out when any of this graffiti changed, we can have a crack at dating it. This skate park looks like it's a key spot.'

'And then try and trace who this is?' says Ally.

'Exactly. You know what, I'm going to send it to Saffron to ask Milo. I've a feeling he's lived in Bristol. If he's still in touch with other artists there, then someone's going to know.' He starts tapping out a message to Saffron, then stops. 'No signal. I'll do it in a sec. Whoever this woman is, Axel cared about her. All these photos of his mum, and then this one.'

'And if Axel took the picture, from the look on her face, I think she cared about him too.'

Just then a gust of wind blows into the van and takes the paper from Jayden's hands. As it flutters to the floor, he bends to pick it up. A glint of something catches his eye, and he bends lower, reaching under Axel's bed.

It's an earring, a small glittery star shape, with turquoise detailing. He holds it up to Ally, says, 'Most likely a woman's, right?'

20

Gus has no need to be at Hang Ten, coming up on closing time, eyeing the sweet treats. He still has half a carrot cake in the tin at home and it's not a bad effort either. He's dipped a toe in the waters of mince pies (dry as you like), brandy snaps (more flop than snap) and croissants (so buttery an independent adjudicator might deem them greasy). All in all, he will not be dissuaded from having a crack, especially when he thinks Ally might appreciate his efforts. The croissants were entirely for her, and for Gus it was as bold a gesture as turning up with a rose in his buttonhole and a limo idling in the driveway. That was a year and a half ago now, when Ally and Jayden were deep in the vineyard case. Gus can still remember how quickly delight turned to desolation; one minute he was sharing a continental breakfast with Ally, bathed in morning sunshine in every sense, and the next he was blundering into her wardrobe – *don't ask* – and discovering she still had all of her late husband's clothes, a sure-fire sign that she wasn't ready to move on. At least that's the assumption he foolishly jumped to. Because then came Ray, thus disproving his theory. And it turned out Ally didn't take too kindly to being second-guessed.

'Tempted, Gus?'

Saffron's face is lit with her usual bright smile. The girl's been through it over the years, but she's never less than chipper.

'No, I won't,' he says, 'I'm already a slice of carrot cake to the wind.'

She looks confused.

'You know, three sheets to the wind?'

Headshake.

'Old saying. To be drunk. Not sure of the etymology . . .'

'You're drunk?'

'No, I . . . Doesn't matter. I've spent the day word-wrangling, Saffron.' He rolls his eyes in a manner that he hopes is self-deprecating; no one can really get away with saying 'word-wrangling', can they? 'Once you start you can't stop.'

Actually, that's not true. Gus finds it frighteningly easy to stop writing. Sometimes he breaks off mid-sentence, mid-*word*. Even though, in the last few months, he's had a certain fire lit beneath him. Ally likes his book. Ally told him to keep going at all costs. So keep going he shall. If he puts his back into it, he'll have the new draft over to his agent in a week or two's time. But quite honestly, he's taken so long with it, she'll probably assign him to the spam folder.

At least Ally likes it.

And if Gus is really honest with himself, he's not sure his nerves could take actually being published.

'Talking of starting and not stopping . . .' Saffron raises her eyebrows.

'Oh God, don't say it.'

'Lovely little foot-highs coming in early next week, Gus.'

Back in the autumn, Gus took up surfing, with Saffron as his patient and ever-positive instructor. But as the water temperature dropped, and his ability failed to rise, he took a rain check. And he hasn't quite found his way back into the water yet.

'Oh, changing the subject . . .' he says.

'Ha, really? Nice try.'

'I saw the woman you sent Ally's way earlier.'

'Yeah? Well, whatever the case is, they've taken it. I got a message from Jayden asking me to get a date stamp on some street art through Milo. They're trying to trace a woman. I figure it's the same case, anyway . . .'

'Gosh.'

Gus surprised himself by hardly thinking about the encounter all day; maybe his novel is capable of sustaining his interest after all. He makes a mental note to drop in on Ally this evening and find out the latest.

Saffron's phone pings. Then again. A third time.

'*Yes, babe*,' she says to herself, 'I knew you'd come through.'

As Saffron messages back, Gus takes his coffee and settles at his usual table by the window. It's a lovely sort of day – candyfloss clouds and bubblegum-blue skies – and they're heading towards a cracking sunset. From here, he can see all the way down the beach, towards the distant dunes. Yes, he'll definitely drop in on Ally later. They're back to being easy like that now. Easy, until Gus thinks of the fact of Ray. The only comfort? Most of the time, Ray is hundreds of miles away in Suffolk.

'They're going to love me,' says Saffron, coming out from behind the counter. 'Well, love Milo. So, Jayden found this random photograph of a woman – cool girl, skater – like . . . less than an hour ago, so Milo puts his feelers out, and his mate has not only confirmed what month it was taken in, but he reckons he can get a name for Jayden too.'

Gus blinks. Milo is Saffron's on–off boyfriend – currently in Paris, by all accounts – and a graffiti artist of some repute. The mere mention of his name is usually enough to make Gus feel about three hundred years old. But now he's simply wondering what a skater girl has to do with the woman on the beach.

Saffron holds up the phone with the picture full-screen.

'That seems . . . an extraordinary feat,' he says. 'Just from that one photo?'

'Street artists,' she says with a grin. 'The fourth emergency service.'

21

Before Mullins goes off shift, he tells Skinner he's meeting Jayden. He treads carefully, but the detective sergeant's moustache is ruler-straight. The thundery mood has gone nowhere.

'Well, you don't have to tell me what Jayden wants.'

And for half a second, Mullins thinks his boss is respecting his right to a social life.

'I can see it a mile off. He's tapping you up, Mullins. He's heard about the body on Lone Island and thinks he's got a mystery to solve.'

'No harm in it,' says Mullins. 'If he and Ally want to waste their time—'

'Ally Bright's coming too, is she?'

Mullins shakes his head. 'No. Just us lads.'

Skinner sits back in his chair and adjusts his tie. It's a new one, skinny as a worm. Mullins isn't sure about it, and by the way Skinner keeps fiddling with it, neither is he. Beside him, the detective sergeant's mobile buzzes with an incoming message; Skinner reaches for it, then changes his mind. He goes back to pulling at his tie.

'Trouble is with that Shell House pair, they're soppy, Mullins. Someone tells them a sob story and they're scribbling it all down in their notebooks, promising the world.'

Mullins obliges with a laugh.

'And we all know most promises aren't worth the paper they're written on.'

Mullins obliges with a *tsk*.

Promises, eh. Murky business.

'Axel Marks, though, he doesn't have anyone, does he?' Skinner continues. 'Even when there's no next of kin, normally we'd have had a call or two through by now. Mates seeing a name they recognised in the paper, wanting more info. For this bloke, though? Diddly squat. Best will in the world, no one seems to care.'

'They care up at Porthmerrin House, though, Sarge. Especially old Edward did.'

'And if you're going to have someone in your corner, then a family like the Greys aren't a bad bunch, I'll grant you that. If their statements are to be believed, anyway. But let's be honest, Mullins, Axel and the Greys weren't bosom buddies. They hadn't seen Axel Marks in fourteen years, had they? So what about who he was with last week, last month, last year? It's like he was a ghost.'

'Off-grid, I reckon.'

'My point is, who's hiring Shell House?'

Mullins rubs at the back of his head. 'Far as I know, no one, Sarge.'

'Twiddling their thumbs, are they? Want something to puzzle over? Well, tell them to pick up a crossword.'

'Could be the woman on the island, I s'pose.'

'Pippa Grant? She didn't know Axel Marks from Adam.'

'But she wasn't happy when we said there was no evidence of suspicious circumstances. She said she was worried there was more to it, didn't she?'

'Best will in the world,' says Skinner again, 'I suspect she's . . . what's the modern word for it . . . catastrophising.'

Mullins nods. *Fair point.*

'But you're right. She's the likely candidate. Or that Elspeth Grey. She struck me as having bleeding-heart potential, despite being married to a toff. Or even that nurse of Edward's, to be fair. Well, there you go, Mullins, you can do a little sleuthing of your own this evening. Find out who's got Ally and Jayden all worked up – and then shut it down. Not that wasting Shell House time is any kind of a criminal offence, mind.'

Mullins hesitates. He knows his boss thinks better of him these days but that's not saying all that much – it was a low bar to start with. But he decides to go for it anyway, with the same gusto that he's planning on sinking a pint of Doom Bar with later.

'Thing is, Sarge, does it matter? If the case is as good as closed from our perspective.'

'Does it *matter*?'

Mullins flinches. Is this the lightning strike out of Skinner's thundery skies? But Mullins stays his course. Because if he's really honest, he thinks Skinner's been a little too quick to write this case off.

'It's what you said when we were looking at the pictures from CSI, Sarge. You said Axel Marks could have been kicked six ways from Sunday, and we'd be none the wiser. You said that what he went through in the cliff fall, and then in the water, is the ultimate wipe-clean. That without an eyewitness, or a straight-up confession, we can't prove a thing. And you said it doesn't matter if you've got fifty people with a motive, in a situation like this.' He hesitates. 'That's what you said.'

Skinner's moustache twitches. That forehead of his has gone from ploughed field to wartime trenches. 'Word for word, was that?'

'More or less, Sarge.'

'So you do listen, then.' Skinner presses his fingers to his temples, and he heaves a sigh that's heavy as a sack of spuds. 'Look, I don't want Ally and Jayden putting a cat amongst the pigeons.

Stirring things up when we all know that, given the circumstances, a charge will never stick. And that's me being generous. Because do I think something's off in this situation? No, I don't, Mullins. I think Axel Marks got unlucky. The world's full of poor fortune. And for Axel, it was probably yet another unlucky strike in a lifetime of them. He got himself wasted, disorientated, and then bad judgement and gravity did the rest. That's what I think.'

'Even with everything else?'

The small matter of about three million quid's worth of property, for one.

'Even with everything else.'

'So, Jay, even with everything else, that's what we think,' says Mullins.

And he sits back, pleased with himself, as he drains his pint. It's hard to tell exactly what Jayden's thinking, but he's probably impressed with Mullins's nippy little summary.

'Isn't that the easy way out, though?' says Jayden.

Typical Shell House.

'The path of least resistance,' he runs on, 'because you both know it'd be difficult to prove anything else.'

Mullins groans inwardly. Never any flies on Jayden Weston. Why can't there be? Just for once? A whopping great bluebottle, landing on his nose.

'You fancy telling that to Skinner, do you, Jay? He's been in a right mood the last few days.'

'He's always in a right mood, Mullins.'

'Well, he's putting in overtime. On the mood, I mean. Not the case.'

Is this where Mullins confides in Jayden that Skinner seems to be going through the motions with this one? Like something else has got his attention, and not a good thing either.

'Look, I get it,' says Jayden. 'You've got limited resources, limited budget, there's no point dedicating a whole load of time to a case when you already know it's not going to result in a conviction. Right?'

To be fair, Mullins's boss said as much himself. If you know a charge will never stick, what's the point of bringing it in the first place? Maybe Skinner's going through the motions because it's a waste of time doing anything else. A strategic decision – or whatever the brass bang on about in the meeting rooms – rather than someone dropping a ball.

'Right.'

'But me and Ally . . . we don't work like that.'

Mullins laughs loudly. 'Yeah, we know how you work.'

But he doesn't actually. Not really. Sometimes it's like hocus pocus, and sometimes it makes more sense than anything that happens down the station. Even when the Major Crimes lot from Newquay swoop in with their slick suits and big shiny watches and bulging biceps. *Except for DS Chang. DS Chang is sound as a pound.* The truth is, if Skinner seconded Mullins to the Shell House Detectives he wouldn't fight it. So long as that pay packet kept coming every month. So long as he got to keep the uniform.

I do like the uniform.

'You'd just be stirring things up, Jay. Putting a cat amongst the pigeons.'

Did Skinner say anything else?

'Too right,' says Jayden.

'But for no point whatsoever. Are you guys really that bored?'

'What if stirring things up results in someone coming forward?'

'Dreamland.'

'Why not?'

'Dreamland,' says Mullins again. 'And it's your round, by the way.'

'In a minute. But it's wild, right? The inheritance?'

'Course it is.'

'And the nurse, Donna Goode. She was hired at random, but it turns out her brother knew Axel back in the day, in the army.'

'We know all this, Jay. You spoken to her yet?'

'What – Donna? No. By the time we'd finished checking the van, she'd gone out.'

'So you don't know that her brother was blown to bits?'

Mullins enjoys the way Jayden's eyebrows go up.

'Curtis Goode. He wasn't just in the same regiment as Axel Marks, Jay, he was in the same section. And if you don't speak "army", that's eight soldiers. Eight soldiers, and two of them are linked one way or another to that night at Porthmerrin House.'

Mullins's tongue is running away with him, but what does it really matter? These weren't facts they sweated hard to get hold of. It doesn't count as divulging confidential information to a third party. *Or does it?* Donna Goode came right out and said it to them, just like she'll probably come right out and say it to Jayden and Ally, once they go and talk to her.

Because, by the look in Jayden's eyes, he is one hundred per cent going to go and talk to her.

'Mullins,' says Jayden, 'that makes Donna a person of interest. Massively so.'

'It makes her a person who's lost her brother, and now, after five minutes reconnecting with an old army mate, goes and loses him too. I felt sorry for her, Jay.'

'And then her patient dies too,' says Jayden. 'Edward Grey.'

'Donna was straightforward. Nothing to hide. She was nursing Edward twenty-four-seven. There was no one-on-one time with

Axel, going over what happened with her brother. None of that. She left the Greys and Axel to it.'

'What happened with her brother? Because Axel was medically discharged from the army.'

'He was.'

'Do you know on what basis?' asks Jayden.

'He was a suicide risk,' says Mullins. 'Now, come on, Jay. Your round.'

Mullins senses a buzzing in his pocket, and he checks his phone. *Skinner.* He can feel Jayden staring at him, absorbing this new fact about poor old Axel Marks.

'I need to get this,' says Mullins.

And Jayden takes his cue and goes to the bar. Noggin no doubt fizzing. *Shell House.* Jayden's going to think there's something in the army connection. Just like he thought there was something in the inheritance.

'Sarge?'

'I just had an interesting chat with a bloke called Fergus Grant.'

There's a weird energy in Skinner's voice.

'Grant. As in Pippa Grant?'

'Pippa's husband. He saw the news – then saw fit to call us immediately. He was worried. Very worried.'

'Right . . .'

'And given what he had to say, I put in a call to Lucas Grey. Remember that outhouse of theirs with the old boats and whatnot? Well, I asked them to go and check it. Count their boats.'

Mullins frowns. He's only had the one pint, but he's not keeping up with Skinner here.

'Erm, Sarge?'

'Turns out there's one missing, Mullins.'

Suddenly, Skinner doesn't sound like a bloke who's about to close an investigation.

'A boat missing?'

'Some knackered old kayak. So first thing in the morning, you and I are going back to Lone Island. We thought Axel Marks was washed up on that beach randomly, but what if he was heading there all along?'

Mullins screws up his nose. 'How are you squaring that with his injuries? Bashed himself in the face with his paddle, did he?'

This time there's a full-throated groan from Skinner.

'Good God, Mullins, use your head. There's no shortage of cliff drops on Lone Island. And he could have gone off any one of them.'

22

Ally sits at the big wooden table in The Shell House, bent over her laptop. Beside her, a lamp sends its reassuring glow, but she feels scattered. She thinks of Donna Goode and her brother Curtis. She thinks of Axel, medically discharged, considered a suicide risk. And she thinks of Pippa, and the eyes of the police now trained upon Lone Island.

All of this new information is courtesy of Mullins, one way or another. Perhaps the constable is glad they're pursuing the case. Or perhaps it was Mullins mining Jayden for information over pints in The Wreckers, rather than the other way round. What did Jayden pass on that Mullins had said, in a somewhat teasing tone: *How much do you really know about your client?*

Ally checks her phone again. She hasn't heard from Pippa since mid-afternoon, when they left the island. She takes a steadying breath and focuses instead on Donna – mostly because she's right here in front of her. Or her Facebook page is, at least. As Ally looks into the woman's eyes she murmurs, 'What do you know, Donna?'

They didn't manage to speak to the nurse at the house earlier. Was Donna taking pains to avoid them by going out on an errand while they were in the van? Ally scrolls back through the page. Edward Grey's nurse is in her early thirties but looks younger. She has a halo of curly blond hair and her styling is a touch 1950s, with wide belts and swingy skirts. Her posts are sporadic but tend towards the cheerful: sunsets, blossom, cocktails. But there's one that stands out, and it's dated just two weeks ago.

Fourteen years ago today. The call we dreaded. My best, brave bro, killed in Helmand Province, gone forever. RIP Curtis.

Then a picture of a young man in desert-coloured camouflage, sunglasses pushed up on his head, grinning at the camera. A sky of untrammelled blue behind. He looks soft-cheeked and wide-eyed; too innocent to be a soldier. But there's a rifle slung over his shoulder.

Ally sits back in her chair, biting her lip.

Surely it can't have been coincidence that brought Donna to Porthmerrin House, Axel's childhood home, of sorts. Lucas and Elspeth spoke of the connection so lightly that Ally can only think that they don't know Donna's brother died in combat; that they have no idea the two men had been involved in a devastating incident at the same time.

Ally scrolls back further through Donna's posts and finds the first entry after her brother died. Her eyes fill as she reads it. It's controlled and factual, as if Donna was aware of army eyes upon it. Helmand Province. The ambush. Improvised Explosive Device. One fatality, multiple injuries. *My darling brother.* She then went quiet on Facebook, but another post, six months later: *Brothers in arms. Some have been brilliant, and some have not, and maybe that's the way it goes, but Curtis had good people around him his whole life and I hoped more than anything that it would be the same in The Rifles.*

Donna doesn't expand on the thought, but the post has had a lot of likes and comments, words of support and love. One comment, from a Nikki Claridge, says: *People deal differently but there's no excuse.*

Ally makes a note in the pad beside her. Writes: *Did Axel and Donna have any contact after Curtis's death? Did Donna know why he was discharged?* The page in her jotter is full of questions. Questions that can only be answered by talking to Donna. *And even then.*

Ally gets up and goes to the kitchen. She fills the kettle, uncertain of her next move.

I feel uncertain full stop.

She could do a deeper dive on Donna Goode, researching Curtis Goode's death in Afghanistan too; it would be useful to go into their conversation tomorrow with their eyes wide open – providing the nurse will speak to them. She could keep trying to find out more about Pippa – who doesn't seem to exist at all on the internet – and her husband, Fergus Grant. Perhaps the ownership of Lone Island is even a factor; Edward's father donated it to the wildlife trust years back. Meanwhile there's Lucas and Elspeth, who stand to benefit vastly from Axel's death.

Ally stands at her kitchen counter, waiting for the kettle to boil, her mind darting this way and that. Instead of feeling energised by this sudden influx of leads, she's left discombobulated. How can they possibly hope to piece together what happened to Axel Marks? Suddenly the landscape of the case feels too large. Axel was found on Lone Island, but his story extends far further than this corner of the world. All the way to Afghanistan? And everything in between is a mystery.

It doesn't matter that they've a number of major cases under their belts, Ally has never felt more of an amateur. And she doesn't quite understand it.

And then an image of the 'For Sale' sign at the cottage on the square comes into her head.

Perhaps I do partly understand it.

Once she's deep in an investigation, everyday life recedes. She's focused, driven. Head down, walking the metaphorical shore, eyes peeled for the glint of something more. But this evening she's tired, and the day sits heavy in her bones. At her fingertips, the internet boggles with its infinite information. Names jostle with one another for her attention. It feels as if they have so much – but so little.

And I don't know how I feel about Ray.

The significance of Ray's phone call this morning returns with full force. So too the uncomfortable feeling that she didn't respond with appropriate, or even fair, enthusiasm. She should phone him, but what would she say? Ally knows that beneath Ray's musings on his next chapter lies a much bigger question. And she's so uncertain of her answer that she's afraid to even hear it asked.

From his basket in the corner, Fox barks. Ally looks over to him, and his nose is in the air, pointed towards the door. Sure enough, there's a knock. Fox settles his head back on his paws, considering his job done.

Ally checks her watch. It's nearly eight o'clock, which would be an early finish for Jayden and Mullins; when he quickly called her with the update, Mullins was just getting another round. As she moves to the door, Ally hopes it is Jayden, because his energy always picks her up. They can get into it all together and do an evening shift in the thinking room.

But she opens up to find Gus. Gus with a bottle of wine tucked under his arm. Her face must look distracted, because his own wide smile shifts, and he says, 'I'm not interrupting, am I?'

'No, no. I'm pleased to see you.'

And as she says it, she realises she really is.

'I'm in a slightly strange mood,' she says, deciding honesty is the best policy.

'Is it this new case?'

'Yes, it's a difficult one,' says Ally. 'A sad one.' She hesitates. *Honesty is the best policy.*

'But, also . . . Ray.'

Because, despite Gus once being not quite impartial when it came to Ray, Ally suspects those feelings have long since subsided.

'Ah now, then I'm glad I brought this,' he says, passing her the wine. 'Because nothing simplifies a situation like a glass or two of wine, in my opinion.'

~

'So that's about the long and short of it,' she says.

'Right,' says Gus. 'Gotcha. That's where we are. Where you are. You both.'

Ally watches him carefully. Was she wrong to go into things about Ray? But while Gus's words are stilted, his face is impassive. He takes another sip of wine. It turns into quite a draught.

'I'm sorry to go on,' she says. 'It's boring really.'

'It's not boring, Ally. Not at all.'

'I suppose you get to a certain age and expect things to be simple. It comes as a perpetual surprise to me that . . . they're not.'

'They could be,' says Gus, turning his glass in his hand. 'Simple, I mean. But I'm very much on the outside, so . . . it's altogether easier, isn't it, to commentate? Well, easier in certain respects.'

There isn't an undercurrent to his comment about being on the outside, and Ally feels a little gust of relief. He's a good friend, Gus. A dear friend. And how she'd have hated to lose him.

'You're right. If Evie was in any such situation, I'd say to listen to her instincts. Which you could say is simple, I suppose. Though it takes a sort of bravery, nevertheless.' She cups her hand to her chin. 'But instincts aren't everything, are they? Sometimes we have to coax ourselves to . . . adjust. Take the next step. Which might be in a different direction to the tried-and-tested one.'

'Like you and the detective work,' says Gus.

'Well, exactly. Like me and the detective work.'

They sit looking at one another.

'Only . . . perhaps not really like that,' he says.

'No. It's quite different, really.'

Gus looks down. 'Do you think,' he says carefully, 'that you feel as if your independence might be threatened, if Ray moved closer?'

Ally smiles sadly. Gus is almost right. From his place over the fireplace, Bill regards her steadily. Her husband's warm and open smile will support her in anything. Except for what she really wants. To have him back.

23

Jayden walks up the last big hill towards home. He's glad he brought his jacket. While the day was full of sunshine, the evening is chilly. The torch beam from his phone bounces off the hedgerows as he strides with purpose.

He's thinking of Axel Marks.

Medically discharged from the army. Deemed a suicide risk. A soldier who lost a friend in his section. *Park the potentially massive significance that it was Donna Goode's brother.* Without knowing the circumstances, Jayden fills in the blanks. Eight soldiers in a section, Mullins said. You're going to be close. You're going to have each other's backs.

It's me and Kieran.

With any case that he and Ally take, they're in it for the victim. It was the same in the police: Jayden joined up because he wanted to help the people who needed it; not to feel important or rise through the ranks, but to make a difference at street level.

From everything that Lucas said, Axel lost his way after he left the army – lost his way and maybe never really found it again. Which Jayden can't help equating to Axel losing his way after his friend died – and his mum, so soon afterwards. After Kieran died, Jayden had plenty of support structures, and still he found it almost impossibly hard.

Did Axel have anyone? Anyone at all?

Jayden was all in with this case before – but now? More than ever. Which is partly about the massive question of the inheritance, and partly about the army connection with Edward's nurse, and partly about whatever the call was that Mullins got from Skinner, chirping about a new development.

And partly about kinship. Which perhaps, when you get down to it, isn't substantially different to Pippa's 'feeling'.

'We're going to solve this for you, Axel,' he says quietly, hands balling into fists as he strides.

Jayden wants to get home now. He wants to *do* something. Go online and do some digging. For tomorrow to hustle on in, so he and Ally can pick up where they left off – pushing forward with adrenalin, no distractions.

He suddenly remembers the call he missed from his mum earlier – *on the subject of distractions* – and listens to the voicemail. It plays havoc with the torchlight, but it'd be nice to walk in and tell Cat that Benji will have one set of grandparents at his party. It feels crazy to Jayden, this sideways movement from someone else's devastation to his own everyday living, but he should be used to it by now. Just because Axel Marks is right up inside his head, it doesn't mean he shouldn't care about Benji having a party. As Jayden listens to the message, he feels his face change. They've booked tickets to a jazz night? One of his dad's favourite musicians, apparently, and they're going *all the way to London for it.* He likes thinking of his parents doing stuff like this, it's cool, but . . . the timing. Cat won't. *But Jayden, we can come down the weekend after*, his mum says, her voice soft with apology. *We can bring him a big cake then!*

He hangs up.

It makes it easier in a way, doesn't it? They'll just shift the party on a week. But he's not sure Cat'll see it the same way.

Seriously, though? It's no big deal.

Jayden looks to the water where there's a far-off pinprick of light. It's probably a boat, but even though it's the wrong direction for Lone Island, he thinks of Pippa alone in her cottage. And all the things they know, and don't know, flood back in.

At first Mullins wouldn't say what Skinner's phone call was about, but then he did that Mullins thing of puffing his chest out, like someone had stuck a bike pump in him. *There's been a development*, he said. But it didn't take long for him to say what was newly on his mind – another half a pint and a bag of beef-and-onion crisps, to be precise – even if it was heavy on innuendo and light on facts. And the line that stuck?

How well do you know this so-called client of yours, Jay?

Turns out the Greys are missing a boat, which has opened up the question of where Axel entered the water. The working theory that Axel fell from the cliffs in the direct vicinity of his van is now being questioned. Only Mullins wouldn't say why. When Jayden said that the Greys hadn't mentioned a missing boat this afternoon, Mullins said, *They wouldn't, would they? We were the ones who told them to go and look.* Then, after a beat, correcting *we* to *Well . . . Skinner*.

All Jayden can think is that they're now looking at the significance of Axel's body being found on the island, because why mention Pippa otherwise? Maybe the pathologist's findings support multiple theories. Like Axel drowning in the water just off the island, and being washed directly in. Or sustaining his injuries falling from the island's cliffs, not those on Porthmerrin land.

Jayden considers it a fail that he couldn't get more out of Mullins on this score. But he does, at the same time, have respect for the constable's professionalism. Though with Mullins, there's probably an element of one-upmanship at play too.

No, it's all good. If the police are headed back to the island tomorrow, then they'll get the full story from Pippa afterwards.

Will we, though?

There's a nagging doubt in the back of Jayden's mind. He can't figure out why he's uncertain when it comes to the island warden. Ironically, perhaps it's Pippa's own certainty causing his unsureness. And no doubt there was something loaded in Mullins's question about how well they know Pippa Grant.

Jayden is aware, suddenly, of a sound behind him in the lane.

The truth? He doesn't love the deserted countryside at night. Give him the hum and crash of the inner city any day. Give him urban sprawl. And it's footsteps he can hear, no question. Footsteps loud enough to cut above the sound of the sea. Loud enough to cut above the low-key rustling in the hedgerows that's probably wind but could be any number of critters. Footsteps that stop when he stops. And start when he starts.

Jayden turns and sweeps his torch beam. But all it picks out is some undefined roadkill that his feet must have missed by inches; the tufted grass in the middle of the lane; the trees waving their arms like drunks on corners.

'Who's there?' he calls out.

Bizarrely, Jayden thinks of Axel himself. But which version? The child who grew up in the grounds of Porthmerrin House? The hopeful young soldier in Afghanistan? The man who was discharged, broken? The drifter in his van? But Axel is dead. Axel will never walk in a lane again.

And Jayden doesn't believe in ghosts.

There was a time, in the weeks after Kieran died, when Jayden heard things. He could be anywhere – their flat, the park, a bus stop – and he'd spin his head, quickly turn, flinch. It didn't last, and while it did he put it down, mostly, to a rational reaction: isn't it smart to have an awareness of peril? Everyone could use 360 vision, right? But he also had enough therapy to know that hypersensitivity is a different thing. Now, deep inside him, something stirs, twitches, like a muscle memory Jayden doesn't want. Do the bad feelings ever fully go away, or do they simply lie dormant? He casts the torch around again.

Nothing.

Possibilities run through his mind. Was someone listening in the pub? No, they kept their voices low, and he scanned the company. And while this lane isn't a private track, there aren't many houses out this way; it's not like in high season with campers running back and forth from the village.

Part of Jayden wants to slow right down. Stop. Wait. And see if there's anything to see. But then he thinks of Cat. How, after last autumn in the sea caves, his wife clutched him to her, and said she understood that some danger was unavoidable, but the avoidable stuff? Don't do it, basically. *Jay, next time, put yourself first. If not for you, then for us.*

So, without knowing if this is danger or not, Jayden breaks into a jog.

24

Ally pours a second cup of coffee, hoping it'll speed away the faint fuzziness in her head. Gus stayed a couple of hours last night, and the bottle he brought soon went. It wasn't as though they only talked about Ray, far from it, but Ally already feels slightly disloyal for voicing her feelings to Gus when she hasn't even broached them with Ray.

Still: it was good to talk.

She wanders out to the veranda, Fox nosing at her ankles, and settles on the bench. She pulls a blanket over her knees. It's early still, and there's a chill in the air. But over the water the sky is a pale wash of blue, without a trace of cloud. The day is set fair.

When Gus asked the question about her independence, he was partly right – and Ally said as much. What she didn't expand on was the other part. That it's not so much her independence as her dependence on Bill. Because, despite the hard facts of the matter, her life is still entwined with her late husband's. Bill is everywhere in this house, these dunes, this place – and always will be. A relationship with Ray, three hundred miles away in Suffolk, is a different proposition to a relationship with him in Cornwall.

With anyone in Cornwall.

And it was talking about this with Gus that made it clear to her. What's not clear is if it's a feeling that can change. And if Ray will be the one to change it.

Gus didn't press her, and they didn't overly linger on the topic. They talked about his novel – and him finally getting the draft ready to send to his agent. They talked about the case. They talked about all sorts, really. The time passed so easily. The wine disappeared. And as Gus tipped an imaginary hat, turned away and walked over the dunes, Ally felt a lightness of spirit. Somewhere an owl, rare out here, rare but not unheard of, said its own goodnight.

'Al!'

Jayden is at the garden gate, swinging his way through, fast feet heading up the path.

'There's coffee still in the pot,' she says. 'Good morning.'

'On it. And morning, Al. Busy day ahead, right?'

'Busy day.'

As Ally says it, she realises she's recharged, despite the mildly fuzzy head. Acknowledging her doubt to Gus has somehow fortified her across the board.

'Saffron and Milo came through for us. Came through with bells on. The woman whose photo was in Axel's van? I've only got a name for you.'

'Jayden!' she exclaims.

'No, Casey,' he grins. 'Casey James. And we know when the picture was taken too. It's recent, Al.'

Jayden explains how an artist friend of Milo's was able to pinpoint the date that the photograph was taken, because one of the graffitied walls in the background – an erupting volcano; an emblazoned word in 'wildstyle', comprehensible only to those in the know – was new. Two weeks later that same wall was sprayed over by another artist. The conclusion? The photograph had to have been taken six months ago, in the first half of October. Moreover, the artist recognised the woman in the picture. She skated the park sometimes.

'So Milo's mate asked around and he got a name,' says Jayden. 'But he wanted to know why anyone was asking, so when Milo said it was a couple of private detectives in Cornwall he went and looked online, and the news report came up. So there's a chance that Casey now knows about Axel's death. I said to pass on my number, but I imagine she'll go straight to the police to find out more.'

Ally pictures, suddenly, a whole group of Axel's friends in Bristol who, for one reason or another, have no idea of his death. Could such a thing be possible, in this supposedly hyper-connected day and age?

'Should we try and speak to Casey James first? Or let Mullins and Skinner know we might have the next best thing to a next of kin?'

Jayden wrinkles his nose. 'Axel kept her photo, but we don't know how much they were really involved with one another.'

'I think she was important to him. She has to have been.'

'Gut feel? I think so too.'

'What about if we try and contact Casey through social media? Does she have it?'

'Already looked, Al. She has an Instagram account – there's a bit of Bristol, a bit of skateboarding, it's her – but she hasn't posted in two years. We could try a message through that, but I reckon our best hope is that she gets in touch with us. Which might be after she's made contact with the police. Mullins said they never recovered Axel's phone, and they're still waiting on the phone company to share records, so once they see that they should be getting in touch with her anyway. If she and Axel were in close contact, anyway. Still, it's progress, right? A nice bit of detective work all round.'

Jayden ducks inside, and Ally can hear him taking down a mug, swapping a few words with Fox. He emerges with a coffee, and plonks down beside her.

'Oh hey, strange thing last night. I think I was followed home from the pub.'

'On foot?'

Jayden nods. 'I wasn't imagining it, and believe me, the thought did enter my head. But . . . no. Definite footsteps.'

'Did you see who it was?'

'No. They were hanging back. But the lanes are weird, right? The acoustics. It sounded close. Anyway, I didn't stick around to investigate. Some detective, right?'

'I'd say that was sensible,' says Ally. 'Jayden, who could it have been?'

'Apart from basically anyone, you mean? I reckon someone we met yesterday. So . . . Pippa, the boatman Trent, Robbie the gardener, Lucas, Elspeth, or Donna the nurse – who we didn't meet but wanted to. And considering Mullins's information, we now *really* want to.'

'But they're all fifteen miles away in Porthmerrin. And Pippa's on the island.'

Jayden shrugs. 'When I got home it even crossed my mind that it was Mullins playing a trick. Swallowed my pride and messaged him.'

'If it was someone we met yesterday, that's telling, isn't it?'

'It is,' says Jayden. 'Mullins said Skinner thought we were going to put a cat amongst the pigeons with our questions – Skinner's words – and going by this, that's exactly what we've done. You know what, it's validating. We're right to be looking into this. Because it's my guess that someone out there doesn't want us to.'

Ally wraps her hands around her coffee cup. 'I can't stop thinking about Donna Goode. And her poor brother.'

'Yeah, me too. Axel . . . had a hard time of it.'

Ally tells him about the Facebook posts. How, reading between the lines, Donna was unhappy with the response to Curtis's death from some quarters.

'It was that line, "brothers in arms", that made me think of his section, specifically. If Axel survived that attack, but then was medically discharged, perhaps those two things are directly related.'

'We're on the same page, Al. I checked out Donna's Facebook last night and saw that "brothers in arms" post too.'

'Did you look at everyone who commented? There was some-one who seemed to understand the subtext.'

'Hold on, I'll bring it up.'

Jayden studies his phone as steam rises from his cup in the crisp air.

'Okay, weird. It's gone.'

'Gone?'

'Gone.' He scrolls up and down. 'She's deleted it. Now that's interesting.'

'I screenshotted it yesterday,' says Ally.

'Nice work.' Jayden takes a sip of coffee. 'Why would Donna delete it? Do you reckon she blamed Axel somehow, for her brother's death?'

'She did seem to blame someone, or some people, for their *response* to Curtis's death. Reading between the lines,' she says again.

Jayden's face is thoughtful. 'When Kieran died, I kept thinking about the things I could have done, or should have done, to prevent it. Even if some part of me knew that wasn't rational. And I fully expected his wife to blame me. Even if it was just . . . for being alive, when Kieran wasn't.'

'You don't feel that way now, do you?' says Ally softly.

Jayden hesitates. 'Not the blame part. But . . . why him and not me? Yeah. I do think that.'

They're quiet for a moment.

'But this is fourteen years on,' says Jayden. 'Elspeth implied that Donna hadn't seen Axel in all that time. There's going to be an emotional charge there, for sure. On both sides.'

Ally thinks again of Axel's tin of photographs. There were none from his time in the army. In Jayden's house, there's a picture of him and Kieran hanging in the hallway. They're out of uniform, laughing at the camera; the image shimmers with youth and happiness and friendship. She remarked on it once, and Jayden just said *Yeah, I like that one.*

'And since last night, something's made Donna go all the way back through her posts and delete this one specifically.' Jayden looks at his watch. 'Alright. Let's get up to the house. According to the Greys, Donna's not going anywhere in a hurry. In fact . . .' He pauses. 'Didn't Elspeth say that Donna wanted to get it in writing, that she could stay on in the house? That doesn't seem like someone who's worried about being discovered. And yet she's thinking twice about her social media footprint. It doesn't add up.'

'Perhaps she's very confident,' says Ally. 'The police had all but given up, hadn't they? Until . . . whatever this new angle is.'

'And that new angle's been keeping me up,' says Jayden. 'You heard anything from Pippa this morning?'

And Ally has to admit that no, she hasn't. Not a peep.

As they drive to Porthmerrin House, they pull in at the jetty where Trent Simms launches his boat. From this distance, Lone Island is as smooth and evenly rounded as a hillock. No suggestion of its jagged rocks and many inlets, or the sheer cliff faces, sharp as teeth, on the seaward side.

'I keep thinking about Mullins saying, "How well do you know your client?"' says Ally.

Beside her, Jayden shakes his head. 'Something, or someone, has put focus on Lone Island. And the possibility that Axel died there. Whatever it is, it's presumably workable with the post-mortem findings, or they wouldn't be wasting their time.'

'And it's enough to get Skinner and Mullins moving on the case.' Ally takes out her phone. 'I should call Pippa, shouldn't I?'

'I wouldn't. Not yet.'

Ally hears the caution in his voice. It's true that Pippa guards her privacy; she's told them what she thinks they need to know for the case, but little more. But it was Pippa who sought them out. Who brought them in. That doesn't seem to fit with someone who has anything to hide.

'How about a text message, saying we're busy making enquiries? It feels strange not to, Jayden.'

'Okay,' says Jayden. 'And I guess she might give us something.'

Ally sends her a message and looks again to the island, imagining Pippa in her tiny cottage, or striding over the clifftops in those big black wellingtons. Alone – for now. But not for much longer, as the days count down to when she has to leave the post.

Unless her appeal has worked.

'The police must have made a connection,' says Jayden. 'A connection between Axel and Pippa.'

'Or Axel and her husband Fergus.'

'Or Axel and Fergus,' echoes Jayden. 'Her *missing* husband.'

'He's not missing. He left.'

'And Trent Simms didn't take him in his boat.'

Even though they have business at Porthmerrin House – Donna Goode, they have to talk to Donna Goode – Ally feels a strong pull towards the island. She'd like to be talking to Pippa, sitting in the cottage with its perfect view from the square kitchen window, or at the cove where Pippa set her flowers between the rocks. But the police will get there first – because they know what questions they're asking – and all Ally and Jayden can do is follow in their wake.

Ally looks at her phone. No reply yet.

'Let's work this through,' says Jayden, tapping a drumbeat on the dash. 'What if Axel was alive when he got to the island? What if Pippa's husband didn't leave two weeks ago? What if Fergus Grant hasn't left at all?'

Ally swivels in her seat. 'And you think Pippa's protecting him? But then why on earth would she come to us?'

'Because maybe she's between a rock and a hard place. She doesn't want to point the finger at her own husband, but she suspects foul play.'

Ally quietly considers it.

'Here's how it went. The police get a report of a missing person, someone considered vulnerable, and under the influence, who parked their van on a clifftop late at night – and that's where Axel was last seen. Then his body is found washed up on Lone Island. The obvious thinking is that he fell from the cliff and the tide took him, right? We said it ourselves, yesterday.'

Ally nods. 'Your friend Occam.'

'Exactly. And there's no witnesses or hard evidence to suggest that *didn't* happen. So it's the most likely scenario. But it's also possible that Axel took a boat to the island – the boat that Mullins said is missing from Porthmerrin – and died there. Lucas Grey said he loved the place.'

'If Axel took a boat, he could have capsized and been thrown against the rocks, couldn't he?' she says. 'Perhaps such injuries wouldn't look that different to if he'd fallen from a great height.'

'Or he could have got to the island and fallen from a great height there.'

The thought hangs. Ally looks again to the island, as if she needs to see it anew. She thinks again of Pippa's flowers in the jam jar. It is, she realises, the image she's holding on to. Reflective of the warden's good intentions.

'The army connection, though,' says Ally. 'It's huge.'

'It is for me too. Come on, Al. Let's go and meet Donna Goode.'

But Ally notices the look he gives the island as they drive away. Jayden is as reluctant as she is to lose it from his sight.

25

It's a short drive up to Porthmerrin from the jetty, but the lanes make a big deal of it, twisting and pitching, the house itself never in sight until the last minute. The verges pop with daffodils, the colour unreal. A deer appears from the hedgerow and springs up the other side, gone before Jayden even has a chance to hit the brakes.

Despite the movement in the case, a percentage of his brain dwells on Cat. He told her his idea about moving the party – *you know, because of the jazz night and Gran Canaria, babe* – but it didn't go down well. *But it's about the day, Jay, the actual day he was born. I wanted all our friends to be there too. A proper bash.* Jayden reminding Cat that Benji would be turning one and has zero concept of time did not seem to help. Nor did his helpful suggestion about perspective; that a man is dead, and aren't the likes of them lucky to be celebrating any birthdays at all?

Yeah, not helpful.

'The date of Benji's party might be moving, Al,' he says. 'But I'll let you know as soon as.'

'I'll be there whenever it is,' she says.

'But we'll crack this case first, okay?'

'Oh, without a doubt.'

As they make the turn into the driveway of Porthmerrin House, through the big acorn-topped stone pillars, two people are up ahead. They draw closer, and Jayden sees they're walking hand in hand.

'That's Robbie,' says Jayden. 'And that's got to be Donna, right?'

At the sound of the engine, the pair drop their hands. Donna stands to one side to let the car pass, but Robbie is slower to shift. No surprise to Jayden. There was an immovability to the gardener yesterday, but Jayden couldn't work out if that was his usual style or a reaction to recent events.

'Let's have a word,' he says to Ally, buzzing down the window as they approach. Then, easily, casually, 'Morning.'

Robbie nods curtly. Donna smiles – but it doesn't reach her eyes. She looks tired, thinks Jayden. Panda eyes. Staying up late deleting Facebook posts, maybe.

'You've missed them,' says Robbie, jerking a thumb towards the house. 'They won't be back till after lunch.'

'Lucas and Elspeth?' says Jayden. 'We wanted a chat with you both, if that's alright. It's Donna, isn't it?'

He smiles at her, but Donna's has fully dropped now. She chews at her lip, then appears to reset.

'Yes. I'm Edward's nurse. It's . . . been an awful couple of days.'

'This about the missing boat?' Robbie bends down to the car window, obscuring Donna at the same time. 'I don't know anything about it.'

'Neither do we.' *Nothing ventured, nothing gained.* 'Fill us in?'

'Lucas reckoned a kayak was missing from the shed. That's all there is to it. If I'm honest, I didn't even register there was one in there. These old outhouses are dumping grounds.' He passes his hand across his mouth. 'Except for where I keep my gear. That's neat as. Anyone so much as took a pair of shears, I'd know it.' Robbie looks to Donna. 'He'd have had a job lugging that thing down to the shore, but it's possible.'

'Axel, you mean?' asks Ally, leaning across.

'Who else?'

'Do you both want a lift back up to the house?' says Jayden. 'We can talk more easily there.'

Robbie looks at his watch. 'I'm meeting a tree surgeon in five. Over there by that ailing oak.'

Jayden looks across the field to a huddle of trees; he can't tell that they're oaks, let alone if they're ailing.

'I can talk to you now, though,' says Donna. 'Lucas said you came by yesterday. Sorry I missed you then.'

Her words are willing enough, but there's something closed about the way she says them. She opens the car door and slides in the back, without looking at Robbie. Ally turns in her seat.

'Pleased to meet you, Donna,' she says. 'And I'm sorry for your loss. The Greys said how close you were to him.'

There's a pause.

'You and Edward,' says Ally.

'He was a dream,' says Donna quietly, tucking a curl behind her ear.

When Jayden glances in the mirror, he sees Donna has her fingertips pressed to her eyes.

'It's been an awful few days,' she says again.

Behind them on the drive, Robbie watches them go. In no time they're parking up and heading for the house. The nurse takes a set of keys from her pocket and lets them in.

'I've never actually been in the house on my own,' she says, stepping out of her shoes. She stands in her pink socks, looking up at the wide, twisting staircase, the elaborate chandelier, the massive, gloomy oil paintings. Her voice sounds very small. 'I mean, it was always just me and Edward. And obviously he never went anywhere. Not by the time I was hired.'

They follow Donna into the kitchen and Ally's struck again by the vastness of it. Light pours in through the wide windows. There are two new flower bouquets since yesterday: white lilies sit in a vase on the windowsill, while a big bunch of pastel-coloured carnations, still in the plastic wrap, lies on the sideboard near the kettle.

'Did Lucas not come down often?' asks Ally.

Donna hesitates. 'Not often, if I'm honest. But they lead busy lives. Do you want tea?'

'Yes, please.'

Ally watches as Donna pushes the bouquet out of the way, then fills the kettle at the sink.

'How did you find the job?' asks Jayden. 'It's not going to suit everyone, a place as remote as this.'

'Oh, I loved it. I mean, I still do.' Her cheeks flush. 'Sorry, it's just everything feels . . . past-tense. Edward. Then Axel Marks. It's overwhelming, actually.'

She busies herself with a teapot, then reaches up for cups and saucers from the dresser.

'So how did you come to be here?' asks Ally again.

'Oh yeah.' Donna turns smartly. 'I was in Devon, no ties, and so I was just looking all over the south-west, really. I saw this job come up and . . . I fancied it. I like being by the sea. Always have. And the house, well, it's a bit different, isn't it? And a lot of nursing isn't.'

'When did you realise the connection?' asks Jayden.

And he drops it in like it's something they've already talked about. *No biggie.*

'The connection?' Donna blinks. Her cheeks flare red, as if a switch has been flicked. 'Oh, you mean The Rifles? I didn't know if you knew that. Yeah . . . that was weird. Um, it came up in my interview, actually. I suddenly found myself talking about Curtis. I mean, he's part of why I got into nursing in the first place, so . . . I guess that's natural. And Elspeth was super approachable, so I suppose I told her more than I normally would. She said she wasn't sure, but that she thought there was a connection with Curtis's regiment and Porthmerrin. Anyway, she checked with Lucas and that's how I found out about Axel Marks basically growing up here. Sugar?'

They both say no thanks.

'If I'm honest, it almost made me change my mind about the job. See . . .' She hesitates, rubs at her arm. 'It was complicated, after Curtis died. You can't imagine. It was right at the end of his tour. Like . . . just a couple of days. We were so excited about having him home and—' She stops, draws in a breath. 'Anyway, it was nuts. The coincidence with this place, I mean. Axel wasn't just a Rifleman, he was in Curtis's section. He was there when Curtis died. But Elspeth told me Axel didn't have anything to do with Edward anymore, though, so . . . I felt okay taking the job.' She shakes her head. 'Sorry, what I mean is, it might have been hard to be face to face with Axel all day every day, you know? Too much of a reminder. A trigger. But . . . he wasn't here.'

And then, suddenly, he was.

A thought strikes Jayden, but before he can ask it Ally has a question of her own.

'So you didn't meet Axel at your brother's funeral?'

My thoughts exactly. Eight soldiers in a section – wouldn't they all be there? Those who came home. If Curtis was killed so close to the end of the tour – a fact that must have made it all the worse – presumably his fellow soldiers would have been back on UK soil and available to attend.

'Apparently Axel couldn't be there,' she says stiffly. 'He struggled afterwards. Ended up leaving the army. I don't think life was very good for him.'

'Because of what happened to Curtis?' asks Jayden.

'What they all went through in Afghanistan. But yeah, Curtis too, I guess, maybe.'

'So when Lucas managed to trace Axel, and bring him back to see Edward, did you know about that plan?'

Donna's pouring their tea and Jayden sees her hesitate: the pot wavers. Ally notes it too.

'Lucas told Edward that he'd try to contact Axel, but he couldn't promise anything. I mean, as far as I understood it from them, Axel had totally slipped through the net. Like, he was off the radar all this time. Couldn't hold down a job. Moving from place to place. Sleeping rough. Lucas didn't have the first idea of how to find him, so he didn't want to get Edward's hopes up for a big reunion.'

She lifts up her cup and blows across the surface. Then takes a tiny sip.

'Anyway, it was easy in the end. Edward had an email address for Axel from back in the day, and Lucas tried that. Two or three weeks later, Axel actually replied.' Donna sets down her teacup, and a little liquid slops in the saucer. 'I can remember the moment when Edward got this phone call from Lucas to tell him that Axel was going to come and see him. It was like . . . he finally had something to live for. That whole day, and the ones after, he was better than I'd seen him in weeks. Bright-eyed, you know? I think that's when I realised how much Axel meant to him. And how much he'd lost these last years.' Donna looks down; she runs her thumb along the rim of her cup. 'I mean, not as much as Axel lost. Obviously.'

'And do you know what Axel was set to gain?' asks Ally gently.

'You mean this place?' She waves her arm. 'Crazy, right?'

'So, what was it like meeting Axel?' asks Jayden. 'Did you get a chance to talk to him about your brother, or was all of his focus on the Greys?'

Because, by then, Edward was near the end. And Axel had just received life-changing news.

'He was focused on the Greys,' says Donna. 'At first, I wasn't going to say anything at all. I mean, I knew he'd been through a tough time. I didn't want to blindside him – bring back . . . bad memories when he was here for a totally different reason. But then it came out naturally, when he was talking to Robbie. Robbie lives in the cottage where Axel spent a lot of his childhood, and . . . Well, yeah. It came out naturally.'

'How did he respond?' asks Jayden.

'He was hard to read. In general, I mean. Lucas said afterwards how quiet he was. That he never remembered him being that quiet. But he was pleased, I think. Pleased to talk to me. It's a bond, isn't it? Soldiers. Even if you've tried to forget all that.'

Jayden thinks of the tattoo: *Swift and Bold*. Axel could have had it removed – but he didn't.

'The missing kayak,' says Jayden. 'Do you think Axel could have taken it, Donna?'

The nurse looks to the window, her eyes fixing on the band of sea. The horizon is smudged with cloud, Lone Island lost inside it. For a moment it's as if Donna is lost too.

'How should I know?' she says, getting to her feet. 'I don't know anything about what Axel Marks would or wouldn't do. Are you finished with these? I'll rinse them.'

As she reaches for her cup she knocks it. It topples like a bowling pin, spinning to the edge of the table with surprising force – then hits the kitchen floor with a smash.

26

'I don't see what that has to do with anything,' says Pippa.

The words come out hard-edged and broken as Morse code. And Mullins doesn't blame her. Skinner's gone in a bit hard, considering.

'If you could just answer the question,' says Skinner, his voice crackling with impatience. 'We'd simply like to be able to eliminate you from our enquiries.'

For a moment, Mullins thinks Pippa is going to make a comment along the lines of 'you've changed your tune' and . . . fair play, if so. Last time they spoke to Pippa, their 'enquiries' were covering the basics, then they were all set to pass off the case to the coroner, no one to blame, et cetera, et cetera. But now? That call from Fergus Grant has changed things. And the call to the Greys? That's *really* changed things.

Pippa sits with her arms wrapped tight around herself, as closed as a clam shell. And she looks at Skinner as if he's wielding a clam knife. Whatever she's done or not done, Mullins feels sorry for her. He offers a sympathetic smile, and Skinner sends him a sideways look. He probably thinks Mullins is going for Good Cop Bad Cop. But, in Mullins's opinion, Bad Cop's got no place here.

'No,' says Pippa. 'I did not think Axel Marks was an intruder.'

'But you had started to feel isolated, living here?'

'No,' she says again. 'That was Fergus. Not me.'

'Fergus said it was both of you.'

Pippa shakes her head, as if she's trying to get something out of it. 'That's not true.'

'But you did purchase some flares?'

'Fergus had been talking about it and so I went and bought some. I wanted to show willing. That we were in this together.'

'And you'd taken to patrolling the island, dawn and dusk?'

Pippa stares hard at Skinner. The phrase *if looks could kill* jumps into his mind. In response, Skinner's face is hard as a tombstone.

'That was my job. *Is* my job. To monitor the wildlife.'

'So you weren't watching the mainland for people crossing by boat?'

'The previous wardens had had some trouble with kayakers coming ashore here. Disturbing the seals. It's important to be vigilant. Like I said, it's one of the main reasons we're here.'

Kayakers. Mullins makes a quiet note.

'Had you seen any evidence of people trying to come ashore in your tenure?'

'No. A couple of times people came closer than they should have. But usually, once they see the nature reserve signs, they maintain a safe distance.'

'And you've never met Axel Marks?'

'*No.*'

Pippa looks to Mullins, and he tries that smile again. She doesn't return it.

'I'm sorry,' she says, turning her attention back to Skinner, 'but I'd like to ask you to leave.'

'Not yet,' says Skinner. 'Unless you wanted to do this down at the station, more formally?'

Pippa sighs, and her thin frame appears to rattle. Mullins doesn't know what he makes of her. He didn't the first time – when she stood on the beach, her face all tear-stained and hands shaking – and he doesn't now either.

What he does know is that Skinner is pushing hard. Maybe just like their colleagues in Gloucestershire did. Because before Pippa Grant lived in Reading, she was Pippa Maddox who lived in Cheltenham.

'Didn't think so. Can I tell you how I see it?'

'That's not really a question, is it?' she says quietly.

And Mullins has to admit, he admires her spunk.

'If I was here all on my own, I'd be a bit jumpy. Especially if I've had violence in my life,' says Skinner pointedly. 'Especially if I'd seen the worst of human nature.' He waits a beat. 'Pippa, if I thought someone was here who shouldn't be, I'd be afraid, but I'd also want to defend myself.'

Pippa drops her head; folds her hands in her lap.

'And a place like this? It's a death trap. I mean, hats off to you for taking it on, I'm sure the wildlife's grateful, but there are fifty ways to hurt yourself before breakfast. My constable slipped just coming up the path now. Didn't you, Mullins? Uneven ground, could have broken an ankle. And I'll let you in to a secret. I don't like heights. Scared witless – and that's the polite version. So you wouldn't see me walking these clifftops, even if it was part of my job. What I'm saying is, accidents can happen. Can't they?'

The fake-mate mode fools no one – least of all Pippa.

'You have to be careful,' she says, with a barely-there nod.

'Very careful,' agrees Skinner. 'So if you throw in various other factors as well, like the fear of an intruder, like the dark, like the unpredictable behaviours of someone who's drunk too much, or potentially has unstable mental health, then—'

'Who are you talking about? I don't drink. Not anymore.'

'I'm talking about Axel Marks.'

'Axel Marks never came to Lone Island. His body was washed up here. He was dead.'

'See, that's been our hypothesis too,' says Skinner. 'But we're investigating the possibility that Axel Marks did, in fact, come here by boat. That his injuries weren't incurred through a fall from a cliff on the mainland, but as a result of a fall here on the island. That his body spent considerable time in the sea but came to be washed ashore in the same vicinity that it first entered the water.'

Pippa stares at Skinner. Then she stands up. Her arms hang by her sides, and she flexes her fingers, as if she's just slung a punch. Mullins shifts on his feet, unconsciously readying himself; Pippa Grant suddenly looks as unpredictable as a wildcat.

'When I found that poor man,' she says, 'I felt very strongly that he'd come to harm by somebody's hand. I told you that. But that can't have happened on the island, because I'm the only one here. And I can promise you I'd never hurt another person.'

Pippa draws a deep breath and her eyes swim. Mullins can't help thinking of that clam shell, that knife, exposing the vulnerable creature beneath. It might be the job, but moments like this, he doesn't love it.

'But then I've told you lot that before, haven't I?' she says. 'And you didn't believe me then either.'

27

Donna walks them into the spring sunshine. She tips her head up and breathes in the air like it's a drink of cool water. She looks relieved to be outside.

Ally thought the nurse's reaction to breaking the cup was overblown. Donna frantically hunted for a dustpan and brush, then knelt to clear every shard, her cheeks bright red. Perhaps the Greys are exacting employers; perhaps she felt uneasy inviting them into the house as if it were her own.

Or perhaps it was their questions that had set Donna on edge. Ally thinks of how, even before they got to talking about her brother and Axel, Donna just shifted that bouquet of flowers out of the way. It smacked of high distraction, or disinterest, because wouldn't the natural reaction be to put them in some water? Especially a nurse, who's used to tending, and who cared a great deal for Edward.

'Robbie's cottage is this way,' Donna says over her shoulder, 'but he won't be there. He'll be out working.'

They follow a path past borders rioting with daffodils, more varieties than Ally can count. They pass a trio of showboating magnolia trees with their soft-pink butter-smooth petals, interspersed with towering palms waving their delicate fronds. The lawn runs on and on, as green and even as Centre Court at Wimbledon. Beyond is the field with Axel's van, where the sheer cliffs and sharp rocks and untamed ocean are a world away from this neat, well-tended space.

Ally tries to imagine Axel here as a boy, playing on this lawn, scaling these trees. Would he have been allowed to have the run of the place, or is a housekeeper's son bound by different rules? With just a couple of years between Axel and Lucas, and neither with siblings, perhaps the two boys would have been thrown together whether they liked it or not. But Lucas told them he went to boarding school, and Axel attended the local comprehensive. So during term time, perhaps it felt as if Porthmerrin belonged to Axel – until his mother died, and he realised it didn't, not anymore; that it never had. Mentally unwell, discharged from the army, his profession and home and family lost to him in more or less one fell swoop.

Just as Pippa now fears.

Could Pippa have known Axel's history? She says not, but there are doubtless similarities and points of emotional connection. Or is all this part of the mysterious tapestry of Pippa's 'feeling'? Her certitude stemming from some deep unspoken shared experience.

And then there is Donna. Just one degree of separation from Axel. Ally thinks of her Facebook post, the mention of 'brothers in arms', the underlying feeling that Donna felt let down by one of those so-called brothers.

And then its deletion.

'Donna, are you still in touch with any of your brother's friends from the army?'

As they follow her down the path, the set of Donna's shoulders is tense.

'Just Staffie,' she says, not quite turning. 'He was with Curtis when they were ambushed. He's always been great. And their platoon commander sends us a Christmas card every year. They're good people. Curtis would have done anything for them.'

'For Axel too?' says Jayden.

'For any of them,' says Donna again. She turns, the emotion clear in her face. 'That's how it is. You look after each other. You're fighting this war but, really, you're fighting for the people alongside you. That's how Curtis saw it.'

'Was the army good to your family after Curtis died?'

Jayden asks the question gently, and Donna blinks. She looks, suddenly, much younger. She wouldn't have been much more than a teenager when her brother was killed.

'Good to us?' Donna gives a small shake of her head. 'Yeah, they said and did all the right things. I remember Mum feeling grateful for that. It gave her comfort, knowing that Curtis was part of something bigger. And that he was valued.'

'And what about you?' says Jayden. 'Did you feel that way too?'

'Nothing would bring Curtis back. And I hated that he was there in the first place. So . . .'

Donna's eyes fill, and she presses her fingertips to the corners. Ally wants to ask again whether she was surprised that Axel didn't come to the funeral, whether she felt let down by him, whether she did, in fact, bear some ill will towards him. But something makes her not want to push it. For all the sturdiness Donna must possess in order to nurse the dying – a practicality, surely? The ability not to balk at the messy parts of life? – there's a fragile quality to her too.

'Donna,' says Jayden gently, 'what's the name of Curtis's platoon commander?'

'Why do you need that?'

'Because a lot of Axel's life, past and present, is a mystery. The more people we can talk to who knew him, the better.'

She hesitates, then says, 'Lieutenant Paul Fairfax. Well, he's a major now.'

'What about Staffie? What's his full name?'

Donna shakes her head, her curls falling across her face. 'Jason Stafford. But these days he lives off-grid in Scotland. I don't even know where. Look, all these questions . . .'

Time to change tack.

'Donna,' says Ally, 'what about Axel and Lucas? What were they like together?'

Donna's eyes still glimmer with tears. She sighs and tucks her hair behind her ear, the sun catching the glint of her earrings.

'Lucas was chuffed to have got him here. Happy to have been able to do something for Edward.'

'Would you have known that they had a shared history, do you think? From how they were with one another?'

'A shared history?' Donna's forehead creases.

'Axel and Lucas,' says Ally.

'Well, yeah. I mean . . . Well, actually, maybe not. You can't always tell, can you? Lucas is quite . . . stiff. Formal. And Axel . . . He seemed kind of quiet. I mean, I don't know, but I guess the inheritance news was pretty overwhelming. It would be for anyone. To be honest, I left them all to it. I'm just staff, aren't I? I didn't want to intrude on family time.'

Jayden catches Ally's eye, his look meaningful, but she can't quite work out what he's trying to convey. She's been following his lead in not mentioning the missing Facebook post – does he want to change direction?

They've reached the cottage, and it's charming. As if from a picture book, a single-storey building with a slate-roof hat, two square windows like eyes, a red-painted door for a mouth. Axel's childhood home – and Robbie's now.

Donna raps at the door but she's already turning, saying, 'He won't be here.'

'If it's alright with you, Donna, we'll wander off and find Robbie in the gardens,' says Jayden. 'Leave you to get on.'

'It's fine, I can come.'

Ally glances to Jayden. She knows he'd rather they spoke to Robbie on his own. He gives her a pointed look, and this time she can read it. *Divide and conquer.*

'Donna,' says Ally, 'could you show me inside the house? I meant to ask before. There are some paintings in the hallway I'd love a closer look at.'

Donna rubs her nose with the flat of her hand; she looks uncertain.

'Lucas and Elspeth will be back after lunch. It's not really up to me to—'

'I'm sure they wouldn't mind,' says Ally.

Donna's eyes sweep the garden, as if looking for a glimpse of Robbie, but then she shrugs. 'Okay, sure.'

As she turns back on to the path, Ally looks to Jayden, expecting him to pop his usual thumbs up. But, instead, he touches his earlobe and sends her a nod. Code for 'listen out'? Just then his phone starts ringing. Ally follows Donna up the path but then she slows her step to listen to him answer.

'I was hoping you'd call,' she hears him say.

Donna turns round. She plants her hand on her hip like a teapot, says briskly – in nurse mode, perhaps – 'Are you coming, then, Ally?'

28

Robbie Cassidy steps into the gloomy interior of the outhouse. The windows are smeared and thick with spiderwebs. It's crowded with junk: stacks of paint pots leaning like the Tower of Pisa; an old bed-frame; a motorboat with a split in its hull. Edward liked his house immaculate, and he sure kept Robbie on a leash with the gardens, but these sheds? Well, everyone can use a dumping ground. He offered to do a tip run once, spruce the place up. *What's the point, Robbie?* Edward said. *I'm not about to convert it into a godawful holiday let, am I?*

So Axel was supposed to have nicked a kayak from here, was he?

It puts a different shade on things, if he did. Lucas was kicking himself for not having noticed earlier, but how could he? An occasional visitor at best, he's not going to keep tabs on all his dad's junk. Robbie couldn't even swear there was a kayak in here to begin with, but then he's never been one to poke his nose where it doesn't need to be.

And that goes for now too.

Robbie didn't like the police being up here. Porthmerrin is his happy place. Just listen to him, as if he's swallowed a greetings card – *My Happy Place!* – but it's true. He couldn't believe his luck, winding up here. Or maybe he could. Because there were enough bumps in the road to get here. The inglorious life of Robbie Cassidy.

And now these two private detectives? He doesn't like that either. So when he was driving back through Porthpella last night after picking up some gear, and saw Jayden Weston all on his own, he thought he'd park and see where the guy was going. Just up the lane, as it turned out, nothing to see, so Robbie soon dropped back.

'Ah, here you are.'

Talk of the devil. Jayden leaning casually in the doorway. Robbie's willing to bet he wouldn't be quite so cool if he knew those cracks in the wall were ram-packed with spiders; ping-pong ball bodies and pipe-cleaner legs.

'Scene of the crime,' says Robbie. 'The missing kayak, apparently.'

'When were the police up here?'

'First thing. They spoke to Lucas and Elspeth, took a look around.'

'Do you think Axel took it?'

'Who else?'

Robbie pushes forward out of the shed, and Jayden walks with him. The sunlight is bright after the gloom, and he shields his eyes. The water glitters in the distance. It's always been so beautiful up here, that's the trouble. A hard thing to let go of.

'He could have done anything,' says Robbie. 'The bloke marched to the beat of his own drum. And I get the feeling that beat was sometimes out of time.'

Jayden nods, as if Robbie's just said something really fascinating. *Gold star for me.*

'Did you speak to him much?'

'He was with the family mostly, but we spoke briefly. I asked him if he wanted to take a look inside the cottage. He used to live in it with his mum, once. I didn't know, then, what Edward had in store for him, did I? No wonder he wasn't interested in the cottage after that.'

'Did Donna tell you about her brother's connection with Axel?'

Robbie rubs at his chin and his stubble-bristles. Is it his imagination, or is this guy Jayden watching him more closely now? He shrugs, but his shoulders feel like lead weights.

'Yeah. A bit. Not really.'

'They knew each other,' says Jayden. 'Fought alongside one another in Afghanistan. That was 2011, 2012.'

'Whole lot of soldiers messed up in that conflict.'

'Literally alongside each other, I mean. They were in the same section. Just a handful of guys.'

Robbie frowns. He feels a headache at his temple, so sharp it's like someone's tapping a nail there.

'Yeah. Donna finds all that hard to talk about. I would too. She's tried to move on from it. But she was pleased to meet Axel. She was pleased he was here making Edward happy.' He hesitates. 'If you want my opinion, the army chewed that bloke up and spat him out and didn't much care about the mess they'd made of him. I've seen it before. The walking dead. Trained killers, but they're gone to mush on the inside. I'm mixing my metaphors, but I'd say he was a timebomb.'

Robbie stops. No need to keep on talking. The pair of them will run round and round, asking their questions, trying to keep up with the cops, overtaking them too, no doubt, but no one any the wiser at the end of it. People like Axel disappear every day; drop clean off the map. Why should his story be different? Because he was suddenly sitting on a mansion?

'Are you and Donna in a relationship?' asks Jayden.

Donna, again.

'What's that got to do with anything?'

Jayden shrugs. 'It hasn't. I just wondered how close you are.'

You and me both, mate, he thinks of snapping back.

For a second Jayden holds his eye and it's Robbie who looks away first.

'Did you see Axel that evening?' asks Jayden.

'I told the police all this. No. I went off early to sleep. I'm outdoors all day so I go out like a light. And before you ask, I was on my own.'

'So you wouldn't have heard Axel if he did take the kayak?'

'Nope. He could have done it in the middle of the night, though he'd have been a fool to try it – or at first light, but even then, he wouldn't have been much smarter. You can launch from the foot of the cliffs, and there's a path down – he'd have known that, living here – but it's not easy street. You'd have to know what you were doing.'

'And if he'd been drinking?'

'A bottle of whisky, that's what Lucas said. No wonder he fetched up dead.'

'So you don't think he could have made it to the island?'

'What, paddled there? Or feet first?' Robbie shrugs. 'It's a mystery, mate. All I know is that he's an idiot. Suddenly he had everything. *Everything.* Handed to him on a plate. And alright, maybe he had some head stuff going on, but if anything's going to motivate you to sort yourself out, it's got to be a gift like this place.'

Robbie can feel the envy leaching into his voice. That toxic green tint. Three years he's worked here, and three years he's been happy. He's never once thought he deserved more. And when Donna came along . . . He stops the thought, feeling the rise of something like dread. But it bursts in anyway, because here's the truth: she was the cherry on the cake. Happy became *really* happy. Robbie knew he was on a timer here, what with Edward Grey falling ill, but he's always hoped that Lucas will keep him on anyway because he's worked his behind off, turned the gardens right around. And all the signs are there that that's what Lucas is going to do. If Axel had inherited this place, he probably would have sold up in a flash, just to get his hands on some cash. And fair play too. No good living in a palace if you're barefooted and empty-bellied. But now that it'll go to Lucas, Robbie can see him and Elspeth making the move down here. Maybe fill the place up with kids too. Robbie wouldn't care, so long as he can stay on. That little roof over his head is the nicest he's ever had.

'Where did you live before this?' asks Jayden.

And Robbie wonders if he knows, because it's cop style, that, to ask a question they already have the answer to. Did he hear the envy come dripping through his voice and now he thinks he has Robbie all figured out?

'All over,' he says, meeting Jayden's gaze and holding it. 'Bedsits, hostels, the streets. I guess me and Axel had that in common.'

And a surge of shame rises up in him. It always does. And even though some days up here Robbie feels like he's got it all – leaning on his spade, master of all he surveys, taking care of the land so it'll take care of him right back – he feels a stinging realisation. It's all so precarious. Because if he loses Porthmerrin, he loses everything. And he loses Donna too.

29

'Right, two things,' says Jayden.

They're clear of Porthmerrin House, turning into the web of steep lanes, heading for the coast road. Jayden's fingers tap a drum-beat on his knees. Pharrell's tune rises from his playlist again: is it a crazy thing to say? No. It makes perfect sense.

'Was it Casey James who phoned you?' says Ally. 'I want to hear everything about it.'

'She did. And you will. But that's the second thing. The first? Donna Goode's lying when she says she barely spoke to Axel. She went to his van, Al.'

'What?' Ally turns her head to look at him and the car swings with her. She corrects, says, 'Do I need to pull over for this?'

'Yeah, maybe. There's more. I don't think I can wait till we're back in Porthpella.'

'Nor me.'

And Ally's bumping the car on to the verge, pulling into a gateway. On the other side, sheep scatter, then turn accusatory looks in their direction.

'How do you know Donna went to his van?' says Ally, swivelling in her seat, giving him her full attention.

He tugs at his earlobe. 'That earring I found under the bed? Donna was wearing the same one. *One* being the operative word.'

Ally wrinkles her brow, probably trying to call to mind Donna's ears.

'She's got multiple piercings,' says Jayden. 'Three on each side. Maybe she hasn't noticed one's missing. It fits, though, right, Al? If Axel was actually there on the spot with Donna's brother when he died, do you really think she's likely to just let that go without a proper conversation? Maybe it is a twist of fate that she ended up at Porthmerrin House, or maybe, just maybe, she came here *because* of Axel.'

'But she can't have known that Axel was ever going to come to Porthmerrin. Lucas didn't know if he'd be able to trace him, let alone persuade him to visit.'

'But maybe Donna didn't know the extent of the separation either,' says Jayden. 'Lucas assumed that it was his dad's idea to trace Axel – a last wish from a dying man – but what if it was Donna pushing it? What if she had her own agenda?'

He can see Ally turning it over. What they know, and what they can only guess at.

'I can absolutely see it,' says Ally. 'And she deleted that old Facebook post. Which is studied, intentional.'

'And it shows she's thinking about how she comes across to the outside world. Or, more specifically, to anyone who might be investigating.'

'But how would it work with Axel taking the kayak? I asked Donna about that again up at the house and she didn't even know until this morning that Edward had one.'

'That I don't know,' says Jayden. 'Robbie showed me the out-house it was taken from. But look, if Donna was inside Axel's van – and that dropped earring is the proof of that – why would she lie about it, unless she had something to hide?'

'Perhaps the earring's a popular style,' says Ally. 'Perhaps it belongs to someone else. To Casey James, for instance.'

'I sent a photo of it to Cat. She'd never seen one exactly like it, not with the turquoise details too. If it was popular, I think she'd know.'

'Wouldn't the police have checked the van for fingerprints?' says Ally.

'It's not a crime scene, because they're not convinced it's a crime. Until this missing kayak, and whatever has made them look in the direction of the island again, they were all set to pass it to the coroner.'

Jayden's still sorting it out in his own brain, but he can always think aloud with Ally – so he lets fly.

'Okay, so what if Donna went to Axel's van late that night? They have a heart-to-heart about Curtis's death, and the way Axel dropped off the radar afterwards. The fact that he doesn't even make the funeral. Maybe Donna gets stuck into that whisky too. If the two of them are drunk, all bets are off, right? Donna's upset, Axel's upset, it's dark, that cliff edge is way closer than either of them realise . . .'

'An accident, then?' says Ally.

'Or . . . Donna blames Axel. Maybe there's something about the way that Curtis died. Like, was it avoidable? Mullins said Axel was considered a suicide risk and that's why he was discharged, but we don't know what led to that. Did Axel feel guilty for something? And Donna felt angry . . . We've got to check out their platoon commander, Major Paul Fairfax. Find out if there's anything more to the situation. I'm even beginning to wonder if the other guy, Staffie, is really off-grid in Scotland.'

'Donna's emotions about Edward dying could very well mask however she's feeling about Axel's death, couldn't they?'

'Exactly. Kind of like Lucas too. He's stressed and agitated, but his dad's just died. It's understandable. Expected. Any complex feelings about Axel can easily be hidden in that mix.'

Ally looks thoughtful. 'So you're still wondering about Lucas?'

'I'm still wondering about all of them. But Donna is one hundred per cent lying to us. Or, like, ninety per cent.'

'I asked Donna about her and Robbie, by the way, as she was showing me the paintings,' says Ally. 'She was rather coy, but said they'd grown quite close.'

'Robbie had his back up when I went near the subject. He made a big deal of saying he went to bed on his own the night Axel died. Which means Donna doesn't have an alibi. Not the obvious one, anyway. One thing was clear: Robbie didn't like talking about Donna and Axel. He was twitchy, Al.'

'Do you think he knows something?'

'Or suspects it? Don't know. Oh, and more info: Robbie's had a rough ride. He said this job is his first permanent one in years. He's been homeless, in and out of hostels. I get the feeling it means a lot to him to be settled here. And he's hoping that continues.'

'Donna aside, if we were looking for connections . . .'

'I don't think there's such a thing as "Donna aside". I think Donna's right in this.'

'. . . could Robbie's past be relevant, Jayden? What if Axel's path has crossed with Robbie's?'

'What, because they've both been homeless?'

'I mean, could they have met at a shelter, or on the streets?'

'It's a thought. But Robbie said he's been in Cornwall for most of his life, and at Porthmerrin – a roof over his head, a monthly pay cheque – for the last three years. Whereas, according to Lucas, Axel left Cornwall years ago and has only been back down this way for a couple of months.'

'You're right, there's no crossover. And we know that, six months ago, Axel was living in Bristol.'

'That's my cue, right? Casey James.'

Ally nods, her face bright. 'That's your cue.'

'Okay, so Casey called. And she's currently on her way to Cornwall.'

Jayden's aware of a car slowing as it comes towards them, even though there's loads of room to pass. A metallic-blue BMW. Maybe they're afraid of scraping that shiny metalwork. It slows then stops. The window buzzes down.

'Hello,' says Lucas. 'Have you guys broken down?'

Elspeth leans across. 'Do you need help?'

'No, we're good,' says Jayden. 'We've just come from yours. We got some time with Robbie and Donna.'

'Ah, good. Though Robbie's rattled at the thought of Axel taking a kayak out,' says Lucas. 'Reading between the lines, I think Robbie thinks Axel brought it on himself.'

'Whatever Axel was thinking,' says Elspeth, 'it was a terrible plan.'

'Is there any way the kayak could have gone missing some other way?' asks Jayden.

'What, you mean someone else took it?' Lucas pulls a face. 'Shouldn't have thought so. I wouldn't have said it'd be anyone's first pick, if we're talking random burglars. Nothing else was gone, as far as I could tell. It was the detective sergeant who made us check. That Skinner chap. He wanted to know if there was any chance Axel could have got his hands on a boat. You went and looked in the outhouse, didn't you, Elspeth? Saw it was gone right away.'

'Edward held on to all sorts,' says Elspeth. 'But that old kayak always amused me. I don't know why. I suppose because I couldn't really picture him ever using it.'

'Was it yours as a boy, Lucas?' asks Ally.

'Mine? No. Never a fan of the water, actually. I suppose it could have been Axel's. I've never dug about in that old shed of my father's. There could be an elephant in there for all I'd know.

Anyway . . . we've been with my father's solicitor all morning. As a consequence, I need a stiff drink. My God, the admin of death.'

'We won't keep you,' says Jayden.

As Lucas puts the car in gear, Elspeth leans across him again.

'What we haven't dwelt on,' she says, 'is why the police might be asking the question in the first place. I asked them if it was because of Axel's body being found on the island, but they were very closed on the subject, which of course is understandable, but . . . it's strange, isn't it?'

'Exploring all options, I guess,' says Jayden.

But hard agree. It's strange.

'Talking of the island, I sent Pippa Grant a message, inviting her for tea. I thought it was the polite thing, but I haven't heard anything back. Is she usually slow to respond, Ally?'

Ally gives a small shrug. 'There's been a lot going on.'

'When you speak to her,' says Elspeth, 'please tell her we don't bite, won't you?'

As the Greys drive away, Jayden raises an eyebrow in Ally's direction. 'So, Pippa's ignoring everybody, then. Try calling her, Al.'

'Are you worried too?'

'More . . . interested,' says Jayden.

But then he thinks of the isolation of Lone Island. And Pippa setting the pair of them in motion, asking questions about a dead man.

'And yeah, okay, a bit worried.'

30

Gus sits at his computer, clicking through the estate agent's photographs of Lighthouse Cottage. It's a fanciful name, of course – there's no view of the lighthouse from that smart little house on the square – but still, he rather applauds the effort. Gus has a soft spot for romantically named seaside properties. The more ordinary the house, and the more picturesque the name, the better. As a boy, he once stayed with his mother in a basic sort of bungalow several cul-de-sacs away from a mud-filled estuary. Playa Blanca, it was called, and even as a child it instilled in Gus a touch of melancholy, and a kind of fondness, that he couldn't understand. And now he lives in All Swell, a weatherboard shack that's just about falling down around his ears. Turns out there is no such thing as a bargain beach house, not round here, anyway. But despite the dry rot, despite the leak in the roof that returns every winter no matter what he does, life here *is* All Swell, thanks very much. Or, certainly, Predominantly Swell.

And this morning? He's feeling an odd mix of Very Swell Indeed and . . . A Touch Uncertain. Because it was a lovely night with Ally, and he felt the two of them were closer than they have been in some time. The way she confided in him about how she was feeling about Ray – or at least how she was feeling about Ray's possible move (but isn't that tantamount to the same?) – means something to him.

Only . . . he's not quite sure what.

Does Ally consider Gus to be impartial on the subject of her love life? Perhaps as objective an observer as, say, Wenna at the shop? Because while that would flatter Gus's ability for masking – it's reassuring, of course, to think that he doesn't present as a lovelorn fool – it would also be inaccurate. And he wouldn't mind Ally knowing that his feelings for her haven't changed, actually. That he is constant. Faithful. Rock-steady. Alright, so he doesn't have the lustrous locks of Ray Finch, but really, at their age, who does? And quite frankly Gus is rather suspicious of Ray's full head of hair. Nor does he have Ray's leather jackets, the gift of infernal gab, the intensely rose-tinted history of being a first love . . . but Gus has other things. Doesn't he?

Ah now.

And this is where Gus falters. Because he has always thought that the sheer convenience of himself might be an appealing factor. All Swell is but a stone's throw from The Shell House. When Gus gets sentimental about it – and he can do that, when the sky blazes towards sunset and the sea is playing its soft music, and he thinks of the sheer *story* of it. Especially when he throws the silver-tongued lyrics of Paul Simon into the mix: Porthpella is Gus's Graceland. And he has reason to believe that he too shall be received, because ever since he got here – getting on for three years ago – this place has felt like an embrace. Gus laid down his hat and perhaps one day he'll push up the daisies, but between the two there could be such riches. There are already such riches. But Ally definitely seemed unsettled that this particular property, Lighthouse Cottage, had come up for sale, given Ray's connection to it. Ally doesn't seem to want Ray in Cornwall, which perhaps translates to Ally not wanting *anyone* in Cornwall. So should Gus, therefore, move to Suffolk?

Oh, for goodness' sake.

He closes down the estate agent page and idly opens up Cornwall Live, where he scrolls through the county's latest happenings, looking for anything new on Ally and Jayden's case. Already, Axel Marks looks to be yesterday's news. Not for that pair, though: their commitment to the truth surpasses even that of Gus's fictional detective DI Larkin, who seems all too eager to put his feet up with a pint and a crossword, plum in the middle of an investigation. Gus scrolls on, frowning at the mugshot of a cruel-eyed thief, then reads about a supermarket's plans for expansion. Then his eye is caught by a photograph of an elaborate old pistol, pictured against the sand, with the headline *Antique firearm washed up on beach.* It's a swashbuckling sort of weapon, the kind a pirate captain might wield on stage during an amateur dramatics production. Only it is, apparently, real. Found by a teenager while walking his dog, about ten miles down the coast from Porthpella. *What a moment for the lad.* Gus longed for a metal detector as a boy, convinced that that single piece of equipment was all that lay between him and the treasures of the ancient world.

Dead bodies and guns washing up on beaches, though? *Goodness me.* No wonder Ally and Jayden are always so busy.

It never ceases to amaze Gus that someone as gentle as Ally is so at home in the world of crime. But then a lot of things amaze him about Ally. As the loveliness of yesterday evening once again settles around him, a line from a poem comes fluttering into Gus's mind: *'Hope' is the thing with feathers.*

Emily Dickinson. Gus's former wife Mona – she of little soul – used to think Dickinson was for softies, but he's always liked this one especially: its message that delicate, birdlike 'hope' asks so little of us, only for a place to exist; a crumb to feed upon, if that.

Yes, Gus has hope. And nights like last night, he hears its full-throated song.

Just then, another thing with feathers – a ruddy great seagull – swoops past his window, screaming its head off and splattering the pane with thick white excrement.

Now, if that's a sign, Gus isn't at all sure that he likes what it's telling him.

31

Casey James is trying to sleep, but sleep is not happening. Instead, she settles for staring from the train window, zoning out, the countryside flashing by like a film she has no interest in. Intermittently the landscape blurs, as the situation hits her anew.

Axel is dead.

Casey can't believe it. But, at the same time – grimly, sadly – she can. Because some days with Axel, it felt like his hold on the earth was so light.

It's the day that Casey first met him that keeps coming back to her, not all the days they've had together since. And she's there, right there. Present tense.

A summer morning down the Deaner, heat of the day already on the rise, the whole skate park shimmering with light, and layer upon layer of colour: some pieces crumbling, some tagged and split, some as vibrant as the day they were sprayed. It's quiet and she's the only skater in the park. Nothing but the sound of her wheels on concrete, the occasional tinkling of a bottle cap as it catches her wheelbase. Or she thought she was the only skater in the park anyway. As she burns round the corner and swoops into the bottom quarter, she sees a guy heading up the steps to the Slab. Simian-long arms, faded jeans, hair that'll fly in his face as soon as he's rolling. He's not someone she recognises, but then Casey doesn't get down here that often, and it's a magnet for skaters all over the city, this place. If he's out early, she figures him for an old guy (she can talk, she's thirty next month). A dad, maybe. A dad with some dim memory of radness, trying to see if he's still got it; if he can still land that kickflip, just one, then he'll have bagged himself a time machine to a better place.

Or something like that.

Casey watches. And it's weird that she does because it's not her usual style. The guys get enough attention without her playing spectator. But there's a kind of camaraderie in the early-morning slot. If he looks her way, she'll nod. But he doesn't. Head down. And as soon as his wheels start moving, she gets why. Full concentration. He's bad. He was never good; there's no muscle memory at play here. Not a total beginner, but not far off. She sees him jump from the board, just avoiding a slam. Maybe he has potential, then, because he lands as lightly as a cat.

And Casey likes that this guy's out, just him and his board, skating badly down the Deaner.

She runs up the quarter, then drops in fast and hard. It's all rhythm now; you could stick her in a tutu, the ballet in these moves. And Casey's not thinking about anything – her mind is emptied, like someone tipped her upside down and shook all the clutter out – all that matters is the here and now. Wheels on concrete. The flow. The flutter of her heart as she nearly sketches out on the coping, heat rushing from her fingers to her toes. But she holds it. She manuals to a stop. She's breathing hard.

And she knows he's watching from up there on the Slab, this guy. He taps his board on the ground – *rat-a-tat* – the universal sign of skater appreciation. He might be rubbish, but he's been in parks.

Casey tips her chin in response, an inverted nod.

And maybe they would have left it there. But there is something about this day. The sun beaming so hard she can feel the push of it, the pulsing colours of the concrete, the painted words she knows from a song, about gusts of wind and jetting. Casey feels good. So she tucks her board under her arm and heads up to the Slab, light as a dancer.

'How long you been skating?' she says.

And the smile he gives her back is magic.

Casey jolts from the reverie, as the train announcer lets her know that a selection of hot and cold sandwiches is available from the buffet. But she couldn't eat a crumb. Axel is dead, and no one knows why. So she's got time off from work – a weird conversation that began: *So my ex-boyfriend died, is that compassionate leave or do I take it as holiday?* – and she's on her way to see the police. But, mostly, she's going to see that guy called Jayden, because he said he wants to help, and when you get down to it, not many people do. Not unless it's in their job description, and even then, some folk are at the bottom of the list. *Even then.*

Casey shifts in her seat, trying to get comfortable. As they cross the Tamar the iron girders of the bridge flash past and she looks down at the deep, dark water and tries not to think about Axel drowning. Tries not to think about what his last thoughts were. And what they should have been, what they could have been, if only she'd trusted him.

I'm a lost cause, Casey. That's what Axel used to say to her, and wouldn't it have been easier to agree? But Casey has never gone for easy, so she'd counter it with her mum's line – *where there's life there's hope.* And then, eventually, at the end, the last straw, one of her own: *But you have to get there on your own, Ax. You know where to find me when you do.*

She rests her hands on her belly and closes her eyes.

They will never find each other again.

'You were never a lost cause, Axel,' she murmurs, as if he's right beside her. Body warm, heart beating. Hers. Theirs. 'Not to us.'

32

'A trade?' says Mullins. 'You're joking, aren't you?'

They're back at The Shell House, with Mullins on speakerphone. The thinking room is calm – despite Mullins's best efforts. Shadows shift gently on the walls: the waving fronds of Ally's palm; stripes from the shutters across the whiteboard and all of their case notes. Finally, they have some information about Axel Marks's recent past.

According to Casey, Axel's ex-girlfriend, they were together for six months, only breaking up in mid-January, which was when Axel got on the road in his van. She knew he was headed for Cornwall; what she didn't know was if he was ever coming back.

She was emotional, said Jayden earlier. *She kept it together, but I could tell she cared.*

He said Casey didn't want a long phone conversation, but she'd told him that when she got to Cornwall they could meet. And she'd keep Jayden posted. That the police couldn't officially treat her as next of kin, even though she's the closest to next of kin that Axel had.

Meanwhile, it was Mullins who called them, to say that Axel's ex-girlfriend, Casey James, had phoned in to the police saying she'd only heard Axel was dead because a street artist was showing her picture around on behalf of some Cornish private detective called

Jayden Weston. To which Jayden replied, *Cornish? No one's ever accused me of that before.*

Their conversation with Mullins has now moved away from Casey, and towards Donna.

'I don't know how you did things up in Leeds, Jay, but we don't do trades . . .'

Ally sends Jayden a look; it's no more than they expected.

'An information exchange, then,' says Jayden. 'You tell us why the boat angle came up, and we tell you why you should be fingerprinting the van.'

Because the kayak is a sticking point. Until Skinner raised it, no one at Porthmerrin House had noticed it was missing. Could Donna have gone to Axel's van, and then Axel took the boat after? The problem is, that doesn't sit with the theory that Donna and Axel had an emotional exchange, resulting in his fall. In a case full of unknowns, the missing kayak complicates things.

And why is the island back in focus?

'You know how much Skinner loves it when you tell us how to do our job, Jay.'

'He loves it when a case is solved, though. Maybe I should speak to him direct. Cut out the middleman, hey, Mullins?'

'See, you always say that, Jay, and then you never do. I think you're a little bit in awe of the detective sergeant.'

Jayden laughs at that. Neither Jayden nor Ally is in awe of Skinner, but they are aware of his authority. Ally likes to think there's a mutual respect between them now – after all, they've collaborated on enough cases – but it's nevertheless a delicate accord. Skinner will always be sceptical of their involvement – until he's given a case-by-case reason to be otherwise.

'It's Pippa who hired us,' says Ally, leaning close to the phone. 'I'm sure she'll tell us why you're interested in the island.'

Will she? Ally's texts from this morning have gone unanswered, and Pippa didn't pick up when she tried calling either. Elspeth Grey isn't the only one being ignored.

'And I'll advise you again to tread carefully with her,' says Mullins.

On Mullins's end of the line the background noise suddenly ramps up, another voice coming through.

'Ally and Jayden. I could have guessed.'

Detective Sergeant Skinner.

'Constable Mullins is on duty. So, unless you have pertinent information, you do realise you're wasting police time, don't you?'

Ally looks to Jayden, and her partner rolls his eyes. But Skinner's voice, while not warm, isn't as cold as it could be.

'Donna Goode,' says Jayden. 'We know that you know that her brother Curtis fought alongside Axel Marks in Afghanistan. Curtis died and didn't come home. Axel did, but only just.'

'I told you all this, Jay,' says Mullins.

And his voice sounds slightly further back, as if he's been crowded off the phone by Skinner. Ally tries to picture where they might be. At Mullins's desk, a wheelie chair and stained ceiling panels and a mug of coffee half gone cold? Or perhaps a meeting room, with a curling flipchart and a wilting plant. She only went to the station once or twice while Bill was there; she always found it faintly depressing, even if seeing Bill surrounded by colleagues who clearly loved him filled her with pride.

'You did, did you, Mullins?' Skinner snaps back, and the constable goes quiet.

Jayden stops a smile. 'It's a powerful connection,' he says, 'and potentially a complex one too. And what are the chances? Of all the country estates with dying patriarchs, Donna has to end up nursing at this one, right?'

'If you're going to misquote *Casablanca*, at least do a better job of it,' says Skinner.

'Donna told us she didn't get any one-on-one time with Axel, but a missing earring says that she did. We found it on the floor underneath Axel's bed.'

'Could be anyone's.'

'It's hers,' says Ally. 'The design is distinctive, and Jayden recognised it when we spoke to Donna this morning.'

The sound of Skinner sighing is like an onshore gust.

'And, what, it's now covered in your fingerprints, is it? This tiny little earring?'

Ally sees Jayden hesitate.

'It's not being treated as a crime scene, is it?' he says. 'But if you fingerprint inside the van, I'll put money on you finding Donna's prints elsewhere.'

'And yours, and Ally's, and anybody else's who's seen fit to trample the place. Donna could have gone in afterwards, just like you two did.'

'Okay, but why would she?' says Jayden. 'When Donna talks, she's missing bits out. And it'll be the same in whatever statement she gave you, right? Which is lying to the police.'

'Even if Axel Marks and Donna had a heart-to-heart that she's keeping under her hat, what's that got to do with Axel nabbing himself a kayak and paddling out to the island?' says Mullins.

'It's just supposition that he even did that,' says Jayden. 'Isn't it?'

Ally can hear Skinner saying something in a low voice. Admonishing, probably. But Mullins has exactly articulated their own confusion on the subject.

'Alright,' says Skinner, 'I'll level with you. This is the investigation that nobody wants, least of all me. There's an almighty black hole in the middle of it, and it's my belief that the only person who can shed any light on it is dead. The victim's body is degraded to a point where we can't make a case for any of his injuries. Slamming rocks, pulled by the tide, hours in the water; the damage is considerable. Forensics are giving us nothing. So all that's left is guesswork. Circumstantial evidence at best. Or someone admitting, straight up, that they know the full story after all. And when does that ever happen, when there's no real threat of consequences? If there is a crime in here somewhere, you could say it's the perfect one.'

'So why ask the Greys if they've a kayak missing?'

'Because we've nothing better to do, Jayden. We thought it'd be a wheeze. Come on, you know how this works.'

'Someone came forward with some information,' says Jayden.

'Bingo.'

'And it's made you look at Lone Island,' says Ally.

'You two are good at this. With a little guidance.'

'Was it Pippa's husband, Fergus Grant?' says Jayden.

Ally's eyes widen. Jayden looks to her and shrugs.

'As I said,' says Skinner, 'you're good at this.'

33

Fergus Grant.

Skinner ends the call abruptly, and Jayden kicks back in his chair. Ally looks worried. Jayden knows she doesn't want this case to be about Pippa. But nor is Ally blindly loyal to her, just because Pippa sought them out.

Now, why would she seek us out?

'There could be nothing in it, Al,' he says. But the reassurance is empty. Skinner was more or less set to close the case. And now he's committing resources.

'It just doesn't make sense to me that Pippa would involve us, Jayden. What on earth have the police got?'

Jayden puffs out his cheeks. It's not like he wants to work for Devon and Cornwall Police – that offer's come his way before, a County Lines task force in Plymouth, but it wasn't for him – but sometimes he wishes they'd bring them in that little bit closer. Silver lining, though? It adds another layer to things, trying to second-guess the cops. Not bad for working the investigative muscles.

'Okay. Fergus Grant must have told them something that's made them view the island, or Pippa, or both, differently,' he says.

'Something that connects either the island or Pippa to Axel?'

'Yeah, maybe. But once the Greys got hold of him – and Lucas said that email was a real shot in the dark – is it likely they'd broadcast it?'

'Perhaps it wasn't generally known that Axel was coming to Porthmerrin House,' says Ally, 'but Casey said he'd been in Cornwall since January. Is it possible that their paths had crossed before? Perhaps he'd even tried to land on the island. Lucas said he'd loved it as a boy, didn't he?'

'*Yes*, Al. Because Axel grew up here.'

And suddenly the thought is obvious. Why hadn't that crossed his mind? That Axel could have come to the area in his van before being an invited guest at Porthmerrin House. Arguably, he could have gone to Lone Island any number of times.

'We know that Edward Grey used to always go and meet the wildlife wardens. And according to Lucas, he and Axel were close. Maybe Axel used to go with him, back in the day. Either way, the island would have been familiar to him. It's the view from his childhood garden. Maybe Axel paddles out there, wanting a trip down memory lane, and there's a confrontation. Pippa's protective of the place, Al, anyone can see that. Maybe she's overzealous.'

'But I can't see Axel doing that directly after learning he was going to inherit the house,' says Ally. 'It's an odd reaction, isn't it?'

'Maybe after a bottle of whisky it was a great idea. Maybe he wanted a view of the house from the water. To see what was going to be his.'

'In the dark?'

'Or at first light?'

'But wouldn't Lucas have spotted him from the cliffs, in that case? He raised the alarm not long after nine o'clock in the morning.'

'Axel could have gone out at eight o'clock. Or seven. The thing is, it's possible. Maybe Axel felt a hell of a lot more at home on Lone Island than he did at Porthmerrin. But . . .' Jayden rubs the back of his head. 'It doesn't fit like Donna Goode fits. Not to me. Okay, try this. What if Axel's on a high after learning about the inheritance, but then Donna brings him back to earth with a bump. She wants to talk about Curtis and what happened in Afghanistan. Axel's all worked up, and decides he needs to clear his head. Let's say he doesn't take the boat out by night, but he wakes in the morning with a screaming hangover and goes out on the water then. A bit of time to himself, away from all the Porthmerrin intensity. He goes ashore, this island that he's known and loved since he was a little kid, and . . . runs into Pippa.'

'Or, what if he got into trouble in the water? With all that alcohol in his system he'd be over the limit . . .'

'. . . over the limit for driving a, erm, kayak?' Jayden laughs. 'Too right.'

'Perhaps Axel doesn't even get as far as the island. Perhaps he capsizes, the kayak drifts out to sea, and he drowns. Pippa finds him washed up on the beach.'

'Sustaining considerable injuries via the rocks on the way. Injuries that fit with a fall from a cliff, which was the cops' previous theory.' Jayden nods. 'It sort of works. But how does Fergus Grant fit into it?'

'Well, like you said, perhaps Axel tried to land on the island before, when Fergus was still there. If Pippa didn't take kindly to it, that's a tangible point of connection, isn't it? Like you said, she's protective. She takes her wardenship seriously.'

'So, when Fergus hears that the same man who Pippa had a confrontation with before has just been found dead on the island, he starts to worry – and calls it in,' says Jayden.

'So the police follow up on it with a call to the Greys. The kayak's missing, and the theory suddenly makes sense. But what doesn't make sense is Pippa involving us in the case, Jayden. Why would she cry foul play, and go to such effort to find us, if she's trying to hide something? She's placing herself directly at the centre of the investigation, when she could have simply been the member of the public who discovered the body.'

'Double bluff?' says Jayden.

But Ally's right: it feels wrong.

'Porthmerrin House,' says Ally. 'I'm trying to think how much emphasis Pippa placed on it the first time we spoke.'

'What, you think she deliberately pointed us in that direction? Anyone would look at the Greys. They were the last people to see him. They reported him missing.'

'But if Pippa wanted to direct attention away from the island, it would help to have us asking questions on the mainland, wouldn't it?' Ally frowns. 'Pippa clearly did her homework on us, Jayden. Perhaps she's not as disconnected as she implies. She said she met Robbie when she and her husband first moved to the island. Maybe Robbie talked about Donna then, perhaps Pippa even knew about the army connection. On the face of it, there's plenty of motive at Porthmerrin.'

'The timing doesn't work, Al. When Robbie met Pippa and Fergus, Donna wasn't even on the scene.'

'Of course. You're right.'

'The other potential reason,' says Jayden, 'is that Pippa has a criminal record. Something that's made the police want to take a closer look at her. Remember the High Tide case?'

'But that was a direct connection between victim and suspect,' says Ally. 'Surely the possibility of that here is . . . remote?'

'Maybe not.' Jayden gets to his feet, frustrated suddenly. 'All this guesswork, and our client could put us out of our misery in seconds. Try phoning her again, Al.'

So Ally tries – but it rings out. She sends him a worried look. 'Nothing.'

Jayden leans over his laptop, taps *Fergus Grant* into the search engine.

'Okay, if Pippa's gone AWOL, we go to Fergus.'

'If they'd arrested Pippa, Skinner would have told us that, wouldn't he?' says Ally.

'Mullins definitely would have. Our client in the slammer? Honestly, I don't think he'd miss the chance to gloat. Okay, I'm going to message Fergus through his website.'

And Jayden's tapping out a few lines. The basics: they're private investigators, they're interested in talking to him as they believe he has some information. He doesn't mention that they've been hired by Pippa.

'Alright,' says Jayden, hitting Send with a flourish. 'Done. Can we get back to Donna? Mullins and Skinner might be all over the island, and sure, Pippa's felt flaky from the start, but Donna potentially has a massive motive, in my opinion. She could blame Axel for the death of her brother. Or blame him for *something* connected to her brother.' Jayden snaps his fingers. 'Major Paul Fairfax. Platoon commander. That's who else we need to find. Hopefully he'll give us an objective assessment of the relationship between Axel and Curtis, and what happened afterwards.'

'Let me,' says Ally, lifting her laptop on to her knees.

Shell House nerve centre. Okay, maybe they don't have resources like the police, but right now they've got leads to chase. Leads a-go-go. Because any case, when it comes down to it, is about people. And he and Ally are good at that part. He knows they are.

'Nice one. Now, bear in mind that we'll have to choose our words carefully with him. He could be defensive. Think we're interfering civilians or something.'

'Like Skinner does, you mean?'

'Major Paul Fairfax is a trained killer,' says Jayden with a laugh. 'With us around, Skinner probably wishes he was too.'

He clicks back to his email, just in case, by some miracle, Fergus has been quick to respond. As he does so his phone beeps with a message – and, because Fergus is on Jayden's mind, he thinks it's going to be him.

But it's Casey James.

Hi. I'm in Penzance. When do you want to meet?

34

Mullins sets down a tea on his boss's desk. The mug says *Top Cop* in faded letters and there's usually a tussle for it in the station kitchen. Skinner doesn't even look up.

'When do you think we'll get the results back on those ashes, Sarge?'

Mullins is treading carefully on this one. Skinner went hard on Pippa on the island, but he was close to matey with Ally and Jayden earlier. Mullins checks Skinner's forehead for those lines, only his fingers are obscuring them now; he has his head sunk in his hands.

'Not a moment too soon, Mullins,' he says in a muffled voice. 'Though, in all honesty, I don't know what we're holding out for.'

'Flipping fibreglass.'

It was Mullins who found the remains of the fire on flat ground up behind Pippa's cottage. He poked the toe of his shoe in the white ash, mind thrumming; if you wanted to get rid of a boat, would you burn it? Pippa was defensive, said she'd cleared some ground and was burning the debris, and all the while Mullins was busy picturing Axel's stolen kayak going up in smoke. But then later, on the boat trip back, Skinner spoilt it all by saying fibreglass was fire-resistant, and if you wanted to ditch a kayak you'd be better off just sending it out to sea, making holes in its hull so it sank to the bottom.

'CSIs are on their way to Axel's van,' says Mullins.

Skinner takes his head from his hands, and grunts like an old man whose nap has been disturbed. 'And a fine mess they'll find when they get there, Ally and Jayden stomping all over the place.'

Mullins doesn't proffer the thought that the police maybe should have done it first thing. But from the statements they took, everything had pointed to Axel getting drunk and going off that cliff all on his own. No reason to suspect a criminal element. And getting CSIs out cost money. You couldn't have them dusting for the sake of it, could you?

Though you probably should.

'But if the nurse's prints are there,' says Skinner, 'then it contradicts her statement, and we'll have no choice but to bring her in.'

'How does that sit with Pippa Grant being involved?'

Skinner shakes his head and picks up his mug of tea, then puts it down again. He looks, Mullins thinks, older than usual. Like all that thundery bad temper has piled the years on him.

'I don't know. I really don't.'

'Could be sour grapes on the husband's part, phoning in?'

'Obviously that crossed my mind. And, of course, we were already aware of her circumstances. But the slant he put on it, we couldn't ignore it. And she was evasive, Mullins. Stonewalled us all the way. I don't know if Pippa was shocked to be under the spotlight, and put there by her ex of all people, or it was old emotions coming back up, or . . . something more.'

'You don't think she'll do a runner, do you?'

'Well, I delivered my favourite line, didn't I?'

Don't leave town.

'I don't love the thought of her on that island all on her own, though,' Skinner says, distractedly. 'Vulnerable sort of spot. Our questions upset her. That much was obvious.'

Is he realising he went in a bit too forcefully? *No 'our' about it, though.*

'You had to ask them,' says Mullins, 'but she didn't have to answer them, did she?'

'No. But then we'd have had to do it down the station.'

'And she's not on her own. She's got Ally and Jayden.'

'Don't get me started there.' Skinner sighs and pushes a hand to his head again. 'Got any paracetamol on you?'

'Sorry, Sarge, no. Want me to nip out?'

Skinner blinks. 'Thanks. Thanks, Mullins.'

'Sarge . . .' Mullins hesitates, conscious that he's overstepping a line, an invisible line where on one side you have people as they want to be seen, and then on the other how they actually are. 'Are you alright? Past the headache, I mean. The last few days . . .'

His boss has dropped his head into his hands again, and his thumbs are circling his temples. Mullins shifts on his feet. He's not very good at this.

'Fergus Grant,' says Skinner quietly. 'They might have only just gone their separate ways, but the marriage could have been on the downturn for a while. There could be all sorts of added layers there. The ways people find to hurt people, the ones we used to love. She looked devastated, didn't she – Pippa? The fact that it was her ex who phoned in. Devastated.'

And the use of that 'we' isn't lost on Mullins. It's nothing like the procedural 'our' before. Was it an accidental slip, or a door held open? A bar stool proffered. The divorce was three or four years back now, but still.

What would Saffron, aka Hippy-Dippy, do?

It's not the first time Mullins has asked himself that question.

'What about you and your ex, Sarge – things all okay there?'

That moustache of his is a dead-straight line. But then Skinner gives a small, sad smile.

'We'll make a copper out of you yet, Mullins,' he says.

35

Saffron sits on her board, slowly lifting and dropping with the swell. Broady is beside her. The biggest thing they had in common before they were a couple is still a bond. When Broady poked his head in the door of Hang Ten twenty minutes ago the waves were perfect peelers, but in the time it took Saffron to guesstimate the lunchtime rush and decide it wasn't happening, get into her wet-suit, flip the sign on the door to 'Gone Surfing', they've dropped. There's no reason for them both to be out here still, but they are. Just in case.

Despite the mostly blue skies and – when the breeze slips – the warm sun, the sea is cold. Broady shakes his head like a dog, and silver drops fly from his wet hair. Saffron laughs. She knows that move.

'Nothing cooking,' she says.

'Patience, my child.'

She laughs again, thinking how nice it is that they can do this, and it's just two people and the thing they love. Same place, same time. Nothing more than that.

'Have you seen the flyers for Jodie's dub night?'

Saffron's housemate is DJing in a tiny basement bar in Penzance tonight. Good tunes, cocktails – obviously she's going. And she's feeling quite lame that this is her roundabout way of asking if Broady's going too.

'Thinking about it.'

'It'll be fun. You should.'

'Milo around, is he?'

'He's in Paris.'

Broady bobs his head. 'That boy and his spray cans sure get about.'

'The art's going really well,' she says.

The trouble is, Saffron still doesn't know how to talk about Milo with Broady.

'Did I tell you Dee's moving back?'

Tit for tat. Okay.

'Dee? No. That's cool. What, permanently?'

Broady's *ex*-ex-girlfriend, the one Saffron was always aware of when they were seeing each other, not because she suspected he still had feelings for her, but because she was insanely beautiful. They stayed at her place in Sri Lanka two winters ago, a beach-shack surf school, all palm trees and hammocks and sundowners. Dee was living her endless summer and loving it. Saffron couldn't imagine her ever giving that up.

'She reckons after surfing became her job she lost the joy in it.'

'Really?' Then, 'Where's she moving to?'

'Back to her folks' in Barnstaple to start with. Then she's not sure.'

Saffron looks over her shoulder, eyeing a shift in the horizon line. She wants a set to roll in, but she also wants to carry on this conversation. See where it ends up.

'You don't feel that way, do you? About surfing being your job?'

Broady grins at her, his white teeth shining out of his tanned face. He keeps his glow all winter.

'I love teaching, Saff. It brings something else to it, like you're passing the love on, you know? Surfing's given me everything. Least I can do is give a bit back.'

'I love that,' she says, feeling herself reflecting his smile.

'It's weird. I didn't know I'd feel that way. I mean, I'm pretty selfish, right? Surfers are. If you want the best waves, you have to be.'

Before they got together, the line round here was that Broady was married to the sea.

'More like . . . single-minded. Driven.'

Saffron's being generous, but hey, she gets it. And it's a whole lot easier to get, now that they're broken up.

'It's an addiction, I guess, and I could have stayed in that loop. But teaching broke it. And you know who I really love doing the sessions with?'

'Kids,' says Saffron. 'The grommets.'

Because she's seen it often enough. Broady jogging down the sand with a whole pack of them at his heels, like a surf Pied Piper. Not just the follow-the-leader stuff, but the tender moments too. The way he helps zip up their wetsuits. Bigs up the pop-ups. Hands out high-fives like free cookies.

'Kids. Exactly. It's even made me think . . .' He looks down at his board, traces a pattern with his thumb. 'Maybe I wouldn't mind a grom of my own one day.'

'Wow.'

Because Saffron never thought she'd hear Broady – the Peter Pan of Porthpella – say that. And suddenly an unexpected feeling descends. A whoosh of emotion that's made of a lot of different things.

Is there a reason he's telling me this?

But then she's saved by the wave, because Broady's calling out 'Incoming!' and as Saffron looks over her shoulder, she sees the horizon is rising, big-time. She drops to her belly and starts to paddle. Fast, strong strokes. Adrenalin pumping, like it always does. Then she's on her feet and thoughts – wanted thoughts, unwanted thoughts, any thoughts at all – are left in her wake as she takes off and flies along the wave. White water chasing her all the way.

36

Morrab Gardens are quiet on a weekday afternoon. Casey said she'd rather they met outside than in a café with people listening in, so Ally suggested this peaceful oasis just back from the seafront. The three of them sit beneath a giant palm tree, spiked shadows at their feet. An office worker, lanyard resting against his shirt, finishes a sandwich on a nearby bench. A young woman with a pram does slow laps of the bandstand. The faint strains of pop music, and clanks of scaffolders, carry on the breeze.

Despite seeing Casey's photograph, the young woman is not what Ally expected.

In one particular way.

When Ally and Jayden first entered the park, they saw the blond-haired woman in a grey hoodie, sitting on the far bench – and they carried on looking beyond her. It was Jayden who tapped Ally's arm, said in a low voice, *Al, I think that's her*. And Ally gave a sharp intake of breath as she took in her slight frame – and the shape of her stomach.

Descendants, Ally said in a whisper. *Axel or his descendants.*

But then Casey spotted them, lifting her hand in an uncertain wave, and Ally returned it with gusto. As they walked towards her, Jayden whispered, *You mean what Elspeth said about the will. 'Axel or his descendants'.*

We can't assume it's his, said Ally.

But the meeting – already charged – had taken on a new energy.

Now, Casey removes the lid from a water bottle and takes a careful sip. Her pale skin is freckled. Her make-up looks freshly applied; her lips shimmer with gloss, and there's a smudge of mascara beneath her right eye. Ally's struck by her quiet dignity – her aura is calm, though inside a storm must be raging.

'When Axel left, I honestly didn't know if I'd ever see him again,' says Casey. 'I figured it was going to go one of two ways. He'd either disappear completely or . . . turn into the version of himself that I knew he could be: Amazing Axel. But that was up to him, not me.'

She takes a steadying breath, rolling the bottle between her palms.

'I expect you think I'm harsh. But . . . it gets to a point where you've got to self-protect. No matter how much you love someone. And . . . Yeah. I did love him.'

Casey looks at them both. She tips her chin, a gleam in her eyes suddenly, and Ally recognises the spirit of the skater girl in the photograph.

'I still don't get why it's you asking the questions,' Casey says.

'Because the police don't know what happened to him.'

'And the woman who found him, Pippa Grant, came to you.'

'That's right,' says Ally.

'I looked you up,' says Casey. 'You solve murders. Does that . . . I mean, you don't think . . .'

'We don't know,' says Jayden gently. 'At this point, we just want to know about Axel. Understand who he really was. Casey, would you tell us about him?'

'Yeah, how long have you got?'

'All the time,' says Jayden.

Casey gives a tiny shake of her head and mouths 'Okay.'

She looks down the park. Between the canopies, the shimmer of the seaward horizon is just visible.

'He was brilliant. If he was here now . . .' Her voice breaks. 'I reckon you would have liked him. He was funny. And handsome. And kind. But he was his own worst enemy too. The absolute worst.' She looks to them both. 'I don't know where to start. Telling you about him, I mean.'

'Why don't you tell us how you met,' says Ally.

So Casey tells them about the skate park last summer – the one from the photograph – and how he seemed like a lost boy; an energy that was frenetic, fragile.

'*This charming smile, all soulful eyes, but he was troubled. I saw it from the off, but I thought I could save him, didn't I? I thought I could be the one to make the difference. Tale as old as time.*'

She speaks of the drinking, how it was always the drinking that was the problem. He didn't do drugs, he wasn't violent, he just had days when he drank and drank, and as he sank beneath the wave of alcohol, Casey could see that this was a man who didn't like himself, who got so sad and defeatist that it didn't matter what she said to pull him back up.

'Six months we were together,' she says. 'We lasted longer than we should have. That's what my friend Saz said. But I believed in Axel. Even when he didn't believe in himself. But that just got so . . . tiring. You know? He wore me out. And I tried. I really did. Because I thought he was worth it.'

Her eyes fill, and she briefly closes them.

'When Axel moved to Bristol, he was in a better place than he had been in a long time, he told me. He said what it was like for him before. How adrift he'd been, and for so long.'

The years in London, never holding down a job, something always coming along to ruin it for him, or ruining it for himself.

The months he spent in a sleeping bag or under cardboard; hostels when he got lucky, temporary housing.

'Axel told me he didn't really feel safe anywhere,' she says, 'but he'd got some help and was finding a way back. He was trying. He really was. He'd got a job in the supermarket, was getting more shifts.'

'Did he talk about leaving the army?' asks Jayden.

'Leaving it? You're joking, right? That's the trouble. He never did.'

She inhales sharply, composing herself.

'He told me once that everything he ever saw in Afghanistan, he was still carrying about, like this massive pack on his back that he couldn't put down. This was like . . . fourteen, fifteen years on. He was barely twenty when he was there. So young. They decided he was a suicide risk, so they discharged him on medical grounds. Gave him a full pension, and a phone number to call at the NHS. I mean, come on, if you're having a mental health crisis, you can't take of yourself, that's the whole point, isn't it? He drank away that pension and he never called that number. And that's on the army. But when he talked about it, he was . . . weirdly loyal. He said he had some of the best times of his life as a Rifleman, as well as the worst. I don't know if he couldn't see what it'd done to him, or he just thought he was lucky to be alive when others weren't.'

'Casey, did Axel ever talk about another soldier called Curtis Goode?'

She shakes her head. 'He never talked about the people he served with.'

'Curtis was in Axel's section in Afghanistan,' says Jayden. 'He died.'

'Oh yeah, okay. Of course. I mean, not directly . . . but I know a particular soldier died and that was a big part of it. But he never told me his name.'

'So the name Donna Goode doesn't mean anything to you either?' asks Jayden.

'Donna? No. You've got to understand, everything I know about Axel's time in the army I learnt in bits and pieces. It was all buried so deep. I wasn't going to push it. It felt like . . . the structure of him, you know? The fundamental structure. The one thing he went into detail about, though, was his mum. When he talked about her, he just lit up. It was tragic, what happened. Totally tragic.'

A man with a Labrador approaches, the dog stretching his lead, sniffing at their feet. Casey waits until they've moved on.

'So, after Axel's tour, he gets back here, in bad shape, and finds that his mum is at death's door. It couldn't have been worse. She died just a few weeks later. So when I said that no one was looking after Axel when he needed it, I meant it. And the same went for his poor mum.'

'Did he talk about being discharged?' asks Jayden.

'You mean how he tried to kill himself?' says Casey, unflinching. 'No. I just know that it was after that tour and after his mum died. He was back at barracks. But . . . someone stopped him.'

They sit in silence for a moment. A light breeze rustles the palm fronds above their heads. Clouds scud fast across the sky, the sun flashing in and out.

'Did he ever talk about his mum's employer, Edward Grey?' asks Ally eventually.

'Not at first, he'd just shut down. I didn't even know that Axel grew up in Cornwall, let alone in this little house in the grounds of a crazy massive mansion. But then it came out one day. He just started talking about it. I couldn't believe it; it was like I was seeing this whole other side of him. A sweet little boy who lived by the sea and some posh bloke who inspired him to join the army.'

'What about Lucas Grey, Edward's son? Did he talk about him?'

Casey tips her head, considering it. 'Not really. I mean, he mentioned him, but Axel was always just focused on Edward. His mum had cancer, but Axel basically blamed Edward Grey for her death.'

'Why did he blame Edward?' asks Ally.

'She was ill for some time, but Edward Grey worked her to the bone, never gave her time off, and she was so under his thumb that she never spoke up, never prioritised getting herself to the doctor. Axel said it was basically abuse. I don't know about that, I guess he wasn't very objective, but then why should he be? It was his mum. And her employer should have taken care of her. By the time she was in the system, getting seen, it was too late. The cancer had progressed.'

Ally looks to Jayden. If this is how Axel saw the situation, it explains the estrangement after his mother's death. It also, perhaps, explains the scale of Edward's final gesture. Was that, in itself, an admission of guilt, that Edward should have done better by her?

'I know what you're thinking,' says Casey. 'He was messed up by Afghanistan, and then he came home to all of that. Maybe he wasn't seeing the situation straight. But he was in a state, and however angry and sad Axel was, Edward Grey didn't try to stop him when he left. It was like, when his mum died, any connection with that place was over – on both sides. And Axel needed Edward Grey, even if he didn't realise it himself. That guy could have made all the difference to Axel. Literally, all the difference.'

There are tears on Casey's cheeks now. She cries silently, but her voice doesn't falter.

'So when the police told me that it was Edward Grey, or his son or whatever, that reported him missing, I couldn't believe it. Because they're the last people I ever expected Axel to want anything to do with. But maybe that was the whole point. Maybe he was going back to the source, facing the problem so he could move forward. I mean, maybe . . . Right?'

'So Axel didn't tell you he was going to see Edward Grey in Cornwall?'

Casey wipes her eyes with her sleeve.

'No, he did. He didn't mention the Greys, but I knew he was coming to Cornwall to try and fix himself. That's how he put it. Because until it all went wrong, he was happy here. That's why he came back. Basically, back in January, we had a row. We'd had them before, but this one was . . . final. It wasn't that he was treating me badly, he never did, it was just how he was with himself, you know? I told him he had to sort himself out if there was any hope for us, and that I didn't want to hear from him again until he had. So that was it. He bought this tip of a van, and about fifty blankets, and went off. But then every week that went past, I thought . . . it's not happening. He's got worse in Cornwall, not better. And he's obviously realised he's happier without me in his life. Because when there's someone there who keeps telling you that you can be better, like you're not good enough as you are, that you're making all the wrong choices . . . I guess that can end up making you feel even worse, can't it? So when he went off in the van, I thought maybe we were better off without him too.'

Casey's hand goes to her mouth.

Was it that 'we'? The emotional significance.

'But I got it wrong. Didn't I? I should have given him a chance to prove himself. And I shouldn't have worried about where the inspiration came from. It wasn't up to me to deny him that. And now he's dead, and I've let them both down.'

Ally's eyes go to Casey's domed stomach. The young woman places her hand on her bump with the saddest of sighs.

'That's the bit I can't forgive myself for. That I've let Axel's daughter down too.'

37

Jayden knows that he and Ally have a good connection, but here's where he wishes he was telepathic. As Casey drops her head, he looks to Ally and sees sorrow in her eyes, and confusion too. Maybe she doesn't know the right thing to do either.

Elspeth Grey said that Edward wanted the house to go to Axel – or his descendants. Elspeth said it to them in passing, because she knew, or thought she knew, that Axel wasn't a father. At that stage, it was a meaningless point in the will.

But it's not meaningless anymore.

While everyone at Porthmerrin knows that Edward intended the house to go to Axel – and the police do too – was this finer detail also widely known? But what if there are clauses attached, meaning a child *in utero* is somehow not valid? It's not the kind of thing that Jayden and Ally can afford to get wrong. So, they're both staying quiet. So far. Meanwhile Casey – pregnant, oblivious – sits between them.

'Was Axel in touch with you at all while he was here?' asks Ally.

'No,' says Casey. 'I thought about messaging him a hundred times, and maybe he did the same with me. But I kept thinking, "No, Casey, stick to what you told him. Sort yourself out, Axel, then come back to me." I wanted to show him I was serious, I guess.'

'Did other friends of yours hear from him?'

She shakes her head. 'He wasn't in touch with my mates directly. While I was with him, we were kind of separate from everyone. He was antisocial, really. And I can be the same.'

'What did your friends think of him?'

'They didn't judge him for his past, if that's what you mean. They saw how good he was to me. I mean, he wasn't good to himself, but when it came to women, Axel was the perfect gentleman. That was how his mum raised him.' She looks up, her eyes shining with tears. 'Did he make friends down here? Or . . . girlfriends? The police said they were struggling to find anyone who knew him, but you know, the police . . .' She pulls a dismissive face. 'Who knows if that's true.'

'So far,' says Jayden, 'we've only been looking at who interacted with him immediately before his death.'

'The Grey family, you mean. The police said he was there for a dinner with them. Edward, and then his son and wife. That he was parked up on their land that night.'

Jayden looks to Ally. Presumably the police didn't mention the inheritance.

'I didn't say this to the police,' says Casey, 'but . . . what if there's a chance that he went there looking for a fight? Like, maybe he wanted to hold Edward to some sort of account. Axel was never, ever violent with me, but . . . he told me back in London he'd had some run-ins. He was a doorman at a club for a bit, all kinds of rough stuff coming through, and he had to get physical sometimes. He lost his job because he took it too far one time. He told me he scared himself. So . . . what if being back in Cornwall did the opposite of what he hoped? What if it brought it all back and . . . he went to see that Edward Grey with some kind of agenda? And, I don't know, they had to stop him or something?'

Subtext? One of the Greys killed Axel.

'As we understand it,' says Jayden carefully, 'Axel was in good spirits while he was at Porthmerrin.'

Casey nods, her hair falling in front of her face. 'They said that, did they? I want to believe it. And to be honest, it's *easier* to believe. Axel didn't leave for Cornwall raging. He got it. He understood why we were breaking up, and he wanted to find a way to turn things around. Maybe he dipped once he was here – you know, the reality of spending winter in a van on his own – but . . . I don't know. Maybe he was open to building bridges with Edward. Because he was dying, wasn't he, the old man?'

'He died yesterday,' says Jayden.

'The cops told me that. Sad.'

'Was Axel a forgiving person?' asks Ally.

'Do I believe that he'd forgive Edward Grey for how he treated his mum, do you mean?' Casey rubs slow circles on her belly with her palm. 'Yeah, maybe,' she says quietly. 'If Axel knew he was dying. Because . . . he was kind.'

Which contradicts what she was saying only a minute ago, about Axel seeking a confrontation. Casey knew him intimately, better than anyone alive, and she can still only guess at what Axel was doing in Cornwall these last two months. She wants to believe he was slowly rebuilding himself, making his peace with the past, but he could just have easily been flying right off the rails and not trying to pick himself up again. Seeking revenge even.

'I'd like to meet them,' says Casey. 'The Greys. I'd like to go to Porthmerrin House.'

Jayden hesitates. Do they have the right to pass on the information about the will to Casey? Not without the details. And probably not even then.

'I mean, I don't know what to think of them, but . . . they were the last people Axel spent time with. And it was the place he grew up, that he loved once.' She looks at them both, her face suddenly determined. 'I think it's where I need to be.'

38

Ally checks her watch. They have half an hour while Casey returns to her bed and breakfast to freshen up, then the three of them will go to Porthmerrin together. Ally doesn't know if Casey going to meet the Greys is a good idea or not. *And Donna, what about Donna?* But if Lucas is the executor of the will, then he needs to know that Axel does have a descendant after all. Or he will have in four months' time when the baby is born, anyway. Isn't it better to learn that sooner rather than later?

'Shall we go down to the seafront?' she says to Jayden.

Ally doesn't often get over to Penzance, but the last time Ray came down, they visited a gallery here. It felt strange, the two of them walking through the town together, like any other couple going about their Saturday-morning business. A coffee with the papers, a look in a gallery or two, a stroll along the seafront. It was nothing they haven't already done in Southwold, or Aldeburgh, but the whole time they were here, Ally felt like somebody else. It wasn't an unpleasant sensation, but nor was it entirely comfortable either. Being here now with Jayden, talking to the ex-girlfriend of a dead man who's yet to discover her unborn child is potentially heir to a vast country estate – now how on earth can that feel more usual?

If Ray moved down . . .

Ally knows she owes Ray a phone call. For all his confidence, he's sensitive, and she's certain her lukewarm response will have hurt him a little. She messaged him earlier to say that they were in the middle of a new case, and Ray replied with a long text saying that he knows she'll be fully absorbed by the investigation and not to think about anything else. A permission slip for her inattention. *I knew when we spoke your mind was elsewhere*, he wrote, *don't give my movements another thought, go forth and detect!* And Ally didn't have the heart to say that the case only came in after their phone call.

'The seafront?' says Jayden. 'Let's do it.'

They wander down through the gardens, then cut into quiet residential streets with elegant townhouses, and smaller terraces of fishermen's cottages. The sea is a broad band of blue, the tide high, waves slapping on the strip of shingle beach. Ally leans on the cool, metal balustrade; a sharp breeze tugs at the ends of her hair. No matter where she is, the ocean is always a balm. Ally watches as a ragged length of seaweed comes and goes on the tide, and she thinks of Axel's body being swept out to Lone Island. How it must feel for Casey to be here, carrying Axel's daughter, looking out at this same sea.

Ally knows Casey is putting on a brave face. If you've always felt someone is vulnerable, subject to forces beyond their control, does their loss feel somehow anticipated? No less sad, but possibly a mite less shocking? Ally cannot say.

'Lucas said that if Axel had a kid, he'd be welcome to the place,' says Jayden. 'Remember?'

'I'm not sure he meant it. And Elspeth knew full well that he didn't.'

'Yeah, she's got his number. The thing is,' says Jayden, leaning on the rail beside her, 'this situation with the will, it's tricky, but it's not a police matter. It's not up to Mullins to tell Lucas that Casey James is carrying Axel's baby, is it? So it has to be down to us, right?'

'Wouldn't it be more appropriate to go to Edward's solicitor? Donna might know who he engaged.'

'Donna, who could potentially be involved? Not sure about that, Al. Look, here's the thing. Pippa hired us to get the full story behind Axel's death. What that basically equates to is us doing the right thing by Axel. And right now, the one thing we can influence is the fact that Axel has an heir. Or . . . has an heir on the way.'

'You're right.'

'So,' says Jayden, 'I reckon we talk to Casey about it in the car. Say that Axel learnt he was set to inherit the house, and leave it to the Greys to mention the bit about descendants. Because let's face it, we can't get that detail wrong, it's too high-stakes. An unborn child might not count, for all we know.'

'You're right. But we're safe telling Casey about Axel finding out he was due to inherit.'

But nothing feels 'safe' about any of it.

'Jayden, do you not think it's strange that the police didn't say anything about the inheritance to Casey when she came forward?'

She watches as he considers it, his dark eyes thoughtful.

'She isn't listed as next of kin. Plus, it's a potentially explosive bit of information to give someone who's in a vulnerable position. And the irony of that statement isn't lost on me, by the way. We'll need to handle it delicately.'

'We will,' says Ally.

She watches as a fishing boat makes its way across the bay, bound for Newlyn. A flock of gulls follow it; iron filings, drawn by the pull of a magnet. She wonders how the information will be received by Casey. Will she see its volatile potential? Or will she believe it means Axel was warmly received at Porthmerrin House?

'Al, what do you reckon to Casey's account of Axel and Edward Grey's relationship?'

'She sounded like she couldn't make her mind up. She said Axel blamed Edward for his mother's death, but she could also imagine him being open to building bridges.'

'Donna and Robbie didn't talk about any big tensions, did they? If there was drama coming from Axel, they'd have been aware of it, right?'

'What Casey said about Axel maybe wanting to confront Edward, we haven't spent a lot of time considering that.'

'Okay, so what if there was a scene, and everyone's lying about it?' says Jayden. 'Lucas, Elspeth, Robbie, Donna . . . They were all loyal to Edward, one way or another. If Axel brought the drama, and Edward's health deteriorated as a consequence . . .'

'. . . someone would hold that against him,' says Ally. 'Agreed.'

'Meanwhile it suits someone like Donna, who potentially has a very different motive, to say that all was well at Porthmerrin, doesn't it?'

'Because it makes Axel's death less suspicious all round.'

Jayden nods. 'And there's a trio of scapegoats. The whisky, the dark night, the cliff edge.'

'The missing kayak too?'

'The missing kayak.' Jayden groans and rocks back on his heels. 'God, Al. My gut's telling me this is about Afghanistan. Because that's the remarkable bit, right?'

'It is. But the inheritance is remarkable too.'

'No, you're right, it is. It definitely is.'

'And whatever Fergus Grant told the police, that must be fairly remarkable too.'

However concerning it is to admit it.

Ally takes her phone from her pocket. There's still no reply from Pippa. But there is a message from Gus. She opens it, clicks on the link. Reads: *Antique firearm washed up on beach.*

'There's a lot of factors,' Jayden goes on, 'but Donna is one hundred per cent lying to us about being in Axel's van. Well, ninety-nine per cent . . . pending the fingerprints results. Ninety-five per cent.'

'If the police investigate it, that is.'

'It's cutting corners not to. Ignoring vital evidence from members of the public.'

Ally raises an eyebrow. 'We're members of the public now?'

'When it suits us,' grins Jayden. 'Hey, what's got your attention?'

'Sorry, it's Gus. He's getting excited about pirate treasure. Someone found an eighteenth-century gun washed up on the beach.'

'Really?' Jayden slips out his phone. 'Hey, speaking of Fergus Grant, I've had nothing back from him.'

'Nor me from Axel's platoon commander. I told you I tracked down his email, didn't I? He's a training officer at Sandhurst now. A desk job.'

'Nice work, Al.'

'And, Jayden, I still haven't heard a thing from Pippa. It feels . . . strange.'

'Are your messages being read?'

'I can't tell because I'm texting her, she's not on WhatsApp. But I know they're being delivered.'

'Try giving her another buzz. If you're still getting nothing, maybe we go back out to the island.'

Ally's already calling; and just like before, the phone is ringing out. She looks to Jayden, shakes her head.

'Okay, here's what we do. First, we brief Casey on the will – the part we know about for sure – and then we ask if she still wants to go up to Porthmerrin House. Sound good?'

Ally nods. 'We've only just met her, but I think I know which one she'll say.'

'Me too. And let's face it, it's the more interesting option, right?'

'Maybe *too* interesting. Are you sure we shouldn't mention the possibility of descendants inheriting? Just so she can be forewarned, if Lucas and Elspeth . . .'

'Freak out? I just worry it's too much of a head spin. And we don't have the full picture. No, let's play it by ear, Al.'

'Okay,' says Ally. 'Then, if we've still not heard from Pippa, we go to the island?'

'It's a plan,' says Jayden. He beats a quick tattoo on the railing, then turns. 'Go on, then, show me the picture of Gus's pirate gun.' His face suddenly changes. 'Hold on, where was it found, this gun?'

And Ally feels an instant thrum of excitement in response – because she knows exactly where Jayden's mind has gone. Because hers is there too.

'Edward Grey,' she says.

'And his antique weapons collection,' finishes Jayden.

39

They meet Casey outside her bed and breakfast, a tall pebbledash terrace in the backstreets of the town. A faded sign announces 'Vacancies', but the curtains are drawn at two of the downstairs windows. A wheelie bin by the door overflows with bags.

'Yeah, it's not the Ritz,' she says by way of greeting. 'But at least there's a kettle and biscuits.'

All the way from the seafront, Jayden and Ally were deep in speculation. Could this found weapon somehow connect to Axel? Did he steal an antique gun and then a kayak and make for the open seas? It feels unlikely. But perhaps that's just the kind of adventure that might have appealed to the one-time soldier – and Lucas already said that Axel had loved Edward's weapons. They don't know for sure that Edward Grey had this exact firearm in his collection. Just like they don't know for sure that the gun hasn't been washing about in the sea for years. But going by the photograph – the wood, the intricate silver – it's in good condition; it doesn't look like it's been dredged up from the deep. For all their questions, as soon as Casey is with them, they refocus their attention on her.

And they refocus on the topic of the will.

They're parked in the street, around the corner from the bed and breakfast. As they climb inside the car, Jayden watches a traffic warden ambling along the pavement and thinks they should get a move on before they get a ticket. The wrong place to drop the bombshell, maybe. But then he's telling her anyway.

Casey doesn't say anything at first. She just stares at Jayden, her mouth open. She's put on more make-up since they met – dark eyeliner that flicks up at the sides – and her eyes are wide as moons.

'But we don't know any of the details,' he says. 'We're just going on what we've heard.'

'Axel inherits a mansion, and the next day he's dead? And meanwhile Lucas Grey gets nothing?'

Casey's voice is quiet, and Jayden thinks of the stillness of the breakdown before the bass drops.

'Lucas got the rest of his father's estate,' says Ally. 'Which presumably is sizeable, because he seemed . . . fine with the arrangement.'

Jayden shifts in his seat, so Casey can see he's giving her his full attention. In the back, Ally leans forward. Her face is creased with concern, as Casey pushes a hand to her forehead.

'You mean he didn't admit to killing Axel there and then?'

Casey makes a strange sound, somewhere between a groan and a wail.

Here's the bass.

'You guys are supposed to be detectives? Seriously? And what about the police? They know all this too?'

'They know all this too, but—'

'My God . . .'

Casey's hands go to her bump, and she cradles it. Jayden can't work out if she's comforting herself, or the baby inside. Perhaps it's the same thing.

'Casey,' says Ally gently, 'I know it's a lot to take in.'

'It's not a lot,' she says, 'it's not a lot at all. It's dead simple. That's what I can't believe, how simple it is and yet here we are . . . and, what, Lucas Grey is just walking around like he's innocent?'

'Edward Grey's nurse had a brother who died in Afghanistan. He was in the same section as Axel when it happened.'

'What?'

'Curtis Goode,' says Jayden. 'Axel didn't go to his funeral.'

Casey's mouth moves but no sound comes out. The silence in the car roars. And Jayden wishes he could take it back, but she has to know there's potentially more to this. She can't go storming in at Porthmerrin, her mind made up.

'Look, Axel probably didn't go to this guy's funeral because his mum was dying. Alright? And he was probably still trying not to kill himself at the same time. So he was busy, okay?' The words are a torrent. 'I think that's what you'll find. That he was really, really busy not dying himself.'

Jayden reaches for her hand but then changes his mind, sensing it's the last thing she wants.

'But you think that's a reason for this nurse to kill him, do you? That he didn't show up?' Casey shakes her head, a tear sliding down her cheek. 'Because that's the stupidest thing I've heard.'

'It's not about the funeral,' says Jayden, 'but the soldiering link is a strong emotional connection.'

Casey looks to Ally, as if wanting to know whether she subscribes to this same mad idea too. Ally nods, backing Jayden up.

'The police didn't mention any of this,' says Casey. 'They said about where he parked his van, right by the cliff edge. The evidence that he'd been drinking.'

'And Casey, there's nothing to say that Axel's death wasn't accidental.'

Apart from Pippa's feeling. And my feeling. Ally's feeling.

'Or self-inflicted? Yeah, right. He's just inherited a massive pile, so he kills himself. That's likely.'

And even though Jayden doesn't think Axel killed himself, they have to stay open to the possibility. So he asks the question.

'Knowing Axel, how do you think he would have felt about being in line to inherit the house? Could it have been . . . complicated?'

Casey looks down. Her hands are folded over her bump, her fingers knitted together. Her pale-pink nail varnish is chipped and scratched.

She mumbles something, and Ally asks her gently to repeat it.

'I don't know,' she says. 'I cut him off, didn't I? I said I didn't want to know, until he was sorted. So maybe he wasn't sorted. And maybe if you're not sorted, getting news like that . . . maybe it is overwhelming. Maybe it is that simple.'

'While you and Axel were together,' says Ally softly, 'did you ever talk about what life might look like for you both? Did you ever live together, or think that you might?'

'We didn't live together,' says Casey. 'But . . . we talked about it.'

Jayden watches Casey carefully. Her eyes are faraway, as if she's reliving a particular moment. She's in a different tune now; something melodic, haunting.

'There was this one time,' she says, so quietly it's a whisper. 'We were in Clifton last summer, this posh part of the city. I don't even know what we were doing there, but it was in the early days of getting together. We were just figuring each other out, you know? I didn't know any of his stuff. And we were walking by all these houses, massive great gates, driveways. I said something dumb like "imagine living somewhere like that". And Axel said, "I can't. No way." I thought he was talking about them being built with slave money or something, and then I felt dumb for saying it, like I didn't care about important history, but he didn't mean that because later, when we were up on the Downs, when we weren't even near those stupid houses anymore, he said, "I don't deserve a life like that." And I didn't even know what he was talking about at first, and then I did. He meant those houses.'

'What did you say to him?' Jayden asks, his tone gentle.

'I told him not to be dumb,' she says. 'That we could have anything we wanted, that we could be anyone we wanted. And that we deserved the world because . . . why not. But later, much later, when I realised, well, when I guess I realised how broken he was, I kept going back to that moment. Because I knew then that he really meant it. Axel felt undeserving of good things.'

'And what did Axel say?' asks Ally. 'When you were so lovely and positive?'

Casey wipes her sleeve across her eyes, smudging her so-careful make-up.

'He said that all he deserved was a drink. So, I guess we went to the pub.'

40

Porthmerrin House looks more formidable than ever as they approach it. Perhaps that's because Ally's seeing it through Casey's eyes, with everything they've told her going through her head. Ally's research says it's Elizabethan, with some later Gothic elements. Castellations hem the steep slate roof like the edge of a decorative quilt; a rampant Virginia creeper crowds the sequences of leaded windows. It's the kind of house you feel you should have bought a ticket to visit: a map in hand, and a souvenir shop on the way out.

What about Edward's antique weapons collection? Lucas only mentioned it in passing, but if it's missing a piece . . . it's another element to this case.

From the back seat, Ally hears Casey mutter something under her breath: a combination of disbelief and disquiet. After her story about the big, smart houses in Bristol, about what Axel had said about himself, Casey seemed to grow heavy, as if the idea of suicide, or a drunken accident, was looming larger.

Some people are born lucky, she said. *Axel wasn't one of those people. He got knocked, time and time again. To be handed a massive house then slip and fall? I can see that. I hate it, but I can see it.*

'Are you sure you still want to do this?' asks Ally.

Casey nods. 'It's the natural thing to do, isn't it? Go to where he was last seen. Meet the people he was last with. It's what anyone would do.' She turns to look at Jayden. 'But we don't mention the will unless they do, okay?'

And this would have been fine, thinks Ally, if she and Jayden didn't know about the conditions of said will, but as it is, they'll be walking into Porthmerrin House with an obviously pregnant girlfriend of Axel's. How can the introduction be anything but loaded? Before they picked up Casey, Ally and Jayden discussed whether they should contact the Greys in advance, to let them know about Axel's former girlfriend, but they decided that felt too much like collusion. Now that they're here, Ally wonders if it would have been sensible, despite that reservation. Or, the better choice all round, to go to the solicitor instead.

Ally's heart flutters as they climb out of the car. Beside her, Casey's jaw is set firm as she looks up at the grandeur of the house. She pulls her thin cardigan around her bump. Ally squeezes her arm, and the young woman responds with a whispered 'Thank you.' Ally feels such a responsibility towards her; every doubt or suspicion that Casey voices, Ally thinks is valid – and she knows Jayden does too.

'Back again?'

They turn to see Robbie coming towards them. Three visits to Porthmerrin and each time it's been the gardener who's met them first. It stands to reason if he's working outside, but nevertheless, there's a watchfulness to Robbie that isn't lost on Ally.

As Robbie reaches them, there's not even the start of a smile at his lips. His eyes take in Casey without interest.

'Back again,' says Jayden easily. 'Are Lucas and Elspeth about?'

'Inside,' says Robbie, nodding. 'If you wanted to catch the cops, they've been and gone.'

'Were they at the van?' asks Ally.

He nods again. 'You know what that's about, do you?'

'They don't exactly keep us informed,' says Jayden. Then, 'Is Donna about too?'

'She's gone into town. Said she wanted something new for Edward's funeral. You'd think she'd be sorted in that department, her line of work.' Robbie gives a dry laugh. 'But Edward was special, I guess.'

Beside her, Ally can feel Casey stiffen at the unintentional implication. Axel? Not special. But according to Jayden, Robbie knows how it feels to be at the fringes of society.

Is it worth introducing Casey to him? Watching Robbie's reaction?

'This is Casey James,' says Jayden, beating her to it. 'Axel's ex-girlfriend.'

Something passes across Robbie's face. Ally can't tell if it's a flash of guilt for being offhand, or a more generalised dislike of yet more visitors to Porthmerrin House.

'Hi Casey,' he says, without emotion.

Casey simply nods, and as Robbie looks down at his boots, Ally decides to take the moment to ask what will, no doubt, seem a strange question.

Unless Robbie knows more than he's letting on.

'Robbie,' she says, 'Edward was a collector of antiques, wasn't he?'

The man's brow furrows. 'Yeah. All sorts.'

'Did he use a particular dealer? Or was he off at auctions and the like by himself?'

'No, Edward always liked to get other people to do the work. He used a bloke in Penzance.' He rubs at his cheek as if there's something on it. 'Why the question?'

'Just interested,' she says. 'You don't know his name, do you?'

'He had a blue van. And a yappy dog that liked digging up my lawn.'

Jayden nods. He'll be logging that as desk research for later.

A movement at one of the downstairs windows catches Ally's eye. Seconds later the door is opening, and Lucas is standing at the top of the steps. He holds up one hand, shielding his eyes from the sun; he looks as if he's at the prow of a ship as it makes its way to harbour.

'There's the boss,' says Robbie, and turns on his heel, feet scuffing the gravel as he goes.

'Afternoon,' Jayden calls out.

And Ally thinks how the three of them must look to Lucas – and whether his mind is already running on, joining the dots. Lucas comes down the steps, then stops still. He stands as if he's the house's guard and perhaps that's exactly how he sees it. So they walk towards him instead.

'Can we introduce you to Casey James?' she says. 'Casey is Axel's ex-girlfriend.'

'Hi,' says Casey, holding out her hand. 'I've heard a lot about you.'

Ally applauds her cool. Lucas, on the other hand, is frozen. Quite frozen. He makes no move to shake her hand. And his face is utterly unreadable.

Casey looks to Ally with an expression of uncertainty. Then she withdraws her hand, turning it into an exaggerated shrug. 'Guess not, then,' she says, with a touch of attitude that is, Ally thinks, wholly reasonable.

'Sorry, sorry.' And it's as if Lucas has hit a switch, reactivating himself. 'God. Sorry.'

He sets one hand on Casey's shoulder and holds out the other. It's a commanding gesture: the move of a politician. And it feels inappropriately intimate. But Casey responds with composure. They shake.

'Good to meet you,' he says. 'Very good.'

'Casey's staying down here for a few days,' says Jayden easily.

'Is she? Good.' He tracks a hand through his hair. 'I don't mean "good", of course. Casey, you said? Casey, I'm sorry for your loss. And you're welcome here. Very welcome. We're devastated about

Axel. And then my father's death so soon afterwards has rather sent us into a tailspin. Forgive me if I forget my manners.'

Lucas looks from Ally to Jayden, then back to Casey. As his eyes linger on her pregnant belly, he gnaws at his lip.

'I'm sorry for your loss too,' says Casey.

'My wife,' says Lucas, 'my wife will make tea. She's much better at this stuff than me. Sorry, "this stuff". I don't know what I mean by that. Come in, come in.'

And he jogs up the steps and throws the door wide, waving with an exaggerated gesture.

'I'd like to see Axel's van,' says Casey, hesitating. 'His things.'

Lucas frowns, his hand dropping.

'Ah now, the police were stomping around in there earlier. I don't know, cataloguing bits and bobs, perhaps. If Axel had a will, then perhaps, well, his estate . . .' He loses his drift.

'Everything Axel owned in the world is in that van,' says Casey.

'Quite.' Lucas pushes his hand through his hair again. 'Then you must see it. But tea first, surely?'

'Darling?'

With a click-clacking of heels, Elspeth appears in the doorway behind Lucas.

'Ellie, now this . . .' says Lucas, 'erm, this is . . .'

'Casey,' says Casey. 'Axel's girlfriend. Well, ex-girlfriend.'

Several different expressions flit cross Elspeth's face, but then she appears to come to a decision.

'We're very happy to meet you, Casey.'

Then she stretches her arms wide and envelops Casey – and her bump – in a warm embrace.

Ally glances to Lucas. He's staring at Elspeth, as she welcomes the woman who'll change everything. Whatever resolve Lucas temporarily gathered has now ebbed, and he looks as if he can't believe what he's seeing. And he doesn't care who knows it.

41

Pippa sits on a hard wooden chair in the darkest corner of an already-dark pub. There's an old seafaring print on the wall opposite, set in one of those knobbly gold frames designed to make you take it seriously. She stares at the image of the turbulent ocean, the lurching galleon with its bloated sails. The brushstrokes swirl before her eyes.

Catatonic. Pippa always thought that word meant 'explosive, wild, chaotic', but has recently learnt it means a state of deep unresponsiveness.

I am catatonic. This pub could go up in flames, and I would not stir.

She takes another drink, and the vodka is hard and cold and tasteless. Before her, the waves hurl. The bows creak. Sailors yell at the tops of their voices as they haul on the ropes. The truth is, Pippa would swap places with any one of them; if she could be beamed up from this sticky-topped table and into that painting, she would in an instant. She'd let it swallow her whole.

Her glass is empty again, and she struggles to get up from her chair. The carpet is uneven. The beamed ceilings shift. And she's pretty sure that man at the bar is looking at her strangely, and she doesn't need that.

No, I don't need that.

'You okay, love?'

She stumbles out on to the street. The light is too bright and the air smells dirty. Towns. She hates towns. A motorbike roars up the street and the loud flash of it scares her; she pointlessly shouts after it: 'Too fast!' A child, his hand in his mother's, turns his wide eyes on her, and she thinks of the seals on the rocks with their doe-expressions and long lashes. Her seals. Her rocks. The one place in the world she wants to be, and she can't.

She had to get away from the island. She was a sitting duck there; her peace, such as it was, too easily breached. So she called for Trent and his boat, and she sat silent and motionless on the starboard side, all the way to the mainland. Then she caught a bus to where nobody knows her, away from prying, preying eyes.

How can her past have taken her present, that gift of an island, from her too?

Pippa makes her way down the street; her eyes are fixed on nothing but her next step. Is it two pubs she's been in, or three? They blur. Everything blurs. The trouble with pubs is people. The looks; the judgement. But she's not the one who can't control herself, is she? Come tonight, half the people in this damn town will be sozzled or on their way to it.

And Pippa? She hasn't been drunk like this in a long, long time.

But the pain. Fergus's betrayal was as venomous as a snake bite, and she knows no antidote. And that police detective's questions? The worst part of her life used against her; unpicking every stitch she's put in herself, her poorly made seams tearing. She thought she was strong enough to withstand it – by God she's been through worse – but it turns out . . . no. She can't stand it at all.

Pippa slips into a supermarket, silent as a shadow, and buys a bottle. The cashier has to take the tag off and Pippa feels him avoiding her eyes. He's a young guy – skinny, spotty, hoops in his ears – and he hands her the bottle without a word. Armed now, she moves more quickly. She exits – expecting the alarm to go off anyway – and scuttles into the street. She crosses steep, uneven cobbles, her feet running away with themselves, and fetches out by a small section of harbour. There's a handful of hardy boys and girls in wetsuits throwing themselves off the wall and into the cold, murky water; as they jump they make a sound as if they're dying, but then they come back up and do it all again. A canoeist – *there you go, there's your bloody kayak* – turns slow circles, like he's a hamster stuck in a wheel. An old man is asleep at the wheel of a mobility scooter while his ratty dog, crouching by his wheels, eyes a gull with intent.

There's life here, so much life, but none of it is for her.

Pippa can see the sea, but that's not what she wants. She had the sea, and she's lost it. So she turns her back on the water and trudges back uphill, back inland, looking for a place to lower herself down and disappear for a while. Soon the streets will be dead; that quiet echoing feeling after the shops close. Everybody with somewhere to go, somewhere to be, except Pippa. Her bottle is heavy in her bag, and it's her anchor point. She pulls out her phone, her loose fingers almost dropping it. She's missed another call from Ally Bright.

Pippa won't face Ally. She can't. She wouldn't be able to bear the questions in her eyes. Because the trouble is, when people think you've killed before, they never look at you in the same way again.

42

Jayden can't take his eyes off Lucas. As Elspeth goes on into the house, ushering Casey along with her, Lucas stays exactly where he is. The guy is rooted, his hands pushed into the pockets of his cord trousers. Jayden can feel the energy coming off him in waves.

'Shall we follow them?' asks Ally.

A rhetorical question, because it's weird that they aren't. But Lucas – and his force field – blocks their path.

'Lucas?' says Jayden.

'What do you mean by this?' Lucas peers through his curtain of hair, his voice hard. 'This . . . ambush?'

'It's not an ambush.'

'Casey got in touch with us,' says Ally. 'She wanted to come. She has no idea about the terms of the will.'

'And nor should you!' cries Lucas.

It was Elspeth who first mentioned the detail about Axel's descendants, not Lucas. He looks from one to the other, his pale eyes furious.

'You'll have to excuse me for not being as magnanimous as my wife in this moment. Forgive me if I'm not down with the . . . the *sisterhood.* This woman, Carrie? Cassie? We know nothing whatsoever about her and she turns up here, staking a claim, and—'

'It's Casey,' cuts in Jayden. 'And she's not staking any claim. Like Ally said, she doesn't know any of the details of the will. *Yet.*'

'And of course you're presuming, I suppose, that the child is Axel's?' Lucas runs on as if he hasn't heard. 'And I expect you've done some rudimentary maths and put two and two together, and, actually, there's absolutely nothing to prove it, is there? A woman like that, she could have shacked up with just about anyone. No, sorry, it doesn't follow at all that there's any entitlement . . .'

Jayden grits his teeth, just stopping himself from voicing his thoughts.

Oh, there's entitlement, and I'm looking right at it.

'All Casey cares about right now,' he says carefully, 'is that someone that she loved has died. I don't know what company you keep, Lucas, but she's not thinking about money. She's not thinking about what she can get her hands on.'

'Oh, you're judging me?'

Lucas's mouth twitches as if amused by the idea. Jayden holds his eye.

'Yeah, a little.'

Lucas gives a bark of laughter.

'It's distressing for Casey,' says Ally, trying to change the tone. 'She's grieving and she's vulnerable. If she senses any hostility . . .'

'Then why the hell did you bring her here? And don't pretend for one moment that you weren't looking for a reaction. When my wife mentioned the terms of the will, she hardly expected you to . . . use it against us. Because not for one moment did either of us ever think we'd be in *this* situation.'

Then Lucas stops, realising he's revealed his cards. It was all too easy to pretend to be sorry for Axel when there was nothing at stake. In the quiet that follows, Jayden can hear the murmur of Elspeth and Casey's voices from inside. He hopes it's a lot more cordial.

'Please see it from my perspective, for just a moment,' says Lucas. His voice is softer now, cajoling. He closes the door carefully behind him, joining them on the steps. 'I go to a great deal of effort to trace a troubled man, because I want to make my dying father happy. And he is, he's very happy when Axel deigns to turn up, and that's wonderful to see. My father is so happy, in fact, that instead of letting his will remain a secret until his death, as I suspect any sane person would do in this situation, he gathers us by his bedside and tells us the news all together. One big happy family. I expect my father was thinking only of how Axel would receive his tidings, not of me. But Jayden, I'm quite used to that. My father was not an emotionally intelligent man. A different generation, perhaps. Or simply, without a wife at his side, there was no one to keep him in check.'

Lucas flicks his fingers through his fringe. He's turned from Ally altogether, as if this is man-to-man talk now. Jayden pointedly moves to stand closer to her, but Lucas's eyes still focus on him alone.

'If I'm honest, I think I always imagined that my father would do something like this in the end. If not give the lot to Axel, then to lame horses or stray dogs or some such. I'm proud to say that my own success is self-made. My father's was not. Silver spoon in the mouth, silver slippers on his feet. He has different notions of deservingness.'

Jayden goes to ask a question, but Lucas holds up his hand. Jayden feels like a kid at school but sucks it up because this is the most Lucas has said since they met. He and Ally swap a look.

Definitely not the right time to ask him about a missing antique weapon.

'So I open my home to this man, but he shirks our hospitality and prefers to sleep in his vehicle. He doesn't shirk our booze, though, does he? Of course not. I refer you to my previous point:

troubled. And off he goes, giddy from the news that he'll be getting his hands on this place, drunk on malt reserve, to that tin can on wheels parked so perilously close to the edge of the cliff. I mean, of all the idiotic things someone could do . . .'

I open my home to this man. Jayden can't help noticing the personal pronoun. The night Axel died, it was still Edward's home.

'But Axel wasn't just any man,' says Jayden. 'He grew up with you here.'

'We hardly grew up together. I was away at school most of the time.'

Maybe Jayden's face does something, because Lucas's mode changes again, his composure short-lived.

'What, you want me to tell you a story where Axel Marks was the cuckoo in the nest? Where I felt sidelined by my father, as he turned his attentions on the housekeeper's son? Watched him grow big and strong and join the army as I . . . didn't? Well, I won't. Because it wasn't like that.' Lucas's cheeks burn red, a blaze of colour creeping down his pale neck too. 'Or even if it was like that, I didn't feel bad about it, because let me tell you, my father's attention was a mixed blessing. Axel was welcome to it.'

The door to the house opens then, and Elspeth appears. She turns a questioning look on her husband.

'Lucas? Coffee's going cold. Oh, and I laid my hands on one of those old albums of Edward's. Casey's found some photos of Axel in there, from when he was a boy. I said you'd see if Edward had any more.'

'Coming,' he says quietly.

Then Lucas trudges past her into the house, head bowed. Jayden thinks of a toddler who's stormed and stormed, then blown themselves out.

'You will come in too, won't you?' says Elspeth, eyeing them both. 'And . . . sorry. I don't know what I'm apologising for exactly, but I suspect it's due. My husband . . .' She gives a brief shake of her head, as if she doesn't want to finish the thought. 'You have to understand, since we got here, it's been one thing after another. It's such a silly cliché, wills causing familial stress, but they say clichés exist for a reason, don't they? Casey seems lovely to me, and of course I feel for her, but if she's carrying Axel's child, it changes a great deal, doesn't it? And that's quite a lot to . . .'

Elspeth's words drift at the sound of an engine, and they all turn to see a police car rolling through the gates. It's Mullins who climbs out, shortly followed by Skinner. The pair stride over the gravel, tiny stones skittering in their wake. They appear authoritative. Purposeful. And as the two officers take in Jayden and Ally, their faces are impossible to read. Even Mullins's.

But then the PC sends Jayden a quick wink.

Lucas appears in the doorway again. Did he hear the engine from inside? Or was he lurking by the door, listening all this time?

'Officers?' says Lucas, in a decent shot at a commanding tone.

'Afternoon,' says Skinner, stepping forward. 'We're looking for Donna Goode.'

Elspeth tips her head enquiringly. 'Donna went into town earlier. What do you want with her, she—'

'Sarge, look,' says Mullins quietly.

Donna is approaching the gates. She walks with her head down, shopping bags swinging in one hand, her phone clasped in the other. She suddenly looks up – conscious, perhaps, of all eyes on her – and stops dead.

The expression on Donna's face is as guilty as any Jayden's seen.

43

As everyone turns towards Donna, Ally can feel the pulsing of her phone in her coat pocket. She discreetly draws it out, hoping it's Pippa at last, but it's a number she doesn't recognise. Mullins and Skinner are walking towards Donna now, and Jayden is watching every move.

'Sorry, I must take this call,' she says quietly to Jayden, and slips away, following a path to the gardens.

What if it's Pippa ringing on a different number? Ally's feeling of unease around Pippa's silence has grown and grown. But police interest in Donna is surely a good sign for the islander.

'Hello, Ally Bright speaking.'

'Ally, it's Major Paul Fairfax.'

With everything that's happened in the last few moments, it takes a second for Ally to place him. Then, *of course*: Axel's platoon commander in Afghanistan, now a training officer at Sandhurst. She quickly collects her thoughts. And wonders if she should use his rank, as he did.

'Paul, um . . . Major, thank you for getting in touch.'

'I was saddened to hear about Axel Marks.'

Which part? His death, presumably, but as someone who was once responsible for the young soldier, Ally wonders if that sorrow isn't significantly more far-reaching.

'I thought it easier to call than email. What do you want to know about him?'

Paul isn't rude but he's certainly brusque. Ally flounders rather. What does she want to know? *Everything.* She wants to know everything.

Meanwhile, looking back towards the house, she can see the glint of handcuffs at Mullins's belt. Is Donna being arrested? Ally knows she can't possibly concentrate on Paul Fairfax unless she moves away from whatever's happening there. She rounds the corner of the building, back to the vast green lawn and the daffodil-filled borders. She stands beneath the canopy of an ebullient magnolia, looking up at its powder-pink petals. *Focus.* Because this is another piece of the puzzle of Axel's past – and an important one.

'I suppose I wanted a sense of the relationship between Axel Marks and another soldier called Curtis Goode,' she says. 'And whether there were any . . . complicating factors.'

Paul starts to reply but his voice falters. The phone signal is poor, and Ally moves again. She needs to hear every word of this. She asks Paul to repeat himself.

'I said they were both good soldiers. Curtis was a great loss, and so was Axel.'

Ally waits for more, but more doesn't come. And this time it isn't the signal.

'So, were they friends?' she asks.

'Every platoon is close-knit. You have to be. A section even more so. And Axel and Curtis were at Catterick together too.'

'Catterick?'

'Infantry training. They passed out – graduated, in layman's speak – at the same time.' He hesitates. 'If you want to know about complicating factors, there was a bit of banter, early on, about Curtis's sister.'

'Donna Goode?'

'That's it. Donna. She and Axel met at Catterick. They may or may not have been involved.'

Ally gives a quick intake of breath.

'They might have been in a relationship?'

'The lads like to let off steam when they get the chance. I think Donna came up and joined them on one or two of their nights out, and she and Axel got a bit friendly. I don't think it was much more than that, in all honesty. If I thought there was a problem between the lads as a result, I'd have ironed it out.'

'Were Donna and Axel still in touch when he and Curtis were in Afghanistan together?'

'No idea. But like I said, there was no issue between Curtis and Axel.'

But was there an issue between Axel and Donna? The nurse gave them the impression that she knew Axel only at a distance – perhaps even only by association. Why the lie?

Perhaps for the same reason that she lied about being in Axel's van.

Is she, even now, in cuffs?

Ally refocuses. As much as her mind is running away with her, she needs to get everything she can from the major.

'After Curtis was killed, was Axel deeply affected?'

Again, the phone line falters. Ally repeats her question.

'Everyone was deeply affected.' And there's a slight note of irritation in his voice. 'But Axel was more emotionally vulnerable than anyone realised. Most of the time, the signs are there, but with Axel . . . no. His mental health deteriorated rapidly in the aftermath, and we had no choice but to medically discharge him for his own safety. It was the right decision, no question.'

'So Axel was there when Curtis Goode died?'

'They were in the same vehicle.'

'Is there a possibility that . . .' Ally hesitates as she thinks of Donna, what she knows and what she believes. 'Could Axel have blamed himself in any way?'

By which I mean, could Donna have blamed him?

There's a moment of silence on the line, where all Ally can hear is the drone of a nearby bumblebee. Instinctively, this time she knows that the quiet is Paul thinking, rather than a break in signal. She waits. She can see Robbie making his way up the lawn, a pair of shears in his hand. He doesn't see her; she's too much in the shade.

Does Robbie know that Donna knew Axel?

'Soldiers are trained for high-stress situations,' says Paul, 'but how a soldier interprets and processes a traumatic situation . . .' He stops. 'Until you've been in it, you can't know. You're never prepared. Curtis Goode was killed instantly. There was nothing any of the lads could have done to stop it. That's a fact.'

The contained emotion in Paul's voice moves her. And beneath the magnolia tree, in a Cornish garden, Ally tries to imagine what any of it would have been like. And she draws a blank, an absolute blank.

'But if you want my personal view, part of Axel died that day too. If we're talking about blame, well, where do we stop? Because it's a hell of a lot more far-reaching, once you start down that road.'

Ally looks towards the house, where Robbie is heading. The green and red leaves of the Virginia creeper; the shimmering grey stone; the lines of leaded windows holding the light of the day. She sees Robbie reach the corner – then stop. Has he caught sight of the police car? Of Donna? For half a moment it's as if he's frozen, then he turns abruptly and goes back the way he came.

'Did Axel ever talk about his childhood?' Ally asks quietly, watching Robbie retreat.

'I gather he and his mother were very close. She died not long after that tour, so he was dealing with a lot of different things.'

'What kind of a soldier was he?'

And her questions are quick-fire now, not wanting Paul Fairfax to leave the line, because he knew Axel, he genuinely knew him. And he was there at what was almost certainly the turning point in Axel's life.

'Axel was a good soldier. But underneath, he was just a boy. A boy playing with toys and he loved it. He absolutely loved it. But then the game changed. It changed when we got to Helmand, and it changed every day we were there and it sure as hell changed the day Curtis Goode died.'

Ally is quiet. In the garden, the bee bumps the rosemary. The magnolia sparkles.

'At the end of the tour we did the usual. Took the lads to Cyprus, decompressed, everyone had their leave. A number of them went to Curtis's funeral. He was killed so close to the end of the tour, it was possible. It . . . isn't always possible. Then it was back to barracks. Back to routine. But Axel was struggling.'

Paul pauses.

'It was the cleaner who found him. He was in the gym. Thought it would be quiet that time of evening, I suppose. He was trying to hang himself, Ally. Look, I'm very sorry to hear that Axel's just died, but honestly? The state he was in when he left the army, I'm amazed he even made it that far.'

44

Jayden watches the police car pass quietly back through the gates and disappear down the driveway. Thanks to the timing of Donna's arrival, it's gone as quickly as it came. He turns back to the Greys.

Elspeth has a look of confusion on her face. Lucas's expression is closed as a fortress. Casey, meanwhile, is still indoors, oblivious.

There's a beat of silence, then Lucas says, 'Now, Jayden, are you going to say you've got no idea about all that either?'

'Axel was with Donna's brother in Afghanistan,' he says. 'In the same section.'

A simple, clear fact. And more or less what Elspeth told them from the off.

'But I told you that,' says Elspeth, as if on cue. 'And Donna told me. There was nothing to hide.' She looks from Jayden to Lucas and back again. 'Plus, we all gave statements, including Donna. Why would the police take her away? It doesn't make sense.'

'Oh, darling,' says Lucas, 'you sound impossibly naive. They've obviously got reason to believe there's something she's not telling them. I mean, we don't actually *know* her, do we?'

'She tended to your dying father, Lucas. And it was me who interviewed her. She had excellent references. So we *do* know her. To say that we don't makes us sound . . .'

'Less than dutiful?' Lucas snorts. 'God forbid. It's a good thing my father's not here to witness this mess. But then again, we've got him to thank for most of it.'

'Where's Casey?' says Jayden suddenly.

'I expect she's still deep in that photo album,' says Elspeth.

'Or she's busy scoping out the house,' adds Lucas.

'Oh, for God's sake.'

And Elspeth gives a tiny, pony-like stamp of her foot as she says it. Jayden almost laughs. *Do people really, actually do that?* But he has no sympathy: Elspeth married the guy.

'I'm glad Casey didn't see the police just now,' says Elspeth. 'She doesn't need any extra drama, especially not in her condition.' She pushes a hand to her forehead. 'I can't actually bear to think of Donna being involved in some way. We placed so much trust in her. The *ultimate* trust for a family, and—'

'Perhaps Donna thought she deserved something a little more than just our gratitude after my father passed,' says Lucas with a shrug. 'After all, she was the one by his side day and night. Oh, Ellie, don't look so worried. I'm sure whatever inconsistencies the police think they've found, it'll all be sorted out by sundown. Whatever their connection, it wasn't Donna who sent Axel off in that kayak of ours, was it? He made his own bad decisions.'

And Jayden notes how Donna leaving with the police seems to have fortified Lucas, rather than distressed him. Beside him, Elspeth looks less certain.

'Casey said just now that Axel was his own worst enemy. She said it with affection, but . . . you're right.' Elspeth sighs. 'Jayden, where's Ally gone off to? Do please both come and have that coffee. I'll make a fresh pot.'

Jayden hesitates, thinking about their next move. Seeing the police pick up Donna means that he was right about the earring, and her prints must have been found in Axel's van. If Skinner and

Mullins were looking for signs of guilt, the way Donna stopped as soon as she saw the police car will have ticked all their boxes.

Is this job done?

Even if it is, doing right by Axel also means doing right by Casey and the baby. And right now, that means joining the Greys inside, because however welcoming Elspeth might be trying to be, Casey's appearance has ignited an animosity in Lucas. It was just a flicker before – but is now fully blazing.

'Darling, Jayden and I will be in in a moment,' says Lucas. 'We're just having a brief chat.'

Elspeth narrows her eyes. 'Alright,' she says, 'but it's going to look rude if you stay out here, Lucas. Casey's come a long way, and—'

'Yes,' says Lucas, holding up his hand as if he's stopping traffic. 'In her condition, et cetera. I'm well aware, darling.'

Elspeth glances to Jayden, mouths, *Sorry*. Then she taps back up the steps in her delicate heels.

Lucas appears to think for a moment before he speaks.

'My wife seems to think it's necessary to keep apologising for me. Does yours do that?'

Jayden shrugs. He could fake it to build a bridge with the guy, but he's not in the mood.

'No, I suppose not. The problem with Elspeth,' Lucas goes on, 'is she doesn't handle disappointment very well. If Donna Goode hasn't been entirely straight with us, then she'll take that hard.'

'Most people don't like being let down by the people they trust.'

Lucas waves his hand dismissively. 'Ellie trained to be an actress, you know, Shakespeare mostly, but she threw in the towel when she didn't get, shock horror, every single part she ever went for. If you ask me, that's the downside of having a childhood where everything is handed to you on a plate. If it doesn't then follow in all aspects of your adult life, it's rather a brutal reality check.'

It's not like what Lucas is saying doesn't make sense, but it's as if all the trappings of his wealth loom larger in this moment. His expensive leather shoes. The watch that glints at his wrist. His gleaming BMW. And the house itself, as big as a palace, rising up behind him. Okay, so it's not in Lucas's name, it might never be now, but it'll always be his childhood home. It'll always be the start he had in life.

'Do you include yourself in that?' asks Jayden.

There's a pulsing at Lucas's jaw. His eyes are hard as rocks.

'You're making presumptions again,' he says. 'Of course you are. You always would.'

'And what does that mean?'

Lucas holds his eye. 'I don't expect you like people like us. Do you?'

'I try not to generalise,' says Jayden, holding it right back.

Lucas gives a shout of laughter. 'Axel, on the other hand, well, I expect you've all the time in the world for him, based on nothing but his inadequacies as a functioning human being.'

Jayden slowly shakes his head.

'What?' says Lucas. 'Say it's not true.'

'Just . . . What you said about welcoming Axel to this house. I can't see it.'

Lucas steps closer to him, so close Jayden can smell the bitter tang of old coffee on his breath. See the bloodshot flecks in his right eye; the tiny, crescent-shaped scar on his chin.

'I found him, Jayden. I brought him here. It was me. All me.' Lucas's teeth are gritted. 'And I did it for my father.'

Donna lied to them. Donna has gone with the police. Donna had a tangible, and emotional, connection to Axel.

But so has Lucas.

45

As Ally rounds the corner, her call with Major Paul Fairfax finished, there's a strange sort of silence outside the house. The police have gone, and Donna, presumably, has gone with them. It's as if Ally's arriving late to a party. The big front door stands just ajar, stoppered with a tall metal hare; its ears are pricked and its nose held high. She supposes it's in place for her benefit.

Ally's discovery – courtesy of Axel and Curtis's platoon commander – that Donna had not only met Axel before but may even have been romantically involved with him for a period of time, is like a piece of treasure that she holds tightly in her hand. She can't wait to tell Jayden. But if Donna has been arrested, perhaps the police already know. Or certainly the information will come out in the interview room.

It's an investigative step forward, but maybe only to reach the point where the police are already.

With that thought, a different problem – the reason they're here – reasserts itself: Casey's emotions, the Greys' reactions. And Pippa. Pippa, who hasn't responded to any of Ally's messages or calls all day long, which troubles Ally, regardless of Donna's arrest. Jayden said they should go out to the island, and Ally wants to do that now more than ever. It has to be before the light fades, or she doubts Trent will run the boat.

Ally pushes open the door and treads into the vast hallway. She takes in the chandelier, the sweeping staircase, the cloying scent of lilies from the elaborate table display. As she passes by, a huge flower-head brushes against her arm – hungry as a Venus flytrap – leaving a rust-brown stain on her jacket. She brushes at it, listening for voices. There's a murmur coming from the kitchen, and she makes her way in that direction. A grandfather clock, at the foot of the stairs, chimes five o'clock. They have an hour before sunset.

'Ally.'

Jayden's face lights up as he sees her, and her first thought is: *what's happened?*

They appear convivial enough. In the middle of the kitchen there's a large island, and Casey sits on a stool, with tea and biscuits and an open photo album. Elspeth is beside her. Jayden leans against the counter, his ankles crossed. Lucas is by the window, lost in his phone.

'He had such a cheeky smile as a boy,' Elspeth's saying to Casey. Then, noticing her: 'Oh, there you are, Ally. Hello.'

Jayden stands upright. 'Elspeth's asked Casey to stay.'

Ally's faintly surprised that that's the first thing he says, not 'Donna Goode has been arrested'. And then surprise over the statement itself sinks in.

Casey looks up from the album. 'I just said the B&B is a bit grim. I wasn't fishing.'

'We'd really love to have you,' says Elspeth. 'Wouldn't we, Lucas? It's the right thing to do. Edward would have insisted on it.'

Lucas looks up from his phone. 'Yes, he probably would have, and once my father makes his mind up . . . Well.'

There's an edge to his voice, but it doesn't seem to bother Casey. She looks, thinks Ally, quite at home.

'We did make up a room for Axel,' says Elspeth, 'only he said he preferred his van. It has a lovely view of the rose garden, Casey.'

Casey drops her head. 'Thank you,' she says quietly.

'What about . . . Donna?' says Jayden, eyeing Elspeth.

'Donna? Oh. Well, I mean, I hadn't thought . . .' And Elspeth suddenly looks worried.

'It'll make for quite the party,' says Lucas.

Elspeth shoots her husband a look, then quickly rights herself. 'I mean, if everything's fine with Donna, then she'll be back here, won't she? Which means . . . everything's fine. But if it's not fine, then . . . she won't be back, will she?'

Despite the veiled language, Elspeth's logic holds. But Jayden's still frowning.

'And what about your stuff?' he says to Casey, his voice still full of hesitation.

'I've got everything I need.'

Casey gives a little one-shouldered shrug, not seeming to pick up on the Donna point. Does that mean she didn't see her arrest?

'I always carry my toothbrush, passport and a spare pair of pants. Since I was a teen. You never know, right?'

Elspeth laughs. 'A modern-day Girl Scout. Ally, I'm going to call Martin, Edward's solicitor. See if he can come up and meet Casey. There's no point delaying, is there? Of course, office hours are as good as over, but I should think we could tempt him after-hours if we open a bottle from Edward's cellar. Did you pair want to stay for dinner too?'

Ally's about to respond when Casey yawns; a big, full-bodied yawn. 'Sorry,' she says, 'I'm done in.'

'Of course you are. It's how many hours by train from Bristol? Five? Not to mention the emotional load. It's a huge amount to deal with, Casey. And in your condition, you need to take extra care of yourself.'

'You really shouldn't have come,' says Lucas, adopting the same consoling voice, 'but of course we all know why you did.'

Jayden pushes off the counter, his face clouded; he's taking Lucas's words quite differently.

'Why don't you have a lie-down now?' says Elspeth, her hand on Casey's shoulder. 'Even if Martin comes more or less directly, I imagine he'll be a good forty minutes. We've plenty to discuss with him anyway. Ally, Jayden, what do you think? Did you want to stay on?'

Before Jayden can answer, Ally says to him, 'Jayden, I was hoping we could see Pippa too. Plus . . .'

I really want to talk to you about Donna and Axel.

He checks his watch. 'Oh yeah. Right. We said that, didn't we.'

'You guys don't need to stay,' says Casey. 'It was really nice of you to bring me up here.'

'You're sure?' says Jayden. 'Because I could always stick around, and Ally could—'

'No, really. We can catch up in the morning. I'm so exhausted I just want to crash.'

'Oh, I think you'll want to meet Martin, Casey,' says Elspeth. And she smiles in Ally and Jayden's direction. 'He always has interesting things to say.'

Part of Ally would like to be here when Edward's solicitor tells Casey the news, but the other part of her very much wants to see Pippa. Because, despite everything with Donna, Ally feels uneasy about Pippa, and Lone Island, and whatever line of enquiry the police are pursuing.

'Elspeth,' says Ally, 'have you heard back from Pippa yet? Your tea invitation.'

Casey chews the end of her thumb, one hand resting on her bump. 'I'd like to meet Pippa,' she says quietly. 'I'd like to thank her. For finding Axel.'

'I still haven't heard a peep,' says Elspeth. 'I'd say it was a little rude, but then there's no playbook for this situation, is there? Not for any of us.'

46

Jayden takes a last glance back before they turn into the lane. In the rear-view mirror, Porthmerrin is like Jazzy's doll's house. Only somehow more lifeless.

'I don't like it, Al.'

'Which part?'

'Take your pick. Leaving Casey there while Lucas clearly isn't happy. Or when Donna could walk back in at any moment.'

'But what Elspeth said about Donna was right, wasn't it? If the police hold her, then . . .'

'Then she won't cross paths with Casey. Yeah. To a degree. But Donna wasn't arrested. She went in voluntarily. She could be under suspicion but still come back to the house.'

'You mean she wasn't in handcuffs?'

'No. But she'll likely be interviewed under caution. Depends what they have.'

And we all saw her face.

And the murder question aside, Lucas in a foul mood doesn't make for good company. But Casey seemed oblivious to the undercurrent – or just didn't care. Maybe that's how she rolled in her relationship with Axel, thinks Jayden – just focusing on the good. Casey's initial suspicion about Axel's death coming so soon after the news of the will, and Donna's army link, soon turned into almost an acceptance that his death was accidental. That he attracted that sort of 'bad luck'. Was that a self-protecting mechanism, or a genuine innocence?

'I do think it's natural for Lucas's reaction to be complex,' says Ally.

So Jayden tells Ally how, when it was just the two of them, Lucas turned aggressive.

'Not physically, but he thought we were goading him for a reaction, bringing Casey here. Now why would that be his default thought? It's the contrast, Al. He made out he had no problem at all with his dad leaving the house to Axel. Once Axel was dead, obviously. But now that it looks like it could go to Axel's heir . . . he loses it. If Elspeth had seen how Lucas let his guard down with me, I don't think she'd be handing out overnight invitations so quickly.'

'Or getting the solicitor up there,' says Ally. 'But then perhaps she knows exactly how to handle him. Nip it in the bud. I don't think Lucas is involved. And . . . I don't think Donna will be back tonight.'

She says it with utter conviction. Jayden turns, his eyebrows shooting high.

'Something in that phone call you took?'

'Jayden, Donna not only knew Axel, but years back she was perhaps even romantically involved with him.'

As Ally relays everything that Paul Fairfax told her, Jayden pictures the two young soldiers, shining in their uniforms, and Curtis's sister falling for Axel's charms. Then, not much more than a year later, Curtis dies – and Axel doesn't show up at his funeral. Which, given the connection, could dial up the emotional intensity big-time.

And it begs the question, was Donna's appointment as nurse at Porthmerrin House really a coincidence?

The sea is intermittently in view now, above the hedgerows. Lone Island a dark smudge as the light fades around it, heavy clouds moving in.

'Do you think the police already know about Donna and Axel?' asks Ally.

'Well, it only took one phone call for you to find out, Al. But then we know they're not digging like we're digging. Or they weren't before, anyway. Depending on what comes out in the interview, they could be looking to build a case – and it'd be a massive part of it. What about Robbie? He won't know about Donna going off with the police, will he?'

'I think he does. I saw him when I was on the phone to Paul, and I was only half concentrating. But I'm sure he saw Donna with them. At least, something stopped Robbie in his tracks and made him turn in the opposite direction.'

The buzzing of a phone fills the car, and Ally says, 'Oh, it's Trent.'

Following up on her message about a lift to the island, no doubt. Jayden eyes the approaching ocean. From here, it looks a little wild. He tunes in to Ally's phone conversation, aware, suddenly, of a change in her tone.

'But it's not that bad, is it?' she says. Then, 'You really won't?'

Jayden glances to her, and her face is fraught. 'What if we paid you double? We're worried, you see. We haven't heard from Pippa, and—'

She stops talking as Trent offers a fulsome reply. But it doesn't look good for getting to the island.

'When was that?' says Ally. 'And she didn't say what she was doing? Did she have luggage with her?'

Pippa.

A bad feeling grows in Jayden. He pulls into the turning that leads to the landing stage. Pointless, really, as they've got the message: there will be no trip to the island. As the lane ends and Jayden sees Trent's boat pulled up far out of the water, he gets why. The sea hurls itself at the shore, spray flying high, spattering their windshield even at this distance.

'He won't make the crossing,' says Ally. 'But Pippa's not there anyway. She came to the mainland at lunchtime, and he hasn't heard from her since.'

They sit in silence for a moment. Out beyond the island, the sky has darkened; clouds as black as tar crowd the horizon.

'I'm worried, Jayden,' says Ally. 'Why's she ignoring us?'

'Yeah, I'm worried too,' says Jayden. *For at least five different reasons.* 'I want to know what's going on in that interview room with Donna, but that door's closed. You know what we do have, though? The flintlock pistol. We're the only ones who've made that connection. Let's do something with that.'

'*Possible* connection. But if it is from Edward's collection, there's a chance Donna could have taken it, isn't there?'

Jayden checks his watch. 'When there's nothing to be done, do something, right? How about we try and catch Penzance's finest antiques dealers, before they shut up shop for the day? There can't be that many.'

'See if anyone recognises Gus's pirate gun?'

'And can trace it to Edward Grey. It's a long shot but . . . it also kind of isn't, you know?'

Not an argument that would stand up in court, but still. And Ally is already tapping on her phone. Jayden knows she'll be looking for signs of weaponry specialism, blue vans, dogs. Breadcrumbs, but maybe, just maybe, the trail will lead somewhere interesting.

47

Mullins and Skinner sit across the table from Donna Goode. Her curly blond hair gives her an angelic look, and her wide blue eyes are all innocence. But the woman lied in her statement. Is she silly enough to lie to them now too?

'I'm sorry,' she says. 'I'm so, so sorry.'

And then she starts to cry. Big wet tears, fat as dewdrops, rolling down her cheeks. Mullins doesn't know where to put himself. Some people look ugly when they cry – people like himself, for instance – but Donna Goode is not one of them.

'It's alright,' says Skinner, sounding almost paternal. 'Just take your time.'

He produces a box of tissues and slides it across the table to her.

'Thank you,' she says quietly, and the detective sergeant nods in response.

Mullins was getting somewhere earlier when he thought that Skinner's defeated mood these past couple of days might be something to do with his ex-wife. But exactly what, he doesn't know. Mullins wasn't going to push it, and Skinner's never been one for a heart-to-heart. That said, Skinner did ask Mullins what he was up to this evening – was that the detective sergeant angling for a pint? Hardly. If Mullins's boss wanted to share a social drink with him – and pigs might fly – then he wouldn't tiptoe, he'd make it an order. And, as it happens, Mullins already has plans.

Mullins is going to a dub night in Penzance.

He saw the flyer in Hang Ten and Saffron said her housemate was DJing. *You should come, Mullins!* And before he knew it, Mullins was telling her he was in. He could have done without Hippy-Dippy's *Yay, I promised Josie I'd drum up numbers, she's worried it'll be dead* – but still.

Note to self: google what 'dub' is.

Second note to self: iron a shirt.

'I did go to Axel's van,' she says. 'But he was fine, absolutely fine, when I left.'

'What time was this?' asks Skinner.

Donna dabs a tissue at her eyes. 'Actually, no, that's a lie. He wasn't fine. He wasn't fine at all.'

Mullins has heard his fair share of interview room confessions, but is it really going to be this easy? All on account of that little silver earring that Ally and Jayden found by sticking their noses in. Again.

Fair play to them. Again.

'I couldn't not talk about Curtis,' she says. 'And I couldn't just lie about how hurt I was when Axel just ghosted me.'

'He ghosted you?' says Mullins.

And in one big whoosh, Donna starts talking about a place called Catterick. Visiting for the weekend, nights out in the bar where all the squaddies went. Meeting Curtis's friend, a brown-eyed, buzz-cut boy called Axel. Skinny as a rope. A laugh that bubbled up out of nowhere. A gentler voice than she'd expected.

'He was gentle in every way,' says Donna.

And then her eyes say the rest.

Skinner leans forward in his seat. 'Are you saying you were in a romantic relationship with Axel Marks, Donna?'

'Not really.'

'I'm going to need you to be more specific. Because so far, your lack of specificity has wasted significant time and resource.'

Donna shakes her head, and those curls of hers bounce. 'A few . . . kisses. Then one . . . night. I knew it wouldn't go anywhere. I didn't want to be with a soldier. Having a brother for one was bad enough. It meant feeling on edge, all the time, and . . . I didn't want that to be my whole life. And anyway, Axel was a free spirit. Not the type to be pinned down. I knew that too. He . . .' She sucks in a breath. 'Oh, what do I actually know? Because the way he was after Curtis . . . I never would have squared that with the Axel that I met.'

'Prior to the last few days at Porthmerrin, when was the last time you had any contact with Axel?' says Skinner.

'June 2012. After Curtis died, I messaged him. And he just ignored me. I asked him to the funeral, I kept reaching out, and . . . nothing. I got nothing. At the time, it felt like he didn't care. And I got in this weird way of thinking – I thought, if this is supposed to be the soldier by Curtis's side, looking out for him, and he doesn't even care, what hope did Curtis have? I know it wasn't Axel's fault that my brother died. I know that Axel will have done his best by him, the others in his section told me clear and true. But . . . it doesn't matter. It didn't matter. I was hurt. And somehow . . . my grief for Curtis got tangled up with my anger at Axel. That he could just walk away like that. Not so much walk away from me, but from Curtis.'

She drops her head, and her curls fall in front of her face.

'But I guess from me too.'

'You know he was medically discharged?' says Skinner carefully. 'He was only nineteen. On the cusp of twenty.'

'I know. I know he was messed up. But . . . I suppose I was messed up by Curtis dying too, because that fact didn't seem to matter to me. I wanted Axel to . . . man up. Like, he was this big tough soldier, and he couldn't even summon a bit of basic courtesy.'

'So it's fair to say you had a grudge against him?' says Skinner.

'For quite a while I did. But then . . . Well, it faded. I got some perspective, I suppose. And I needed it. I really did.'

'Did you know Axel was connected to Porthmerrin House when you took the job?' asks Skinner.

'Yes,' says Donna. 'It felt like a mad coincidence, and it almost made me change my mind about wanting to work there. But it was only a really remote connection. Elspeth said he was basically estranged, so I felt okay about it. And I never gave a hint that I even knew Axel, to be honest.'

'Whose idea was it to find Axel, to invite him to Porthmerrin?'

'Edward's.' Donna sighs. Her hands rest on the table in front of her, her thumbs biting at one another. 'Edward told me all about him, and I listened with gritted teeth. I never said I knew him. I guess Elspeth never mentioned the Rifles connection to Edward either. I tried to put Edward off, actually. But then I could see how much it meant to him. Edward asked Lucas to try and find him, because he wanted Lucas to feel involved, he said. Course, we didn't know at that point what Edward was planning with his will, but with Edward so sick, Lucas just seemed really happy to be able to do something for his dad.'

'And how did you feel, knowing you were finally going to come face to face with Axel, after having had such strong feelings towards him?'

Donna tips her chin. 'I'd made my peace with the fact that people deal with trauma, with grief, differently. Axel had had a really tough time of his own, and I wasn't going to judge him for that.'

And Mullins believes her – hook, line and sinker.

But then I also believed her when she said she never went to his van.

'But then, when I was actually with him, I felt different. A lot of stuff came back up.'

There it is. Mullins the mug.

'And he wanted to talk about Curtis. So we just . . . got into it. Went deep. He started to tell me about the day it happened. In minute detail.' She presses her fingers to her eyes. 'I was there, right there, with them in that truck in Helmand. And it was so hard to hear. The way Axel talked about it, it wasn't just facts. It was poetry. Like, the saddest poetry.'

'What about you and him?' says Skinner. 'Did you talk about that too?'

'A bit,' says Donna. 'He was sorry about how he cut me off. He felt bad. But that was nothing compared to Curtis. Not for either of us.'

Is Donna Goode the kind to hold a grudge? Situation like that, Mullins is pretty sure it'd feel like insult to injury. *And the rest.*

'Were you drinking together?' asks Skinner. 'There was an empty bottle of whisky in the van.'

'He offered me some, but I don't drink whisky.'

'Was Axel drunk at that point?'

She nods. 'He was. But not . . . senseless. He was . . . It was like he just went to this other place. He told me that he'd never really talked about what happened that day. I know part of it was seeing me, and me bringing it all up, but I get the feeling as well that with everything with Edward, and learning about his intentions with the will, it was like Axel was sorting through things in his head. As if, in order to accept this good thing, he had to accept the bad too. Does that make sense?'

Mullins nods, and beside him Skinner does the same. Quite honestly, Mullins is hanging on Donna's every word.

'Was Axel happy about the will?' asks Skinner.

'I think it felt too big. He said he didn't want it.'

'He was shocked, then?' says Mullins.

'He was shocked.' Donna heaves a breath. 'Overwhelmed. Anyway, I was there for . . . maybe forty-five minutes. Perhaps an hour. Then I left.'

'And how was he when you left?'

Donna opens her mouth to speak, then closes it again. She takes a long moment to reply.

'I don't think Axel knew how to feel. But then . . .'

Silence hangs in the interview room. Mullins holds his breath. Donna looks to the left.

Does that mean lying? Or is that to the right?

'The next morning,' she says, 'when Lucas said that he was missing, I thought . . . I know exactly what's happened. And if Axel jumped off that cliff after talking to me, that makes it my fault. Doesn't it?'

48

'Ah now, I've already been in touch about this. Absolute mystery.'

The man behind the desk – who, with a slightly damp handshake, introduced himself as Laurence Fentiman – pushes his half-moon glasses on top of his head and looks at the article on Ally's phone. A Yorkshire terrier lies at his feet, a rubber chicken wedged between its paws. A blue van was parked on the kerb outside the shop.

Fentiman Antiquities is their second port of call. The first stop promised much on the face of it – specifically citing antique and ornamental firearms among their wares – but on arrival at the Chapel Street shop it was already closed for the day, metal shutters unequivocally drawn.

'Really?' says Ally. 'Who have you been in touch with?'

And in the low light of the crowded shop, Ally sends Jayden a hopeful look; she's not sure it carries. How anyone could make a detailed appraisal of anything in here is beyond her, but perhaps that's the idea. All manner of imperfections could be hidden in this gloom.

'Eighteenth-century flintlock pistol. Intricate silver and gold finishing. Ivory detailing, as was the fashion then. Sidearm likely carried by a pirate captain. Simply gorgeous. Worth a bob or two as well, of course. And an absolute travesty that it could have been lost at sea.'

Laurence hands the phone back.

'Were you interested in purchasing something similar, then?'

To which Ally shakes her head and repeats her previous question.

'Who have I been in touch with? The customer who bought it from me.' He repositions his glasses; a smile lifts the corner of his mouth. 'I'd recognise it anywhere. And I suppose I was fascinated at how on earth it ended up in the deep blue sea. Fascinated and appalled.'

'Are you able to tell us who that customer was?'

'I'm sorry,' he says, shaking his head. 'Patient confidentiality.'

'Patient confidentiality?' says Jayden.

Laurence laughs lightly, and it sounds like the ringing of the bell.

'I'm joking, of course. But I do exercise discretion when it comes to my customers. That's just good business.'

'Thing is, it might be connected to a murder investigation,' says Jayden.

'Murder?' Laurence's mouth drops and makes a small but perfect 'o'. 'Oh, that's absurd. Any firearms I sell are purely for ornamental purposes. They haven't been fired in more than a hundred years. Two hundred, for goodness' sake.'

'Not used as a weapon,' says Jayden. 'But . . . we're looking for a connection between this artefact and Porthmerrin House.'

'Ah now. I read about the man who drowned, of course. You can't mean that?'

And it strikes Ally that Laurence has shown more concern for the thought of the antiquity being lost at sea than the human being.

'Is Edward Grey one of your customers?' she asks.

'Is Edward Grey one of my customers?' he repeats. He appears to be buying time rather than obstructing. But having to work out how to respond to a simple question is revealing in itself.

Edward Grey is almost certainly one of his customers.

'I've known Edward for many years,' he says.

They wait.

'And yes, very well, he is a much-valued customer.'

'*Was* a much-valued customer,' says Jayden gently.

'What? He hasn't died? Oh, dear me, he has, hasn't he? I knew he was very ill, of course. I met that lovely nurse of his. Ah now, that explains it, then. That explains it.'

And for a moment a strange image drops into Ally's mind: a burial at sea, a sailor's weapon going down with him.

'Nobody answering my call, I mean,' he says. 'As soon as I heard about the find, I tried to get in touch. I was fascinated, I suppose, as to how on earth this treasured object of Edward's could end up washed up on a beach. For a moment I imagined Edward taking to the sea, re-enacting scenes of skulduggery. But of course that was just me being fanciful. Oh dear, Edward. Poor chap.'

'What did you think could have happened?' asks Jayden.

And Ally wonders if he's studiously not mentioning the possibility that Axel Marks – or 'that man who drowned', as Laurence knows him – took it.

'Absolutely no idea,' says Laurence. 'It makes no sense to me whatsoever. The only thing I can think . . .'

He hesitates, takes off his glasses and wipes them carefully on his waistcoat.

'. . . is that a fool of a robber broke into Porthmerrin, didn't realise the value of what they had, and tried to dispose of it. But someone would have reported a robbery, wouldn't they? So you wouldn't be here now, asking me questions, if that were the case.'

He wrinkles his brow then, a new thought appearing to cross his mind.

'Hold on, how did you know to come to me, if Edward is dead?'

And Ally mentions Robbie the gardener.

'Oh, the gardener,' says Laurence. He looks thoughtful for a moment. 'I suppose, if we're looking for a thief, he could be your culprit. He was homeless not so very long ago, you know. Didn't have a penny to his name. Edward gave him a roof and a job. Though if he's paid attention to my visits, as you say he has, then he'll know the pistol was worth something. No, no. It can't be him. Because he wouldn't have tossed it into the sea, would he?'

'What made you say "murder"?' says Ally, once they're a few steps from the shop.

'That line about patient confidentiality,' says Jayden. 'It annoyed me. He only sells a bunch of cracked vases and miserable paintings, right?'

'And immaculate flintlock pistols,' says Ally, with a smile.

She wraps her coat around her. Dusk is creeping in, and the wind is up now; it's a physical presence, pushing and pressing. Once again Pippa darts into her head. They still haven't heard a word. They've paused by an alleyway; there's a faintly sour smell, and broken glass crunches underfoot.

'I wanted to shock him into a response. And it worked. It belongs to Edward Grey. Nailed it, Al.' Jayden shakes his head. 'Gus to the rescue once again. We're going to need to get him on the books.'

Ally smiles. *Good old Gus. He's such a help to her in other directions too, like nipping in to let Fox out on a long day away like this one.*

'I didn't like the way Laurence talked about Robbie Cassidy.'

'Me neither. But Al, it's got me thinking about Robbie. Specifically, Robbie and Donna.'

Robbie and Donna. The thought is like a perfect crescent moon appearing between clouds on a dark night. It's so bright, it's hard to believe it couldn't beam through everything.

'You think Robbie knew about Donna's connection to Axel?'

'They're in a relationship. This old flame suddenly pitches up. Set to inherit everything too.'

Ally thinks of how, when she was on the phone to Paul Fairfax, Robbie stopped at the corner of the house – then abruptly went in the other direction.

'You know how I said I thought Robbie spotted Donna with the police? Jayden, if he cares for her, I'd have expected him to rush in, to try and find out what was happening.'

'And if he was too late, to ask one of us.'

'Unless he already knew.'

'Robbie was keen to set forward the view that it was suicide,' says Jayden. 'Then, when the missing kayak came up, he ran with that theory too. Has he been deliberately shifting attention?'

Ally tries to order her thoughts. 'Are we saying Robbie could have acted without Donna's knowledge? Or that, somehow, they're involved together? Because so far, it's only Donna who we know has lied.'

'You're right. And right now, she could be telling the police everything she knows. Or lying still. Okay, let's just focus back on this pistol, see if we can connect it. When Laurence sees the article, he tries calling Edward, wanting to know how it's ended up in the sea, and gets no reply at the house.'

'Wouldn't a natural next step have been for Laurence to contact the police?' asks Ally. 'To confirm that it's not ancient treasure, and he knows the owner?'

'I guess he thought there was no point. According to the article, the gun was handed to the police by the parents of the boy who found it. Which was sensible, because they weren't to know it couldn't be fired, right?'

'Would the police have made the same connection that we did, do you think?'

'I don't see how,' says Jayden. 'The only reason we ever put antique weapons together with Porthmerrin House is because Lucas said his dad and Axel bonded over his collection, back in the day.'

'And Lucas said it so passingly. Jayden, no one at Porthmerrin can have noticed it's gone, otherwise they would have mentioned it.'

'Along with the missing kayak.'

'Exactly.'

'Unless . . .' Jayden stops. 'Unless someone doesn't want its theft to be noticed.'

'What do you mean?' says Ally.

Jayden rubs the back of his head, and his razor-short hair crackles.

'Not sure.'

'A second ago, you said "they weren't to know it couldn't be fired",' says Ally.

'Yeah, I was talking about the people who found it washed up on the beach.'

'What if Axel didn't know it couldn't be fired?'

'And he took it as a weapon? It's possible. But as a former soldier? I doubt it. Maybe he just admired it as a kid. Maybe he'd always wanted it and took it as a memento.'

They're back at the car now. Before long they'll be back in Porthpella, and back in the thinking room, where they can put their thoughts up on the board and try to make sense of them. But there's a question that's bothering Ally.

'Just because it was found in the sea,' she says, 'doesn't mean it went in with Axel, does it?'

Jayden's hand pauses on the car door.

'Keep talking, Al.'

'Well, what if someone else took it and brandished it like a weapon? What if someone threatened Axel with it on the clifftop, and that's why he fell?'

49

As they drive back towards Porthpella, Jayden turns the facts over in his mind. Donna lied about being in Axel's van and knowing him. Robbie appeared to see Donna leave with the police and reacted strangely – or, more accurately, *didn't* react. Lucas has much more complex feelings about Axel's place in the will than he first made out – and he one hundred per cent has a short fuse. And the flintlock pistol, washed up on a beach between Porthmerrin and Porthpella, belongs to Edward Grey; no one at the house has reported it missing – unlike the kayak.

'I had a message from Casey,' he says to Ally. 'She said all's good. She's being made to feel welcome. She didn't mention the solicitor.'

'So presumably she doesn't know about the clause about Axel's descendants in the will yet?'

'No.'

'I haven't tried Pippa again,' says Ally. 'I don't want her to think we're hounding her, but . . . she's disappeared on us, Jayden. And she's not responding to Elspeth either, when she seemed so keen to have contact with the Greys before. Should we mention it to the police?'

'If they're treating her as a suspect, or at least a person of interest, they'll be keeping tabs on her themselves,' says Jayden.

'Oh gosh,' says Ally, 'what if they have arrested her and that's why we haven't heard a word?'

'We talked about that, Al, and it's like we said: there's no way Mullins would have missed the chance to tell us he had our client in the clink.'

But Ally's right, it's strange. It's *all* strange. And now they've got an antique gun in the mix too. Jayden drums his fingers on the steering wheel. There's a lot of players on the pitch. A lot of moving parts.

'What about if our tip-off led to a confession?' asks Ally. 'I'm talking about the police. And Donna. And them telling us.'

'If they had this solved, they'd say. But either way, soon as we land at The Shell House, I'm tapping up Mullins. Man, I need a coffee. Al, shall I let Cat know it's going to be a late night?'

'Can you do a late night?'

'Sure. Cat knows we're deep in a case.'

Cat messaged earlier to say sorry for, as she put it, 'being stupid about Benji's party'. Her new suggestion is that they have two: One for friends, one for family! Which means double to do, so once this case is over, can I give you a list?

Jayden told her she could give him two lists.

It's only early evening, but over the water night has fallen. The sea, to their left, is a band of black, distinguishable only by the flecked lights of far-off boats. Presumably larger craft that can handle the swell, unlike Trent Simms's boat. Lone Island lies in total darkness.

'I'm thinking more about Donna and Robbie,' says Ally.

'Go on,' says Jayden.

'What if they both went to his van, then confronted him on the clifftop. Then threatened him with the pistol.'

'What's their motivation, if they're in it together?'

'Donna is emotional. However illogical, she blames Axel for her brother's death. And Robbie . . . Robbie's in love with her.'

Okay. Jayden thinks it through.

'Or it was Donna who confronted Axel, but Robbie knows the truth,' says Ally. 'Perhaps Robbie made her dispose of the weapon.'

Weapon. Jayden can practically hear Laurence Fentiman correcting him: *it's strictly ornamental.* But on a dark night, if someone's waving a gun in your face, you're not to know that, are you?

'Or Robbie acted without Donna,' says Jayden. 'As far as he's concerned, Axel's all-round bad news. Former lover of his girlfriend, suddenly back on the scene. Set to get very rich. He wants him gone.'

What bothers Jayden is that Axel was a trained soldier. While the man might have had complex feelings about his time in the army, a gun wouldn't have been likely to provoke such instant fear in him as with a civilian, perhaps. *Unless I'm underestimating how bad his mental health was.* So . . . what if the pistol was used in a different way?

'He could have been hit over the head with it, right?' says Jayden. 'Someone could have come up behind him, struck him, then pushed him off the cliff. Then thrown the pistol in after him.'

'Wouldn't that have shown up in the post-mortem?' asks Ally.

'With all his other injuries, a single strike might not. But let's push it with Mullins and Skinner. Get them to raise it with the pathologist, this time knowing exactly what they're looking for. Now we know categorically . . .' He hesitates. '. . . *potentially* . . . that a specific weapon was involved.'

After hours and hours at sea, it'll be too much to hope for fingerprints on the pistol, but maybe it could be matched to a specific laceration or impact. Another piece of the puzzle.

'In fact, I'm thinking now's the time to update the police on a few things. They might be getting something from Donna, but they need to take a closer look at Robbie too. And they need to know Casey and Axel's unborn child is potentially in line to inherit.'

'It sounds like you're passing the case, Jayden,' says Ally, with an arch smile.

'As if.'

'It's still possible, of course, that it was Axel who took the pistol, along with the kayak.'

'Yeah, it is. That's why we need the pathologist to take another look.'

As they crest the hill, the pinprick lights of Porthpella appear in the distance. Jayden thinks of those footsteps in the dark, as he walked home from The Wreckers last night. Could that have been Robbie? Already worried, perhaps, that they were asking too many questions? The gardener could easily have followed them from Porthmerrin to Porthpella, then waited for him to leave the pub. Did he think Jayden would make a phone call on the walk back, debriefing Ally after seeing Mullins? Did he just want to know what they knew – or something more sinister?

But then it could have been Lucas.

And the thing about the pistol? It feels personal. Of all the things to brandish as a weapon – kitchen knives, clifftop rocks, any number of garden tools – an antique firearm isn't an obvious choice. But maybe it was a deliberate one.

'Al, Lucas hated how Axel and his dad bonded over the weapons collection. We both sensed that, before we knew any significance. And he hated that Axel got to be the hero by joining the army. I'm wondering if the flintlock pistol was chosen because of what it represented on a more emotional level. And if that's the case, it'd mean the most to Lucas.'

They make the turning for the dunes. Their headlights pick out the soft alps of sand, the tufted marram grass. The road narrows to a lane, then a track. They pass All Swell, Gus's place, where there's the faint glow of a lamp at the window. Sea Dream – the immense glass-fronted house that's seen its fair share of action since it was built – lies in darkness; another luxury rental sitting empty.

'Or to Axel,' says Ally.

'But if Axel took it, then what? Lucas and the inheritance factor is huge. And it's been there since the beginning.'

They pull up at The Shell House, headlights playing across Ally's giant palm. Jayden's itching to get into the thinking room. Lots of coffee. And a no doubt punchy chat with Mullins.

'I agree. But it's also so obvious.'

'Sometimes it is the most obvious thing,' says Jayden. 'Occam's razor, the sequel. Look, we're presuming that Elspeth and Lucas were each other's alibi that night. At the moment, Elspeth doesn't have any reason to suspect her husband, but if we started asking questions, it'd be interesting to see how she'd react, right? Elspeth didn't like the thought of being let down by Donna. She almost took it personally. If we're going to point the finger at Lucas, I think Elspeth will either say we're crazy or go completely to pieces.'

'And either response could be revealing, couldn't it?'

'Exactly. So, while the police follow the Donna line – and the Robbie one, when we give it to them – how about we turn our focus to Lucas. But go in via Elspeth. Plan?'

He holds out his fist, and in the dark of the car they bump knuckles.

'Plan,' says Ally. 'But Jayden, if there's anything in this, it puts Casey in danger, doesn't it?'

Casey and the baby.

50

'Salad?'

Elspeth proffers a bowl of spiky-looking green and purple leaves, scooping a generous serving when Casey nods. Her plate is heaped with spaghetti that doesn't look up to much, but she's already snuck a forkful and it's delicious: olive oil that actually tastes of olives, slabs of Parmesan, garlic and chilli. Part of Casey is guilty that she has an appetite at all, but it's the baby. The baby makes her ravenous.

Our baby.

Is it a consolation to believe that Axel was happy here, for a time? Perhaps not when he first drove through those wide gates, but afterwards, when the dying Edward told him his intentions. *He was flabbergasted*, said Elspeth. *I've never seen a smile so wide.* And as Casey's eyes filled, Elspeth's did too: call and response. Casey didn't expect to like anyone connected to Porthmerrin, but maybe she needs to learn to park her preconceptions.

Casey talked to Elspeth about Axel earlier, and how the two of them met. Her tongue ran away with her. Skate sessions. Movie nights. Tubs of ice cream. *Axel really loved ice cream. Mint choc chip.* Then, *Sorry, why am I even telling you that?* But Elspeth was a good listener. *I can tell how much you cared about him*, she said, a sad smile on her face. To which Casey replied that she wished she'd had the strength to stick by him, because that would have been really caring. Because that's the basic truth of it, isn't it? And even Elspeth didn't have an answer to that.

'It's a nightmare cooking in someone else's kitchen,' says Elspeth now, slipping off her apron. 'Edward's tastes were always very simple, even when he was in full health. He was a meat-and-two-veg man, wasn't he, Lucas?'

Lucas grunts. 'Famously so.'

They're sitting at the kitchen island, perched on stools. Casey said she was comfortable when Elspeth asked, but she was mostly being polite. She'd kill for a stack of cushions, her feet up on a sofa. But a strange sensation has come over her since walking into this house, one she doesn't even really understand herself. Casey wants to please her hosts. No, correction: she wants to please Elspeth – because the woman's treating Casey as if she's come home, and for a moment, Casey lets her imagination drift to if Axel had lived, if he really had gone on to inherit the house, if he'd turned it all around and the three of them had lived here in harmony; their child, having the run of the gardens as Axel had once – not as the housekeeper's son, but as the little lord of the manor. But it's all too crazy to imagine. Even if Axel had lived, it would still be too crazy to imagine.

Casey could tell that Ally and Jayden didn't really want her to stay here, but she wanted to see it all for herself. *Really* see it. And maybe she's just tired and sad – bone-achingly tired and sad – but being at Porthmerrin makes her feel closer to Axel. Closer to the child he was before loss and conflict destroyed him. Whatever mistakes Edward made, those photos in his albums show a real fondness. Axel with his muddy knees and shining eyes, and laughing, always laughing. He had still been that boy, somewhere far inside. Occasionally Casey had caught flashes, and it was like lightning in a bottle.

'Darling,' says Elspeth, as Lucas slurps his spaghetti, noisy as a pre-schooler. 'You're forgetting your manners.'

'Am I not at home?' he says.

Casey twirls the pasta on to her fork and watches him from beneath her fringe. She was preset to dislike Lucas but he's a lot less of a force than she imagined. All mouth and no trousers, as her mum would say. There's something pitiful about the slope of his shoulders, the dip of his head, the heavy bags beneath his eyes. He looks like he's carrying the weight of the world.

Well, his dad did just die.

'Yes, dear, you are at home,' says Elspeth, patting her husband's arm but not meeting his eye. 'And of course Donna Goode . . . isn't. Quite honestly, I can hardly believe it.'

'Ridiculous charade,' says Lucas. 'I don't know what the police are thinking.'

'I want to say "poor thing", but . . . what if it's not a charade?'

'It's a charade,' says Lucas, with bullish confidence. 'Trust me.'

'Casey, it doesn't upset you, does it? Us talking about Donna, and, um . . .'

'And Axel?' She shakes her head. 'No. Not really.'

The truth is, Casey feels like a sponge which is so soaked through it can't take on anything more. So, what, this nurse of Edward's, this person whose brother knew Axel, has gone off with the police? Well, Casey is full, sodden; she has no reaction left to give. And maybe that's because deep down the thought remains: *Axel was unlucky. Axel just fell. Oh, Axel.*

'Because we can change the subject,' says Elspeth, 'change it entirely, and talk about something very polite and English, like . . . the weather.'

Casey gives a slow smile. 'The truth is, with Axel, I've already felt pretty much every emotion there is to feel. When he was alive too.'

She stops herself. It feels like a betrayal.

'He wasn't always easy?' asks Elspeth.

He could be. Easy like a Sunday morning, and they had a few of them. Rolling over in bed, his warm back, his skin that smelt like hazelnuts. The way he held her, and she felt like she was in the safest place in the world, wrapped in those long arms. He'd make her triangles of toast and, once, a bunch of daisies on a tea tray, picked from the pavement outside. But then chaos blew in, chaos like the most unwanted of guests, and in those moments the Axel that Casey knew disappeared. She watched a zombie movie once, full of the possessed, and she thought that was Axel: eyes glazed, stopping at nothing. He tried to explain it to her once: *It's like someone shows me a brick wall and says go on, run at it, run at it full pelt, and so I do, again and again and again, until the pain gets so much I can't feel it anymore.*

'Not always, no,' she says quietly.

'It was over between you, wasn't it?' says Lucas. 'Long over.'

Casey flinches. 'Is that what he said?'

And she regrets the question as soon as it's out of her mouth. She doesn't need to ask this man about her own relationship. Even if she didn't hear from Axel for two months. Even if. She knows what they had together. But she's also wise enough to know that any thoughts of what they could have had together were nothing but whispers of smoke. Coming to Porthmerrin House might have been an important step for Axel, but he left with a whisky bottle. He'd turned nothing around.

'Axel said no such thing,' says Elspeth, reassuringly.

'He didn't mention you at all,' says Lucas, setting down his cutlery with a clatter.

And Casey catches the reproachful look that Elspeth sends him.

'Changing the subject,' says Elspeth, 'I keep thinking back to when I interviewed Donna. I helped with the hiring, you see.

But there was nothing, absolutely nothing, that she said to give me alarm.'

'Of course there wasn't,' says Lucas. 'Give enough monkeys typewriters, and one of them will eventually churn out a page of Shakespeare. That army connection is completely bloody random. I'm sorry, Casey, but we all know what happened to Axel.'

'Do we?' she says, carefully setting down her fork. 'Because one day I'm going to have to tell his daughter, and . . .' Her voice breaks. 'I won't know what to say. I won't know what to say about how he died, and I won't know what to say about how he lived either. Because he was full of contradictions.'

Elspeth is by her side, a hand on her arm.

'I think,' says Elspeth, 'that how the living choose to remember the dead is up to us. Isn't it? That's what I told myself when my father died. *We* decide. You tell your little girl whatever you want, Casey. And you believe it too.'

Axel as a hero? Well, he was. He could be. In flashes so neon-bright they lit you up inside and out.

'You don't have to worry about her,' says Elspeth, 'this daughter of yours. Does she, Lucas? She'll be just fine. By the way, Lucas, Martin hasn't got back to me yet. Let me try him again.'

'Take the hint and leave him to his evening,' says Lucas.

Elspeth ignores him. Getting up from the table, she looks to Casey, says, 'We're talking about Edward's solicitor.'

But by the look on Lucas's face, Edward's solicitor is a guest even less welcome than Casey.

After dinner, Casey lies back in the bath, trying her hardest to relax. Elspeth has lit her a scented candle – she says she always travels with scented candles – and the smell is so delicious Casey would bite the air if she could. Vanilla and coconut and burnt sugar. She closes her eyes and tries to bring to mind desert islands and swaying hammocks and the kiss of a sunset. But despite the candle's best efforts, Casey thinks of swirling salt water and crashing rocks and dead drops. Full stops. The terrifying endlessness of it.

The solicitor didn't join them in the end, a fact that seemed to irritate Elspeth but please Lucas. And, actually, it pleased Casey too, because once her hunger was sated her energy ebbed, and suddenly, perching on that high stool felt like balancing on top of a needle.

A bath and bed, said Elspeth. *That's what you need.*

Now, Casey's domed belly sits above the water, and she rests a hand on it: the baby kicks as if in response.

'Hey you,' she says softly. Then, 'This is all so strange, isn't it?'

Casey closes her eyes. She could so easily drift off. She tries to empty her head of everything except the warm and silky water, the feeling of her daughter moving inside her. Not think about the past, or the future, just now: this moment.

This place that was Axel's beginning.

But then a voice from downstairs cuts in, sharp as a knife. Casey snaps her eyes open. She can't catch the words, but it's Lucas. Then Elspeth, quieter. Then Lucas again, louder still. And even with his barely disguised gruffness earlier, the pair of them sound nothing like they did at dinner. The contrast is shocking, as though the curtain between their private and public lives has been ripped and torn away. Part of Casey wants to slip underwater and lose the voices entirely. Part of her wants to tune in to every word, sadistically fascinated.

Casey knows about arguments; she and Axel had some wall-shakers in their time. But never with anyone else so obviously in earshot. Maybe Lucas and Elspeth credit this massive house with thicker walls and floors. Or maybe they just don't care. Casey knows she isn't the kind of person that anyone tries to impress.

The voices ricochet back and forth, bouncing up the stairs and down the hall. Each is giving as good as the other, and Casey's quietly impressed by Elspeth's steel. They go on and on. This isn't a storm passing quickly overhead; it's foul weather that's set in. Relaxation is futile now, Casey thinks. She was stupid to think it was possible for even a second. A tasty spaghetti, a hot bath, and suddenly she can pretend everything is well in the world? *Idiot.*

She grips the sides of the bath and carefully draws herself up and out. Her wet feet leave cartoon-like prints on the mat. Wrapping a towel around herself, she treads to the door and leans in. She still can't make out what they're saying. Holding her breath, she carefully slides the bolt back, then turns the handle. The door just ajar, she peers out into the dark hallway.

All is quiet.

Perhaps it's blown over. And Casey feels a push of relief. She doesn't want more drama here. She wants the bed that Axel should have slept in, the bed he would have been safe in, with the fresh cotton sheets and the view of the rose garden.

Or is it that they've heard me?

Are they standing, this very second, with their ears cocked to the floor above? Being caught eavesdropping is never a good look, and even though mild embarrassment is a pretty inconsequential emotion given the competition right now, Casey's cheeks flare at the thought. She's about to close the door and get dressed when she hears the fast clacking of heels over a hard floor.

'Elspeth! You stop when I'm talking to you!'

It's a roar so guttural it makes the hairs on the back of Casey's neck stand up. Suddenly, Lucas doesn't seem so mild.

Mouth *and* trousers.

The footsteps stop. Elspeth starts to say something, when Lucas cuts in again:

'Elspeth, she's *playing* us, you bloody fool. And I don't for a second believe that the baby's his.'

Casey's hand moves to her belly in an instinctive gesture of protection. And just as instinctive is the certainty that rises up: *I need to get out of here. Like,* now.

51

Saffron glances sideways. She hasn't been in a car with Broady for months and months, but he messaged last-minute asking if he could get a lift, so here they are, swinging into Penzance for a night out. The lights twinkle at the harbour, and with the window down the cool air blows in. Soon they'll be in the basement bar, Jodie's records spinning, walls glistening as the crowd get their groove on. Words swapped for moves. Not that there's been very many words in the car. Saffron turned the stereo all the way up and they threw their heads back and sang along. Easier that way.

Saffron is with Milo.

Dee is moving back.

Broady wants a family.

Just plain facts. And the second two shouldn't have any bearing on the first.

Mullins leans forward, stuffing his head between the seats. Saffron turns the stereo down.

'Are we there yet, Mum and Dad?'

Saffron laughs, and as the lights turn red, she swivels in her seat. He's a good distraction, old Mullins. He's put a little gel in his hair, and he's wearing a white shirt that looks like standard school-issue. How long ago was it that they were actually at school together? Seven, eight years? If you'd told her to scan their class back then and take a guess at who'd end up being a police officer, there's no way she'd have picked out Mullins. First in custody, though? Maybe, although there was competition for that. But then, if you'd told her to take a guess at whose lovely mum would die, leaving her daughter all alone in the world, she wouldn't have picked out herself, would she? Life moves in mysterious ways: the good, the great, the bad, the ugly. The desperately sad.

'Mullins, I thought the deal was I'd only give you a lift if you promised not to talk?'

'That's on the way home,' he says, settling back in his seat. 'When I'll be snoring.'

The lights change, and Saffron moves forward – then slams on the brakes. She jerks against her belt, and beside her Broady swears. A pedestrian is weaving across the road, their steps ragged, totally oblivious to any traffic. Saffron glances in the rear-view mirror in case she's about to get rammed, but there's no one behind her. Her heart's beating fast. It was close. Too close. The person, a woman, appears to drop something in the middle of the road and bends to pick it up; she stumbles, off balance, her bag slipping from her shoulder.

'Gotta love after-hours in Penzance,' murmurs Broady.

'Hold on,' says Saffron, 'I recognise her.'

And she's pulling over, flicking on her emergency lights.

'That's Pippa Grant, that is,' says Mullins, craning to look out the window.

'Ally and Jayden's client,' says Saffron.

'And my suspect,' says Mullins, with trademark bluster.

Saffron's hand is on the door. The woman, Pippa, has made it to the other side, but not without a delivery moped screeching by, honking its horn.

'What do you mean, your suspect?'

'Well, we had questions for her, put it that way,' says Mullins.

'And did she answer them?'

Mullins blows out his cheeks – he looks like a pufferfish.

'Some.'

Saffron taps his arm. 'Mullins, is she genuinely a suspect?'

Mullins hesitates, and Saffron gets out of the car anyway. A lone woman, stumbling into traffic and near open water? Saffron's not going to just leave her.

'Wait,' says Mullins, climbing out too. He moves closer to Saffron and drops his voice. 'Look, she was in a domestic violence situation, okay? She testified against the husband and then moved away. Got a divorce while he was inside. But one week after he was released, he was killed in a hit-and-run back in their hometown. The police brought her in, but there wasn't enough for a charge. He's got a nutty family who've never forgiven her for getting him arrested in the first place, and they one hundred per cent think she was behind the hit-and-run. So Pippa's paranoid as you like, thinking they're going to come after her one day. That's why we were talking to her.'

Saffron stops. 'But what's all that got to do with your case?'

'Because she's on her own on that little island, and when a strange man pitches up, she's going to defend herself from any perceived threat, isn't she? That was Skinner's theory, anyway. For a bit.'

Saffron looks towards Pippa. She's standing on the pavement, digging in her bag. She sways on her feet. Right now, she doesn't look as if she could defend herself against anyone.

'Do Ally and Jayden know all this?'

'Doubt it,' says Mullins. 'Unless Pippa's told them.'

'You haven't filled them in?'

'Police confidentiality.'

'But you're telling me?'

'I'd tell you anything, Saff.'

There's a note of pure silence, as they both realise what he's said.

'I mean, because you're bossy.' Under the street lights, his cheeks are two red apples. 'You don't give anyone any choice. Look, shut up. Are we going to speak to her or what?'

And he hustles off down the pavement, all wide-boy swagger. But then Saffron sees him slow down, stop a few feet from Pippa and say gently, 'Pippa, it's Officer Mullins. Are you alright there?'

He sounds professional. Trustworthy. Kind. And maybe she shouldn't be surprised at that by now, but she is.

The passenger door opens and Broady thrusts his head out. His face is all impatience as he says, 'Babe, what's the hold-up? Just leave her, yeah?'

52

Ally pours their coffee, the perfect almost-burnt aroma filling the room. The lamps are on in The Shell House, and it's suffused with a warm glow. A light rain taps melodically at the windowpanes and every so often the wind makes itself heard. It tears at the palm fronds, bothers the chimney, and the rain becomes handfuls of grit then; a sharp key-change.

They've had their fair share of wild nights out in the dunes, but this a far cry from the worst of them. It's just everyday weather, battering Ally's outpost. She thinks of the high seas and Trent Simms's grounded boat. And Pippa's cottage lying dark and quiet; it doesn't take much for the island to be cut off. At least they know now that Pippa made the crossing earlier, but Ally can't help wondering if she's now stranded, or has willingly gone AWOL.

They know, at least, that Casey is alright. Jayden messaged her earlier and she said Elspeth was making dinner. It sounded like Lucas was behaving too.

Fox is curled in his basket, head on his paws; Gus reported that he had a little run earlier but was eager to get back to being cosy. Meanwhile, Ally and Jayden make their way to the thinking room. Ally takes Bill's armchair, the leather emitting its habitual creak of welcome, as Jayden assumes his position at the board, marker pen in hand. He writes *Antique flintlock pistol taken from Porthmerrin and washed out to sea*, then: *Who took it?*

'That about the size of it, Al?'

'That's about the size of it.'

'Time to call Mullins, drag him away from his TV dinner. I'll put him on speaker.'

Ally folds her hands in her lap. For all their success, she always feels oddly nervous when they share their theories with the police. But they've gone directly up against the local force on more than one occasion, opposing even Skinner's directives, and Ally is always surprised that her desire for getting to the truth far outweighs any notion of toeing the line. Just because she was married to a devoted sergeant, just because she fundamentally believes in the good of the police, doesn't mean her loyalties are skewed.

As the dial tone fills the room, Jayden drums his fingers on the table.

'This is Tim's phone,' says an oddly formal voice for Mullins. 'Leave me a message and I'll get back to you.'

'Mullins,' says Jayden, 'Ally and I want to fill you in on a few things. Directly relating to Donna Goode, and . . . a new development. Call us back?'

He sends Ally a questioning look, and she nods. She loves their silent communication.

'In fact, time is of the essence, Mullins,' says Jayden, 'so here's what we have. Feel free to run it up to Skinner. Donna Goode not only lied about being in Axel's van, but she also lied about having met him before. They knew each other from years back, possibly intimately. You might have got that out of her by now, but we're interested in what that means in the context of Robbie, her current boyfriend. Ally observed him as Donna went off in the patrol car, and he didn't react like you'd expect. He laid low. Which, for our money, suggests he knew exactly what was going on with Donna.

Or he wanted to keep himself out of the picture for a different reason. Either way, you're going to want to bring him up in your Donna interviews. Next bit, Al?'

Ally moves closer to the phone.

'You'll have seen the news report of an antique gun washed up on the beach about ten miles from here,' she says. 'We have it on good authority that it comes from Edward Grey's collection. And we can't help thinking it's connected to Axel's death. Whether he had it with him when he went into the water or, more likely, an assailant threatened him with it.'

'Much more likely,' says Jayden, taking the baton. 'Now, we know you said the autopsy showed significant damage to Axel's body, consistent with a cliff fall and time in the water, but now we've got a potential weapon. No, scratch that, Mullins, we're putting our cards on the table: an *actual* weapon. So you'll want to get the pathologist looking specifically for any lacerations or wounds that could have been caused by this particular pistol. Like a semicircular imprint, a depression on the skull that matches the butt, say. Easy to miss the first time around, with all the chaos of his other injuries, but now you know what you're looking for. If you haven't still got the weapon in evidence, then you'll know exactly where to source it – a teen called Max Clemence has his picture in the paper for finding it. Now, in other news, Casey James is—'

But then they're cut off, Mullins's voicemail reaching its limit.

'Call him again?' says Ally.

'Or Skinner . . .' says Jayden, rubbing at his chin.

Jayden's phone beeps with a message then, and they both jump at it. *Mullins!*

But Jayden frowns as he reads it. 'Casey again,' he says. 'Things are kicking off at Porthmerrin House.'

'What? Between who?'

He holds up the phone. 'Lucas and Elspeth. A massive row after dinner. Casey thinks it's about her.'

Then he's immediately calling Casey, but instead of ringing it goes straight to voicemail.

'The signal's unreliable up there,' says Ally, taking in his worried face. 'It kept cutting out when I was talking to Paul Fairfax.'

'Damn. We shouldn't have left her – not knowing what we know. And what she doesn't. That's on us, Al.'

But Casey had been determined. It wasn't up to them to stop her. But was it up to Ally and Jayden to share what they knew about descendants, after all? Ally feels hot suddenly, a flare of anxiety. The weight of these decisions they have to make; sometimes, it feels wrong even when they're getting them right. But was this irresponsible, leaving Casey under-informed?

'Do you want to go to Porthmerrin?' asks Ally. 'Or . . . call the police?'

'Let's go and get Casey,' says Jayden. 'I want her out of there.'

Just as they're getting to their feet, Ally's phone rings.

'Tim,' she says.

'I know Jayden's been trying to get hold of me,' says Mullins, 'but first . . . Saffron thought you'd want to know that we've seen Pippa Grant in Penzance.'

Ally can hear the wind in the receiver. Mullins is outside.

'She's a bit worse for wear. Soon as we tried to talk to her, she made off.'

'Made off?'

'Ran away. I wasn't going to chase her. I mean, she's done nothing wrong, has she?'

'But you were suspicious of her for a while?' says Ally carefully, trying to take the accusation from her voice.

'A line of enquiry, that's all. Anyway . . . Saffron thought you'd want to know. Truth be told, I don't like the thought of Pippa wandering up and down the seafront in a state like that. Drunk as a sailor, Ally. Vulnerable as you like. She's had a bit of a time of it in the past, and—'

Mullins's voice is temporarily lost in the crackle of wind.

'. . . if we had the resources, I'd try and get a female officer dispatched but . . . there isn't anyone. Saffron's doing her best, but as far as Pippa's concerned, she's just some random stranger, isn't she?'

Ally's not getting this one wrong.

'I'll come right away,' she says.

She looks to Jayden. He has his car keys in his hand and is popping on his toes, wanting to be gone. Porthmerrin and Penzance – ten miles of country lanes between them. But he's heard the conversation, and he nods. Mouths, *You go, Al.* Divide and conquer.

'Tell me where you are,' says Ally, 'and I'll be there. And Tim? You need to listen to our voicemail.'

53

Casey crosses the vast hallway, her heart hammering in her chest. The storm has moved to a different part of the house, but Lucas's voice still reverberates like trapped thunder. She thinks of the female bond – *should I go to her?* But Elspeth's voice is raised too, and what couple likes their arguments interrupted by a third? Especially when that third person is, apparently, the topic of the fight. Casey knows that's self-protective thinking, but she's carrying Axel's baby. It's the only way to be.

As she closes the door of the house behind her and feels the outside air on her face, a gust of relief blows in. *No one saw me*. She moves fast across the lawn, the torchlight from her phone showing the way. The grass is wet, and she can already feel it seeping through the toes of her trainers. The trees that hem the garden throw eerie shadows and she jumps at every single one of them.

Come on, Casey, it's scarier inside than out.

Axel's van. That's her safe space. Even though it's charged with emotion, she knows it's where she needs to be. It's where she should have been all along.

She's messaged Jayden, but she hasn't had a reply yet. As soon as she gets to the van, she'll call herself a taxi. And then she'll get as far away from Porthmerrin House as possible.

What Casey doesn't understand is why Lucas is so angry about her pregnancy. What's it to him? What's it to anyone? Casey's tough enough not to be taken down by one idiot's words, but she hates thinking that Axel spent his last hours in the company of someone who can be this foul. Casey's original feeling rises up, from before she started thinking on bad luck and all the trouble Axel could get himself into on his own: *the inheritance*. If Lucas can turn on his wife like this, he could just as easily have turned on Axel.

As Casey clambers over the stile into the field, her torchlight just picks out the dim shape of Axel's van in the distance. The grass is longer here, and her jeans are sodden too; her trainers slip on the wet ground. The rain is a fine mist on her face. She can hear the sea, and she tries to pretend it's the hum of the M32: a familiar soundtrack back home. Not a dark beast, clawing at the cliff, seeking prey. Claiming lives.

Claiming life.

Casey has a sudden feeling of being caught between perils. The house and the ocean. The further she gets from one, the closer she is to the other. But the van is near now; her torch picks out the stickers on Axel's battered bumper. The curtain at the rear window, made from an old dress he found in an Easton charity shop. She sewed it for him, and they hung it together. Her throat burns at the memory.

As she rounds the van, she sees a stray end of police tape, madly dancing in the wind.

He died here.

She's taken by a weird feeling. A desire – no, a *need* – to retrace Axel's steps. She wanted to do it earlier, but she was seduced by the Greys' hospitality, the warmth and comfort. She told herself she'd do it in the morning. What, after a lie-in and a luxury breakfast? What was she playing at, being part of this?

The invisible sea is a riot of sound, far below but all around. She's reminded, all of a sudden, of being caught in the wrong crowd after a Bristol Rovers match when she was a tiny girl. Her hand slipping from her dad's. Pints spilled over her shoes. Big men pushing and shoving and swear words raining down all round her. Her instinct, then, had been to curl up in a tiny ball until the storm passed. And hope that her dad found her, a limpet in the depths of the stadium.

But now? Casey the grown-up walks away from the van, towards the cliff edge. She's no fool, she won't go anywhere near the drop, but Axel was here. *He was right here.* And maybe she'll get some feeling of what really happened. Because here's the truth of it: sometimes being with Axel felt like magic. That's why she kept going back for more. That's why she tried, so hard, to help him. Because she could see the beauty of the unscarred boy in him. They say everyone's made of stars, but with Axel, honest to God you could see the twinkle.

She checks her messages again. There's one from Jayden, but it won't load. *No signal.* She walks a few paces, holding the phone high. Still nothing. She makes a sound of frustration, one which quickly turns into a scream as her feet go from under her. She falls hard on one ankle, the breath juddering from her, as if she's been punched.

For a second, Casey can't move.

She knows slams. Go anywhere near a skateboard, and you've got to make friends with the ground. Skinned elbows and bruised haunches: that's her. But not in the dark, not near a cliff edge, not when you're carrying the most precious cargo in the world.

Her ankle burns like wildfire, but Casey's hand goes to her belly.

'I'm sorry,' she breathes. 'I'm so sorry.'

Uneven ground, the slick of rain: that was all it took. And suddenly, compared to such things, the raging, resentful Lucas seems like no threat at all. Throw in a bottle of whisky?

Axel had no chance.

Did he fall or was he pushed? The question pings around her brain and it's not what she needs; not even close.

Focus, Casey. The here and now.

She tries to lever herself up, but pain spikes in her ankle with the slightest pressure. Casey's phone slipped from her grip with the fall, and she casts around for it. The grass is long here, the ground uneven, and it must have fallen with the torch beam facing down because she can't see it. Her fingers clutch at wet grass and nothing more.

The sea shouts louder, and Casey wants to tip her head back and scream with it. But instead, she whispers, one eye on the dim and distant stars above.

'Kick,' she says to her baby. 'Please, please kick.'

54

There are lights on inside Porthmerrin House, but no one answers Jayden's knock. He stands on the steps trying to call Casey again; this time it rings at least, though there's no answer.

He tries the door: locked. He bends to lift the letterbox, trying to hear anything from inside, but all is silent.

'Is anyone there?' he shouts out.

His voice sounds thin, and he calls again, with more muscle this time.

This is on us.

There's the sound of an approaching engine, and Jayden turns. Headlights play over the gravel, and it takes him a moment to recognise who it is.

Robbie and Donna.

So the police had no reason to hold her. Did Donna leave the station before Mullins heard Jayden's voicemail? The pair climb out, the security lights showing their wary faces. Robbie folds an arm around Donna's shoulders and tips his chin up defiantly.

'No one's answering,' Jayden calls out by way of greeting.

'There's been enough excitement around here,' says Robbie flatly. 'They'll be lying down. Wringing their hands.'

Jayden takes the steps two at a time.

Of all the questions he could ask Donna, he settles for this: 'Are you okay?'

Her face is blotchy, her eyes are red.

'Course she's not okay,' cuts in Robbie. 'She's been made to feel like she's to blame for that bloke dying.'

'I am to blame,' says Donna.

'You're not!' says Robbie with heat. Then, to Jayden, 'I keep telling her she's not. Free will. That's all we've got, isn't it? If a man wants to off himself—'

'Robbie,' says Donna, 'you think you're helping but you're not.'

'Were you both questioned?' asks Jayden evenly.

'I went to pick her up,' says Robbie. Donna wilts against his shoulder, and he presses a kiss to her crown. 'She was in pieces. So I took her for a stiff drink after.'

'Robbie thought I was involved. I mean, I am. I know I am. If I hadn't brought everything up with Curtis, and Afghanistan, then Axel wouldn't have lost it. But . . . Robbie thought I was hiding something more. He was that worried.'

Jayden stares at Robbie. He has his head down, feet scuffing at the gravel.

'Alright,' says Robbie, 'I admit it. I thought Donna was acting weird, and I knew Axel wasn't an easy proposition for her, so . . . I put two and two together and made some stupid number.'

'I'm still to blame, though,' she says quietly.

'Sweetheart, you are not,' says Robbie.

Jayden's brain works quickly. Can he square this position of Robbie's with what Ally observed of him? *Kind of.* But not so much that Jayden's going to wipe him off the board. He might be doing a good impression of a dutiful boyfriend right now, but jealousy and envy could just as easily have fired through Robbie's veins.

Jayden looks back to the house. No change. No new lights flicked on. No figures at the window. And still no call from Casey.

'The police haven't confirmed it was suicide, have they?' says Jayden.

'Well, no . . .' says Donna, wiping her sleeve across her eyes.

'Ally and I believe Axel was murdered,' says Jayden.

He lets the statement hang a moment.

'And I'm looking for Casey. Axel's ex-girlfriend. Robbie, did you see her on your way in? She's not picking up.'

'You think she did it?' says Robbie, rubbing at his chin.

'No, I don't think she did it,' says Jayden pointedly. Then, 'Donna, you have a key to the house, right?'

55

'Ally,' says Saffron, 'you're here.'

But Ally can already see that Pippa is not. She can't help wondering what Saffron and Mullins are doing in Penzance together of an evening. *No wonder Mullins wasn't answering his phone.* Not a date, surely? But they are dressed up. Saffron in a tiny tie-dye dress and leggings; the pink streaks in her hair glowing. Mullins is in a creased white shirt and jeans; short back and sides glistening with gel. Behind them yachts shift on their moorings at the quayside. Rigging clinks and rattles. Light rain flickers in the street lights, darting like fireflies as the breeze blows in off the water. Whatever forces brought the pair of them here, Ally is grateful.

'Where is she?' she asks. 'Where's Pippa?'

'We lost her,' says Mullins. 'Sorry, Mrs Bright.'

'She ran off,' adds Saffron. 'I tried to talk to her, but she didn't want to know.'

'Not your fault, Saff.' Mullins turns to her. 'She was all over the place.'

'Sorry, though, Ally,' says Saffron. 'She went along the seafront. I tried to follow but I just felt like I was making things worse. She was really edgy. And Mullins was great with her. Really gentle. But it didn't make a difference.'

Beside Saffron, Ally sees Mullins glitter a little.

'Did Pippa go that way?' Ally points towards the town.

Saffron nods. 'Ally, I've got my car, do you want us to keep looking? We totally can. Right, Mullins?'

'Sure,' says Mullins. 'Nothing better to do. I don't even know what dub is.'

Saffron rolls her eyes. 'My pal Jodie's DJing. Broady's gone on ahead. I'll message him, tell him we're helping look for Pippa instead.'

'Found Pippa, lost Pippa, looking for Pippa,' says Mullins. 'By the way, Mrs Bright, I listened to your and Jayden's message. Donna's been released without charge.'

Ally raises her eyebrows. 'What did she have to say?'

Mullins hesitates.

'Come on, Mullins.' Saffron nudges him. 'Teamwork makes the dream work.'

'Alright, Donna's all cut up, thinks it was her pushing the subject of her brother that made Axel jump. And that's the headline. Donna thinks he jumped.'

'What about Robbie?'

'They're copping off.'

'I mean what about Robbie acting strangely?'

'Oh, that. We'll follow it up and all that, but honestly? I reckon he's proper lovey-dovey for her and didn't want her being made to feel any worse by us lot.'

'Tim, Jayden's gone up to Porthmerrin House. Casey sent a message saying Lucas and Elspeth were having a big row, and the subtext . . .'

'Can't expect me to go to Skinner with that,' says Mullins. 'Married couple have words. It's not exactly . . . news. But the pirate gun? That was news. The connection with Edward Grey, anyway.'

'So Skinner's checking with the pathologist?'

'I did that,' he says quickly. 'Interrupted the bloke's chicken dinner. He wasn't best pleased.' Mullins looks like he's about to say something else, then changes his mind. 'Anyway, the ball's in his court now. But that was a decent bit of detective work, if it comes to anything or not.'

'You needn't sound so surprised about it, Mullins,' says Saffron.

'Tim,' says Ally, 'I can look for Pippa on my own. I think Jayden would value the back-up from you.'

'Back-up? What's that based on?'

Instinct, thinks Ally. But before she puts it into words, Mullins is nodding.

'Alright, we'll go straight up there.'

Ally looks down the deserted seafront. The tide is high, and waves are flinging themselves at the quayside. The rain is harder now, falling in fat spots. And Pippa feels like she has something to run from.

'Was Pippa wearing her blue coat?'

'She was,' says Mullins. 'Grey hiking boots and brown trousers. She had a blue bag with her.'

'A tote bag,' says Saffron. 'With a leaf pattern.'

'Tim, I can't get this next bit wrong. I'm going to need to know what made you look at Pippa in the first place. There must be more, beyond the missing kayak.'

Ally sees Saffron's look to Mullins, her eyebrows raised – and firmly on her side. A burly officer of the Devon and Cornwall Police, and it looks like they've got him cornered.

Ally drives slowly along the seafront, eyes everywhere. To her left, the sea thrashes at the shingle beach, hurling spray high in the air. To her right, the myriad streets of the town unwind. Pippa could be anywhere. On such an inclement evening, there are few people about to ask. Ally stops two backpackers in matching anoraks, but they haven't seen anyone like Pippa. Ditto a man in a suit, holding his briefcase over his head to shelter from the rain. Ally's struck by how all three seem mildly alarmed, then inconvenienced, to be stopped and asked a question. No one wants to know why she's racing about town on a wet night, searching for a lone woman. Instead of asking Mullins to go to Porthmerrin, should Ally have kept him here, looking with her? And Saffron too?

Ally sees, then, a man in a big coat sitting on one of the pebble sculptures along the promenade. He's huddled against the weather, no umbrella; motionless, he could be a sculpture himself. Ally pulls over the car and flicks her warning lights on. She hurries over to him, rain stinging her face. As she says 'Excuse me' the man peers up at her from beneath a wide hood. The street light makes his pale skin sallow; his eyes are dark as night. When he smiles, he's missing teeth and it's impossible to tell his age. There's a sudden movement at his chest and she leaps back, startled. A small dog pokes its nose out of his coat and she's immediately ashamed of her reaction, as if somehow a homeless man is scarier than any other.

'Keeping him dry,' he says. 'You stay in there, bud.'

Ally asks if he's seen a woman matching Pippa's description and he nods.

'She was leaning on the railing just over there. Made off when I sat down here. Well, I'm used to that.'

'How long ago was that?'

'Not long. Five minutes?'

'You didn't see which direction she went in, did you?'

He jerks his thumb behind him. 'Turned up the street there. I watched her go. She shouldn't be hanging about on her own, night like this.'

'Thank you so much for your help,' says Ally. Then, carefully, not wanting to be seen to be jumping to conclusions, 'Have you got somewhere to sleep tonight?'

The man regards her from beneath his hood. He doesn't say anything. Ally takes a note from her purse, then hesitates; she takes out everything she has, pressing the money into his hand. 'Thank you for your help,' she says again. 'I really appreciate it.'

As she walks away, she glances back. He has his head bent, his nose pressed to his little dog's head. The rain keeps coming down; needles falling from the sky.

56

Lucas shuts himself away at the very top of the house, in the room he had as a child. He hates rowing with Elspeth; hates, hates, hates it. He becomes a version of himself he doesn't recognise – although that suggests his temper hasn't flared before, and he can't pretend that. But no one cuts him down to size like his wife – except for his dearly departed father – so is it any wonder that he exploded? And now here he is, a one-inch man, a lily-livered boy, cowering away. Faced with the truth, there's nowhere else to go but back to where it all began. His childhood sanctuary. The one room in the house that Lucas made sure Axel never set foot in when they were boys.

It's a time trap in Lucas's old bedroom, and he breathes in the dust of it. The little wooden bed. The desk. The globe. The shelf of books. He knows better than to think his father kept it preserved this way for sentimental reasons; he simply couldn't be bothered to turn his attention to it; had forgotten, probably, that it even existed, this upper-floor box room, with leaded windows and gaping floorboards and the walls holding every single sorrow Lucas ever brought here.

Not a lot of fun knowing, no matter what you did, it was never enough.

Even less fun knowing a servant's son was considered your better.

In all the ways that Lucas has tried to shake off the effect of his father, he's never quite managed it. He'll never forget the day he launched his own marketing firm. The phone call to his father, his need dripping through the phone: *Automotive clients, Dad, direct marketing strategy for luxury cars.* Edward had laughed, said, *Oh, you mean junk mail, do you? The stuff that goes straight in the bin?* Whereas Axel, running around pretending to be a soldier – then actually a soldier, and finding out he couldn't hack it after all – was the golden boy. The golden boy with a golden goose, eventually. His father's last play, executed with cruelty and precision.

Laughable, that Axel should ever be deemed worthy of Porthmerrin. A sick joke.

I'm sorry, but you have only yourself to blame, Lucas, Elspeth said, as Lucas railed at her in the kitchen. *If you'd fostered a better relationship with your father . . .*

He doesn't know where Elspeth is now. He doesn't care. They've argued before and come back from it – but this time it feels different. This time, Lucas feels like his wife has seen him for who he really is.

His darkest, most broken parts.

And that she hates him.

But how could Lucas not be furious, as that scrap of a woman with her pregnant belly sat at his table? That ridiculous clause in the will, coming back to bite them all with the sharpest teeth. How could it not all come rearing up?

From somewhere deep in the house, Lucas hears his name being called and shakes his head. *No more.* He goes to the shelf and takes the key that's been sitting there for decades. It's coated in dust, and he blows it as he makes his way to the door. He locks himself in, and huffs with childish relief.

No one can get at me now.

It's the exact thing he used to do as a child. And he experiences the same feeling he did as a child too; only, his wife's disapproval, her disappointment, her disdain, will never cut as deep as his father's. As Lucas makes his way back across the room he trips on the rug, and he's that much on edge that he staggers and cries out. A fall of millimetres, for goodness' sake. *Nothing like Axel's dead drop*. As Lucas flails, pathetically, his fingers part and the key slips from them. It lands with an odd-sounding thunk, and when he looks for it, it's nowhere. Lucas gets down on his knees.

Oh, come on.

Between the gap in the floorboards, no more than the width of a pound coin – or, indeed, a key – he sees a dim glint in the darkness. He couldn't reach it if he tried.

'Lock me up and throw away the key,' he says out loud. The key, the only key, is a goner. Lucas slowly gets to his feet, laughing bitterly, for it couldn't be more apposite, could it?

He turns and rattles the door handle, but of course it's not going to give. He vaguely thinks about banging, of calling out, but then that feeling of peace reasserts itself.

My sanctuary.

No one can get at him now – whether he wants them to or not.

57

Jayden turns Donna's key in the lock and carefully lets himself into the house. He catches the pungent scent of lilies from the massive display in the hall. The chandelier glitters above his head. He closes the door quietly behind him, wincing as his wet trainers squeak loudly on the tiles.

Donna has gone with Robbie to his cottage. Jayden guesses she was headed there all along, but as she said to him, *I don't like drama.* She wasn't altogether comfortable handing over her key. If Robbie hadn't been by her side, Jayden would have told her about the flintlock pistol. He'd have asked if she'd ever seen Lucas interacting with the collection. But he's not about to give that detail away in front of Robbie. Not while that avenue's still wide open.

Inside, the house rings with silence.

Could they all have left?

A grim image lurches into his head, and Jayden shakes it away. There is nothing to indicate that there has been violence here. Innocent explanations are possible for everything. But then there's instinct. There is, as Pippa might say, *feeling*.

Jayden slides his phone from his pocket, checking it's on silent. Still nothing back from Casey. He tries calling her again, because what if he can hear it ringing somewhere in the house. But he can't. Then the signal cuts out again.

He goes through to the kitchen. The bright lights make it feel like a stage set. There are the remnants of a meal on the sideboard. The dishwasher has its mouth wide open. A half-empty bottle of wine sits in the middle of the table. Butted up against it, a wine glass lies on its side like a bowling pin; it's broken but not smashed. And it's a small crack in an otherwise ordinary scene.

Jayden heads back to the hallway and methodically checks all the rooms downstairs. Two sitting rooms, the first of which is formal in its arrangement, and looks as if it's rarely used. The second has a fire burning low in the grate. Candles flicker on the mantelpiece. A newspaper lies open on the coffee table, and a wheelchair, presumably Edward's, is parked in the corner. Paintings of fox-hunting scenes, interspersed with galleons and warships, decorate the walls. Jayden treads on down the hallway, passing a small bathroom, a laundry room, then a dining room with a long wooden table and eight straight-backed chairs; a dresser lined with the kinds of plates that would probably get Laurence Fentiman all excited. Then into a wood-panelled room with a snooker table. He pauses, hand resting on the baize: was that a sound from above? But all he can hear is his own breathing.

It's a heavy-feeling house. Stuffy and unfriendly. Despite Lucas and Elspeth staying here this past week, there's little evidence of their belongings about the place. And presumably Donna, a resident for some months, keeps her things in her own room.

For all Elspeth's welcome, why would Casey want to stay here?

A thought darts into his head. Another grim one. Surely Casey hasn't meted out some vengeance? Did she engineer the overnight stay? *No, that's stupid, Jayden.* It's this place – it's making him uneasy. There was an estate in Leeds where the police used to hate to go; he and Kieran answered a call once, dodging bottles and bricks; a firework going off like a shotgun. He was right to be cautious there, but this lumpy old mansion in Cornwall? *Get real.*

He resets, heading to the stairs. He takes them two at a time, soft-footed as a panther. As he turns on to the landing he pauses by a window. It faces the garden, the field beyond, the sea. And he can just make out a tiny, bobbing light. Down near Axel's van.

Jayden pulls his phone out again and sees missed calls from Ally and Mullins. He looks to the light again and makes a quick decision. He heads back down the stairs and out into the dark garden. As Jayden crunches over the gravel, he pauses, sensing he's being watched. A rising of the hairs at the back of the neck. He looks up at the windows of the house. Has he made the right call? Then he runs fast towards the light.

58

Ally takes the street the man pointed out. It's narrow and dimly lit, and she hurries along, her eyes open for Pippa. When Ally sees her in the distance, standing beneath the halo of a street light, she has to stop herself from shouting out. The last thing she wants to do is alarm her.

Mullins told Ally what happened with Pippa's first husband, Liam Maddox. The abuse she suffered, and how she eventually testified against him. Then how, four years later, he died in a hit-and-run, not long after his release from prison – and the police lens focused firmly on Pippa. Despite the fact that by then she had a new life in a different part of the country; had a new partner too: Fergus Grant. Mullins only told Ally the basics, but Ally can't help wondering if there is more to the story. That investigation was six years ago. Why, all these years on, is it – or was it – considered relevant?

For some reason, Ally imagines Jayden phrasing the question – perhaps because she knows she'd be most inclined to listen if it came from him.

Could Pippa have killed before, Al?

'Pippa,' she says softly. 'It's me. Ally.'

Pippa turns. Her hair hangs in sodden tendrils. Her lips move, but no sound comes out.

'It's alright,' says Ally. 'I was worried about you, that's all. I wanted to be sure you're okay.'

Pippa's initial look of relief changes and she peers past Ally as if she expects someone else to appear.

'It's just me here,' says Ally.

'Those other people . . .'

'They're friends. They knew I was looking for you.'

'Where's your partner? Where's Jayden?'

'Jayden's with Axel's former girlfriend. We managed to find her, Pippa. She didn't know that he'd died. She came to Cornwall as soon as she heard.'

Pippa closes her eyes. 'Poor woman,' she says quietly. She has one hand holding on to the lamp post, as if she's anchored; she sways slightly. 'Everything went wrong, Ally. I came over and then I couldn't get back.'

'Trent's not running the boat because of the weather?' says Ally, framing it as a question.

Pippa nods; chews at her lip. 'He warned me. But then I stayed longer, and . . .' She pushes a hand to her head, as if a sudden piercing headache has landed. '. . . lost track of time.'

Ally steps closer. 'Pippa, I've a thermos of hot coffee in the car,' she says carefully. 'Why don't we get out of the rain, and I can tell you where we are with the case.'

Pippa looks down at her feet. She's wearing hiking boots.

'Do you know who killed him yet?' she asks softly.

'Not for sure. But there've been some developments. Shall we go and get dry? Have some coffee. I'll update you.'

'I feel a bit drunk, Ally.'

'I know. Let's get you warm and dry.'

'I don't drink. Not now. I used to once, a lot, and . . .'

Pippa starts to quietly cry. Ally folds an arm around her and the woman feels birdlike, brittle.

'I'm sorry I ignored your messages.'

'Really, it's alright.'

'The police came to see me.' Pippa looks up at Ally; her eyes are amber under the glow of the street light. She rubs a hand across her mouth. 'They thought I'd done it. The way they made me feel . . . It was like I had a black mark against me. Like I was . . .'

Pippa stops. Ally waits, wondering what she'll tell her – if anything. The rain falls heavier. Somewhere nearby a gutter splutters and spills as though it's Niagara Falls.

'Where's Jayden?' asks Pippa abruptly, as if a new thought has come down with the rain. 'Jayden, and Axel's girlfriend?'

'They're at Porthmerrin House.'

She nods. 'Because someone there has the answer, don't they?'

Ally waits for more. Pippa has a faraway look in her eyes, and Ally thinks of that feeling of hers on finding Axel's body; her intuition that something was wrong.

Ally trusted that intuition. Was she right to?

'You should be there too,' says Pippa. 'Shouldn't you? They need you.'

59

Casey clutches her phone in her hand. By some miracle, she managed to find it in the wet grass. She still has no signal, but even just the weight of it in her palm feels like connection. It feels like hope. And the torchlight: Axel's van gleams with it, looking a far brighter white than it ever did by day.

Casey crawls forward, trying to keep her left ankle off the ground. Trying not to think about the giant, yawning space just a few metres behind her. The roar of the sea fills her ears; the rain slicks her hair across her face. But she has torchlight, and she can make it to the van.

And maybe then my baby will kick.

Casey can taste salt, and she knows it's half from the sea wind blowing over the clifftop and half from her own tears. An old song comes into her head: 'Help Me Make It Through the Night'. A bunch of different versions, but it was Kris Kristofferson's that Axel loved. Kristofferson's husky tones, jangly guitar; that old cowboy swagger. Casey starts to quietly sing as she crawls painstakingly forward on her hands and knees.

She's in touching distance of the van when she stops and cocks an ear to the wind, as if she's a street fox. She catches a scent of something but isn't sure what. She swings her torch beam, heart banging in her chest.

She hears footsteps. Fast, running footsteps. And sees a light coming this way.

Casey thinks of Lucas, the roar of his voice – and his venom as he spoke of her and the baby. Did Lucas follow her out? Did he see her light? She turns off her own, afraid that it's too late and that she's already been seen. With this injury, she's defenceless. She can't stand, let alone run. So Casey shrinks to the side of the van. She curls up in the darkness, holding one hand to her middle. The smell she caught a moment ago is stronger now.

Smoke.

The footsteps stop. She can hear breathing. Then torch-light crosses her like a lighthouse beam. She hears a sharp intake of breath.

'Casey,' says a familiar voice, a kind voice. 'It's okay.'

And, as if in response, she feels a kick inside her.

60

'First time I've been on a shout with you, Mullins,' says Saffron. 'Am I allowed to break the speed limit?'

She turns a grinning face to him as they careen through the narrow lanes. Briars brush the metalwork. A fat moth dances in their headlights, then against the odds makes it away.

Mullins is loving this. Loving, too, the fact that Broady's currently nodding his head and shuffling his shoes at the dub night all on his own. It's not that Mullins dislikes the guy – you've got to feel for him, losing a girl like Saffron – but he doesn't exactly *like* him either.

Mullins is just cooking up a witty response when his phone goes. *Skinner.* Always the party pooper.

'I've just had a call from Roger Cunningham,' says his boss by way of greeting.

The pathologist. And Mullins never took him for a tell-tale.

'Told me you'd been bothering him out of hours.'

And now you're bothering me out of hours, thinks Mullins. *I'm at a dub night, aren't I? Only I'm not. I'm on my way to some not-quite suspect's house – a fact you'll like even less. With Saffron. Because basically I'll do anything she tells me to. How's that for you, Sarge?*

The lip on me.

'Yes, sorry, Sarge. I didn't want to trouble you with it until I knew if it was something or nothing.'

'That's not how we work, Mullins. Everything goes through me.'

'Yes, Sarge. Sorry, Sarge.'

Mullins can feel his ears going red, as Saffron looks at him sideways.

'Missing firearms, for goodness' sake. I can only presume Ally and Jayden put you up to this.'

'Ally and Jayden? Erm . . .'

Mullins can smell a lose-lose situation coming on. He elects not to finish the sentence. Which is no problem for Skinner, as, apparently, he's not done yet.

'As it happens, I've never heard Cunningham so contrite. He went back over his report and called me immediately. Turns out there's evidence of an impact and laceration consistent with the butt of a pistol. Missed it entirely, in amongst the other injuries.'

Mullins breathes in sharply. *Ally and Jayden were right.*

'So, someone clobbered Axel with Edward Grey's gun?'

'A hypothesis supported by forensic evidence. This changes everything, Mullins. It's a misstep from Cunningham. And a bloody nuisance for us.'

'There's got to be only a few people who knew about that weapons collection, Sarge.'

'And even fewer who had reason to wish Axel Marks ill.'

The high stone wall of the Porthmerrin estate comes into view.

'We're here,' says Mullins quietly, pointing ahead. 'Left turn, Saff.'

'And it focuses attention back on Porthmerrin House,' says Skinner.

Saffron turns into the driveway, and they bounce between the stone pillars. Tall trees line the track, neat as soldiers.

'Course, there's no chance of fingerprints on the thing, but we'll go through the motions anyway,' Skinner goes on. 'And we'll need to talk to them all. Robbie Cassidy, Lucas Grey, Elspeth Grey.

I think we can strike the nurse off the list. But we're going to need to approach this very carefully. Wouldn't be at all surprised if the DCI is going to want Major Crimes involved. But Mullins, first thing in the morning, you and I . . .'

And suddenly it feels like a very bad idea to be hurtling up to Porthmerrin House – whatever mess Jayden has got himself into.

Beside him, Saffron winds down her window. She pokes her nose out like a dog and sniffs.

'Smoke, Mullins,' she says.

Porthmerrin House comes into view, and there's a weird glow behind the windows. Mullins can smell it too now, the smoke.

'Fire,' he breathes. 'It's on fire.'

At the end of the line, Skinner suddenly sounds very far away. Mullins sees a flame lick out from a downstairs window. Plumes of smoke rising into the night sky. For a split second, he thinks it's eerily beautiful. Then it makes his stomach roil, like he's eaten something dodgy and is going to pay and pay.

Saffron already has her phone out. 'I'm calling 999.'

'Fire at Porthmerrin House, Sarge. You'd best get up here.'

Skinner goes off on one, questions coming at Mullins like bullets, but then he sees a figure streaking from the house. The person staggers into their headlights like an apparition, her pale arms thrown up to shield her eyes. Mullins buzzes down his window.

'Please!' Elspeth screams. 'Please help! My husband's in there!'

Mullins feels dread land like a punch.

'Where is he, Elspeth? Where's Lucas?'

'The third floor. He's trapped. Locked in. He—'

Then she turns and makes to run back towards the house. Her hair streams like ribbons, her nightdress flutters at her knees; she looks as if she'll fly away over the grass if he doesn't catch her.

Mullins jumps out of the car and goes after her; grabs hold of her shoulders. 'Elspeth, you stay put. The fire brigade's on its way.'

'They won't get here in time, they won't, I have to . . .'

She wriggles in his arms, quick as a wildcat, and Mullins feels the spikes of her nails.

'You can't go back in there, it's dangerous,' he says, and the way she's moving, trying to hold her without hurting her is really hard.

'We've got to wait for the professionals,' says Saffron, by his side. She's trying to sound calm, and it'd fool most people, but Mullins can tell her voice is fraught with fear. 'They'll be here soon . . .'

But earlier on the radio he heard of a factory fire out at Camborne. So it's not likely to be all units dispatched to Porthmerrin; not at the push of a button. Wrong uniform, but right now Mullins is all they have. And if Skinner were here, wouldn't he be shrugging off his suit jacket, striding towards the scene? It's their job to evacuate. To keep people safe.

'The professionals?' Elspeth cries, and it's pitched as high as a scream. She spins on her heel, pushing her palms against Mullins's chest. 'Then what are you supposed to be?'

It's more plea than jibe. Her eyes are huge and liquid – and Mullins is her only hope.

'Tell me exactly where he is,' he says.

The words taste hot in his mouth, like he's already in there. As Elspeth gabbles the layout, he feels weirdly calm. *Up the stairs. Take a left. Follow it down. Door at the end.* It's his method of entry training – plus video-game mode.

I can do this, can't I?

Then, before he can change his mind, Mullins blazes towards the house.

61

Jayden is at the wheel of Axel's van, Casey beside him. They were forced to take a looping route, out via the field gate and back on to the driveway. The fire engines are on their way, but the rush of triumph Jayden felt as he finally got some signal and the call connected soon fades as they draw closer. The scent of smoke is a stench now. The sky behind the house is thick and dark and shifting. Behind the windows, the fire rages.

'Jayden, they were both in there,' says Casey. 'Lucas and Elspeth.'

As they spin on to the gravel, Jayden makes out a small cluster of people on the lawn. Robbie is hauling a garden hose that looks up for the task of watering a rose garden but not much else. The way he's working it, though: the guy's trying.

'There's Elspeth,' he says. 'Elspeth's safe.'

And, weirdly, it's Saffron who has her arm around her. *What's Saffron doing here?* Elspeth stares up at the house, her hands clasped to her head; she's barefoot and dressed for bed, her nightdress fluttering at her knees. Donna, coming from the direction of Robbie's cottage, hands Elspeth a big coat, and she and Saffron help her inside it as if Elspeth is a small child.

Jayden runs a quick mental roll call. No Mullins. Ally was going to Penzance to meet him and Saffron, so why is Saffron here, and Mullins and Ally aren't?

'Casey, I want you to stay in the van,' says Jayden. 'You don't want to breathe in the smoke. I need the others to get back too.'

Because he's thinking of this big old house splitting apart. Masonry raining from the smoking sky; showers of burning sparks as the wind switches direction. Jayden looks back down the drive, wanting, more than anything, to see the approach of blue lights.

'Jayden, where's Lucas?' says Casey in a small voice.

Jayden's climbing from the van, eyes on the house. He freezes; swears under his breath. A window is opening on the third floor, and a figure appears in the frame like a dark ghost; arms waving, scream carrying on the smoke-filled air.

'He's up there,' he says grimly.

Casey's eyes are big as planets.

'Jayden,' she says, catching his arm, 'don't risk anything.'

Who, me?

'Stay in the van, Casey,' he says. 'Promise me.'

Then he's running towards the group and their collective desperation. Robbie has a scarf tied around his mouth and nose as he brandishes the useless hose. Donna's face is all fear as she tends to a crying Elspeth. Only Saffron is a calm centre, and for a split second Jayden wonders if she's really there. *Because if she is, where are the others?*

She turns to him, pink hair whipping in the wind.

'God, I'm glad to see you, Jayden. Mullins has gone in. He's crazy.'

'Mullins is in there?'

'The owner's trapped . . .' Saffron gestures to the window, and it looks even higher from this angle. 'And his wife was trying to get back in, so Mullins went instead.'

Lucas waves his arms as if in semaphore; his scream is as high and long as a wolf's howl. Then disappears again.

Jayden assesses. The fire must have spread to the stairs. A few metres away, an abandoned ladder lies on the grass; Robbie must have tried it and found it too short. *Way too short.*

'Jayden.' Elspeth pulls at his arm. 'He's locked in. I couldn't get to him. I tried, I tried, but he said there was no key, that he had it and dropped it and now he can't get it. I mean, how's that possible? How? It's as if he has a death wish, I don't . . .'

Her eyes are hectic, her voice scattergun. Panic has hold of her. Jayden needs to get her safely away from the scene, and Donna too. Saffron can take them to the cottage.

'Elspeth,' he says, 'is there another key to that room?'

'I don't know. How should I know? It's not my house. It fell between the floorboards. That's what he said. This stupid old place – I don't . . . Someone needs to help. Please! That policeman hasn't been able to do anything, he's in there too now, and . . .'

She gasps for breath, and Jayden fills in the blank.

And this old house is going up like a tinderbox.

62

Inside the burning house, Mullins is trying not to breathe. Which isn't really working out. He lifts the chair and runs at Lucas's door again with all of his might. The blasted wood panelling splinters but holds. All Mullins wants is to suck in a lungful of air, but already the black smoke is on the third floor. Putrid, choking.

Mullins isn't stupid; he has one eye on the stairs, and the flames aren't spreading as quickly as they could. His mum's voice comes into his head: *Proper furniture, none of this synthetic junk, Tim.* Wherever this fire started, Edward Grey's house is doing its best to hold it off, as if there are centuries' worth of toffs saying, 'Not on our watch.' And Mullins? He's just got to get through this door, get Lucas, and get both of them out into the open air.

No biggie.

Sweat runs from his forehead. His eyes are watering, stinging. Any second he's expecting to be hauled out of here by the fire crew. *That's going to happen, right? Any second.* Mullins isn't trained for this. He's got none of the gear. He knew all that when Elspeth turned to him with her desperate plea, but in he went anyway, like an idiotic have-a-go hero. And now? Now he's not much more than a mad bloke trying to batter a door down with a chair. Scared for his life.

'Lucas!' he shouts. 'Get back!'

And Mullins goes at it again. Full force. Bull, china shop: that's him. The wood splinters again, and he can see inside the room now. The shape of Lucas, hopping from one foot to the other as if he's trodden on a jellyfish. Mullins throws the chair aside and aims a big kick at the door.

No police-issue boots tonight but a pub shoe. Because Mullins was on his way to a dub night, and he thought he might need to do something or other on the dancefloor. Suede, if anyone's asking, little bit smart, not too fussy – and about as much good as a silk stocking for this. He kicks again, then goes at it with his shoulder too. Pain smashes up his arm, but he's doing it. He's doing it.

I've bloody done it.

He's through, landing on the hard floor on the other side, the wreckage of the door all around him. For a second, he's winded, and he pushes his fist to his mouth, fighting the temptation to gulp in the poisoned air. He coughs, and it rasps in his throat.

Lucas comes towards him – and then he's past him.

He's out the door.

Lucas Grey has only bloody left him behind.

Mullins wants to laugh. To say to Jayden, *You'll never guess what he did, mate.* Over a pint, he'll do that, for sure, and throw in a bag of Scampi Fries while you're at it. He gets to his knees, then his feet. He storms through what's left of the door – with what's left of himself – and runs smack into Lucas's back.

Oh, he waited for me after all. What a gent.

Then Mullins sees why Lucas's exit was aborted. Fire climbs the stairs ahead of them like the live thing it is, puffing black smoke and stopping for nothing.

Despite the insane heat, Mullins goes cold from head to foot.

'Is there another way out?' he shouts.

It's loud, fire. That's what they don't tell you. It's really, really loud.

Lucas's face is skeleton-pale. Mullins can't hear him, but the headshake says it.

No way out.

Mullins grabs hold of Lucas, pulls him back into the room.

'Alright,' he says. 'It's got to be the window.'

Mullins leans out and sees Jayden and Robbie Cassidy on the grass far below. Mullins can't make it out, but they're dragging something big between them. A mattress?

That'll do it.

'Mullins!' yells Jayden, cupping his hands round his mouth. 'I tried getting in but there's no way—'

'The stairs are cut off! This is the way out.'

Mullins estimates it. Three floors. Maybe ten metres. It's a drop, alright. It's a drop.

'We'll position it, okay? How's your aim, mate?'

'Spot on,' yells Mullins. He wheels round to Lucas. 'Alright, here's the plan.'

Over Lucas's shoulder Mullins sees the little wooden bed and sprints to it. He drags off the cover and gets a hold of that mattress too. He hoists it to the window, pushing at it to force it through. He coughs with effort, throat burning – even though, normal times, he could lift a thing like that with his little finger.

Meanwhile the tick-tick-ticking bomb of the fire on the stairs, and it's heading in only one direction.

'Every little helps, Lucas,' he says, with a grin that probably comes out as a grimace. 'Right? Jayden, incoming!'

With a push, the skinny single mattress twirls through the air, buckling on impact. Jayden and Robbie rush to position it. Their landing has now increased by maybe twenty per cent.

'Okay, Lucas. This is it. Let's go.'

But Lucas isn't moving.

'Lucas, mate? It's a straight jump. Easy.'

The guy shakes his head. He looks more afraid than when Mullins burst into the room. How's that even possible?

'Lucas, we've got to go. That fire's not stopping. We've got seconds for this. That's it.'

Or we die.

Did he say that last bit out loud? It's got the bloke moving, anyway. Lucas edges forward, plants a hand on the sill and grips hold of it. He leans out, then quickly back in.

'Can't do it.'

'You can do it,' says Mullins.

'Not heights. I'm scared of heights.'

'Don't love 'em myself.'

'Terrified of them.'

'This is the way out. The only one. Come on, mate. You've got this. It's a straight jump.'

Lucas shakes his head. He makes a strange sound and his shoulders bounce. The bloke's trying not to sob.

'Lucas, we've got to do this.' He claps a hand to him, pulls him in. 'Trust me, it's a straight drop. Easy. Just get up here on the sill, I'll hold you steady, then let yourself go. The guys have got the mattresses. See? Just down there. It'll be like a bouncy castle. Like soft play. Alright?'

Lucas peers over again, his whole body shaking. Over his shoulder, far below, Mullins can see Jayden and Robbie in position, ready to adjust if they need to. Couple of pros. They've got this.

And they must be wondering why the bloody hell we're not already jumping.

'Lucas, now or never. Seriously.'

The sound, the heat, the smoke. Tick, tick, tick.

Lucas says something and Mullins leans in to catch it. It sounds like 'You go first.'

'Go on,' says Lucas, louder, and Mullins's eardrum crackles. 'You go first. I want to see you do it.'

'I'm not leaving you, Lucas. You're getting out first.'

'You don't trust it, do you? I'm not going to be your guinea pig.'

The bloody idiot.

'I trust it,' says Mullins. 'I trust it all day long. That bloke down there, Jayden, there's no one better. He's going to look after you. So, you're going to jump, and you're going to be all good.'

Lucas shakes his head. His eyes are glazed over; cheeks wet. Mullins takes a different tack; laughs and cuffs his shoulder.

'Look, if you so much as break a little finger, I'll give you fifty quid, Lucas. How's that?'

Definitely going to break a finger.

'No. No, no, no. You have to go first.'

Mullins stares at him. There's no way he's jumping first. He's police, he protects others, and that means getting Lucas out. Mullins would be in a world of trouble if he jumped first. And besides, he couldn't forgive himself.

'I'm only doing it,' says Lucas, lips wobbling again, 'if you go first.'

And Mullins wants to shake him. Get hold of his shoulders and shake the bones of him. Because if they don't move it, they are going to die. Right here, right now. Dead. Because this bloke won't jump.

'Mullins!' Jayden is yelling from outside, at the very top of his voice. A lion's roar.

'I mean it,' says Lucas, grabbing hold of Mullins, his nails biting at his arm with surprising force for a skinny bloke. 'You go first. Show it's safe. I need to know it's safe. Then I'll go.'

Mullins looks behind. The fire's not in the corridor, not yet. But the smoke is, the smoke is everywhere. His eyes burn.

'You don't jump first,' says Lucas, pushing his face close to his, 'then we both die. You want that on you, do you?'

Well, I'd be dead, so . . .

Mullins groans, defeated. He takes one long look at Lucas – his streaming eyes, his quivering chin – then he climbs up on to the sill. Mullins doesn't like it. He doesn't like it one bit.

'Lucas, you go straight after me. Okay? I'll land, test it, like you say, then get clear. Then you go. Promise me.'

'Got it. Show me it works.'

'It'll work.' Mullins hesitates. 'Lucas, please. You've got to go first. This is all wrong.'

He hates the pleading in his voice.

'It's the only way I'm doing it,' says Lucas.

Immovable.

'Swear you'll follow me.'

'I swear.'

Mullins shifts his position, readying himself. Looks back over his shoulder.

'Swear?'

Lucas nods.

So Mullins drops.

His arms and legs flail and he hits the ground like he's an egg smashing on a kitchen floor. But then he feels the give of the mattress, more hands – gentle hands, this time – on his shoulder, and he's gasping. Pain shoots down his arm.

Alright, maybe a little finger broken.

'Mullins.'

Jayden's there. Jayden's hands are on him. Mullins rolls to his knees, falls clear of the mattress and he's on the wet grass. He staggers to his feet, Jayden catching his arm and just holding him.

'Lucas,' Mullins shouts up. 'See that? Easy. Your turn.'

The sky is swirling with black smoke now, the flames pouring out the second-floor windows. Lucas is at the window. One leg appears over the sill. He stops. The one leg dangles. He freezes.

'That's it!' Mullins yells. 'You've got this, mate. Just take a seat up there, then it's a straight drop, you just—'

His voice breaks, and Mullins explodes in coughing. He feels Jayden's hand in the middle of his back, rubbing slow circles.

'Lucas!' yells Jayden, taking over. 'Three, two, one. Okay? You've got this.'

The leg stays frozen.

'Lucas!' yells Jayden.

The leg goes back inside.

Mullins pounds at his chest as he coughs and spits on the ground.

'Lucas!' he shouts, his throat burning like the fire is inside him. 'Lucas! You swore! Lucas!'

But Lucas is gone from the window.

Mullins is still shouting the man's name as two fire engines blast on to the lawn. And he's still shouting it as Jayden folds an arm around his shoulders and walks him to the waiting ambulance. By the time the firefighters stream out with a stretcher, Mullins's voice is gone altogether.

63

Ally picks her way through the emergency vehicles. The air is still thick with smoke, and she can taste it at the very back of her throat. Her eyes sting, and she feels a mix of relief – and guilt. As she and Pippa pulled up in the driveway, a firefighter met them. One fatality, he confirmed. And Ally thought straight away of Jayden, because he's always the one who runs towards danger. It's always him. And she felt Pippa's hand on her arm.

It won't be Jayden, Pippa said.

It's the owner, said the firefighter.

And Ally thought then of Casey's unborn child – and in the confusion of it all, the stress, she must have cried out, but then it was Pippa saying calmly, quite soberly, *You mean Lucas Grey.*

Now, Ally sees Jayden coming towards her. He holds out his arms and she steps into them. He tells her what happened, and that Mullins is on his way to the hospital with a broken collarbone and smoke inhalation.

'He's in a bad way,' he says.

And Jayden explains how Lucas refused to jump unless Mullins first proved it was safe. But then Lucas couldn't do it. By the time the fire engines arrived, the flames had engulfed the room he was in.

'Mullins is devastated,' says Jayden. 'He thinks Lucas's death is all his fault.'

'But what else could he do?'

'Nothing,' says Jayden. Then, 'Same circumstances, I'd have done the same. Lucas gave him no choice.'

'Where's Elspeth?' asks Ally.

Before Jayden can answer, Skinner's beside them. He claps a hand on both of their shoulders, then he eyes Pippa, who's standing off to one side. He shakes his head, as if none of it – none of it at all – makes sense.

'Elspeth Grey says her husband locked himself in. Then managed to lose the key.'

'But how's that possible?'

'She said something about Lucas dropping it between the floorboards,' says Jayden. 'She was panicking, not very coherent, and—'

'Well, I'm glad you were on the spot to tell us how it was, Jayden,' snaps Skinner. Then he presses his hand to his forehead. 'Sorry. But . . . this whole case is a mess. This whole place is a mess. And I've got a constable who—' Skinner stops.

'Mullins went above and beyond,' cuts in Jayden. 'He wasn't even on duty.'

'That I know. Which begs the question . . .'

'It was me,' says Ally. 'I was the one who asked him to come. I knew Jayden was here, and—'

Skinner holds up his hand as if he doesn't want to know.

'Before you pair rush to his defence, it'll all be going in his statement, when he's well enough to make it,' he says. 'In the meantime, I expect Mullins told you about the amendment to the post-mortem findings?'

Skinner's voice has softened a notch. Ally and Jayden look to one another. They shake their heads.

'Looks like you were right on the flintlock pistol being used as a weapon. Which might go some way to explaining why Lucas

Grey locked himself in his childhood bedroom. In fact, that's the only logical explanation. Beating us to the damn punch.'

'Casey, Axel's ex, said that—' begins Jayden.

'I know who Casey James is, thank you very much.'

'She said that Lucas was yelling at Elspeth. A huge row about the inheritance. Casey was afraid and left the house.'

'At that particular point, why would Lucas be yelling about the inheritance? He had what he wanted.'

So Jayden explains that part to Skinner too. Ally watches as the detective processes the information – and then starts to pace.

'So . . . Lucas Grey strikes Axel with the pistol, pushes him off the cliff, and is set to get his so-called rightful inheritance, until you two turn up a new heir. And so then he loses it. His wife doesn't appreciate his reaction, hence the row . . .'

'Lucas didn't like that Elspeth was kind to Casey,' says Ally.

'So Elspeth's cooing over Casey James, meanwhile Lucas is raging. Because it turns out he killed Axel all for nothing. So they have a big barney, and he shuts himself up in his old bedroom and throws away the key.'

'Drops the key,' says Jayden. 'Random act. That's what Elspeth said.'

'And then fire breaks out. Early indication is that it was candles in the lounge. Simple as that. And then all hell breaks loose.'

Jayden drops his head. 'I saw the candles when I went in,' he says. 'I should have—'

'Is this how you always do things, Detective Sergeant?'

They turn to see Elspeth Grey standing there. She's wearing a dark coat that swamps her, and her face is red from crying.

'Mrs Grey,' says Skinner. He coughs awkwardly.

He's clearly wondering how much Elspeth has heard. By the look on her face, Ally suspects most of it. But then there is grief too, and shock. Ally immediately goes to her side, but Elspeth looks all the way through her – and fixes on Skinner.

'While I don't appreciate your manner, you might have . . .' Elspeth holds a hand to her mouth and stops. She closes her eyes.

Ally feels a bolt of adrenalin. *Elspeth knows.*

'You think he killed Axel Marks,' says Skinner, as if reading Ally's mind.

'My husband isn't here to defend himself, but the things he said . . .'

'You believe he killed him,' Skinner repeats, quite undaunted.

'Yes,' says Elspeth, in all but a whisper. 'Yes. He said he killed Axel. He didn't set out to, but . . . Oh God.'

As Elspeth breaks down, Ally and Jayden meet eyes. *It was Lucas all along.* But the revelation, in this moment, brings no satisfaction.

'Elspeth,' says Ally gently, 'why don't you wait to talk to the police properly, when—'

But Elspeth shakes her head. She shakes, in fact, her whole body, as if composing herself from top to toe. She draws a long breath.

'Lucas was so incredibly hurt by his father's decision about the house,' she says, speaking each word slowly, carefully, as if it's an effort of great will. 'I . . . had no idea how much until tonight. He hid so much from me, he . . .' She stops; breathes. 'I thought I knew his heart. It's a horrible shock to discover that . . . I didn't.'

'And when he did reveal those true feelings,' says Skinner, 'did you challenge him about Axel, Elspeth? Was that the row?'

Ally looks to Jayden, to see if he agrees that Skinner should be pulling back. But Jayden's eyes are on Elspeth.

Elspeth holds a shaking hand to her cheek. Did Lucas strike her there? Was the row physical? Past Elspeth, Ally can see Pippa watching too, her face crumpled with pity. They're all so horribly spellbound.

'We argued,' says Elspeth, tucking her chin into the collar of her coat. 'Lucas just came out with it. He blamed his father, of course. He couldn't take responsibility, even for a thing like that, and . . .' She looks up, her eyes glittering with a new wave of tears. 'I had no idea what an unhappy man he is. Was. *My God.* As his wife, don't I have to bear some responsibility for that?'

'And you didn't think to call us there and then?' says Skinner. He gestures behind him. 'Before all this?'

But he's being unfair now. The police knowing the truth about Lucas wouldn't have stopped the fire.

Ally turns to see Casey, Donna and Robbie approaching. *Skinner has an audience now.* Casey goes to stand beside Elspeth and puts an arm around her shoulders in comfort.

She can't have heard Elspeth's admission.

'I'm so, so sorry, Casey,' says Elspeth, turning to her. 'And to you too, little darling . . .' She places a careful hand on Casey's bump. 'And now there's nothing left. Nothing at all.'

Ally takes in the confusion on Casey's face as Elspeth quietly sobs. Ally feels a flash of anger for Skinner. It wasn't right to let this scene unfold here.

None of this is right.

Behind them, the house is a blackened ruin against the sky.

64

Jayden watches as Elspeth leaves with Skinner. She insisted on making a formal statement there and then, despite Skinner telling her that it could wait. Was it a way of avoiding the reality of Lucas's death, or an attempt to atone for her husband's actions? Beside the detective sergeant – a hi-vis jacket over her nightdress – Elspeth looks both helpless and determined.

Jayden feels a tug at his sleeve, and it's Donna.

'Sorry, but we don't know what to do now,' she says, gesturing at the ruin. 'Me and Robbie. I mean . . .'

Porthmerrin House has no need for nurse or gardener. Porthmerrin House is no more.

Jayden suddenly feels very tired. He saw those candles burning unattended. Why didn't he think to stop and blow them out? Mullins is busy blaming himself for Lucas's death, but what about the fire in the first place – could that have been avoided too?

'I guess just stay in the cottage,' he says. 'Or don't, if you have somewhere else. It's up to you. Elspeth's in charge now, but she's got other things on her mind, so . . . I'd give her space.'

'I don't want to stay here,' says Donna. 'After everything that's happened. Three people dead in three days.'

A grim statistic.

Next to Donna, Robbie drags a hand across his eyes. His hair stands on end and there's a smear of soot on his cheek that looks like the mark of a cross. He beams exhaustion. Robbie worked hard tonight, doing everything he could: trying with the ladder, the hose, making all the difference with the mattress. And he felt the weight of seeing Lucas at the window – that leg over the sill – then drawing back inside too. None of them can unsee that.

Pitching up here tonight, Jayden wasn't ruling Robbie out. Not by miles. But now he has to, and it feels a lot like relief. He holds out his hand, and the gardener shakes it.

A limp grip. Maybe he sustained an injury. Maybe he's just got nothing left in the tank.

'Rob, can we go?' says Donna. 'Sleep somewhere else tonight, like a B&B, or . . .'

'I don't want to leave.' Robbie passes his hand across his mouth. 'This is my home.'

His tone cuts like a blade. Jayden glances to Ally. She's all eyes on Robbie too.

'This place is all I've got.'

Donna laughs uneasily. 'Not all you've got. You've got me, Rob . . .'

'It's my home,' he says again.

And then he shoulders off into the darkness.

Donna turns to them, wide-eyed. 'He's emotional,' she says, her voice full of apology. 'I know he loves it here, and without it he's afraid that he'll have nowhere. He said the one good thing about Lucas getting the house instead of Axel was that Lucas wouldn't sell up.' She glances to Casey. 'Oh God, I'm sorry. That sounds so rough. What I mean is that Robbie thought Lucas would want to keep it in the family. He wanted to still be gardening this place when he was old and grey. So I get it. I get why he's gutted that it's gone . . .' She stops; rubs her nose with the back of her hand. 'It's all just so crazy. I mean, it makes no sense. Why would Lucas be locked in a room? Why would he do that? Are you sure that someone didn't . . .'

The unfinished sentence flutters in the air.

'I know,' says Jayden. Because it's not like the same thought hasn't crossed his mind. 'But . . . Lucas confessed. Maybe he was punishing himself. No one could have foreseen the fire . . .'

'It's all such a mess,' croaks Donna. She turns, following Robbie into the dark. Then abruptly stops. She rushes to Casey, puts her hand in hers. She whispers something Jayden can't catch and Casey nods, murmurs, 'Thank you.'

Jayden sighs. There are no winners in this. Not a one.

You okay? he mouths to Casey, and she nods. She's leaning on a stick, her ankle still off the ground. The medics looked at it for her. They suggested she gets an X-ray tomorrow, but they reckon it's just a bad sprain. The pain is zero compared to what she's carrying: the knowledge that Axel came to Porthmerrin with an open heart – and was killed for it.

'Jayden,' says Ally, 'Pippa's going to stay at The Shell House.'

There's still a lot they don't know about Pippa, but Ally filled him in on what Mullins said, and their conversation in Penzance.

'I'll go back to the island in the morning,' says Pippa. 'If the boat's running. Ally, are you sure? After all I've done. All I've . . .'

'Pippa,' says Jayden, 'if it wasn't for you, none of us would be here.'

He realises that's come out wrong. They're standing in wreckage, every one of them. But what he means is that Pippa was the one who wanted answers for Axel. And, somehow, they've got them. But there are more explanations to come. Because, despite

Elspeth's words, and Elspeth's hand on her bump, Casey still doesn't know what her daughter stands to inherit.

The ruin of it all.

Jayden turns to her; takes a breath.

'Casey,' he says. 'We need to talk.'

65

'Tim, we're keeping you under observation for the night,' says the doctor.

Mullins nods. His throat's too sore to speak much anyway. He closes his eyes, but as he does the scenes of the night rush back in and so he opens them again.

Beside him, Saffron puts her hand on his. The other one's done up in a sling, on account of his busted collarbone. Her touch is so warm.

'You should go,' he says, moving his hand away.

'I've got nowhere else to be.'

He can't look at her.

'Cheers, Saff, but I'm just going to go to sleep.'

There's no way he's going to sleep. He's bone-tired, but his head's too noisy.

'I'll be here when you wake up,' she says, and he knows she's giving him one of those smiles. He can hear it in her voice.

'I don't want you here,' he says. Then, 'Not personal. I don't want anyone here.'

And then he jams his eyes shut. He hears the soft shuck of the chair as she gets up, the squeak of her trainers.

'Rest up, Mullins,' she says.

And then he feels a featherlight kiss on the top of his head.

Then she's gone. Just like he wanted, apparently.

~

Light's streaming into the room when Mullins wakes. For a split second he thinks it's a fine and standard day, then he remembers. He plummets. Only this time with no mattress to break his fall. Miraculously, he dreamt of nothing at all last night. But the way it all rushes back in now makes any nightmare look like a let-off.

With his good arm, he checks his phone. His mum's staying with her sister in Truro, and as far as she knows everything's hunky-dory: just Mullins plodding about being Mullins; bit of bother with the body on the island, maybe, but all in a day's work. He wants to keep it that way, though she's got a sixth sense, has Jenny Mullins.

But there's only a message from Jayden: How are you doing, mate? Want a visitor?

'Ah, Sleeping Beauty awakes.'

Skinner, holding a Styrofoam cup, nosing through the blue curtain at the end of his bed.

Mullins pulls himself up. He feels stupid in the hospital gown. A busted collarbone and a bit of smoke? It's hardly bad, is it?

Skinner rocks on his heels, looking uncertain; stroking the ends of his moustache.

This is it. Any second now, it's coming.

'Earlier yesterday evening, Lucas Grey admitted to his wife that he killed Axel Marks.'

Mullins blinks hard. He was so sure Skinner was about to fire him. Dereliction of duty: failing to protect and support a member of the public. Gross misconduct; saving your own skin.

He still might.

'Elspeth Grey made a full statement, Mullins. And given the situation . . . with the perpetrator being . . . deceased, well, it's case closed.'

Skinner holds out a hand and it takes Mullins a beat to understand that he wants them to shake.

'Look,' says Skinner, and he eyes the chair beside the bed and dumps himself in it. Then he shifts forward, hands on his knees. 'Look,' he says again.

Here it comes.

'You did what you could, Mullins.'

Just get it over with.

Mullins has the bedclothes pulled up to his chin. He eyes Skinner sideways. He doesn't want to, but it's probably insubordination not to look at him. Not that that matters right now.

'This is not on you, Mullins.'

The back of Mullins's throat burns.

'What happened to Lucas Grey is not your fault.'

Mullins grits his teeth. He tastes metal. And smoke. *I can still taste smoke.*

'I've got your back, Tim. When you're up to it, you'll make a statement. Jayden has already. He said . . . Well, he said how hard you worked up there. He said how hard you tried.'

The room's blurring now. Mullins can feel his lower lip wobbling like a five-year-old's.

'The way you played it, I'm not sure I would have done it any different. The bloke had you between a rock and a hard place, didn't he?'

'He promised me,' mumbles Mullins.

But maybe the word of a killer isn't worth much.

'Elspeth knew about the pistol, did she?' he croaks.

'She didn't know Lucas took it, if that's what you mean. But she was aware of Edward's collection. And that's what'll make the charge stick. Not that there'll be a charge, it being posthumous and all that. But that bloody pirate pistol, together with Take Two on the pathologist's report, categorically confirms foul play.'

Mullins nods. He feels a wash of fatigue sweep over him; it takes him like a rip tide, and he lets it. It's what Hippy-Dippy said before that one and only surf lesson of theirs: *You get taken by a rip, Mullins, you go with it. Alright? You relax, and let it take you. It'll spit you out along the shore and you'll be fine. Just fine.*

For the first time since being admitted to this hospital, Mullins feels safe.

But the way he was with Saffron last night? He needs to apologise. Big-time.

'I need to apologise,' says Skinner.

Mullins blinks again. Interior and exterior worlds, blurring weirdly.

'This whole case. I haven't been on my A game.'

For a second, Mullins wonders if this is, in fact, all a dream. A hallucination. Like in a minute Skinner will start barking like a dog, and Lucas Grey will run in, then the ceiling will fall, and they'll all go up in flames. No one getting out of it, least of all him.

'I was too quick to dismiss it,' says Skinner.

'You always said it was a thankless one. No evidence, no way of proving anything . . .'

'But there was evidence, wasn't there? And there was proof. Shell House to the rescue once again. We should be used to it by now, Mullins. I should be used to it. Ally and Jayden saving the day.'

Skinner has a strange smile on his face. Or maybe it's not strange, it's just . . . a smile. Mullins isn't used to seeing it.

'They're good detectives,' he says.

'Ah well, you know who else is?' Skinner shuffles in his seat. 'This missing-A-game business, well, it's not an excuse, but . . . you were on the money when you said you thought it was something to do with Meredith.'

Meredith. She's always just been 'the wife' or – mostly – 'the ex'.

'I had a bit of a shock,' says Skinner. 'Last weekend.'

Mullins fully looks at Skinner, in the way he thinks Hippy-Dippy probably would. Listening face. Kind eyes too, if he can find them, because Mullins figures he owes him.

'See, she always told me she didn't want kids. She's a good few years younger than me, Meredith, but our whole marriage, that's what she said. Then we parted ways, as you know, and she gets herself in a new relationship. No problem with that, you've got to move on. But then I saw her on Saturday, down at the new shopping centre. First time in nearly two years, I reckon. And . . . she's got a kiddie with her. She's got a kiddie with her, and it's hers.'

Skinner stops. He drains his coffee.

'I tell you what, Mullins, nothing prepared me for that.'

'Sarge,' says Mullins quietly.

'I wanted them, see. Kiddies. But she didn't, so . . .' He passes a hand through his thinning hair. 'Lovely little lad he was too. Lovely.'

Mullins doesn't know what to say. Jayden would. Hippy-Dippy definitely would. She'd be getting in there with a hug.

Or a little kiss, right on the top of his head, where he'd least expect it.

'It's not too late for you, Sarge.'

'What, to make it up with Meredith? Oh, that ship has sailed.'

'For kids, I mean. To be a dad.'

But as he says it, Mullins wonders how old Skinner actually is. He's one of those blokes you just can't tell. Was there a fiftieth birthday a while back? A shiny new tie?

'I think that ship's gone and sailed too.' Skinner shakes his head, crushes his coffee cup in his fist. 'Anyway, now you know. I always say don't ever let the personal interfere with the professional, especially in our line of work. Fact is, you were in this case with both boots, Mullins, and me? I was only half in the room.'

Skinner gets to his feet, then pats Mullins on the shoulder.

'I'm sorry I let you down, son.'

And he's gone before Mullins can think what to say back.

66

Ally sits on the veranda, watching over the bay. There's a silky quality to the morning light. Sand martins dip and weave. The waves roll in in lines, perfect as the pleats in a skirt. Ally has her phone in her hand; she really does need to call Ray. He messaged yesterday: What do you think, Al? If it's a coin toss, I was rather hoping you'd make it double-sided. She marked it with a heart emoji – very modern of her – but is yet to reply properly. And the case is no longer an excuse for the delay.

Pippa appears in the doorway, peering shyly as if she's interrupting. Fox gets up from his spot and pushes against her legs as Pippa bends to stroke him.

'I've phoned for a taxi,' she says, looking up. 'And I've booked Trent too.'

'Oh, what time's the taxi coming? Let me at least make you a coffee.'

Ally knows she sounds disappointed, but she wanted to make Pippa breakfast; wanted her to know that there is no need to rush away. Pippa told Ally her full story last night. She talked of her violent first husband, Liam, and the damage to her confidence that had lasted far beyond the physical harm. How she fell too readily for Fergus in the aftermath, knowing they weren't suited really. She spoke of the trauma of being under suspicion when Liam was killed in a hit-and-run accident just after his release from jail. *My mum was taken ill, and so I'd been back in Cheltenham when it happened,* Pippa said, *so I understood why the police had to question me. As far as they were concerned, I had means, motive and opportunity. And honestly? Some part of me probably did wish him dead.*

Ally thought of Pippa's mention of her first husband having died, when they first met at The Shell House. That glance of hers towards Bill's photograph that seemed too deliberate. *The way you spoke of it then,* she said to Pippa, choosing her words carefully, *I would never have guessed the complexity of the situation.* And Pippa looked contrite. She admitted that she had so badly wanted to connect with Ally, just so she would take the case.

After the call from Fergus, Mullins and Skinner had latched on to Pippa's ongoing fear of Liam's family punishing her – a fear that was there after her testimony sent Liam to jail and, according to Fergus, only increased after his death. In that light, Ally could see how the police thought Pippa might have been wary of any trespassers on the island, especially when she was alone there. The narrative of Axel being alive when he came ashore had been worth exploring, even if it sounded as though the police approach was rather heavy-handed. As for Fergus, he'd never replied to Jayden's message; he talked to the police, but that was where his interest ran out.

Pippa apologised to Ally for disappearing as she had. For giving all the wrong impressions, as messages and calls went unanswered; how she felt embarrassed, too, for the state in which she'd been found.

Ally might have taken her in last night out of sympathy, but she feels they ended the evening as friends. The woman is a survivor.

'Oh, yes please to a quick coffee,' says Pippa. 'I haven't had a hangover in years. It's just awful.'

'You really don't need to rush off, Pippa. You can rest here.'

'Thank you, but . . . if you can understand it, I want to enjoy the island while I still can.'

'You never know,' says Ally, 'you might not have to leave after all.'

Pippa's appeal to the wildlife trust is still ongoing. Ally suggested that she request a trial period, to show that she can handle things solo. *I feel safe on the island*, Pippa told her, *I always have. Fergus could never tolerate the idea that I can cope on my own, because at the point in my life that I met him, I couldn't.*

Now Pippa leans against the balustrade, as Fox settles at her feet. 'The last few days . . .' she says, 'I can't make sense of them.'

'What do you mean?' says Ally.

'I keep wondering if Axel came to me for a reason. I'm trying to take some . . . positive, from all of this dreadfulness.'

Ally thinks of Axel's terrible death. Edward's passing. Lucas burning. Pippa's own trauma resurfacing, adrift in the streets of Penzance. *All this dreadfulness.*

But a glimmer too.

'Well,' she says, 'if you hadn't found Axel, and pushed for answers, then the truth would never have come out, Pippa. Casey would never have known what happened. Their child would have grown up never knowing too.'

Pippa dips her head. 'Thank you, Ally,' she says. Then, 'I told you Casey wants to come over, didn't I? Later today or tomorrow, when her ankle's a little better.'

'You did.'

To see the place where Axel came ashore, that's what Pippa said last night. Ally thinks of the spring flowers in the jam jar on the rocks. Pippa sitting with Axel's body. Lone Island and its warden took care of him as best they could.

'And I suppose Elspeth would never have known what kind of a man she really married either,' says Pippa. 'Or perhaps she would have, eventually. I hope she would. At least she can start again. In time.'

'A long way away from here, probably,' says Ally.

Ally can't help wondering what will happen to Porthmerrin House now. Whether any part of it is salvageable, and whether insurance might fund a rebuild. There is still the land, at least. While Ally doesn't know the specifics of Edward's will, the property will presumably still belong to Axel and Casey's daughter. And it would be worth a huge amount of money.

Casey simply couldn't take the news in last night. *That can't be right*, she kept saying. *It can't be.*

If Edward's solicitor had been able to attend dinner yesterday evening, would this small change in the rhythm of the evening have provoked a different outcome? Perhaps in the presence of another person, Lucas would have been forced to keep his composure. Perhaps he and Elspeth would never have argued, the dispute escalating to an extent no one foresaw. Perhaps Lucas would never have stormed off to his childhood bedroom; never locked the door nor lost the key. Perhaps Elspeth wouldn't have been so upset and distracted that she went to bed, leaving the candles burning downstairs. Perhaps, perhaps.

But if Lucas had survived the fire, would Elspeth still have told the police what he'd done? Ally pictures her standing in front of Skinner, somebody else's coat over her nightdress, her face shining with tears, her voice wavering but firm. Ally has a feeling that Elspeth couldn't have brought herself to lie for her husband, no matter the circumstances.

'Oh!' cries Pippa. 'It's here early.'

The blue taxi, so out of place here in the dunes, rumbles down the track. Ally goes to Pippa; hugs her hard.

'Please stay in touch,' she says. 'You're welcome here anytime.'

'And you're welcome on the island. I mean . . . as long as I'm still there. If you'd ever like to stay a night, there's a serviceable sofa . . .'

'I'd love to,' says Ally.

To feel the dark come down around the island at nightfall, see the far-off glint of the shore. Know the seals are sleeping on the rocks. The quiet, folding around them. Then first light; the luminescence of the watery dawn. The Shell House takes some beating, but Lone Island is a world unto itself.

At the gate, Pippa holds up a hand in farewell. Fox watches her go, his nose in the air.

'You liked her, didn't you, boy?' says Ally softly. 'I did too.'

Ally watches the taxi pull away, the dust from the track rising in its wake. And out of said dust comes Jayden. His dear loping stride. He has his hands in his pockets and his head dipped. Lost in apparent thought, he barely registers the taxi.

Time for their debrief.

Ally steps down from the veranda. It's another case solved, but it doesn't feel like a success. And by the look of him, she suspects Jayden thinks the same.

'Coffee?' she says by way of greeting.

'Coffee,' he says. 'And a question.'

67

'Top shelf, please, Wenna. The Shoreline Vines sparkling.'

Gus is after a bottle of wine. And not just any bottle, but a Pinot Noir courtesy of their local vineyard that is, after new investment, thriving once again. Costs a pretty penny too, but it's worth it.

'Ooh, bubbles, is it?' Wenna regards him over the top of her specs. 'What's the occasion?'

'No occasion,' says Gus. Because he likes to maintain an air of mystery where Wenna is concerned: the woman's a wicked gossip. Plus, Gus doesn't know how much of what went on up at Porthmerrin House last night is common knowledge yet. It's certainly not on the front page of any of the papers in Wenna's rack. But Gus heard the news hot off the press, as he messaged Ally earlier. She sounded rather downbeat, he thought, not exactly air-punch territory. But then a man had died. Even if he was the killer.

And goodness, poor Tim Mullins being put through it as well.

It was your flintlock pistol news that did it, Gus, Ally wrote in her message. And he must confess that made him glow.

Gus is just settling up when he throws in a Terry's Chocolate Orange for Mullins.

'Much obliged, Wenna,' he says, tipping an imaginary hat. Then he's out the door, hugging his wares to his chest.

Then he stops dead.

A young man in a slick blue suit is wrestling with a 'For Sale' sign outside the very house that Gus was snooping at online yesterday. The very house that, last spring, Ray Finch rented for himself after charging into town. *Lighthouse Cottage.* Gus watches as the man takes the sign out of the ground, hoists it over his shoulder and sticks it in the back of his car.

'Excuse me.'

Gus can feel the Chocolate Orange starting to slip from his grip, and he clamps his elbow to his side to trap it.

'It hasn't . . . been sold, has it?'

The young man grins. 'You bet. Was only on the market thirty-six hours.'

Gus feels slightly sick.

'Who on earth bought it?'

'Some bloke from upcountry. Impulsive chap. Love it.'

'Londoner, I suppose?' tries Gus, mentally crossing his fingers. 'Classic second-homer, is it?'

'No, he says he's moving down here lock, stock and barrel. Not from London . . . Somewhere else.'

'Where?'

Gus is aware he sounds faintly desperate.

'Sussex?' The man shrugs. 'Could be Sussex.'

It's bloody Suffolk, isn't it.

The Chocolate Orange slips from his grip, bouncing on the pavement before jumping into a puddle. Gus stares at it dimly as dirty water seeps into the cardboard.

'Wet chocolate,' says the man.

Accurate, but unnecessary.

'Yes,' says Gus, stooping to retrieve it. 'What was I thinking?'

And he shuffles away, stuffing the soggy box in the kerbside wheelie bin of godforsaken Lighthouse Cottage as he goes. What was he thinking, indeed. How is a cheap bit of chocolate recompense for escaping death by the skin of your teeth? Nevertheless, Gus'll drop back in at Wenna's and replace it; he can't let the lad down. And he might just ask for a refund on his bottle at the same time. Because what's the point in toasting anything if Ray Finch is moving to Porthpella?

'Brownies for Mullins,' says Gus. 'That's a lovely thought.'

Gus has taken his sinking heart to Hang Ten, where he's usually assured of a pick-me-up.

'Just a little thing,' says Saffron, as she cuts them into giant hunks and carefully sets them in a white cardboard box. Gus counts seven, eight, nine, ten – and she keeps them coming. 'They're his favourite, aren't they? Hey Gus, you wouldn't do me a massive favour, would you?'

'Of course.'

'Drop them at his place?'

'He's out of hospital, then, is he?'

'Not sure . . .' Saffron chews her lip. 'I don't want to bug him, and . . .'

'Ally said you were with him last night when he went in.'

'Well, yeah. But I think he's had enough of my face by now.'

And Gus studies said face. Saffron doesn't look herself today, he thinks. He's certain he doesn't either – *not since the godforsaken Lighthouse Cottage* – but then perhaps such changes are less noticeable in his old mug. Saffron is sunshine, but today the clouds have blown in.

'I don't believe that for a second,' says Gus.

Because, apart from anything, they all know how Mullins feels about Saffron. Even if she appears not to.

'He is alright, isn't he? Mullins, I mean. You're not worried, Saffron? Because Ally said he'd broken his collarbone, but other than that . . .'

Saffron folds the box closed. She fiddles with the card-board fastener.

'I am,' she says. Then she looks up, her eyes swimming. 'I actually am. For literally the first time in my life, Gus, I'm worried about Tim Mullins.'

68

'Lucas was petrified, Al. In the true sense of the word.'

They're back on the veranda, coffees in hand. Out in the bay, big sets are rolling in; lines darkening until explosions of white-water fly into shore.

'If you were that scared of heights,' says Jayden, 'so scared that even when your life is at stake you can't jump down on to a soft landing, would you pick a cliff edge as a place to attack someone?'

Ally lets the question sit. She watches a distant speck of a surfer get up on a wave – dance and dance then fall. Jayden has explained that last night he couldn't sleep. He kept going over and over it – and it didn't sit right.

'Because even if Axel was drunk, and weakened, he'd fight back, right?' he says. 'He's ex-army. Okay, it was a long time ago, and maybe he wasn't in the shape he was once, but there's a physique, a basic strength . . . and Lucas knew that. There's every chance Lucas could have gone off the cliff instead of Axel. Or both of them. But Al, honestly, I can't see Lucas even going anywhere near the edge of a sheer drop. Not after what I witnessed last night. And I know Mullins would agree.'

Jayden's right. But last night there was a fire raging. Last night Lucas was in pieces because he'd admitted to his wife that he'd killed

Axel. Under those circumstances, couldn't an everyday healthy fear of heights turn to something more debilitating?

But when Ally says this, Jayden gives a shake of his head. 'I witnessed it first-hand, Al. And so did Mullins. It was the height that scared him, even more than the threat of the fire. Which seems crazy, but . . .'

'But why would Lucas confess to Elspeth if it wasn't true?'

Jayden raises his eyebrows. 'Al?'

'I know, I know, we've only Elspeth's word for it, but . . .'

Elspeth lying. The concept doesn't sit comfortably, because everything Ally's seen of Elspeth has made her trust her. But shouldn't Ally know by now, to trust no one? Not when it comes down to it.

'You can't think she locked him in the room?' she says.

'No, because Mullins confirmed it. Lucas managed to do that to himself.'

She pictures Elspeth telling Skinner – with all of them listening – what Lucas did. The tears on her cheeks; her slight frame standing firm, bare feet planted in the grass. How Ally's heart went out to her, admiring her strength in the moment but all too aware of her vulnerability. Ally wanted to protect her.

'Lucas told me that Elspeth used to be an actress,' says Jayden, as if reading Ally's mind. 'If I'm right about this, her performance last night was virtuoso.'

Ally thinks of how Elspeth didn't usher Skinner away to confide in him in some private place. She laid it all out there in the open – surrounded by an audience.

And they were captivated.

'What if they were both involved?' she says. 'What if it was Elspeth who attacked Axel, but it was Lucas who masterminded it.'

'Maybe. But why does it have to be Lucas who masterminded it? Why not Elspeth?'

'Would she care that much?'

'Sure she would. Money, status, power . . . That's what a house like Porthmerrin represents.'

'Or,' says Ally, 'what if Elspeth misconstrued it? What if she was so appalled by Lucas's reaction to Casey and the pregnancy that she presumed the very worst of him?'

Ally watches Jayden consider it.

'Lucas was unstable last night,' he says. 'He ran upstairs and locked himself in the bedroom he had as a kid. I mean, that's just weird. Okay, maybe you're right, maybe he was ranting away, and in the middle of all that Elspeth got it wrong. Lucas hated Axel, so by default he hates Casey and the fact of the baby, but he didn't actually go and kill the guy. Yeah . . . it's possible. But I still think it's strange, the way Elspeth came out with it all so soon after Lucas's death.'

'Could it have been shock?'

Their eyes are on the water. Clouds have blown in and the early blue-sky promise of the day is blotted out. The waves keep charging. And Ally's mind keeps changing. She's with Jayden on his theory that Lucas's fear of heights rules him out. But does it necessarily rule Elspeth in? If Elspeth did misconstrue Lucas's confession, is the real killer escaping scot-free?

'You know, until we focused on the pistol, and Lucas's personal connection to it, Robbie was looking suspicious,' she says. 'He was visibly upset last night, Jayden. And we both heard what Donna said about why.'

'Yeah.' Jayden rubs at his chin. 'I see where you're going with this.'

He's on his feet now. As he paces, the boards of the veranda creak.

'Okay, so Lucas is in a right state, and Elspeth gets it all wrong. Meanwhile Robbie, no one's looking at him . . . And his motive is a simple one. He thought he'd lose his job and his home if Axel inherited, because he presumed Axel would sell up for the cash.'

'It'd be a fair assumption of Robbie's,' says Ally. 'The upkeep on a house like Porthmerrin would be huge. If you're not being left any reserves with which to maintain it, then if I was in Axel's position I'd probably sell too.'

'So, what, Robbie's thinking that to keep his job and home he needs Lucas to inherit? And he doesn't know about the clause in the will, he doesn't know about Casey, so it seems simple. Get rid of Axel and Lucas inherits. Lucas keeps the house. Robbie keeps his job and home. Status quo maintained.'

'Although there's nothing to say that Lucas would have kept the house,' says Ally. 'I don't think his childhood memories were especially happy ones, were they?'

'That's an understatement. Okay, so it'd be a gamble from Robbie, but maybe it was the best he could come up with. Plus, Robbie knows Donna and Axel used to be close, so maybe he's feeling uneasy on that point too. And he knew about the antique firearms collection, Al. As staff, he'd have had easy access to the pistol, especially as he's close to Donna who had the run of the house.' Jayden stops. 'And it could have been Robbie following me the other night in the lanes. It was someone with a heavy tread. Not Elspeth, for sure.'

'The police haven't given Robbie a second glance, have they?' says Ally.

'No. And it's case closed, as far as Skinner is concerned. And Al, I'd love it to be case closed too, but it's just . . . Lucas and heights. That's what kept me up all night. That's what I still can't get past now. Lucas and heights.'

'I agree. I do. Just . . .'

Ally pictures Robbie, and the way he appeared to witness Donna leaving with the police but made no attempt to go to her, instead turning in the opposite direction. Was that the behaviour of someone who hated seeing his loved one under scrutiny for a crime that he himself committed? Perhaps.

Robbie didn't seem to know much about Axel, other than snippets from the Greys. But did Donna tell him more? How he'd drifted since his discharge, never found his place, suffering spells of homelessness. Wouldn't Robbie have felt some kinship, if aspects of his own past weren't dissimilar – or is that reductive thinking? The fact is, no matter how much or how little Robbie knew about Axel, deciding to murder him, within hours of discovering that he was set to inherit, would have been a bold and impulsive act. There was no long-held animosity there. *Unlike with Lucas.* Just utterly ruthless opportunism, based on a gamble for future decisions.

Is that Robbie? The quiet, reflective, really rather grumpy gardener? Who has tended those gardens so beautifully, so lovingly; all those borders, singing with narcissi.

Is that him?

'Look, Al, Casey said Elspeth was excited about getting the solicitor up last night. Presumably to communicate the news about the will officially.'

'You're back thinking about Elspeth?'

'No, I'm still on Robbie. Which means I'm trying to rule out Elspeth. And the fact is, Elspeth getting the solicitor up there isn't the action of someone who's unhappy about where the will's at.'

'Oh, of course. You're right.'

Ally watches another surfer enter the water. Dipping low on their board and stroking out; duck-diving beneath the waves. The rain is moving in light drifts now. Pattering on the roof, misting the windows, blowing lightly through the pillars of the veranda.

'Unless Elspeth lied,' says Ally, 'and she never contacted the solicitor at all.'

Jayden stares at her. 'What, so she wanted to give the impression of being all in with Casey . . . so was faking it. But why? Why bother? Because she's playing for time? Trying to work out what to do next?'

'Like set fire to the house,' says Ally with a light laugh.

'Because if Elspeth and Lucas can't have it then no one can,' says Jayden. 'You know what, Lucas said that Elspeth has always had a problem with disappointment. That she quit acting because she hated that she didn't get every part she went for. At the time, I was focused on Lucas, thinking how rich it was for him to be going on about somebody else's entitlement when there he was, the little posh boy . . . but now?'

'If Elspeth has a problem with disappointment, what must she have made of her husband? Failing to inherit his house from his own father.'

'Yeah, put like that, a profiler would be having a field day.' Jayden slaps a hand on the balustrade. 'Al, we need to speak to that solicitor. If he confirms the invite to Porthmerrin last night, then I think Elspeth's off the table, because getting him and Casey together makes no sense. But if he doesn't confirm it . . .'

'Then we're on to something,' finishes Ally.

69

Ten minutes later, and they have the number of Edward Grey's solicitor, Martin Fellowes. Ally suggested they tried the antiques dealer, Laurence Fentiman, in the hope that he might know who Edward used. He did, and – in exchange for a first-hand account of the fire at Porthmerrin House: *That fine collection of his! Up in smoke! What a travesty* – Laurence was happy to tell them.

Martin Fellowes, on the other hand, wasn't available. They left a message with his receptionist, and now? Nothing to do but wait.

'Have you heard from Casey today?' asks Ally, as she sets about making more coffee.

'Yeah, we spoke this morning. Her ankle's better at least, but she's still kind of blown away by it all. I don't think Casey ever really believed that Axel could have been murdered. That's why she initially felt okay staying at the house last night. She's not sure how long she's going to stay down here now. I don't think the will stuff feels real to her.' He bites the corner of his lip. 'She'll need to talk to this Martin Fellowes, I guess.'

'Not with Elspeth as chaperone?' says Ally suddenly.

'I don't think Casey wants to be anywhere near Elspeth. It's too complicated.'

Because as far as Casey will see it, Elspeth is grieving Axel's killer.

'But what if Elspeth wants to be near Casey?' asks Ally, her voice urgent.

'Don't worry, I already briefed Casey. As soon as I thought it didn't add up with Lucas, I told her not to have any contact with anyone from Porthmerrin. She's lying low at her B&B. Which she's now decided is a whole lot nicer than Lucas and Elspeth's hospitality.' He pauses. 'You know what, while we're waiting, why don't we get up to Porthmerrin? Check in with Robbie and Donna. Get talking to them. Because . . . Robbie, right?'

'That's a perfectly natural thing to do,' says Ally. 'Given the circumstances.'

'Totally natural. Because if this Martin Fellowes calls and says sure, Elspeth invited him for dinner but he couldn't come, then Robbie's our prime suspect. And right now, he's sitting there thinking he's got away with it.'

Ally can just imagine how Skinner will respond to this one. But maybe the detective sergeant will surprise them. Perhaps the same thought has even struck him, if poor Mullins has given his full account by now.

'I feel dreadful for Tim,' she says now. 'I hope Skinner was kind.'

'Same. I've never seen Mullins affected like that.'

'You know, if we prove Lucas isn't the killer . . . will that make him feel worse about what happened?'

Jayden rubs at the back of his head. 'I think he'll feel bad either way. But everything he went through with Lucas refusing to jump, if that's what ultimately gets us to our breakthrough, that's something, right?'

Ally's reply is interrupted by the ringing of her phone. It's a Penzance number, and she answers it. As Martin Fellowes introduces himself – his voice clipped, impatient – her heart climbs in her chest. *So much hangs on this one detail.* She explains that they're private detectives, investigating the death of Axel Marks.

'A very sad business,' says Martin. 'From start to finish.'

'Martin, were you due to be at Porthmerrin House yesterday evening?'

The direct question appears to take him by surprise.

'Yesterday evening? No, no. I only saw Lucas and Elspeth that morning.'

Ally goes cold, goosebumps breaking up and down her arms. Across the table, Jayden's eyes widen.

'Elspeth didn't invite you for supper?' she says.

'No. Might I ask why . . .'

'She didn't get in touch with you at all yesterday evening?'

'Unless she left a message with my office and it wasn't passed along.' He hesitates. 'But that's unlikely, because the Greys have my mobile.'

'Could you check with your receptionist?' asks Ally. 'Just to be sure?'

The solicitor gives a click of frustration, but then Ally can hear him speaking to someone in the background in a low voice. He comes back on the line.

'Nothing at all from the Greys after I met with them in the morning.'

Ally knows she needs to end the call. She has what she needs, and she doesn't want to arouse suspicion.

'Could I ask you not to mention this conversation if Elspeth gets in touch with you?' she asks.

The request is entirely on trust. Because for all Ally knows, Martin could be loyal to Edward Grey and his family; loyal beyond all bounds.

'I need to send my condolences to her,' says Martin. 'It's remiss that I haven't already.'

Ally waits.

'But . . . fine. Though if she were to directly ask whether you and I have spoken, I shan't lie.'

'Of course not,' says Ally, eyeing Jayden. 'Martin, one last question. Did you know that Axel's former girlfriend is here in Cornwall?'

'Former girlfriend?' He gives a low laugh. 'Well, we all have them. But no, I didn't. As far as I knew, he was quite alone in the world.'

As Ally hangs up, Jayden's already on his feet.

'Elspeth lied,' he says.

'She lied.'

Jayden's practically bouncing.

'You know what, all that stuff about the missing boat, Al . . . That came from Elspeth, didn't it? She was the one who said there was a kayak missing when the police asked. I'm thinking now . . . what if there was never any kayak in that shed? Lucas said he couldn't remember. Even Robbie couldn't say for sure. Elspeth could have completely made up the existence of a kayak to throw the police off.'

'And it worked. They were suddenly looking at the island. And Pippa.'

Jayden takes a deep breath. 'Right. Okay. I need to call Casey and tell her categorically not to have any contact with Elspeth. And if she comes to the B&B, not to open up.'

'You don't think Elspeth would do anything, do you?'

Jayden considers it. 'If she wanted to hurt Casey and the baby, I think she would have done it last night. But we don't know how unstable she is right now. And we don't know where she is either.'

'Jayden, she could be anywhere. The last we saw of her, she was going off with Skinner to make a formal statement.'

'Skinner. We've got to bring him in on this, Al. Him and Mullins.'

'Are you calling him?'

'Detective Sergeant,' he says, his phone to his ear, with a nod to Ally. 'Morning.'

Ally watches as Jayden talks through his theory to Skinner. Her partner is considered and straightforward in his approach. There's no sensationalism; just the facts. And as far as Ally can see it, there are two facts that are utterly unarguable. One: Lucas was terrified of heights, which rules out the clifftop. And two: Elspeth lied to Casey when she said she'd contacted Edward's solicitor.

Ally can't hear Skinner's response, and Jayden doesn't put him on speakerphone. Jayden nods, his face grave as he says 'No, okay' once, then twice. And then he hangs up, his mouth turned down.

'Okay,' he sighs, 'so he says he sees where we're coming from . . .'

'Good.'

'But he thinks we should leave it, Al. He says he's closing the case. He's got Elspeth on record saying Lucas confessed.'

'Which makes her guilty of lying to the police too.'

'Unless, like you say, they were in it together. So she's not really lying, she's telling a version – insert air quotes – of the truth.'

'But she did lie about the solicitor.'

'But how do we prove that? It's circumstantial. Less than that, even. Al, we've got everything and nothing.'

'So we build a case. Don't we?'

Jayden rubs his face with both hands.

'Jayden, you came in with such conviction this morning. You *know* Lucas can't have hit Axel with the pistol and pushed him off the cliff. So surely we—'

Jayden's phone rings again. His eyebrows shoot up. 'Skinner.'

This time he puts him on speaker.

'Alright,' says the detective sergeant, as though he's still mid-conversation with Jayden, 'I'll bring Elspeth Grey back in for a formal interview. We've only got her word that it was her husband who killed Axel, and you've highlighted enough inconsistencies for us to hold her for twenty-four hours.'

Stranger things have happened at sea, but Skinner doing a U-turn? Ally and Jayden lock eyes. This is real.

'So that's what we've got, Shell House. Twenty-four hours to come up with some hard evidence.'

'We'll get it,' says Jayden.

Somehow, somehow.

'And one last thing. I know a constable on sick leave who might appreciate being kept up to speed. You know, just if you happen to be passing Ocean Drive.'

70

'I want in,' says Mullins.

He says it through an enormous mouthful of brownie. It was his mum who found the box of cakes on the doorstep, because even though Mullins told her that he was feeling A1 – *mostly A1* – she steamed back from Truro as soon as she got his text. And when she carried the whacking great box in, she said, *Someone must really like you, Tim*.

'And we want you in, mate,' says Jayden. 'But are you sure you're up to it?'

'What, sitting in a car and trundling up to what's left of Porthmerrin? Yeah, I'm up to it.'

Mullins sees Ally and Jayden swap a look and he reads it like a comic book. *I'm being managed.* In fact, now he's thinking about it, them being here at all doesn't feel quite right.

'Skinner suggested it?' he says again.

'Believe me, we're as confused as you are,' says Jayden.

But then Mullins thinks of what Skinner admitted in the hospital: of not being fully in the room on this one. Maybe he's making up for it. Maybe he wants to make sure he's got his best cop chaperoning, if Ally and Jayden are running amok. And Mullins has got to admit, Shell House have a point with this theory. They've got several points. Mullins can personally vouch for Lucas's fear last night: it was the third in the room, and it was much bigger than either of them.

'Brownie for the road?' he says, offering the box. 'Best ever, I'd say.'

'Saffron's?' Jayden takes one. 'Nice.'

'Special delivery,' calls out his mum from the kitchen, clearly earwigging. 'What do you make of that? Now, you'll look after him for me, won't you? Not sure I like the idea of all this, he's only been discharged five minutes, and they can't even give him a cast for that arm . . .'

If his mum knew they were going back to Porthmerrin, she'd be all kinds of worried. Mullins hasn't told her everything about what happened up there. Maybe he will one day.

'We'll look after him,' says Ally.

'And it's a collarbone, Mum,' says Mullins, giving her a peck on the cheek on the way out.

'What's the play, then?' he says as they climb into Ally's little red car. Jayden offers Mullins the wingman spot up front, but he knows his place. He dumps his rear in the back.

'Between Robbie and Donna, they've been closest to Lucas and Elspeth since they got to Porthmerrin,' says Jayden. 'We need to get their take.'

'And I think after everything last night,' says Ally carefully, 'they'll want to help.'

'Right on,' says Mullins, leaning through the seats.

Earlier, Ally and Jayden talked him through the alternative theory that Robbie had motive for wanting Axel dead, but Mullins said he wasn't feeling it. *It's the phony dinner invite to the solicitor, isn't it? She dug her own grave with that one.* Then he fell quiet.

And now they're cannoning out of Ocean Drive. Nippy driver, Ally Bright. Soon they're on the coast road, the sea flying off to the right, swell lines like crinkle-cut crisps. Then into the maze of lanes. In less than half an hour they're passing through the gates of Porthmerrin, Mullins holding his breath as the blackened, ruined shape of the house looms ahead.

'Alright?' says Jayden, turning to him.

'Great, mate.' Then, quietly, 'Feels a bit weird. Seeing it again.'

'Me too. And I wasn't even in it like you were.'

Mullins forces a laugh. 'In it to win it, wasn't I?'

As they park up and open the doors, Mullins swears he can still smell smoke. He grits his teeth.

Easy now, pal.

They head on down to the cottage, Jayden's hand on his shoulder. *His good shoulder, mind.* If he went anywhere near the collarbone, he'd have to swing for him.

They knock, and when Donna opens up, she looks as wide-eyed and pale-faced as a doll. It's Ally who does the talking, and before Mullins knows it, they're all crowding into the titchy living room, with its low beams and sagging sofa. Axel grew up in this little house, so the story goes, just him and his mum. So Mullins and Axel have that in common. Just like Jayden lost a mate on duty, same as Axel. Maybe none of them are that different to Axel Marks, when it comes down to it.

Robbie gets up from the sofa. His hands are fists, and his cheeks are bright red, like he's a little kid with colic. Mullins gets the feeling they're interrupting something.

'Sorry,' says Donna, 'we've just had some bad news.'

'We've been sent packing,' says Robbie. 'In short order.'

'Elspeth?' says Jayden.

'Elspeth,' says Robbie, nodding grimly. 'Lucas has been dead five minutes and she's going back on what he said to us.'

'Was she here?' says Jayden.

'Didn't have the guts to do it face to face. Phone call.'

'Her husband did just die,' says Donna softly, 'and she did just discover he's a murderer, so we have to cut her some slack . . .'

'Anyway,' says Robbie, 'we've got until the end of the week to be out of here, so . . . sorry, not much time to chat and all that.'

And Mullins can feel the anger – *no, the sadness; the great ruddy sadness* – coming off the bloke.

'Cheers for what you did last night, Robbie,' he says. 'With the mattress.'

Robbie nods. 'You alright, are you?'

'I'm alright. So, look . . . We wanted to talk to you about Elspeth, as it happens. Didn't we?'

And Mullins turns to Ally and Jayden beside him. The pair of them take the baton smooth as athletes, and Donna and Robbie listen. If there were ever two people who would now want to take down Elspeth Grey, Mullins reckons it's Robbie and Donna.

'I see what you're saying,' says Robbie, rubbing hard at his stubble, 'but she's a hell of a faker if that's the case. Like, Oscar-level acting. Wouldn't you say, Don?'

'She trained as an actress,' says Donna. 'She told me. Shakespeare and everything. But she gave it up in the end. Said it felt too shallow.'

Mullins grunts in amusement.

'Donna,' says Ally, 'the night you talked to Axel, after you left his van did you go back to the main house or to here?'

'The main house. I was rattled. I wanted to be on my own. Stupid, really, Robbie would have been great to me, but . . . I just knew I'd churned everything up with my talk about Curtis and Afghanistan. I felt so bad about it.'

'And when you went back into the house, are you sure you didn't see or hear anyone?' asks Jayden.

Donna shakes her head and those curls of hers bounce. 'Nothing. But I had a lot on my mind. I just went to my room.'

'Robbie, what about you?' says Mullins. 'Were you expecting Donna here, or . . .'

'No, she said she wasn't coming over that night. Full disclosure, I knew there was a weird charge about her because of Axel. I didn't mind staying out of that. I'm not always great at . . . emotions.'

Mullins nods like he understands.

They've got a lot to answer for, emotions.

'And you didn't hear anything?' asks Ally. 'If anyone was coming from the house, they'd have to have passed this way, wouldn't they?'

'Nothing,' says Robbie. 'But then maybe they went a different way, if they were trying to avoid being seen and all that.'

'Is there another way?' Jayden's at the window, peering out over the lawn to the fence at the end, the tall trees, the field where Axel's van was parked. Then the dead drop.

'You could go round the side of the house and through the rose garden. Out into that line of trees for cover, then over the fence on the other side. It's twisty enough, but if you were trying not to be seen it's a hell of a lot safer than heading clean across the lawn.'

They stare out the window dumbly, as if the answer's out there, just waiting to show itself.

'Oh my God!' cries Donna suddenly. 'Robbie, the roses!'

Robbie pushes a hand to his head. '*Damn.* You're right, Don.'

Mullins looks to Ally and Jayden – they appear as confused as he is.

'Is it even still working?' says Donna.

'I reckon. Got to be worth a check.' Then he rubs his hands together, like they've really got something. 'So, about a month back, something was getting in and ravaging the roses. I reckoned deer – they love the new shoots, see. It was driving me nuts. Edward loved his roses.'

'So you had an idea, didn't you, Rob?'

'I said to Edward that we should get one of those trail cameras. You know, the motion-capture ones. Infra-red lighting, the lot. Well, he loved that idea, didn't he? He insisted on having it connected to this old phone of his and he liked fiddling with it from his bed. And it showed us exactly what we wanted to see. Deer. Decent-quality shots too. So I got some new fencing put up, whacked on a new gate, and on we went.'

'Are you saying there's a chance that camera is still in place and running?' says Jayden. 'That it's still working on motion-capture?'

Mullins can hear the excitement in Jayden's voice. Ally's eyes are sparkling like she's got the bug too.

'Edward took a turn for the worse,' says Donna, 'and after that he lost interest in it. And Robbie had fixed the deer problem anyway.'

'I was that distracted with Edward,' says Robbie. 'He was always good to me, and I was worrying about my future here too, I guess. I forgot about the damn camera. So, yeah . . . there's a chance it's still running.'

'Hold on,' Mullins cuts in, 'we asked the Greys about cameras. Lucas said there weren't any. He was ticked off about it too, said his dad was flaky about security.'

'Lucas didn't know anything about my little trail camera,' says Robbie. Then, after a pause, 'Nor did Elspeth. If she went through the rose garden, there's a good chance we've got it on camera.'

Mullins looks towards Ally and Jayden – *this is it! The evidence!* – but Ally's face clouds suddenly.

'You said the footage linked to Edward's phone?' she says.

As Robbie nods, Ally points out the window, towards the blackened wreck.

The penny drops.

'Bums,' says Mullins. 'Then it's gone up in smoke, hasn't it?'

71

Motion-capture footage would have been the dream. Motion-capture could *still* be the dream.

Jayden turns to Robbie, says, 'But it must be stored on the camera too, right?'

Robbie nods. 'One hundred per cent. We don't need the phone. The footage will be on the memory card in the camera.'

Mullins holds up his good hand for a high-five and Robbie obliges, then says, 'I'll go and get it. But you know this is still a long shot, right? I was out cold the night Axel disappeared – Elspeth could have strolled right by my front door and I wouldn't have known.'

'But if she was being careful, she'd have cut through the rose garden?' says Ally.

Robbie nods as he pulls on his coat and heads out the door.

'I think she was a very careful person,' says Ally, turning to Jayden. 'And I think she's had us all fooled from the moment we met her.'

Jayden thinks of how welcoming Elspeth was the first time they came to Porthmerrin, how she said how grateful she was to Pippa for asking questions about Axel's death, and how she was afraid the police were dismissing him as a lost cause. She was so convincing.

But it was sheer confidence, and arrogance, shining through. She was sure she could never be caught.

But Casey turning up? Casey's pregnancy ruined everything. Because of the clause in the will, Elspeth killed for nothing.

What was Elspeth's game plan there? Did she even have one? Last night she folded Casey into the house, and her talk of inviting the solicitor up reassured him and Ally of her good intentions. Had she planned to harm Casey too, all along? When the fire broke out, Elspeth never once mentioned Casey, yet she couldn't have known that she'd slipped out and gone to Axel's van. Or was the fire a genuine accident, and Elspeth wanted only to watch and wait, perhaps getting to know more about Casey and Axel's relationship to determine if the baby was definitely his? Either way, Elspeth would have demanded a DNA test.

Jayden's phone pings. Skinner.

Picked up Elspeth as she was swimming lengths at some fancy hotel. She's delighted to help with our enquiries, obviously

Jayden resists the temptation to reply saying they might have something.

Might.

'Elspeth's in custody,' he says to Mullins.

And Mullins pops a thumbs up, then checks his own phone. His mouth seems to turn down at the edges when there are no messages for him.

'And you're sure Casey's safe?' asks Ally.

'I'll call to be sure,' says Jayden.

A brief chat confirms that Casey is watching TV in her room, with a potential plan of heading to the island later to see Pippa Grant, if her ankle's up to it.

'She's safe,' says Jayden.

'Axel told me about Casey,' says Donna. 'That night in his van.'

'Did he?'

'He said they were split but . . .' Donna touches her nose with her knuckle, gives a small sniff. '. . . he hoped one day they'd make it back together.'

'That was after he was told about the inheritance, right?' says Mullins with a laugh. 'I reckon she'd have been in, am I right?'

Jayden rolls his eyes.

'Axel didn't want the house,' says Donna. 'That's what he told me, and I believed him. All he wanted was some silly old fake pistol . . .' Then she claps her hand to her mouth.

But Jayden's on it. 'Axel had the flintlock pistol when you saw him in the van?'

'He took it,' she says quietly. 'I didn't want to get him in trouble for it.'

Jayden ignores the 'Erm, hello, he's dead?' look on Mullins's face.

'Axel and Edward bonded over the army stuff, back in the day. Edward loved showing him his collection. That pistol was his favourite. So Axel took it. He didn't think anyone would miss it. The whole house was set to be his, but all he wanted was that stupid little gun. It couldn't fire, though,' says Donna, looking up quickly. 'I'd never have left him with it if it did. Not after what we talked about, bringing everything with Afghanistan and Curtis back up. I never would have . . .'

Jayden turns it over in his mind. So Axel had the pistol at the van. Did Elspeth find him with it, and take it from him? Use it as a weapon to bludgeon him? Suddenly it makes sense. Jayden knew it must have felt personal for someone. Even if, for Axel's attacker, it was a simple case of opportunism.

'Should I have said something earlier?' says Donna quietly.

And for once, Mullins stays quiet.

'It's okay,' says Jayden. 'We're putting it together now.'

Five minutes later, Robbie returns. 'Sorry guys,' he says. 'No luck.'

Before Jayden even absorbs the disappointment, Robbie pulls his hand from behind his back and holds up the camera in triumph. Says, 'Not really!' Then he slips the back panel from it. 'And here's your memory card. You're going to want my laptop now, aren't you?'

As Robbie fetches a heavy old laptop from his bedroom, the five of them gather round. The card loads, and he clicks on a file with thumbnails of hundreds of night-time photographs.

'It's busy round here, see? We got the deer beat, but look: fox, badger. What's that, a field mouse? Tiny thing. What date am I looking for? Three nights ago, right?'

'The twelfth,' says Jayden.

'These are from the twelfth,' says Robbie.

He opens up a slant-eyed fox, one foot poised mid-air. A fat-bellied moth, bumping so close to the camera it's a blur. Then . . . they see it. Wellington boots. Not a standard gardener's wellie, but slimline, with a flower pattern and a clasp at the top. Skinny jeans. A fast stride, caught on camera at 1.20 a.m. Then a raincoat, the swing of her hair, as the figure walks away.

There's a collective gasp as, on-screen, Elspeth turns her head. Why? Did she catch a crackle in the undergrowth? The rustle of a creature? Maybe it was a whistle from a god, playing for their side. Whatever it was, she's face on to the camera.

'Elspeth,' whispers Donna.

'Gotcha!' shouts Mullins, and punches the air with his good arm. Then, 'Shotgun on making the call to Skinner.'

72

Elspeth sits in the interview room. There's a wall of glass and she knows she has an audience. She holds her head high, tears glinting behind her eyes. Her role here is the grieving widow: a widow whose grief is complex – *my husband confessed to murder, after all* – but nevertheless one who is humouring the police as they blunder around looking for answers they'll never find. And the strange thing is, Elspeth isn't having to try very hard.

As much as she attempts to keep a hold on her thoughts, she can't help thinking about Lucas. Weak, weak Lucas. He took up so little space in life, and yet in death he seems much larger. If she was superstitious, she'd say that her husband was asserting himself from beyond the grave – outraged at her false accusation. His absence is like a yawning crevasse, drawing her into its depths. If she thinks about it – *I won't, I won't* – she feels quite sick at the plummet.

It'll pass.

Just like this ridiculous detective's questions will pass too.

When DS Skinner put the suggestion to her just now that Lucas was too scared of heights to accost Axel on a clifftop, Elspeth handled it perfectly. She bowed her head and said that she'd been thinking about this a lot too, and could only conclude that her husband had wanted to die. That he saw the fire as his just deserts. And while he needed Axel gone, Lucas hadn't been a stone-cold killer. *He wanted that young officer to be safe*, she said. *Of that, I'm sure*. And she batted her eyelids at the grizzly old detective across the table from her, as if she, and Lucas, really cared about the boys in blue.

The nausea that swelled in her stomach had no visible symptoms. Except, perhaps, for a draining of colour. But that worked to her advantage.

Starring role! The grieving, appalled widow.

Back when Elspeth was still acting, in the early days of her relationship with Lucas, she just missed out on playing Lady Macbeth in a summer run of Shakespeare in the Garden. And how that had stung, because wasn't she born for the role? She has always had a manipulative streak, even as a pigtailed child, but people mistook it for persuasion because she learnt to be sweet along with it. She would have been perfect: *Out, damned spot! Out, I say!* Lucas was no Macbeth, though. Elspeth knew he wouldn't have it in him – not even to be a meagre accomplice, let alone a vessel – so when she made her plan to dispense with Axel, she made it all on her own.

Look like the innocent flower, but be the serpent under it.

A line she spoke not to her husband, but into the mirror. And her performance was pitch-perfect.

As for the dratted Martin Fellowes, Elspeth never thought anyone would actually bother checking with the solicitor. She clamps her jaw hard now as she thinks of Ally and Jayden. But she has explained this away as well. That in all the excitement of having Casey there, it slipped her mind to send the message to Martin. Not quite adequate, but unproveable either way. The fact of the matter? It was a glitch. But Elspeth was desperate by then. Playing for time. Wanting to keep Casey close, so she could ascertain whether this situation was as disastrous as she feared. Of course there would be rigorous DNA testing to prove the kid's paternity. There would have to be, with this much at stake. But not until after it was born – and what was Elspeth expected to do, spend the next four months in the purgatory of faint hope? *No, thank you.* Because for one so liberal with her lies, Elspeth knows the truth when she hears it. And in the hours that she spent with the woman, it was quite clear: Casey James loved Axel Marks. *Just like I loved stupid Lucas.* The baby is Axel's.

And that's where this story ends, really.

There is a baby. And Edward was so sentimental, so absurd, so unfeeling towards Lucas, that by inserting that clause he showed how he preferred to have a total unknown – fifty per cent of a broken soldier – inherit his family home.

Elspeth is not a monster. She was never going to harm Casey or the child. Though did the thought flit across her mind, just for a split second, like a shadow in an already darkened room? *Perhaps.* But Axel? He was a no-hoper, and he set himself up for his fall. It was absurdly easy, which just shows it was meant to be. Elspeth had planned to summon him from his van that night, knowing he'd be drunk, doddering, pathetic. She'd planned to ask him to talk, and the two of them would wander along the clifftop together, deep in a heart-to-heart, then, at the right moment, she would strike: hit, push, then watch him fall. Only, when Elspeth turned up, Axel was an emotional wreck, undone by Donna Goode and her talk of the past. He was bent and remorseful, pacing along the clifftop, tottering on his feet. He saw no threat in Elspeth, because she'd made sure to be kind to him from the moment he set foot in Porthmerrin. *Kill them with kindness.*

Axel was clutching an old pistol in his hands, and she recognised it as one of Edward's antiques. Pilfering little fool. *This was always my favourite*, he told her. She pretended to admire it, asked to hold it, as if it were a guinea pig and she were a child on a playdate: feed it a carrot. Then, as Axel briefly turned, she cracked him over the back of the head with it. She didn't even have to push him. He staggered forward at the blow – and fell.

It was, Elspeth thinks, as if Axel grew wings and took off, sailing into the darkness by his own free will. Perhaps, on one level, she did the man a favour. He could never have coped with a house like Porthmerrin. Nor could he have coped with all the money from selling it either. Some people are destined to fail, no matter how much – or how little – they try.

And she was getting away with it. Even when that hopeless woman on the island piped up. Even when Ally Bright and Jayden Weston came sniffing around. Not even Lucas suspected a thing, and why would he? He always thought Elspeth wore a halo. And he could be so extraordinarily gutless that it never crossed his mind that, instead of whingeing and whining, some people *acted.*

But then came Casey James and her big swollen belly, and Elspeth decided that if she and Lucas weren't to have Porthmerrin House, then no one would. *Enter the candles.* The gesture of a toddler, really; one who rips a doll away from another – then pulls its head off. *Not yours, mine!* Nobody's. Of course, Elspeth wasn't thinking about insurance. Wasn't thinking about how a sizeable pay-out would fund a rebuild.

Not fair!

None of it is fair.

Elspeth never intended for anyone to be hurt in the fire. She'd wanted the house gone, not her husband. Not Lucas. Is there some strange poetic justice at play? Because Elspeth certainly meant it when she told Lucas that the situation was all his fault; that if he hadn't been such a failure in the eyes of his father he'd have inherited the house like a normal son. *I meant that.* But what she didn't say to Lucas? That she loved him anyway. Against reason, she loved him anyway. She tells herself that she has the house in Windsor. She has Lucas's life insurance. She has Lucas's share in his tinpot marketing agency. Elspeth will not starve.

But what I don't have is Lucas.

Tears flood her eyes. Real tears, the kind that hurt. It had seemed so easy, but somehow it all got so complicated.

Lost in this inconvenient reverie, Elspeth jumps as Detective Sergeant Skinner walks back into the room. *Dotting i's and crossing t's*, he said to her ten minutes ago. He's holding a paper file, and he sets the tape going again. He passes her a Styrofoam cup of coffee, and she wipes her eyes, trying to muster a grateful smile – one in keeping with that grieving, appalled widow – but she can feel it straining her face and she can't hold it. Meanwhile Skinner's ugly moustache is lifting in a smile of his own, and he drums his fingers on the table with a measure of jauntiness.

She experiences another swell of nausea and her throat burns.

Lucas is dead.

'So, Elspeth,' he says, 'let me go over something again. You said you never left the house the night that Axel died, correct? You went straight to sleep after dinner, and the first thing you knew of his disappearance was when your husband raised the alarm the next morning.'

'Correct,' she says.

'Are you quite sure about that? You're saying you never left the house in the middle of the night?'

Elspeth feels her left eyelid pulsing. It flutters uncontrollably, like a moth caught at a window. She pictures herself walking back into their Windsor home all on her own; footsteps echoing in those big empty rooms. The wide bed. Lucas's toothbrush in the pot. His dressing gown hanging on the peg like a ghost.

It wasn't supposed to be this way.

'Quite sure,' she says.

Skinner nods. He opens the file and slides out a black-and-white picture.

At the sight of it, the nausea tilts her as if she's out at sea.

'For the benefit of the tape, I'm showing the suspect a photograph,' he says. 'Motion-capture footage, from one-twenty a.m. on the twelfth.'

The nausea strengthens. No longer the feeling of being at sea but instead tipped overboard; a wave crashing over her head, heavy as a wardrobe.

It's. Not. Fair.

As Elspeth stares at her eerie face in black and white, turning to the camera as if to give it a wave, she feels the fight go out of her like the last air in her lungs. She opens her mouth to speak.

And the deadly water flows in.

73

Jayden and Ally drop Mullins outside his place on Ocean Drive. As the car idles at the kerb, Jayden sees the flicker of a television set through the window. Then Mullins's mum is tweaking the net curtain, peering out, giving a little wave. Mullins waves back. Then he swivels and faces the pair of them.

'Got lucky there, didn't we, Shell House?'

'We did,' says Jayden, with a smile to Ally.

Mullins appears to be back to his old self. Aided, for sure, by the news from Skinner that – faced with the photograph – Elspeth faltered, broke down, then confessed.

They were lucky with the trail camera – no doubt. But they also put themselves in the way of luck. They kept on pushing. If they'd left this one to the police, Jayden has a feeling no one would have been arrested at all – let alone the right person.

'I'm vibrating,' says Mullins suddenly, and with his good arm he pulls his phone from his pocket. He gives a shout of laughter, looking in that moment just like a little kid. 'Okay, so Skinner wants to take us all for bacon baps at Hang Ten. Meeting in an hour.'

'Does he really?' says Ally.

'Has Skinner even ever been to Hang Ten?' says Jayden.

'Erm, no.'

'Has Skinner ever suggested getting food?' says Jayden.

'Erm, no again. And, no offence, definitely not with you guys.' Mullins hesitates, looking a little dreamy all of a sudden. 'Maybe he's just feeling good about what he's got, not what he hasn't.'

Jayden lifts his eyebrows. The guy's full of surprises.

'Or maybe he wants to gloat that it was his interview skills that finally got Elspeth to crack?'

'Yeah, that's more like it.' Mullins winks. 'Still, we're all in, are we?'

'Absolutely,' says Ally.

As they drive away, Jayden glances in the rear-view mirror. Jenny Mullins is halfway down the path in her slippers, and Mullins is stepping in for a hug.

'Well,' says Ally, 'I don't know what to say.'

'Another case nailed, Al.'

There's satisfaction, of course. And relief. But Jayden doesn't feel celebratory; not out and out.

'Do you think the charge will stick?'

He wrinkles his nose. 'Elspeth's confessed. Even if she retracts it, she's on record lying multiple times. Forensics may turn up something more. Plus, they'll seize her laptop, her phone. Skinner's going to be all over it.'

'After he's had his bap at Hang Ten, you mean,' smiles Ally. 'Jayden, I need to make a phone call first. I've been putting it off and it's not fair. But I'll come straight away afterwards.'

'Everything okay?' he asks.

They turn into the track for the dunes. A flock of starlings swirls through the sky as one, dipping low ahead of them. The sky is trying to be blue. Ally is slow to reply.

'Yes,' she says eventually. 'Sorry. Yes. Absolutely.'

Jayden can take a hint, but, as they pull up outside The Shell House, curiosity gets the better of him.

'Is it Ray stuff?' he asks.

~

Jayden turns his key in the lock, and his daughter hurtles to meet him. Jazzy streaks ahead of her little brother, throwing herself at Jayden's legs and holding on.

'Do the walk!' she shrieks. 'The Dadatz Walk!'

And as she places her small feet on his much larger ones, he takes big swinging steps. Benji tumbles up to them, laughing at nothing, at everything, and Jayden scoops him up too, carrying him like a rugby ball. He is a man made of children. And the thought that strikes? Axel should have had this. It was the inheritance that got him killed, but Axel already stood to be the richest man on earth. He just didn't know it.

I wish I told him about our baby, Casey said last night. *I wish so much.*

'Jay, hey,' says Cat.

And then she gets in the mix too. They're a human pile-up; eight arms, eight legs. Jayden holds on with all he's got.

'Middle-of-the-night hunch paid off, then?' she says, as they finally come apart.

'It paid off. Tonight, though, nothing's keeping me awake. Nothing at all.'

'Double party planning is going to keep you awake, Jay. The to-do lists are long.'

'Nothing I can't handle. I'm thinking two playlists, by the way. No crossover. And it's the friends who get all the bangers.'

'That's fair. The price the grandparents pay for having their own lives.' And she kisses him. 'Hey, I'm about to take the kids for an ice cream at Hang Ten. Come with us?'

Jazzy starts shouting with pleasure, and Benji joins in just because.

'Yeah, they do look like they need the sugar lift. Funnily enough, Ally and I have just been invited there for a bacon bap. By Detective Sergeant Skinner, of all people.'

'What?' Cat's eyes dance. 'That's a first.'

'Right?' says Jayden. 'Come on, let's get your coats.'

74

Saffron peers out of the rain-soaked window. The horizon line has disappeared. The dark sky feels like a lid that's screwed on too tight.

'Would you be offended if I closed up early today, Gus?'

Gus has been sitting at one of the corner tables for hours, bent over his laptop. After he delivered Mullins's box of brownies for her, he came and holed up at Hang Ten. *Misery loves company*, was what he said, and Saffron said cheers to that, and gave him a flat white on the house. Whatever's been driving Gus today, it's paid off in the work, she thinks. His fingers have been flying over the keys, the tap-tap-tap giving her electro-beats a run for their money.

'Do you know what,' he says, not hearing her, 'I think I'm just going to bloody send it.'

'What, the book?'

'To my agent. I'm going to say this is as good as it's going to get, so take it or leave it.'

Saffron comes out from behind the counter.

'Is it as good as it's going to get?' she says.

Gus sits back with his arms folded. He tips his head, eyes reading back over what he's done.

'Now, there's a question. There's probably more I could do, but . . . For instance . . . Oops, yes, probably best not to repeat the word *laconic* twice in three sentences, is it? Dear me, no,' he says, tapping at the keys again. 'In retrospect, I'm not sure my fine-toothcomb approach is quite as fine as it could be.'

'So keep working on it, Gus. No stress. Go at your pace. What's the sudden rush anyway?'

'I don't know, Saffron,' he says quickly. 'Maybe to make something of my life?'

Saffron frowns. She's underserved Gus; he's been here for most of the day and she hasn't asked what's eating him. She's been too much in her own head, that's the trouble. Because the one person she's wanted to hear from is Mullins – and when has that ever been true? She wants to know he's okay; to know that she can expect his big silly self to come back in here soon.

'Is everything alright, Gus?' she asks.

Gus waves a dismissive hand. 'Oh, just stuff. Like all these emmets coming here from upcountry and liking what they see so much that they stay forever.'

Saffron grins at him. 'Yeah, uh-huh, Gus. I hate it when people do that.'

He rubs a hand over his pebble-smooth head and sends her a smile back. It's got a bit of the old twinkle in it as he says, 'I know, I know, pot calling kettle.'

But nevertheless, Saffron wonders what's prompted it. With Gus, it's usually an Ally thing.

'You're right,' he says, staring at his screen. 'What's the rush? Knee-jerk. I'm being foolish. Which of course is my modus operandi, in some respects. Just . . .' He sighs. 'I'll keep trucking on.'

'You know, Gus, good things take time.'

'Yes, I suppose they do.'

'You've just got to hang in there. When the time's right, it'll happen.'

Gus sends her a quizzical look. 'Are you still talking about the book, or . . .'

Saffron's attention is caught by stomping feet along the boardwalk, and a flash of black at the window. A grey-haired man in a suit, looking completely out of place at the beach, is wrestling with a big umbrella; the wind whips and turns it inside out like it's playing for laughs. Then the door's clanging, and it's Cat and the kids and Jayden and, oh yes, Detective Sergeant Skinner – minus his broken umbrella. Then, bringing up the rear, Mullins.

Mullins in a tracksuit jacket, his sling wet through. And he's all smiles.

Saffron smiles back, and the relief is like a sudden burst of sunshine. For a second she forgets herself, but then she's righted: they need coffee, and they need it now. She heads behind the counter, gets the beans grinding, the milk frothing. Pots of ice cream for Jazz and Benji. And how many bacon baps?

'Ally's on her way,' says Jayden. 'Gus, you going to join us?'

As they all settle at a couple of tables, Skinner wedged between the two ice-cream-licking kids, Saffron heads to the fridge. She hauls out enough bacon and eggs for five. As she closes the door she turns and jumps.

Mullins. Just standing there with a look on his face that's a little bit different.

'Sorry,' he says. 'For being a plonker. A class-A plonker.'

She bites the corner of her lip. 'Is this, like, a catch-all apology, for school and everything since, or . . .'

'Yeah, go on, then. But mostly for yesterday.'

And Saffron tells him that yesterday, at the hospital, is the one thing he doesn't need to apologise for. 'The rest, though? I'll take.'

'Telling you to leave me alone, though . . .' He shakes his head. 'Of all the people.'

'Right? Of all the people.'

Skinner's calling his name then, and Mullins taps the counter with his good hand. Then he's squeezing in amongst them all, Jazzy straight away putting down her ice cream and climbing into his lap.

'Mullins, she appears to like you,' says Skinner, as if he's witnessing something incomprehensible.

'Yeah, well, Jazz and I go way back, don't we, flower?'

Flower?

Saffron bites down a smile and gets on with the order. The rain keeps tapping at the windows but it's not coming in. The bacon hits the grill and the aroma is instant. She traces leaves, tulips and hearts in the foam of the coffees and carries the tray over. It doesn't matter who gets what, does it? But somehow, Mullins ends up with the heart.

75

Ally steps outside The Shell House. The wind is up, and giant banks of cloud are moving fast across the sky. She fastens her hood and dips her head, then she changes her mind and yanks it back. She turns her face to the driving rain and closes her eyes.

Fox twines around her legs, and as she opens her eyes, she sees he's off, trotting in the direction of Hang Ten.

As Ally walks, her boots sink in the sand. She feels tired, and heads closer to the shore, to the hard-packed stuff where the going is easier. If it weren't such a rare invitation from DS Skinner, she suspects she would have cried off completely.

The case has taken it out of her. But so too has the phone call.

Ally, he said, *your silence spoke volumes.*

Ray's tone wasn't injured, or irritated, it was just . . . sad. Ally apologised. Not just for the delay, but for the lukewarmth of her initial response.

It was unfair of me, she said. *You deserved more.*

You always expect me not to understand, said Ray, *but I do. You're used to being on your own now. That's what it is. And if I were to move to Cornwall . . .*

But that's not quite it. Ally has always enjoyed her own company, she has always valued her solitude and independence. But being alone? That she has had to learn to live with, and there isn't a day that goes by when she doesn't wish that Bill were still by her side. And the image she had of Ray being in Cornwall all the time – dropping by, stopping over, eventually saying, 'Isn't it silly, us having two places?' – felt wrong to Ally. And she doesn't even quite know why, because this last year reconnecting with Ray has felt, in so many ways, like a wonderful adventure.

Ally looks ahead up the beach. There's a trail of footprints left by her little dog and already they're fading in the sand. He's old now, Fox, and right now Ally feels old too.

Old and tired.

So, look, said Ray, *I adore you, Ally, you know that. But I'm no glutton for punishment. My daughter's twisted my arm on St Andrews, but honestly? She didn't have to twist very hard.*

They talked for a while after that. He made a joke about sleeper trains. Beachcombing spots on Mull, on Skye. It isn't the end of their friendship. But their intimacy? Yes. She suspects it is the end of that.

Ally whistles for Fox, and he stops and waits, his tail waving. His fur bristles in the wind, as if he's trembling from head to foot.

'Come here,' she says, and scoops him up into her arms. She buries her nose in his wet fur.

'As if I'm on my own,' she says, 'when I've got you.'

Ally carries him for a bit, until she remembers she has a ball in her pocket. She throws it and he pelts after it. He pelts like a young pup, just with a little glitch in his stride. They make their way to Hang Ten that way: throwing, fetching, throwing, fetching; playing on the beach in the rain. By the time Ally pushes open the door, her cheeks are bright, and she's smiling.

She sees everyone crowded around two tables, and it looks more like a gathering of old friends than a debrief with Devon and Cornwall Police. Cat and the children are there too, and Jayden's wife is talking about a party they're planning, to which everyone's invited. And in the middle of them all is Gus, holding Benji on his knee, for all the world like a proud grandad.

Jayden looks up and gives Ally a look that's so full of warmth that she wants, inexplicably – or perhaps explicably – to cry. He pops a thumbs up and she nods.

As if I'm on my own.

'Ally!' sings out Saffron. 'Coffee?'

'Bacon baps are go!' roars Mullins, apparently back to full throttle. 'I'm starving.'

And then she's pulling up a chair, and Skinner is rising to shake her hand with vigour, and Gus – Gus is concentrating very hard on baby Benji, as though the two of them are locked in a conversation of great importance. But then he looks up and meets Ally's eye, and they swap a simple smile.

'You haven't been waiting for me, have you?' she says, looking around at everyone.

'Of course,' says Gus. 'Always.'

Epilogue

Six months later

Casey rolls the pram through the Deaner, her favourite skate park in all of Bristol. It's early, and there's nothing but the sound of her wheels on concrete. The place will fill up later – it's one of those September mornings that still feel like summer – but for now it's all hers.

All theirs.

Casey hasn't been on her board in months, but she knows it's waiting for her, the day she feels like skating again. She stops pushing and looks down at her tiny daughter in her pram, with all her immaculate, unimaginable beauty. Her baby looks back, nearly smiling; her eyes are a startling hazel, almost amber. *Jeanie.* Named for Axel's beloved mother. It was an easy choice. Plus, it's just cool, isn't it? Jeanie James.

They walk past the banks and ramps, the rails and wedges. The concrete is cracked and chipped and spray-painted to pieces – and it's radiant. All the colours here, all the life. Casey casts an eye up to the Slab, the place where she first saw Axel. It's empty, but not to her. She can see him, kick-pushing, knees bent, eyes all focus; how she liked that he wasn't very good, but he was doing it anyway, loving it anyway.

'Today's the day,' she says quietly.

Casey has been putting off the DNA test. She doesn't need a piece of paper to know that Axel is the father of her child. But the solicitor does need it. And while she felt like walking away from Porthmerrin and never, ever looking back, that wouldn't be fair to her daughter. And it is a lot of money – like, an eye-boggling amount. For the land, let alone the house – which is, in part, salvageable. According to the terms, it'll be held in trust until Jeanie turns eighteen, which feels so far off as to be almost unbelievable. Like a fairy story: only one of those tales with a dark and frightening undercurrent. But Casey is trying not to think like that. Because while Edward Grey's bequest may have been driven by guilt and neglect, and Axel's death the result of greed and disgust, Jeanie is only here because of love. That's all.

Pure love.

This afternoon, after the test is over and done with, Casey and Jeanie will have a visitor to their little flat. Pippa is making a rare excursion from Lone Island to come and meet her goddaughter for the first time. The woman didn't know what to do when Casey first asked her to be her godmother, saying *There must be someone better*, to which Casey replied: *How could there be? You were the one who found him.* Casey would love to take Jeanie to the island one day. Maybe when she's toddling, and she can look for shells on the shore, marvel at the fat-bellied seals. While Casey doesn't know how she feels about Porthmerrin itself, the island is different. The island, she has come to appreciate.

The wildlife trust people didn't want Pippa working there on her own – Health and Safety, or so they said – but they were open to hiring someone to work alongside her. It turned out that Robbie Cassidy was looking for a new position and he got the job. He lives on the mainland with Donna, in a cottage that's also owned by the trust, and goes over by boat each day – unless the weather stops it running. It's a trial arrangement on all sides, but so far? Apparently, it's working out.

Meanwhile Elspeth Grey is in prison for life, convicted of the murder of Axel. And the manslaughter of Lucas. And arson.

After all that Axel survived, to die in that way – at the hands of that woman, and for such a reason – feels unreal to Casey. But six months on, Casey accepts that the unreal and the unfair are stitched into the fabric of what it means to be human. Knowing this does not diminish their tragedy, nor does it lessen her pain. What Casey feels, instead, is a resolve: she will not let the death of Axel, her daughter's father, be the death of her too. One day she will have to find a way to explain it all to Jeanie, but not yet. Not for a long, long time yet.

As she passes through the gates at the bottom of the park, Casey sees the word *hope* spray-painted in big, bright letters down one of the pillars. It stops her in her tracks. It'll be sprayed over again soon because that's how it works round here – a coloured concrete carousel – but while she still can, Casey lays her palm on the sun-warmed stone.

Hope. At times, Axel had so much of it. At times, he had so little.

And Casey? She has Jeanie. And all she can do is try to love her enough for both of them. That is, in fact, the only part that feels easy.

From inside the pram there's a soft bleating.

'Come on then, babe,' she says. 'Let's go home.'

ACKNOWLEDGEMENTS

Thank you to everyone who's been part of this novel's journey, from the first idea through to the book you have in your hands – or in your ears, if you're listening to Kristin Atherton's fantastic narration.

Thank you to my wonderful agent, Rowan Lawton, and all of the team at The Soho Agency, for always being brilliant. This is our eleventh published novel together, and I'm grateful to have you by my side.

I'm very lucky, too, to be part of the Thomas & Mercer family. For *The Lone Island Mystery*, I had the benefit of a fabulous trio of editors: Vic Haslam, Victoria Pepe and Laura Gerrard – my story and I could not have been in better hands, from start to finish. Thanks also to the wider team at Thomas & Mercer, including Nicole Wagner, Gemma Wain, Silvia Crompton, Will Speed, Rebecca Hills and Sammia Hamer. Meanwhile artist Marianna Tomaselli has created yet another absolutely stunning cover: thank you.

Thank you to all of my dear friends who always offer inspiration, camaraderie and kindness, and the cherished writer pals who so generously support these novels, and me; you make it all so fun. A special mention to Lucy Clarke, who always reads my first drafts, along with my husband Robin Etherington: what a killer duo; I'm so appreciative of your combined insight and encouragement.

If I ever have a crime writer's emergency – aka a 'real world' procedural question – I'm lucky to have my CSI friend Zoe and my police constable friend Oli on hand, book on book. Any inaccuracies are, as ever, down to me. I'm also hugely grateful to Will Greswell for so generously answering my questions on army life throughout the writing process and helping me make sure Axel's experiences ring true.

A couple of scenes in *The Lone Island Mystery* unfold in Dean Lane skatepark in Bristol. The 'hope' pillar described in the epilogue was real (and beautiful). It was painted by Nic @nancyandbelle in 2023, and while it's been sprayed over now, I always think of it as I walk through the gates of the Deaner with my board under my arm. Skate Club, this book's dedicated to you.

Much love and gratitude to my family, as always – the Halls, the Green-Halls and the Etheringtons – for your unending love and support in every way. Big, big thanks to Robin – my husband, my creative partner in crime, and such a big help with these books – and my son, Calvin, who is quite the budding murder mystery fan. You're simply the best.

Thank you, lastly, to my readers. Whether you're new to the Shell House series or have been here since the beginning, I'm so very, very grateful. It's no exaggeration to say that these books wouldn't exist without you.

ABOUT THE AUTHOR

Photo © 2022 Victoria Walker

Emylia Hall lives in Bristol with her husband and son, where she writes from a hut in the garden and dreams of the sea. She is the author of the Shell House Detectives Mysteries, a series inspired by her love of Cornwall's wild landscape. The first, *The Shell House Detectives*, was a Kindle Top 10 Bestseller, with the rights being optioned for TV. *The Lone Island Mystery* is her seventh crime novel. Emylia has published four previous novels, including Richard and Judy Book Club pick *The Book of Summers* and *The Thousand Lights Hotel*. Her work has been translated into ten languages, and broadcast on BBC Radio 6 Music. She is the founder of Mothership Writers and is a writing coach at The Novelry.

Instagram: @emyliahall_author

X: @emyliahall

Follow the Author on Amazon

If you enjoyed this book, follow Emylia Hall on Amazon to be notified when the author releases a new book!
To do this, please follow these instructions:

Desktop:

1) Search for the author's name on Amazon or in the Amazon App.
2) Click on the author's name to arrive on their Amazon page.
3) Click the 'Follow' button.

Mobile and Tablet:

1) Search for the author's name on Amazon or in the Amazon App.
2) Click on one of the author's books.
3) Click on the author's name to arrive on their Amazon page.
4) Click the 'Follow' button.

Kindle eReader and Kindle App:

If you enjoyed this book on a Kindle eReader or in the Kindle App, you will find the author 'Follow' button after the last page.